NAT ENOUGH

MARIA SCRIVAN

graphix

An Imprint of

SCHOLASTIC

For you, reader.
You are more than enough.

All rights reserved. Published by Graphix, an imprint of Scholastic Inc.,
Publishers since 1920. SCHOLASTIC, GRAPHIX, and associated logos are
trademarks and/or registered trademarks of Scholastic Inc.

The publisher does not have any control over and does not assume any
responsibility for author or third-party websites or their content.

No part of this publication may be reproduced, stored in a retrieval
system, or transmitted in any form or by any means, electronic, mechanical,
photocopying, recording, or otherwise, without written permission of the
publisher. For information regarding permission, write to Scholastic Inc.,
Attention: Permissions Department, 557 Broadway, New York, NY 10012.

This book is a work of fiction. Names, characters, places, and incidents are
either the product of the author's imagination or are used fictitiously, and any
resemblance to actual persons, living or dead, business establishments,
events, or locales is entirely coincidental.

Library of Congress Control Number: 2019936057

ISBN 978-1-338-53821-2 (hardcover)
ISBN 978-1-338-53819-9 (paperback)

10 9 8 7 6 5 4 3 2 1   20 21 22 23 24

Printed in China 62
First edition, April 2020
Edited by Megan Peace
Book design by Phil Falco
Publisher: David Saylor

CONTENTS

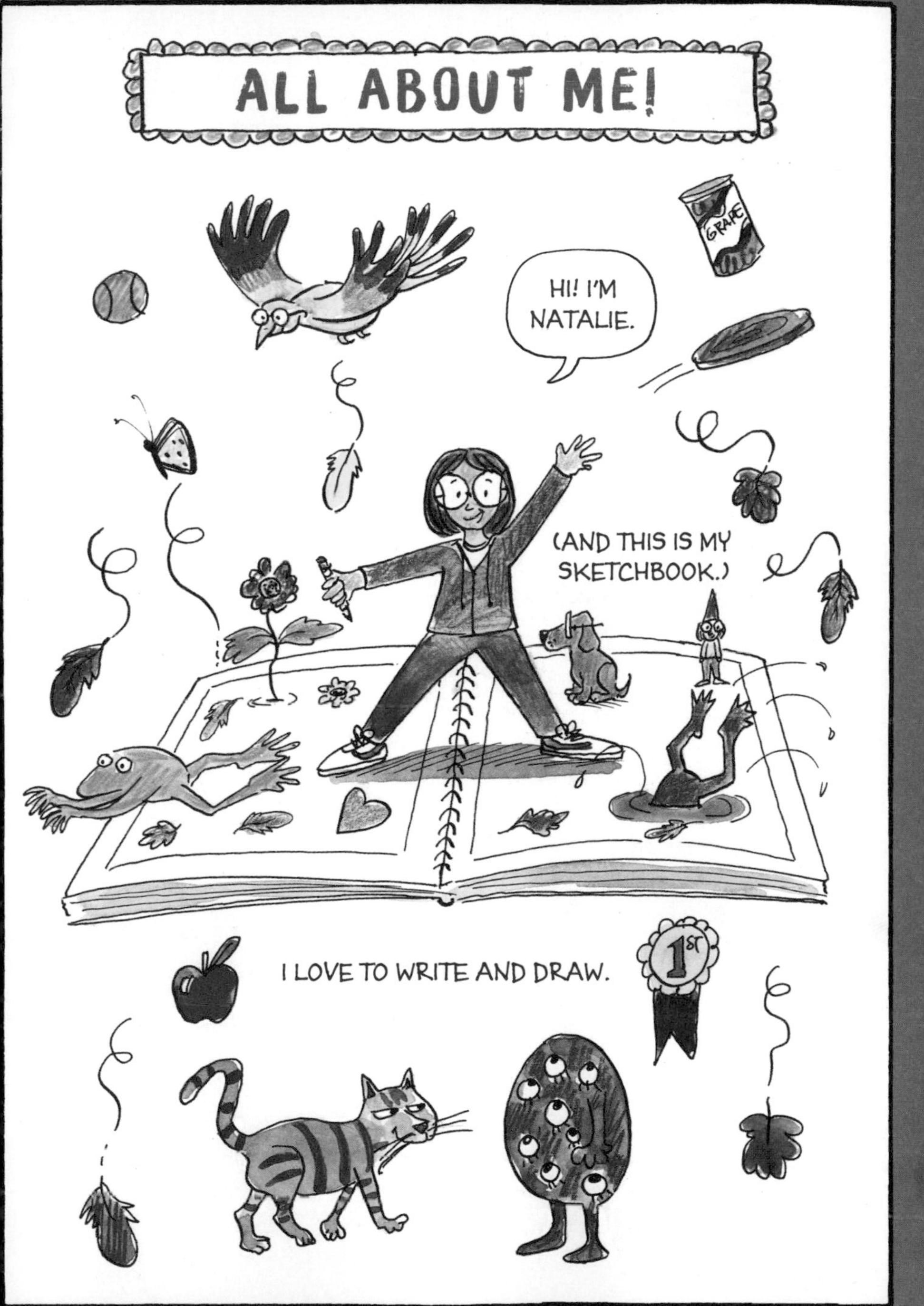
ALL ABOUT ME!
GRAPE
HI! I'M NATALIE.
(AND THIS IS MY SKETCHBOOK.)
I LOVE TO WRITE AND DRAW.
1ST

I ALSO LOVE TO PLAY WITH MY CAT AND DOG,

RIDE MY BIKE,

AND HANG OUT WITH MY BEST FRIEND, LILY.
MORE ABOUT HER IN A MINUTE.

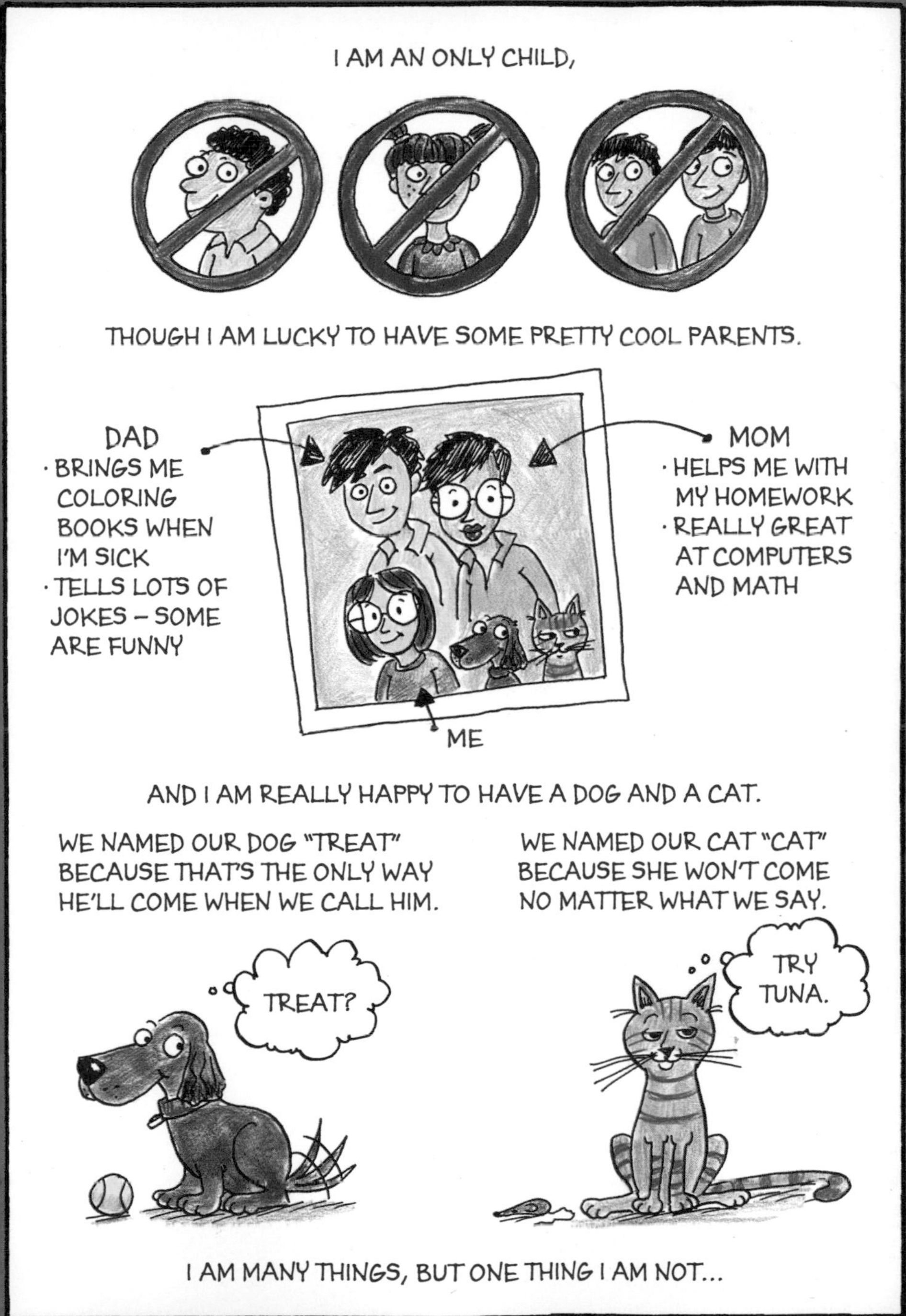
I AM AN ONLY CHILD,
THOUGH I AM LUCKY TO HAVE SOME PRETTY COOL PARENTS.
DAD
· BRINGS ME COLORING BOOKS WHEN I'M SICK
· TELLS LOTS OF JOKES – SOME ARE FUNNY
MOM
· HELPS ME WITH MY HOMEWORK
· REALLY GREAT AT COMPUTERS AND MATH
ME
AND I AM REALLY HAPPY TO HAVE A DOG AND A CAT.
WE NAMED OUR DOG "TREAT" BECAUSE THAT'S THE ONLY WAY HE'LL COME WHEN WE CALL HIM.
WE NAMED OUR CAT "CAT" BECAUSE SHE WON'T COME NO MATTER WHAT WE SAY.
TREAT?
TRY TUNA.
I AM MANY THINGS, BUT ONE THING I AM NOT...

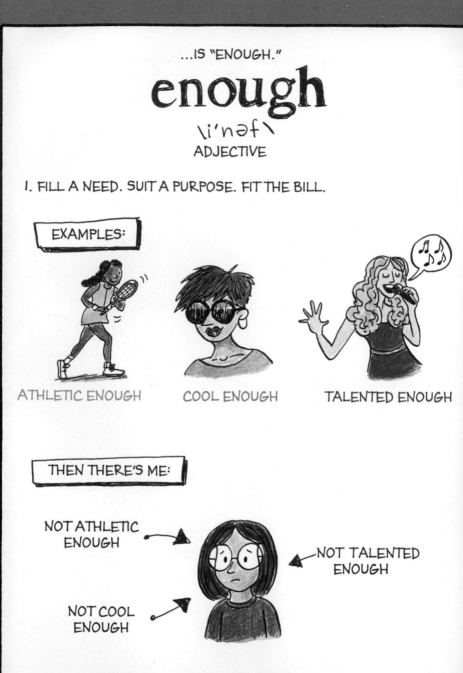

...IS "ENOUGH."

enough

\i'nəf\

ADJECTIVE

1. FILL A NEED. SUIT A PURPOSE. FIT THE BILL.

EXAMPLES:

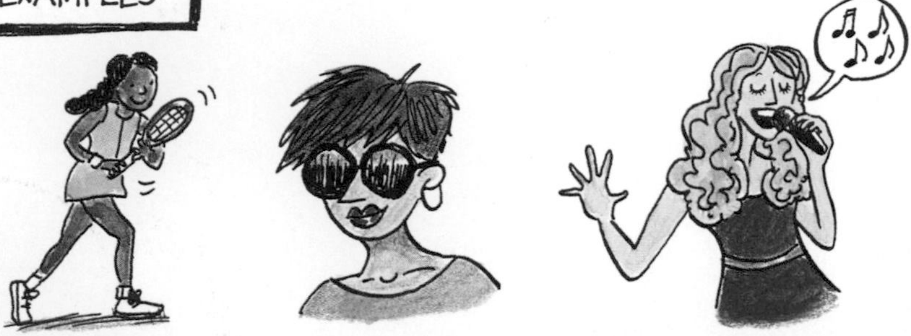

ATHLETIC ENOUGH

COOL ENOUGH

TALENTED ENOUGH

THEN THERE'S ME:

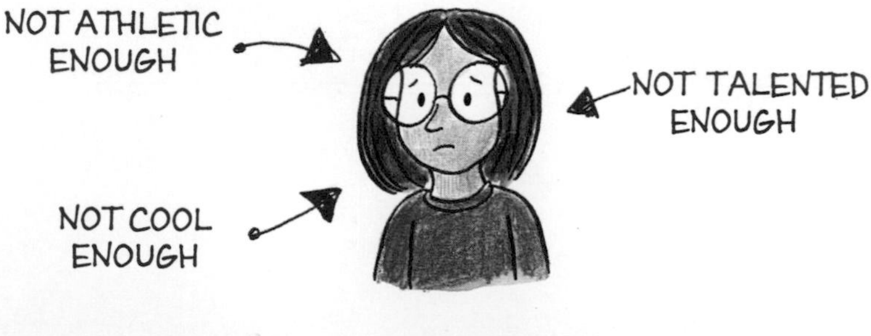
NOT ATHLETIC ENOUGH
NOT TALENTED ENOUGH
NOT COOL ENOUGH

SEE ALSO: NERDY, CLUMSY, AWKWARD.

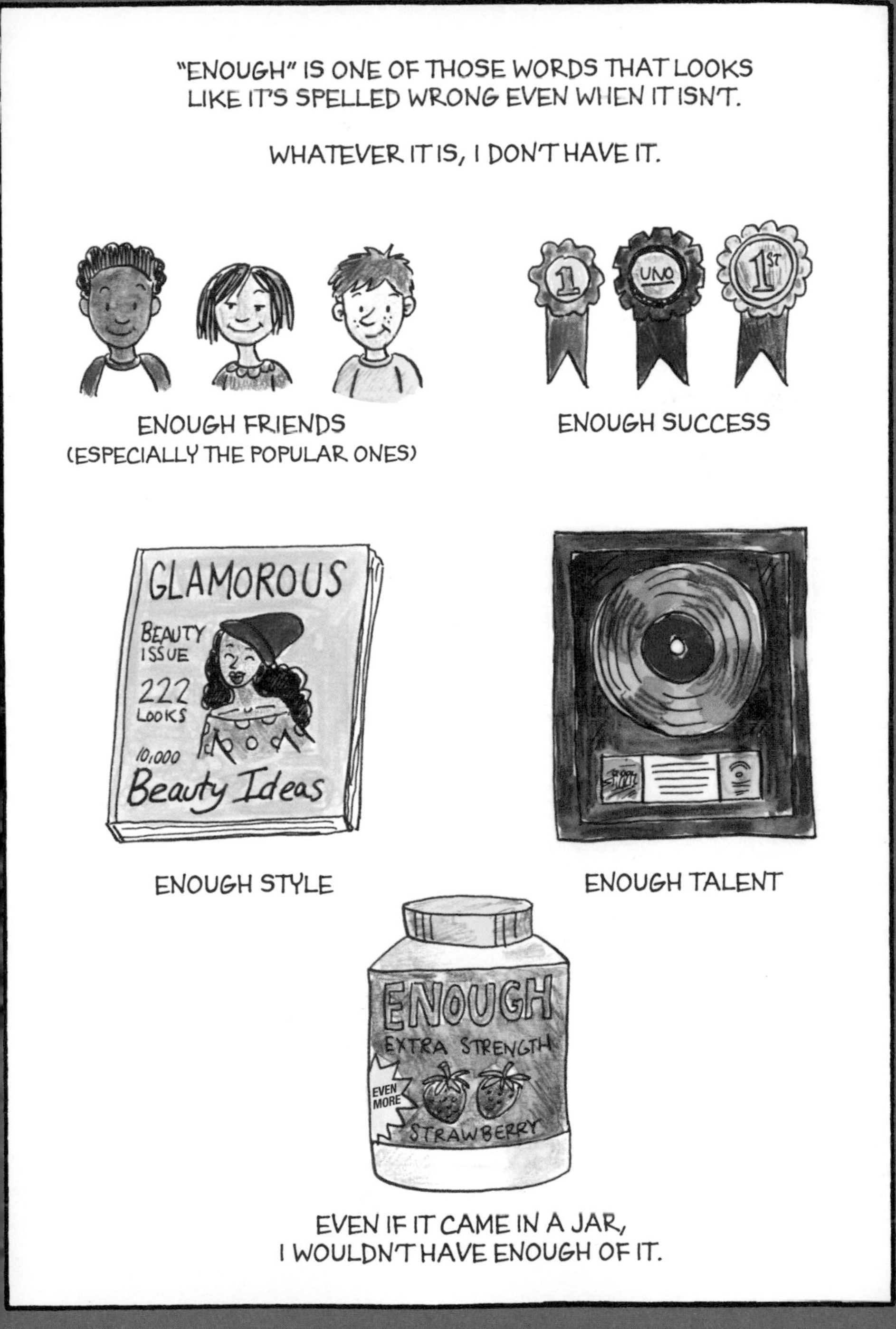
"ENOUGH" IS ONE OF THOSE WORDS THAT LOOKS LIKE IT'S SPELLED WRONG EVEN WHEN IT ISN'T.
WHATEVER IT IS, I DON'T HAVE IT.
ENOUGH FRIENDS (ESPECIALLY THE POPULAR ONES)
1
UNO
1ST
ENOUGH SUCCESS
GLAMOROUS
BEAUTY ISSUE
222 LOOKS
10,000 Beauty Ideas
ENOUGH STYLE
ENOUGH TALENT
ENOUGH
EXTRA STRENGTH
EVEN MORE
STRAWBERRY
EVEN IF IT CAME IN A JAR, I WOULDN'T HAVE ENOUGH OF IT.

BUT AT LEAST I HAVE LILY.

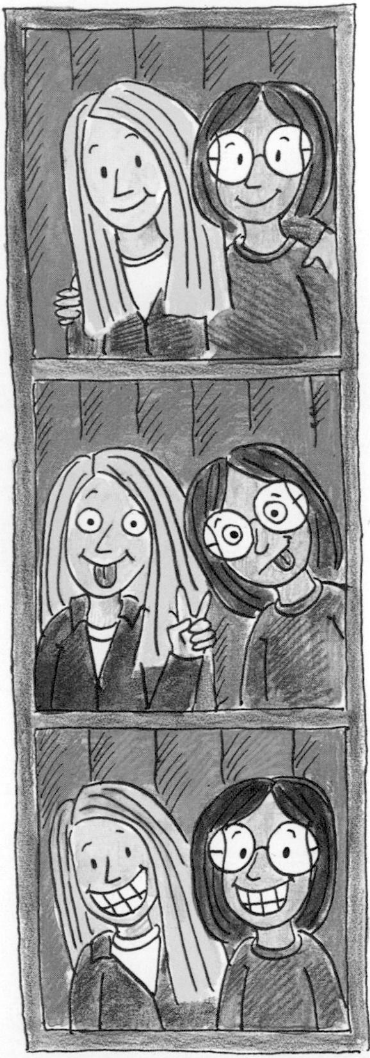

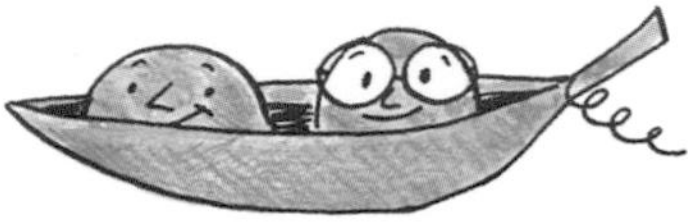

WE'RE TWO PEAS IN A POD.

AND WE'VE BEEN BEST FRIENDS SINCE SECOND GRADE.

WE DO EVERYTHING TOGETHER. WE EVEN HAVE A CLUB.

EVERYTHING IN THE CLUB IS PURPLE BECAUSE THAT'S LILY'S FAVORITE COLOR. (I LIKE PINK.)

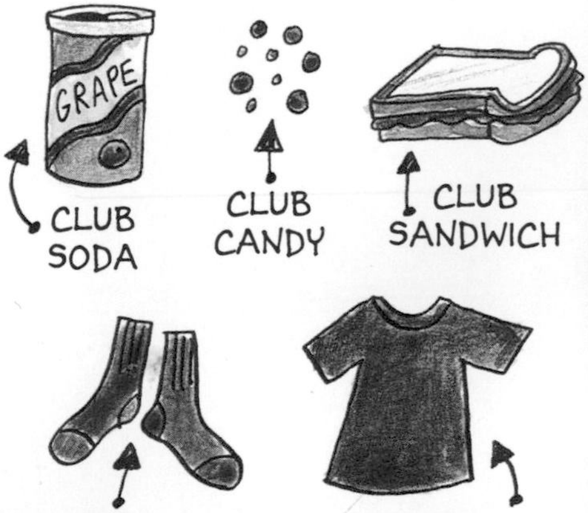
GRAPE
CLUB SODA
CLUB CANDY
CLUB SANDWICH
CLUB SOCKS
CLUB T-SHIRT

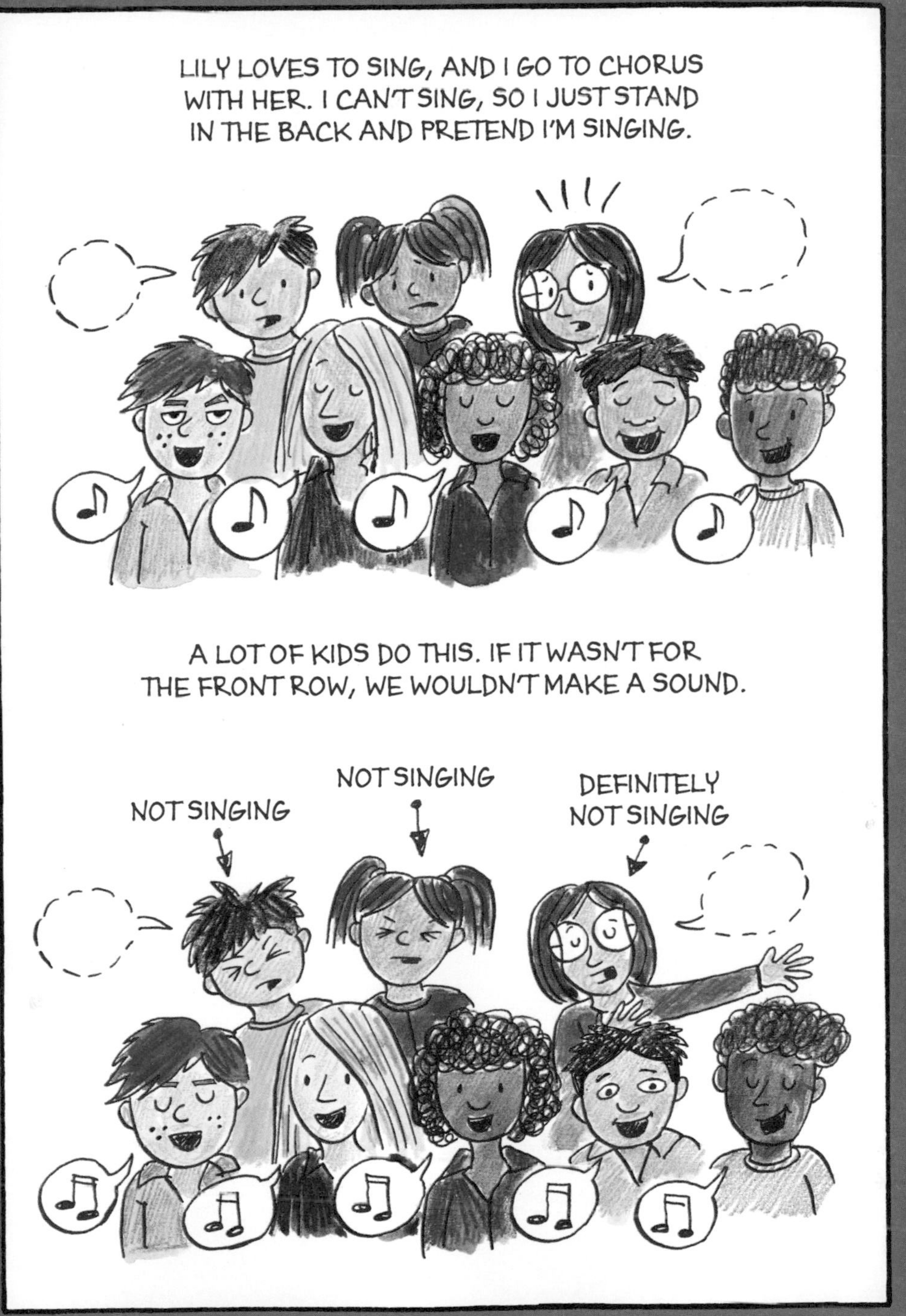
LILY LOVES TO SING, AND I GO TO CHORUS WITH HER. I CAN'T SING, SO I JUST STAND IN THE BACK AND PRETEND I'M SINGING.
A LOT OF KIDS DO THIS. IF IT WASN'T FOR THE FRONT ROW, WE WOULDN'T MAKE A SOUND.
NOT SINGING
NOT SINGING
DEFINITELY NOT SINGING

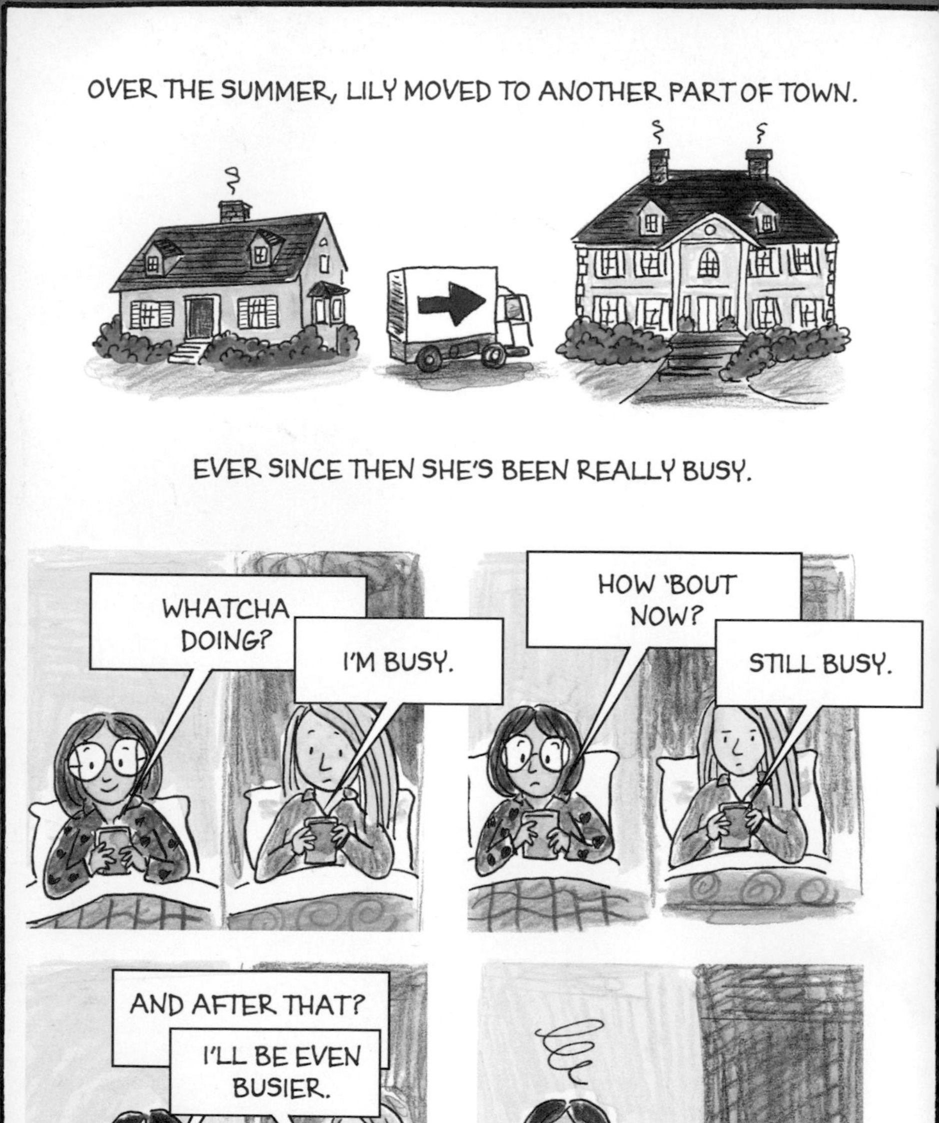
OVER THE SUMMER, LILY MOVED TO ANOTHER PART OF TOWN.
EVER SINCE THEN SHE'S BEEN REALLY BUSY.
WHATCHA DOING?
I'M BUSY.
HOW 'BOUT NOW?
STILL BUSY.
AND AFTER THAT?
I'LL BE EVEN BUSIER.

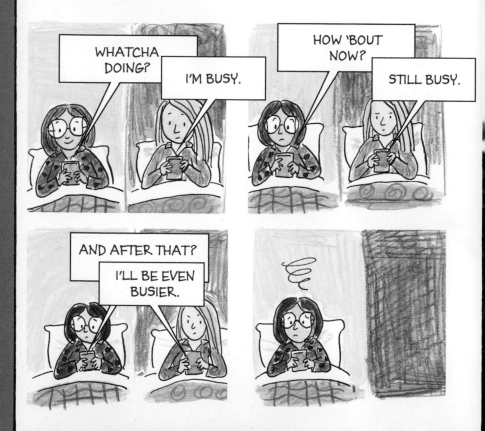

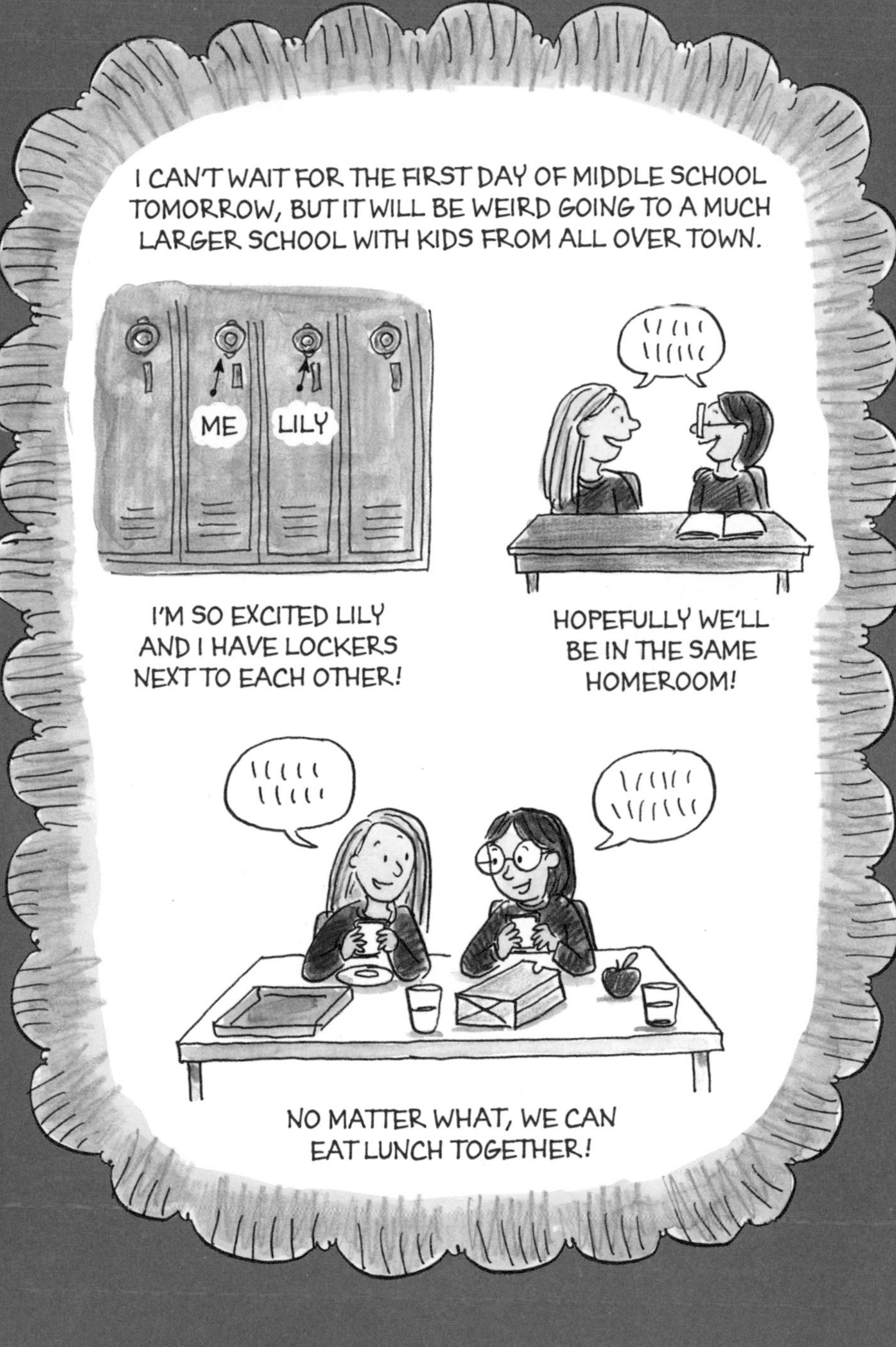
I CAN'T WAIT FOR THE FIRST DAY OF MIDDLE SCHOOL TOMORROW, BUT IT WILL BE WEIRD GOING TO A MUCH LARGER SCHOOL WITH KIDS FROM ALL OVER TOWN.
ME
LILY
I'M SO EXCITED LILY AND I HAVE LOCKERS NEXT TO EACH OTHER!
HOPEFULLY WE'LL BE IN THE SAME HOMEROOM!
NO MATTER WHAT, WE CAN EAT LUNCH TOGETHER!

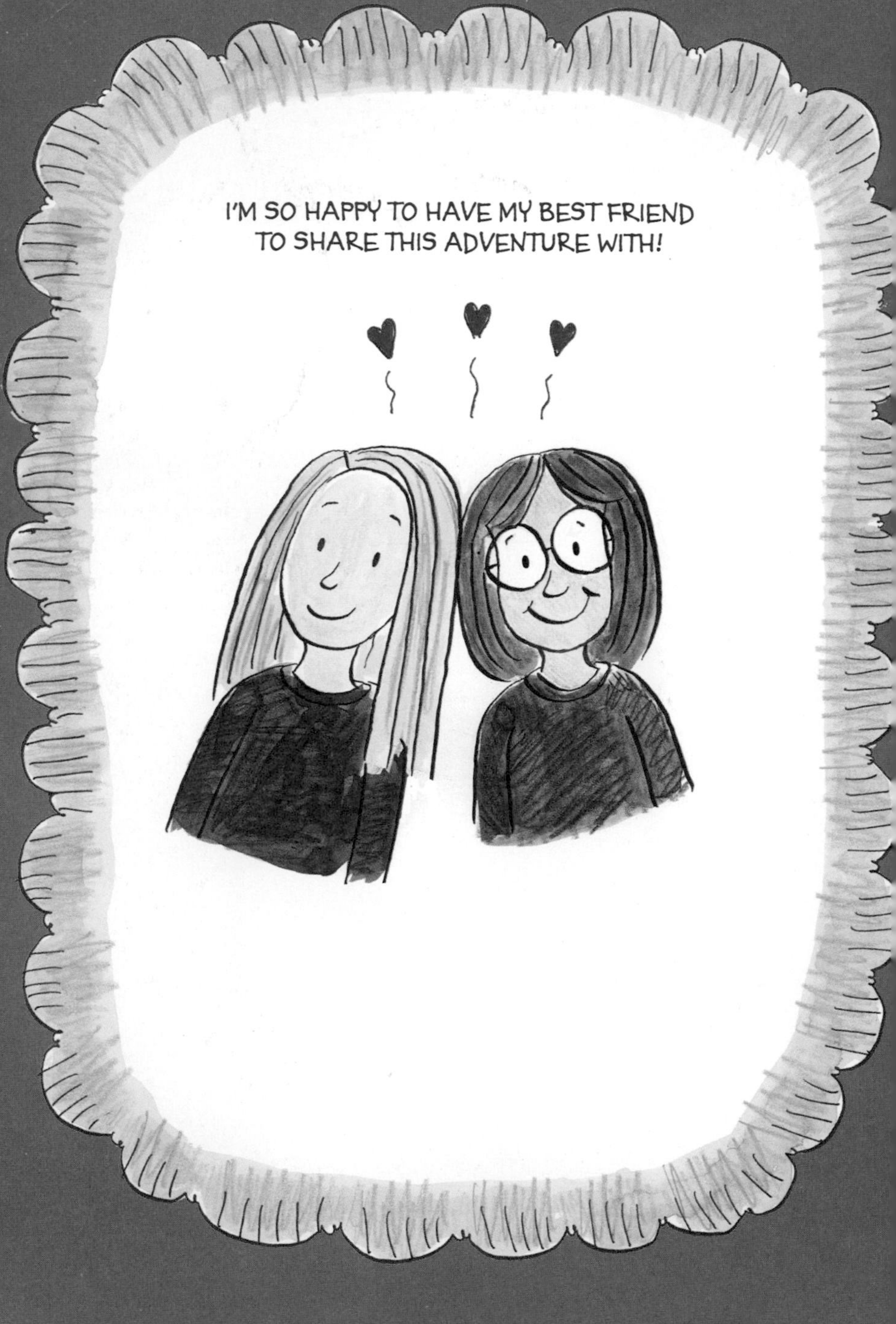
I'M SO HAPPY TO HAVE MY BEST FRIEND TO SHARE THIS ADVENTURE WITH!

CHAPTER 1
MAGAZINE GiRL

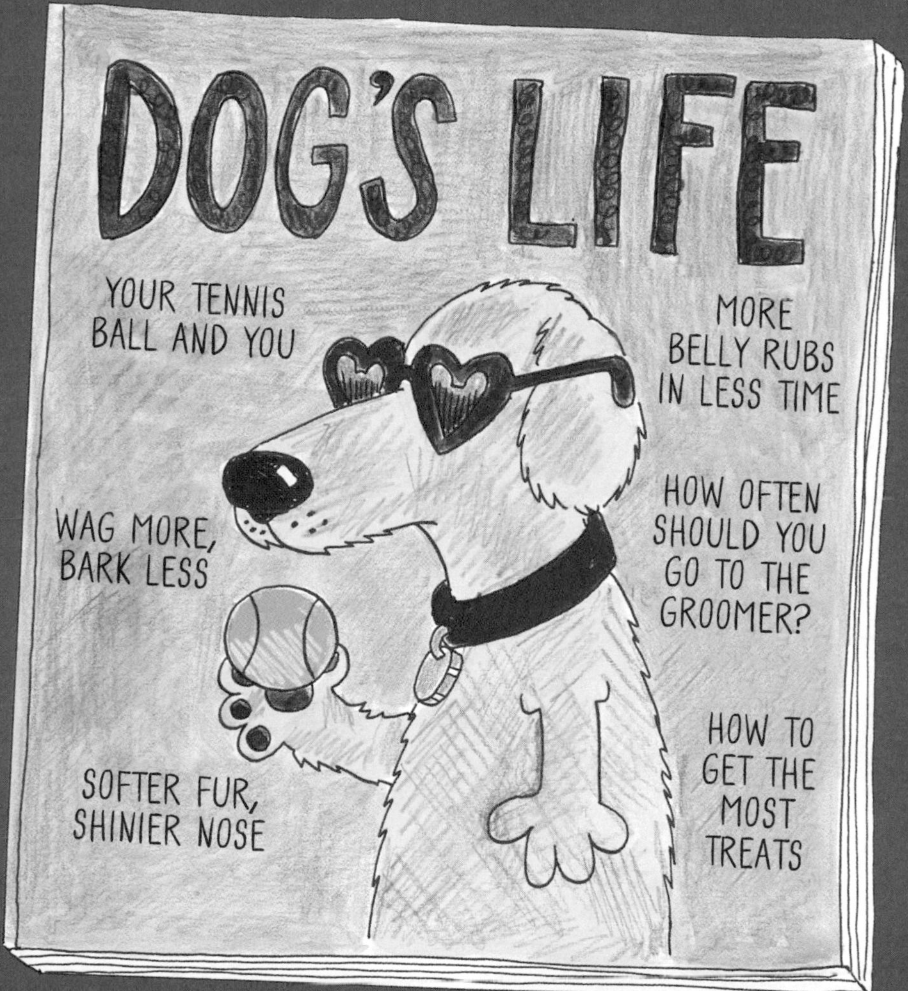
DOG'S LIFE
YOUR TENNIS BALL AND YOU
MORE BELLY RUBS IN LESS TIME
WAG MORE, BARK LESS
HOW OFTEN SHOULD YOU GO TO THE GROOMER?
HOW TO GET THE MOST TREATS
SOFTER FUR, SHINIER NOSE

THE NEXT MORNING I GOT READY FOR SCHOOL...

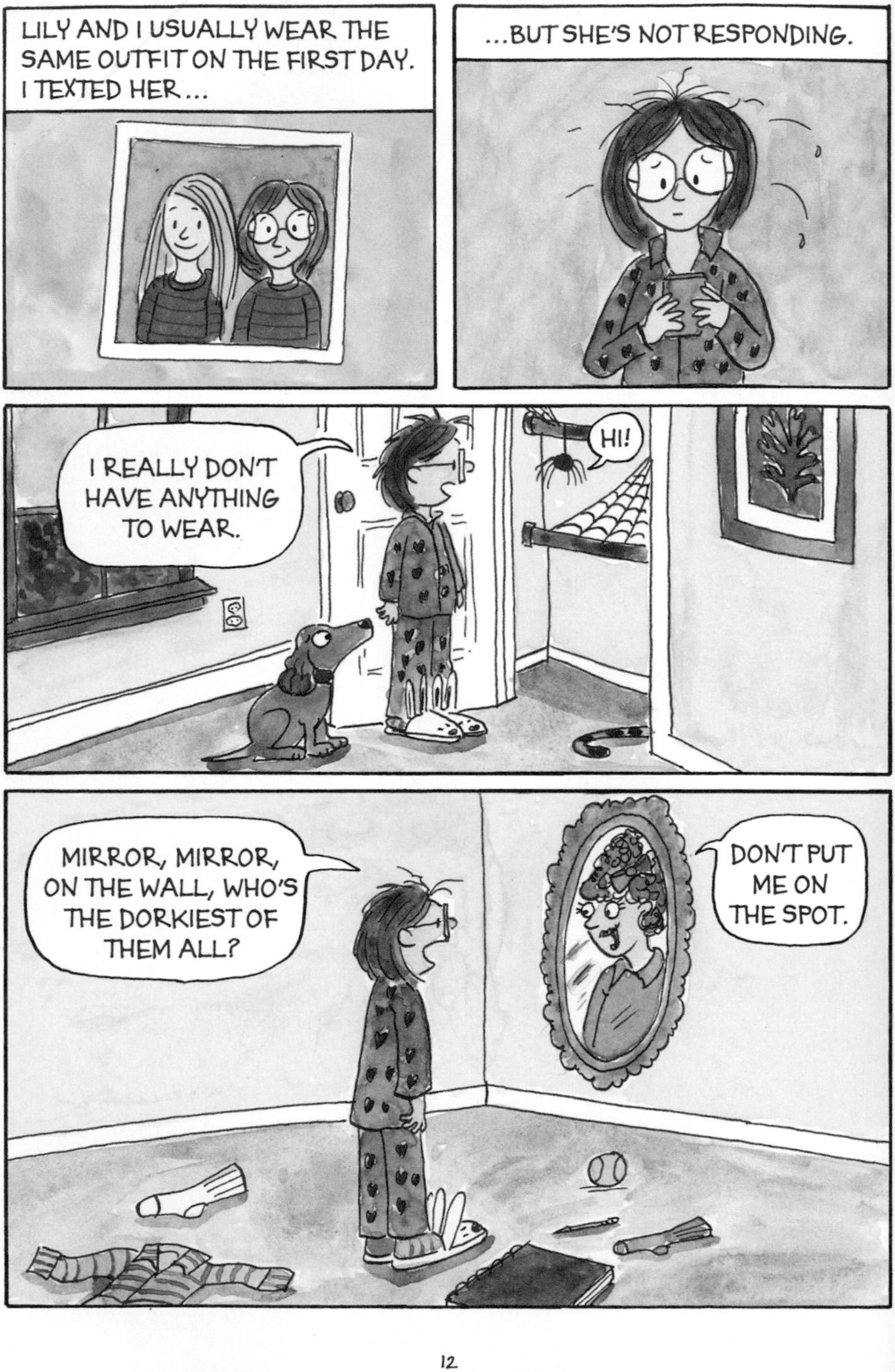
LILY AND I USUALLY WEAR THE SAME OUTFIT ON THE FIRST DAY. I TEXTED HER...
...BUT SHE'S NOT RESPONDING.
I REALLY DON'T HAVE ANYTHING TO WEAR.
HI!
MIRROR, MIRROR, ON THE WALL, WHO'S THE DORKIEST OF THEM ALL?
DON'T PUT ME ON THE SPOT.

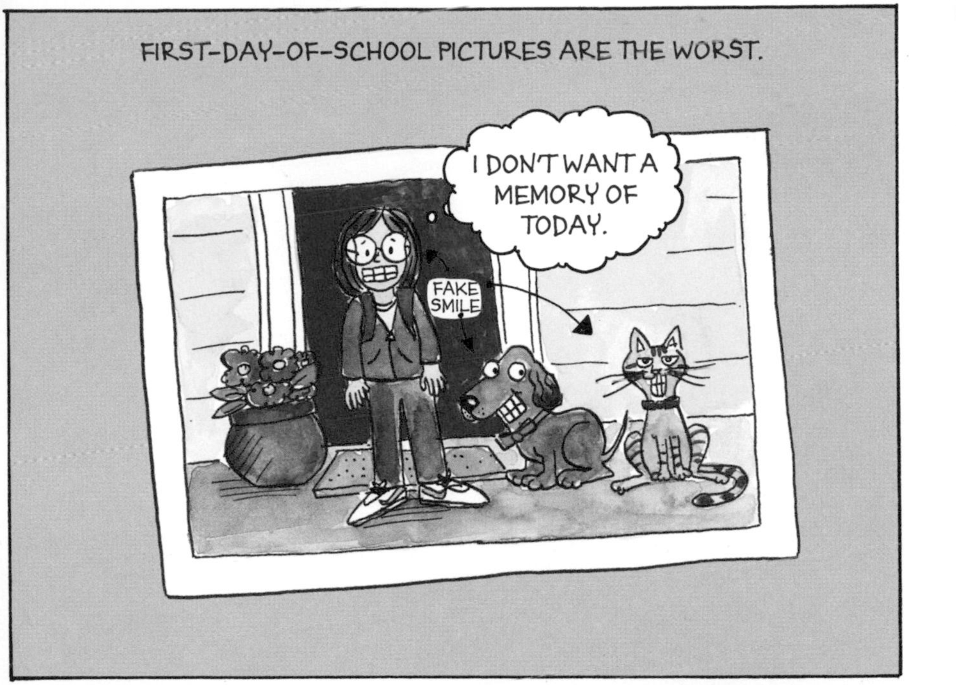
FIRST-DAY-OF-SCHOOL PICTURES ARE THE WORST.
I DON'T WANT A MEMORY OF TODAY.
FAKE SMILE

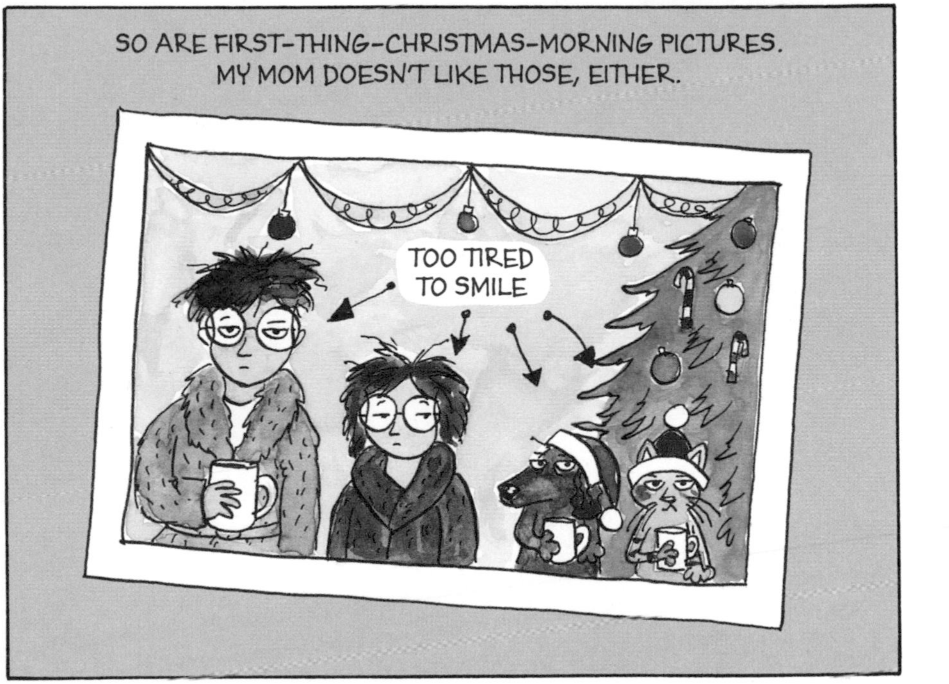
SO ARE FIRST-THING-CHRISTMAS-MORNING PICTURES.
MY MOM DOESN'T LIKE THOSE, EITHER.
TOO TIRED TO SMILE

I HOPPED ON MY BIKE, EXCITED TO GET TO SCHOOL AND SEE LILY.

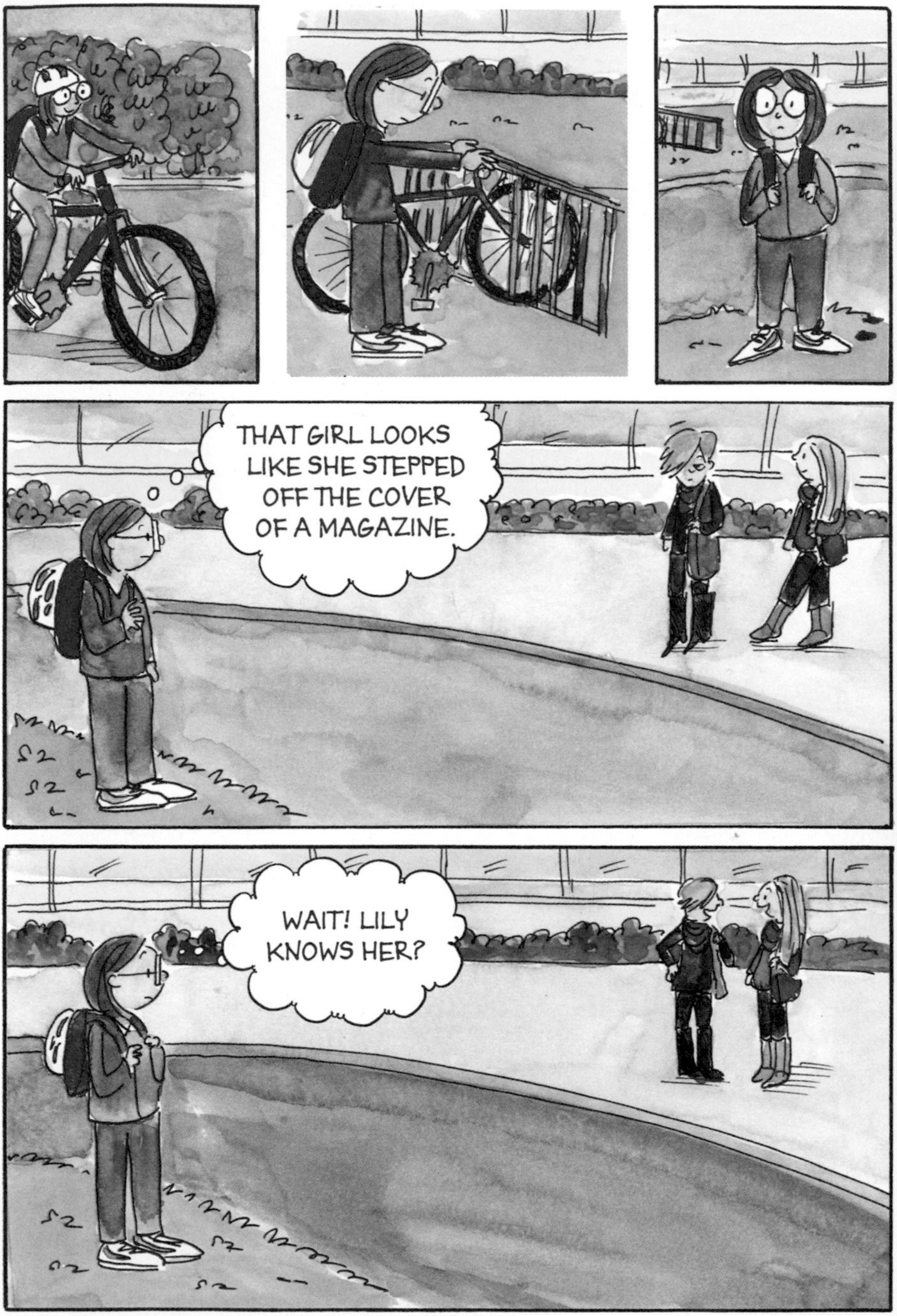
THAT GIRL LOOKS LIKE SHE STEPPED OFF THE COVER OF A MAGAZINE.
WAIT! LILY KNOWS HER?

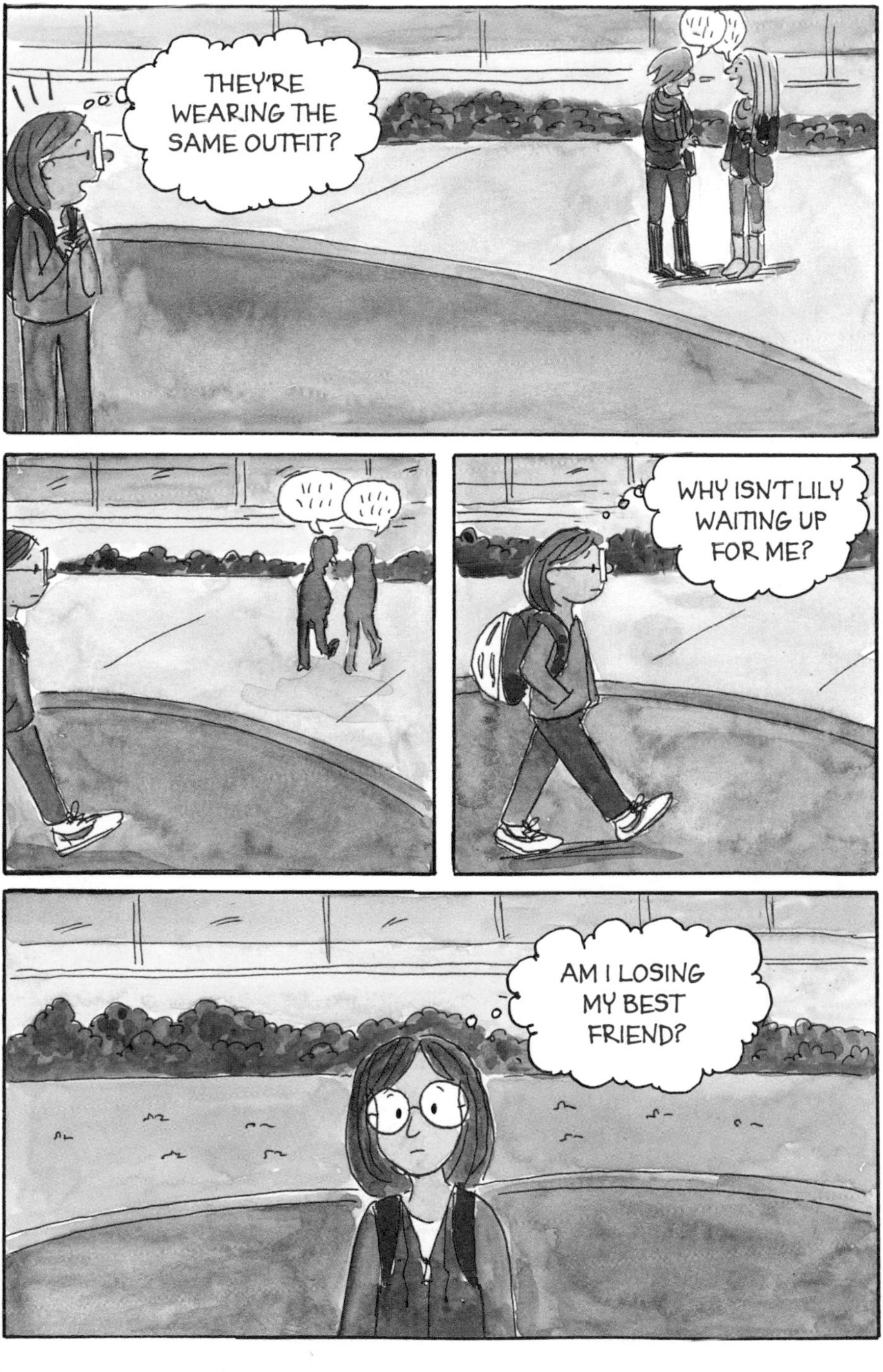
THEY'RE WEARING THE SAME OUTFIT?
WHY ISN'T LILY WAITING UP FOR ME?
AM I LOSING MY BEST FRIEND?

MAGAZINE GiRL

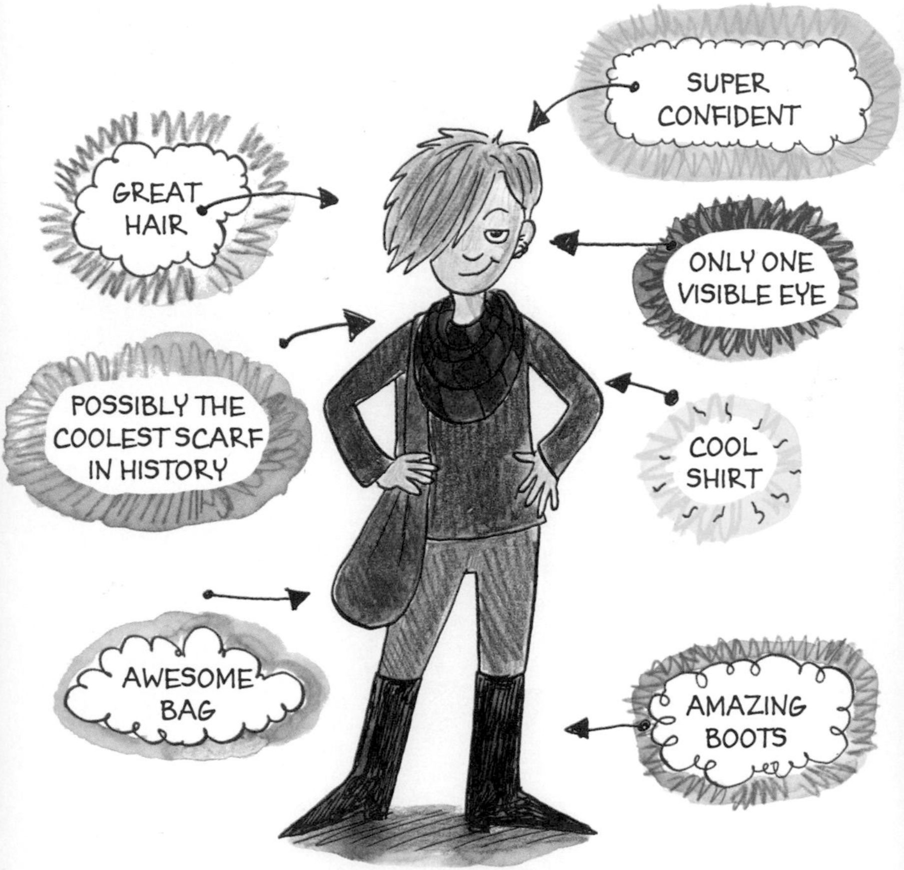
SUPER CONFIDENT
GREAT HAIR
ONLY ONE VISIBLE EYE
POSSIBLY THE COOLEST SCARF IN HISTORY
COOL SHIRT
AWESOME BAG
AMAZING BOOTS

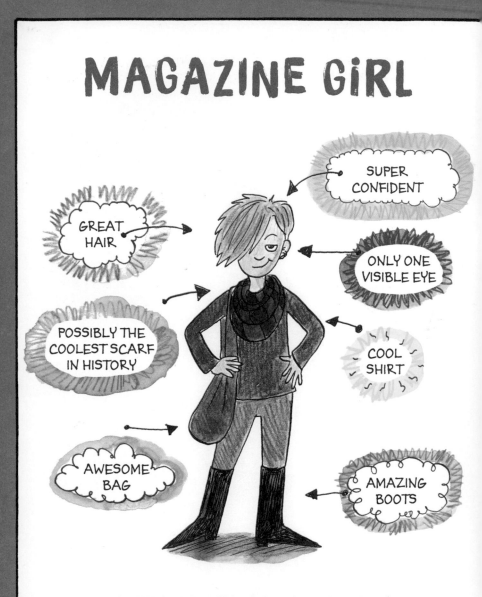

MAGAZINE GIRL HAS HAIR COVERING ONE EYE.
PEOPLE ARE MYSTERIOUS WHEN THEY COVER ONE EYE.

MAGAZINES ARE FUNNY. THEY'RE ALWAYS TELLING PEOPLE HOW TO LOOK AND WHAT TO WEAR AND THINGS THEY SHOULD BE DOING.

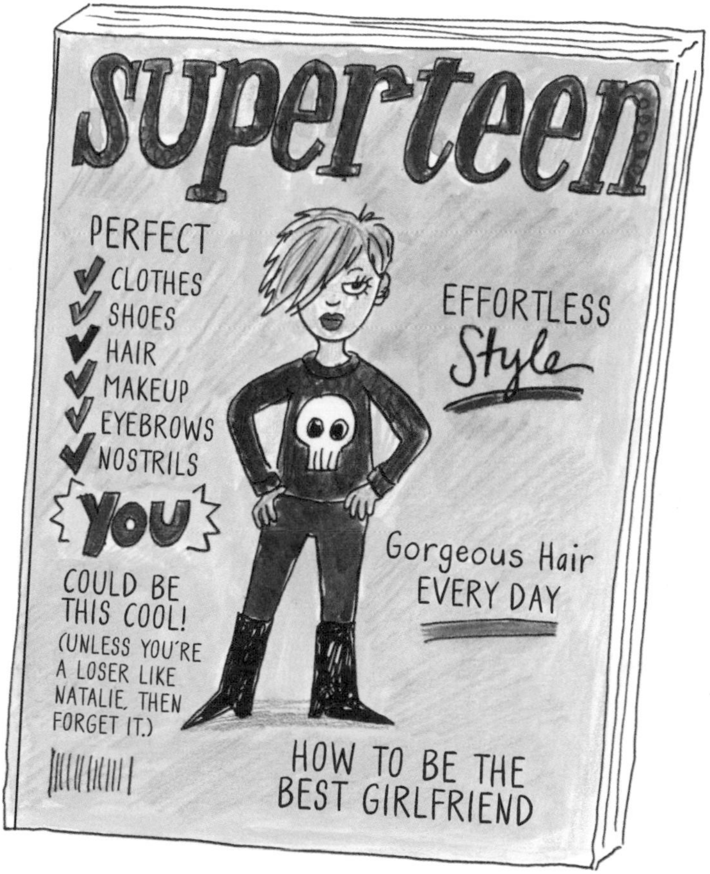
superteen
PERFECT
CLOTHES
SHOES
HAIR
MAKEUP
EYEBROWS
NOSTRILS
YOU
COULD BE THIS COOL!
(UNLESS YOU'RE A LOSER LIKE NATALIE. THEN FORGET IT.)
EFFORTLESS Style
Gorgeous Hair EVERY DAY
HOW TO BE THE BEST GIRLFRIEND

MAGAZINES TELL ME THAT MY CLOTHES AREN'T COOL ENOUGH, MY TEETH AREN'T WHITE ENOUGH, MY HAIR ISN'T EDGY ENOUGH, AND MY NOSTRILS AREN'T CUTE ENOUGH. ALSO, I HAVE TOO MANY PORES. (DON'T WE NEED PORES FOR SOMETHING?)

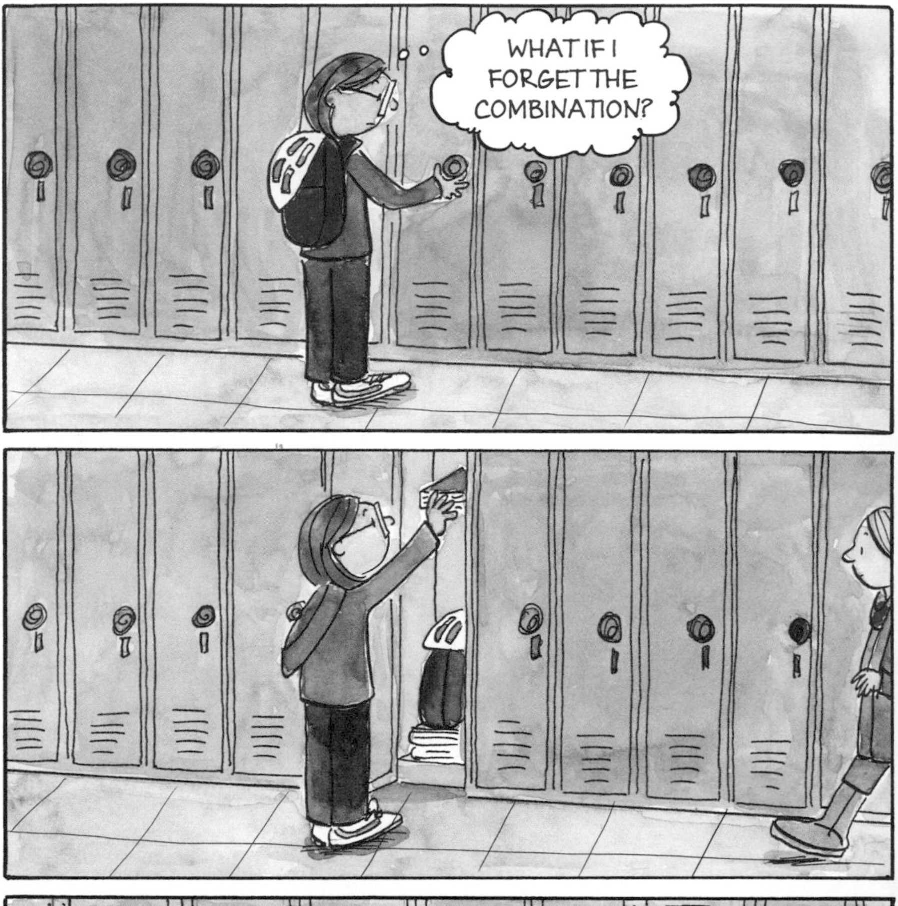
WHAT IF I FORGET THE COMBINATION?
HEY, LILY! AREN'T YOU HAPPY THAT WE'RE LOCKER NEIGHBORS?
WHATEVER.

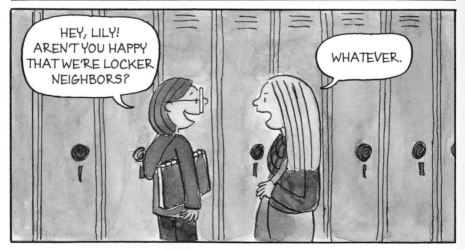

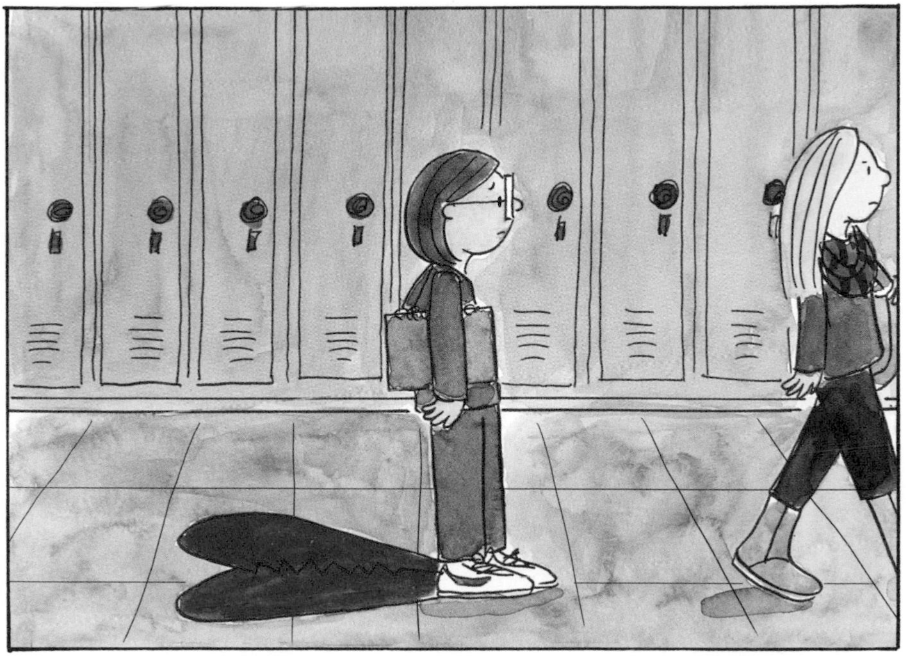

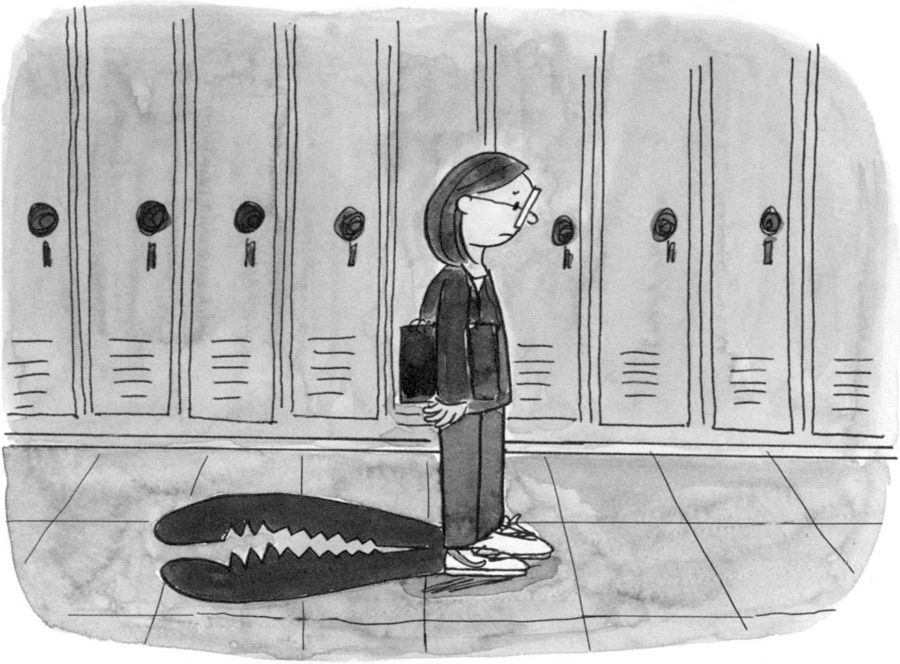

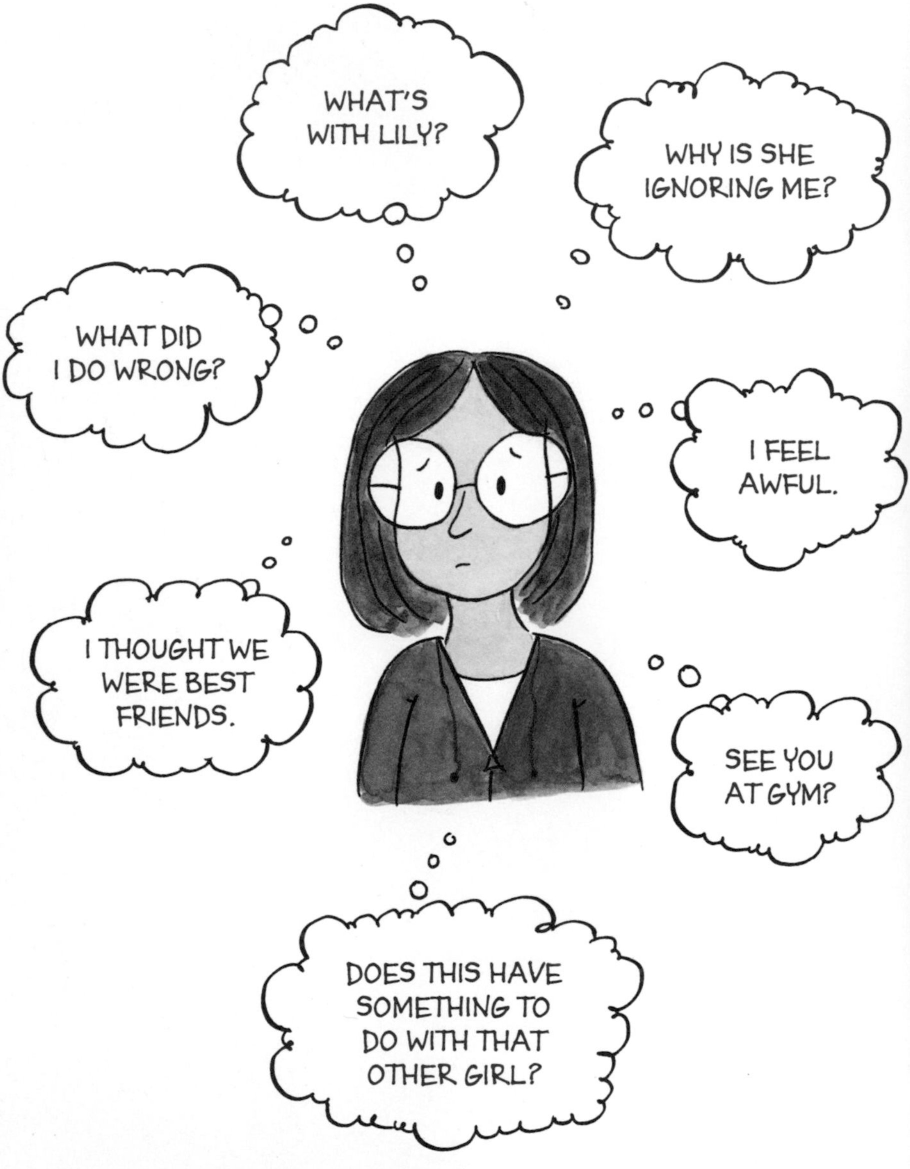
WHAT'S WITH LILY?
WHY IS SHE IGNORING ME?
WHAT DID I DO WRONG?
I FEEL AWFUL.
I THOUGHT WE WERE BEST FRIENDS.
SEE YOU AT GYM?
DOES THIS HAVE SOMETHING TO DO WITH THAT OTHER GIRL?

CHAPTER 2
HURDLES AND OTHER OBSTACLES

DOG EXERCISES

CAT EXERCISES

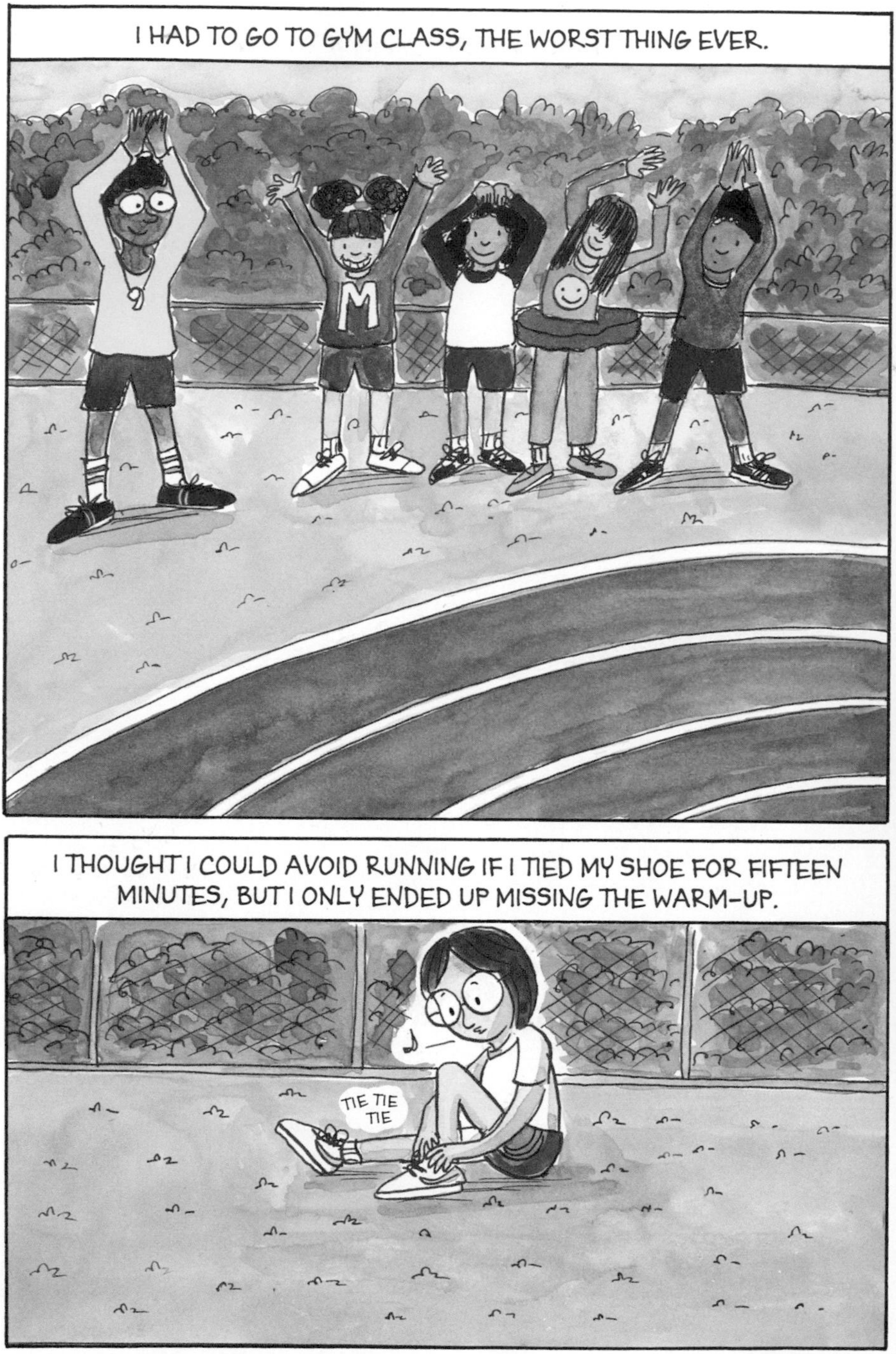
I HAD TO GO TO GYM CLASS, THE WORST THING EVER.
I THOUGHT I COULD AVOID RUNNING IF I TIED MY SHOE FOR FIFTEEN MINUTES, BUT I ONLY ENDED UP MISSING THE WARM-UP.
TIE TIE TIE

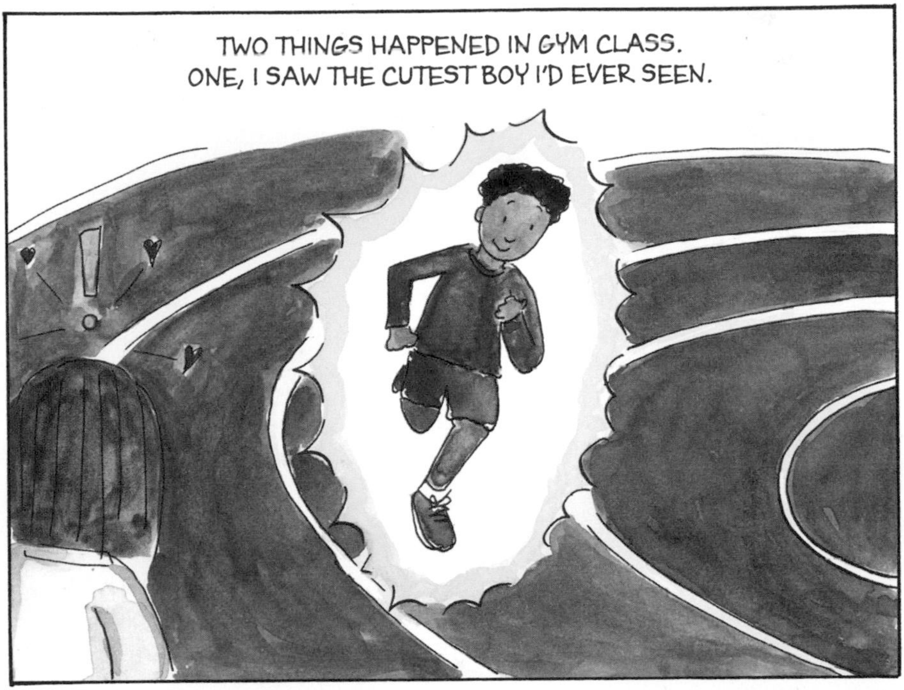
TWO THINGS HAPPENED IN GYM CLASS.
ONE, I SAW THE CUTEST BOY I'D EVER SEEN.

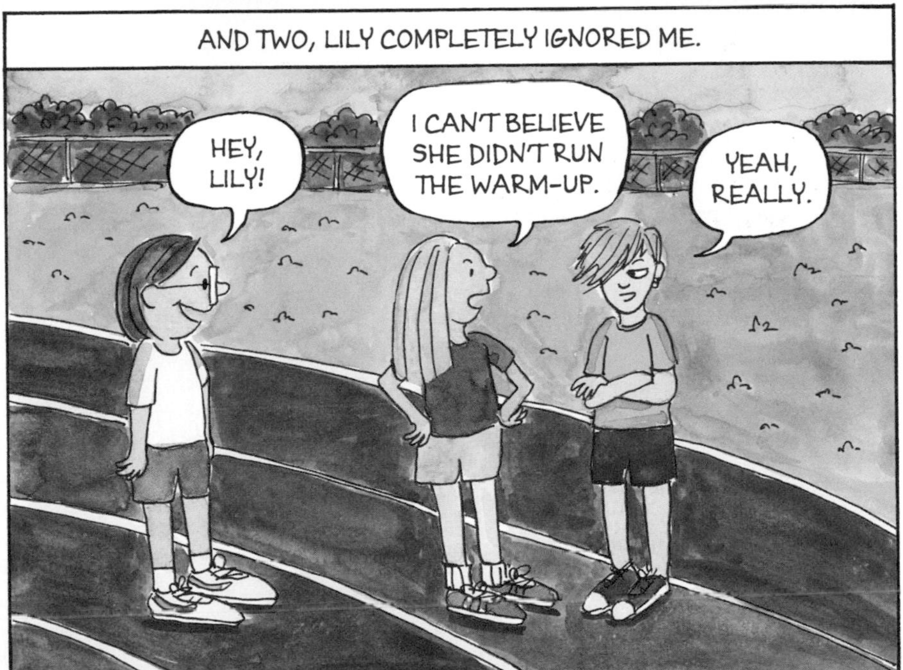
AND TWO, LILY COMPLETELY IGNORED ME.
HEY, LILY!
I CAN'T BELIEVE SHE DIDN'T RUN THE WARM-UP.
YEAH, REALLY.

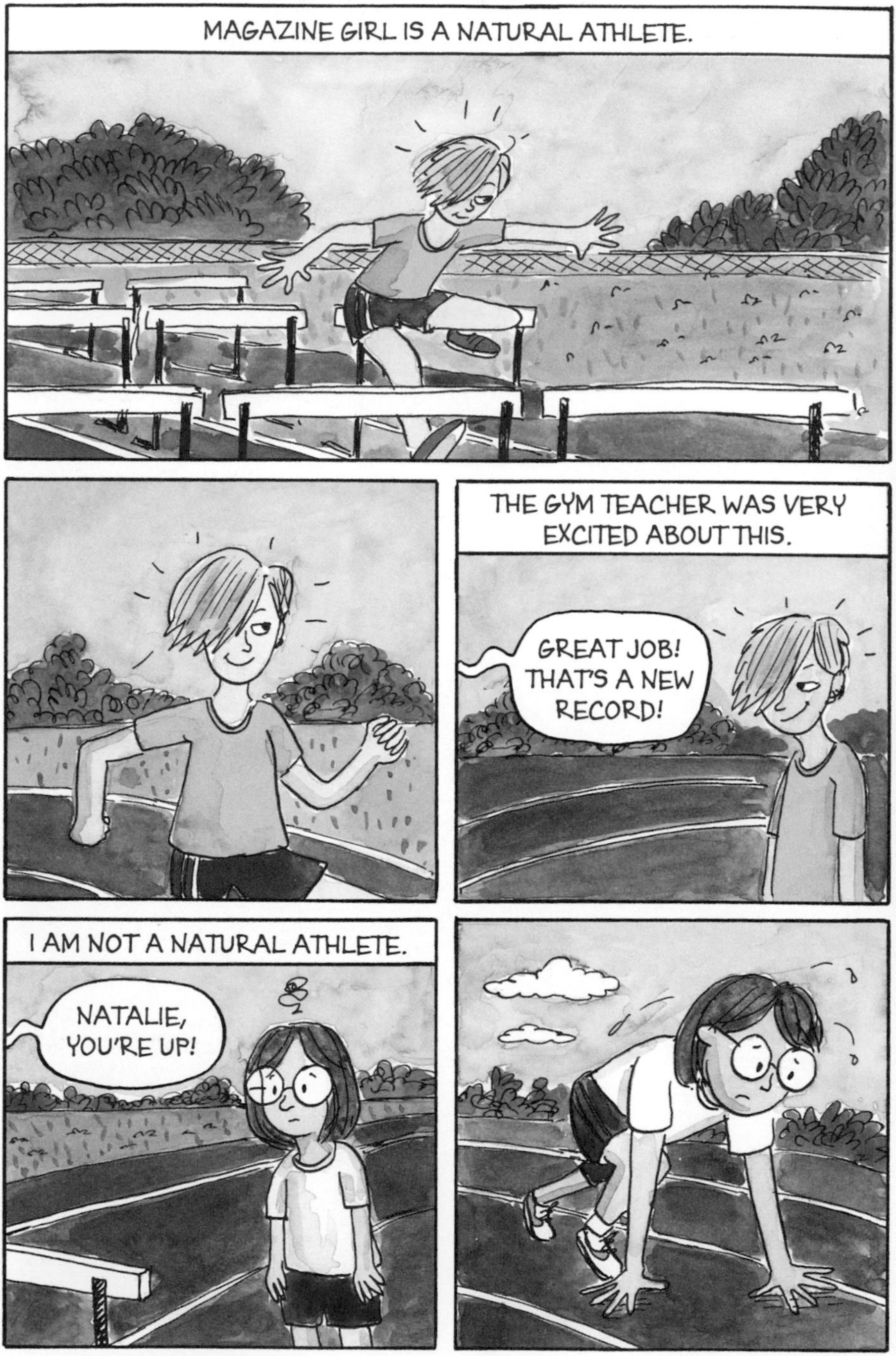
MAGAZINE GIRL IS A NATURAL ATHLETE.
THE GYM TEACHER WAS VERY EXCITED ABOUT THIS.
GREAT JOB! THAT'S A NEW RECORD!
I AM NOT A NATURAL ATHLETE.
NATALIE, YOU'RE UP!

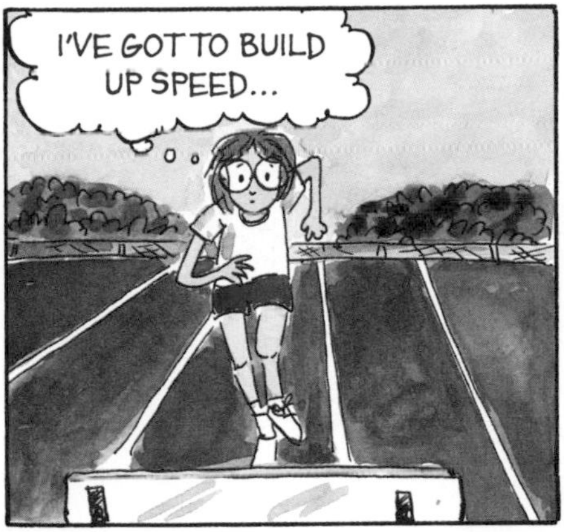
I'VE GOT TO BUILD
UP SPEED...

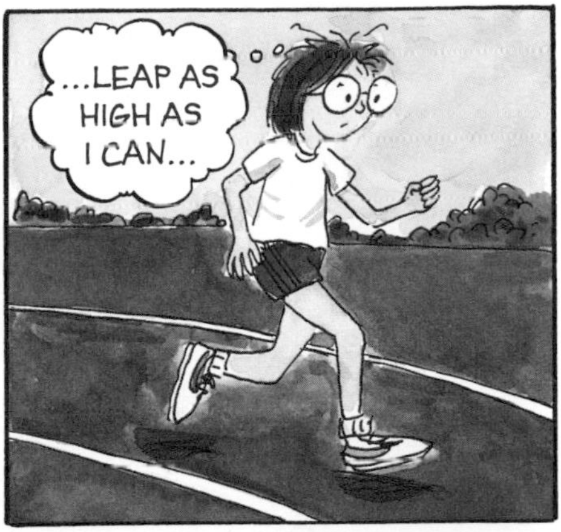
...LEAP AS
HIGH AS
I CAN...

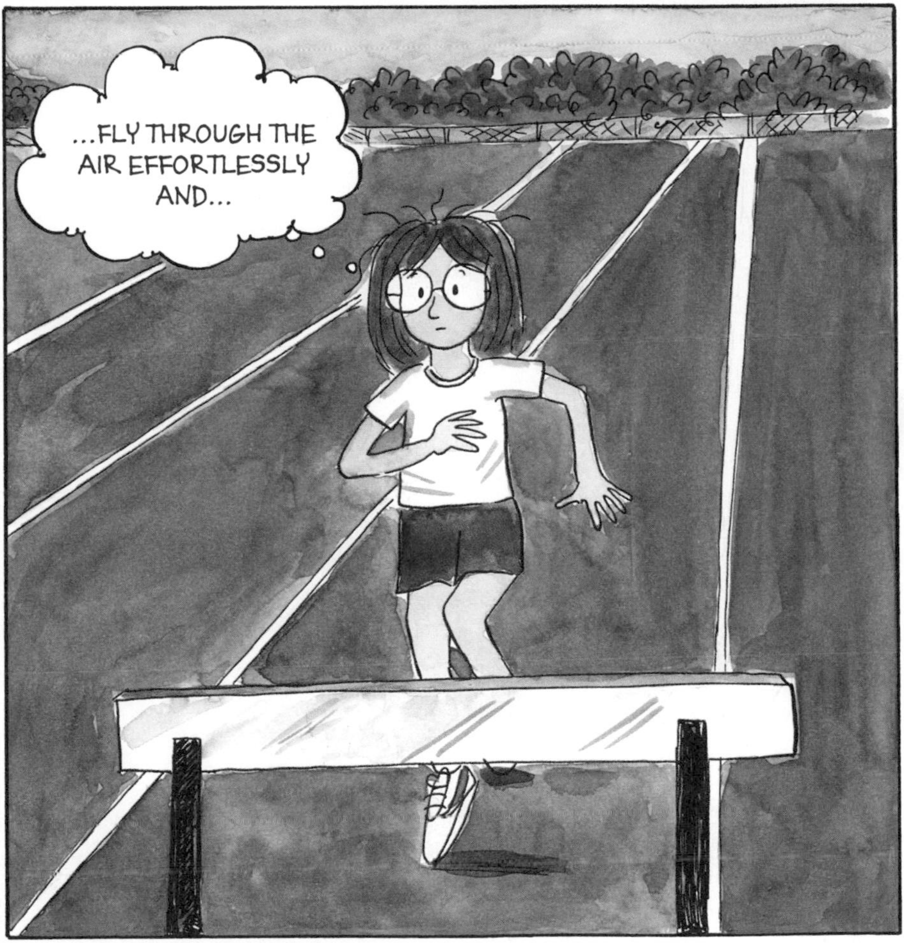
...FLY THROUGH THE
AIR EFFORTLESSLY
AND...

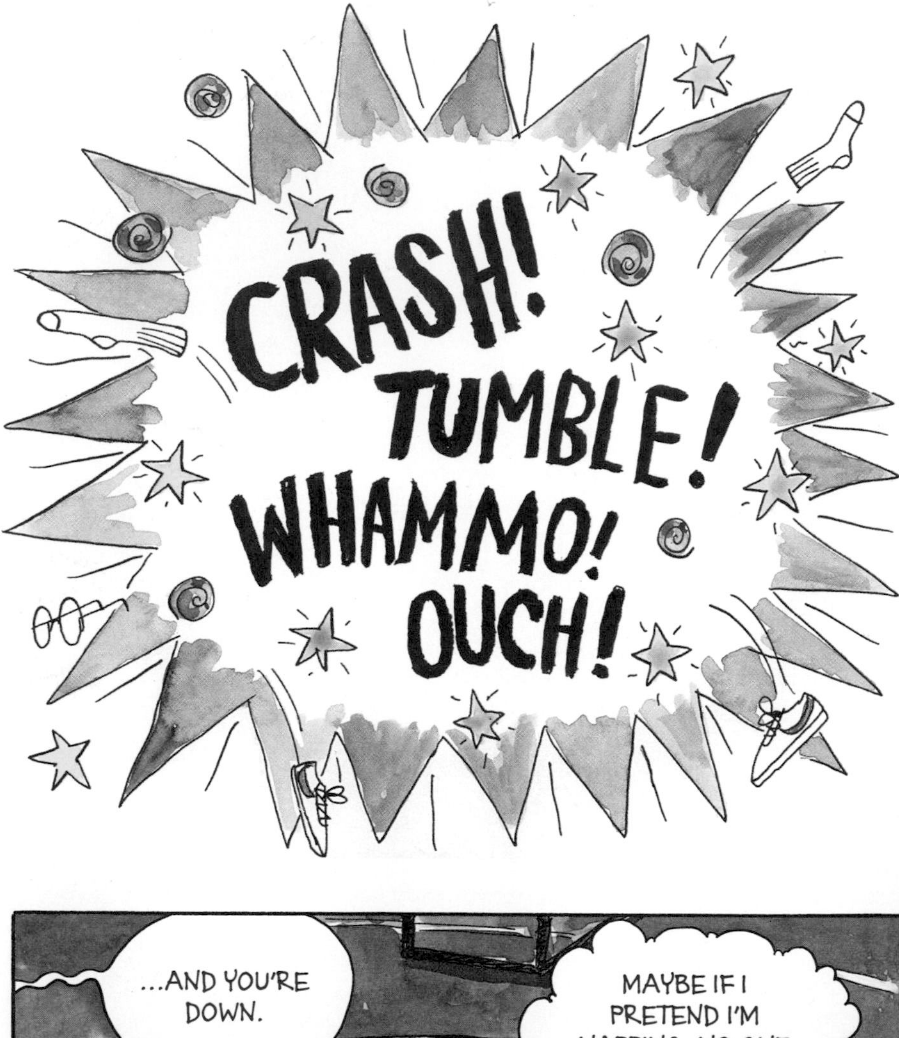
CRASH!
TUMBLE!
WHAMMO!
OUCH!

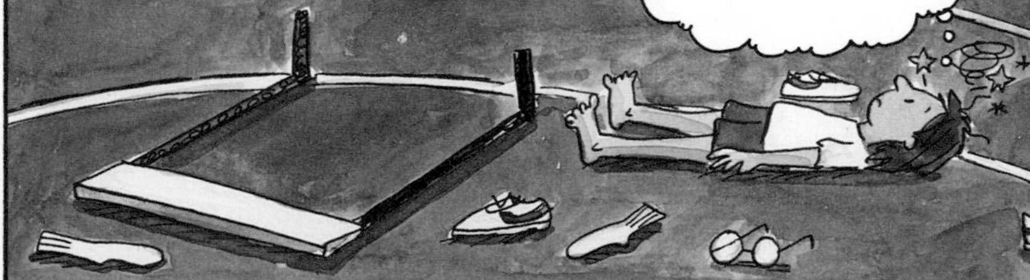
...AND YOU'RE DOWN.
MAYBE IF I PRETEND I'M NAPPING, NO ONE WILL NOTICE.

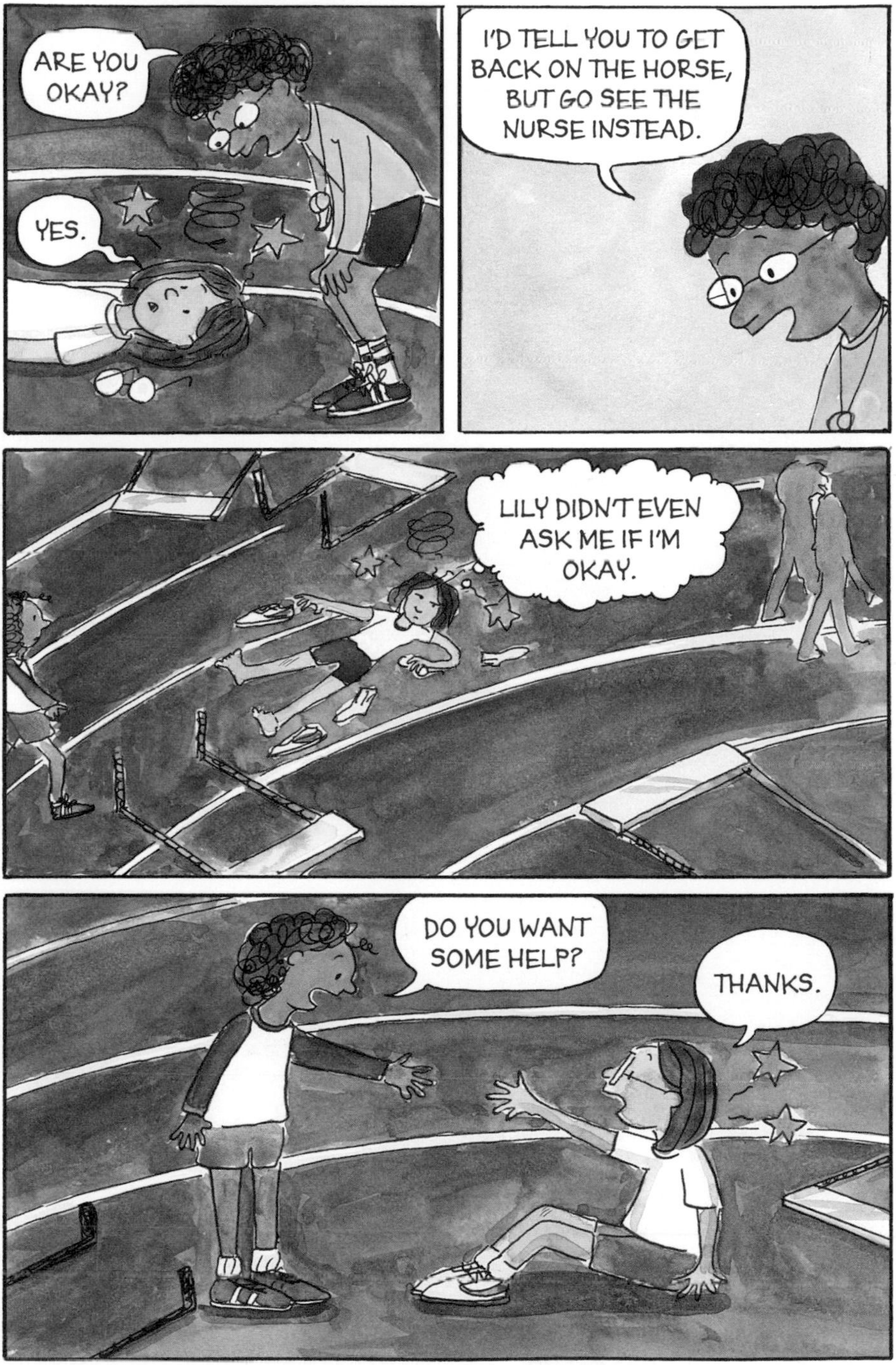
ARE YOU OKAY?
YES.
I'D TELL YOU TO GET BACK ON THE HORSE, BUT GO SEE THE NURSE INSTEAD.
LILY DIDN'T EVEN ASK ME IF I'M OKAY.
DO YOU WANT SOME HELP?
THANKS.

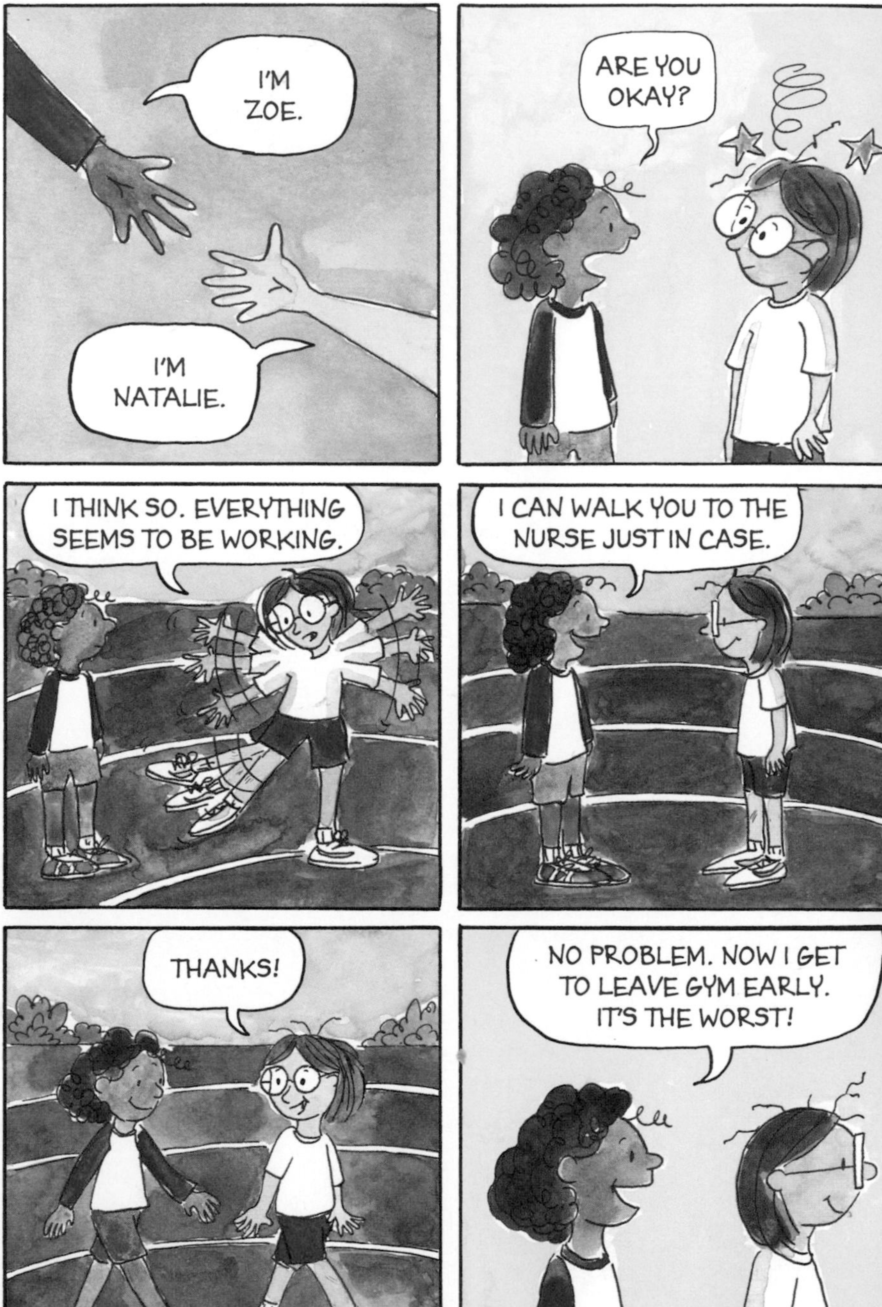
I'M ZOE.
I'M NATALIE.
ARE YOU OKAY?
I THINK SO. EVERYTHING SEEMS TO BE WORKING.
I CAN WALK YOU TO THE NURSE JUST IN CASE.
THANKS!
NO PROBLEM. NOW I GET TO LEAVE GYM EARLY. IT'S THE WORST!

CHAPTER 3
SNOOZEFEST

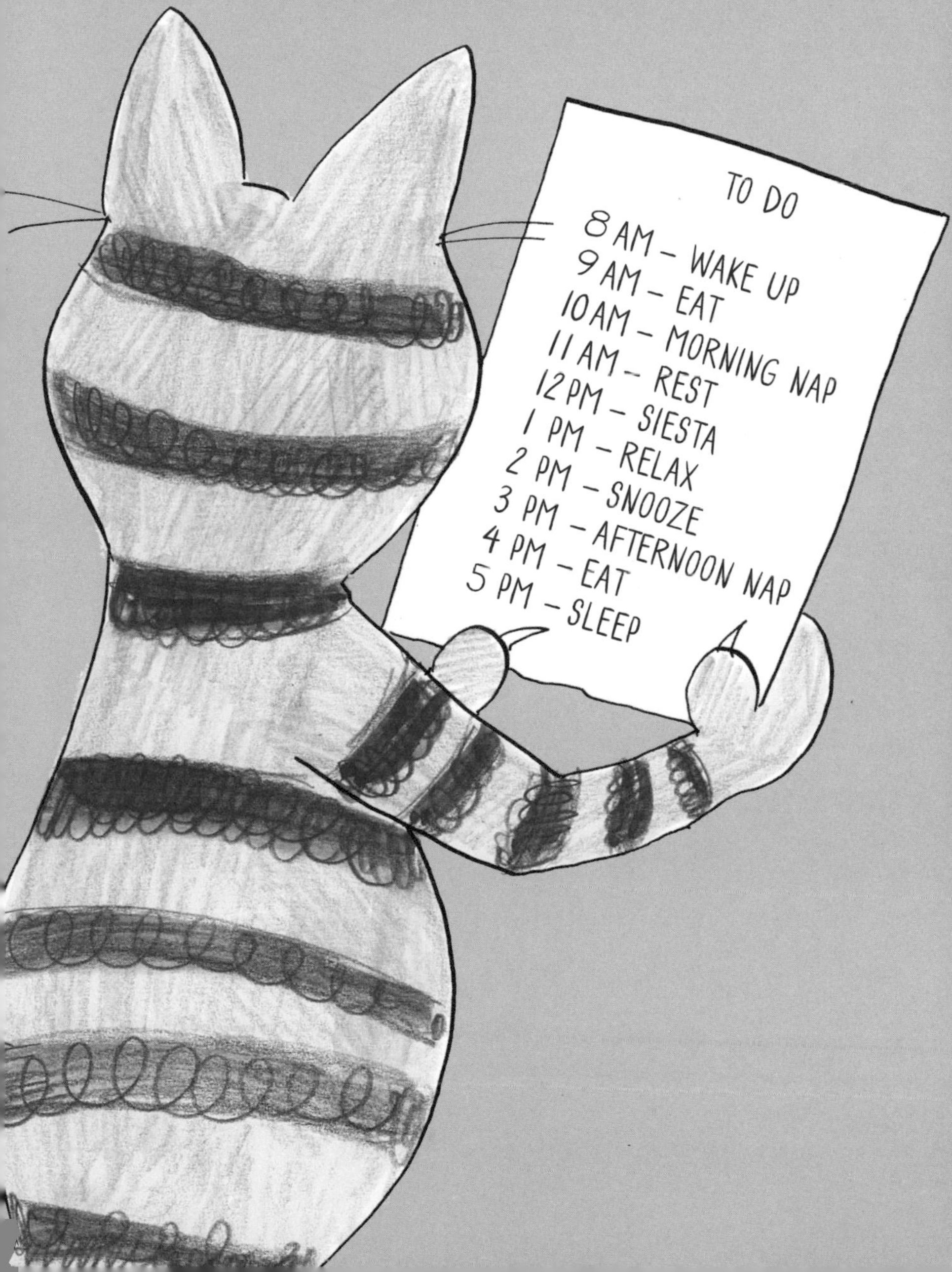
TO DO
8 AM – WAKE UP
9 AM – EAT
10 AM – MORNING NAP
11 AM – REST
12 PM – SIESTA
1 PM – RELAX
2 PM – SNOOZE
3 PM – AFTERNOON NAP
4 PM – EAT
5 PM – SLEEP

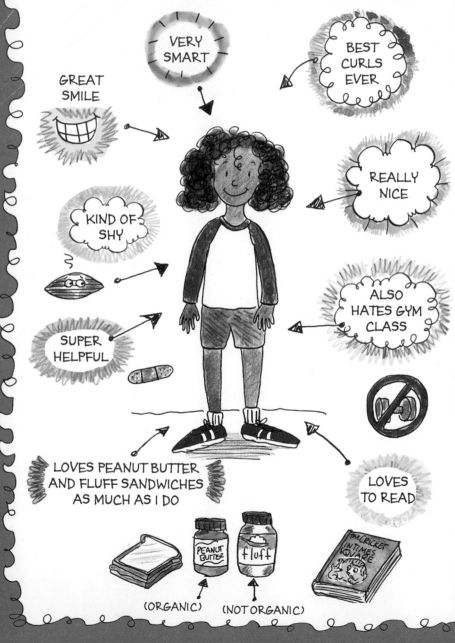

ZOE IS FROM ONE OF THE TWO OTHER ELEMENTARY SCHOOLS THAT FUNNELED INTO MIDWAY MIDDLE SCHOOL.

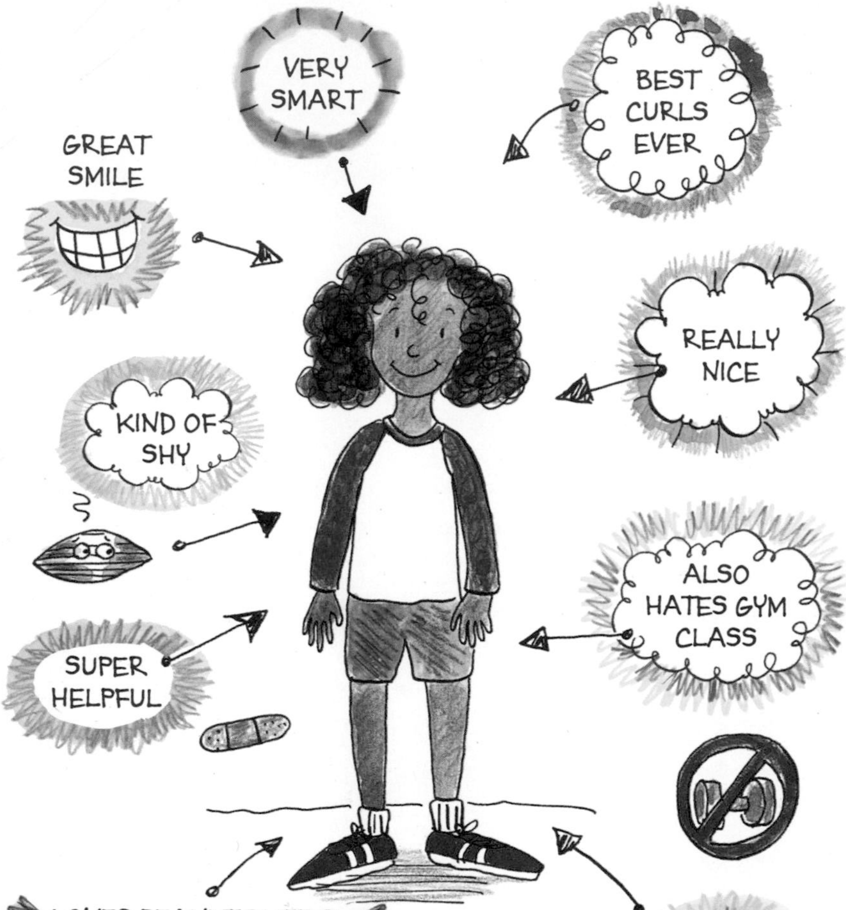
VERY SMART
BEST CURLS EVER
GREAT SMILE
REALLY NICE
KIND OF SHY
ALSO HATES GYM CLASS
SUPER HELPFUL
LOVES PEANUT BUTTER AND FLUFF SANDWICHES AS MUCH AS I DO
LOVES TO READ
PEANUT BUTTER
fluff
THE CRICKET IN TIMES SQUARE
(ORGANIC)
(NOT ORGANIC)

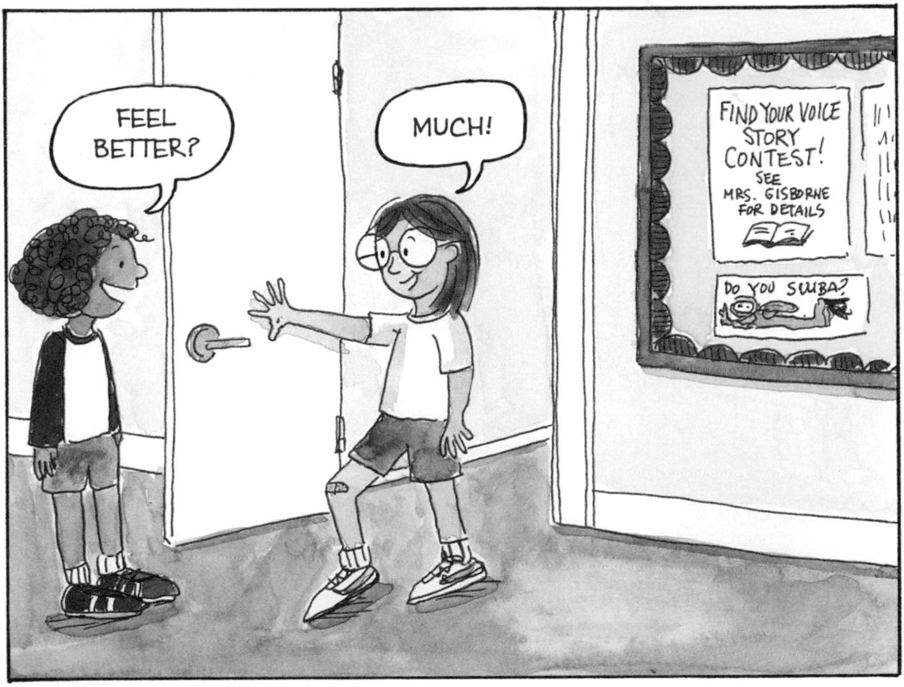
FEEL BETTER?
MUCH!
FIND YOUR VOICE STORY CONTEST! SEE MRS. GISBORNE FOR DETAILS
DO YOU SCUBA?

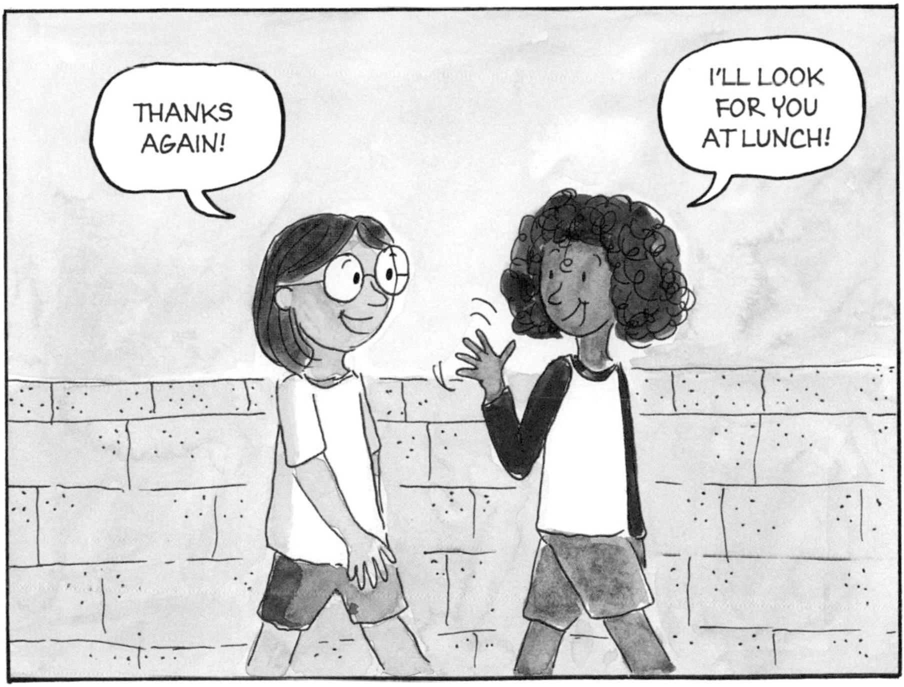
THANKS AGAIN!
I'LL LOOK FOR YOU AT LUNCH!

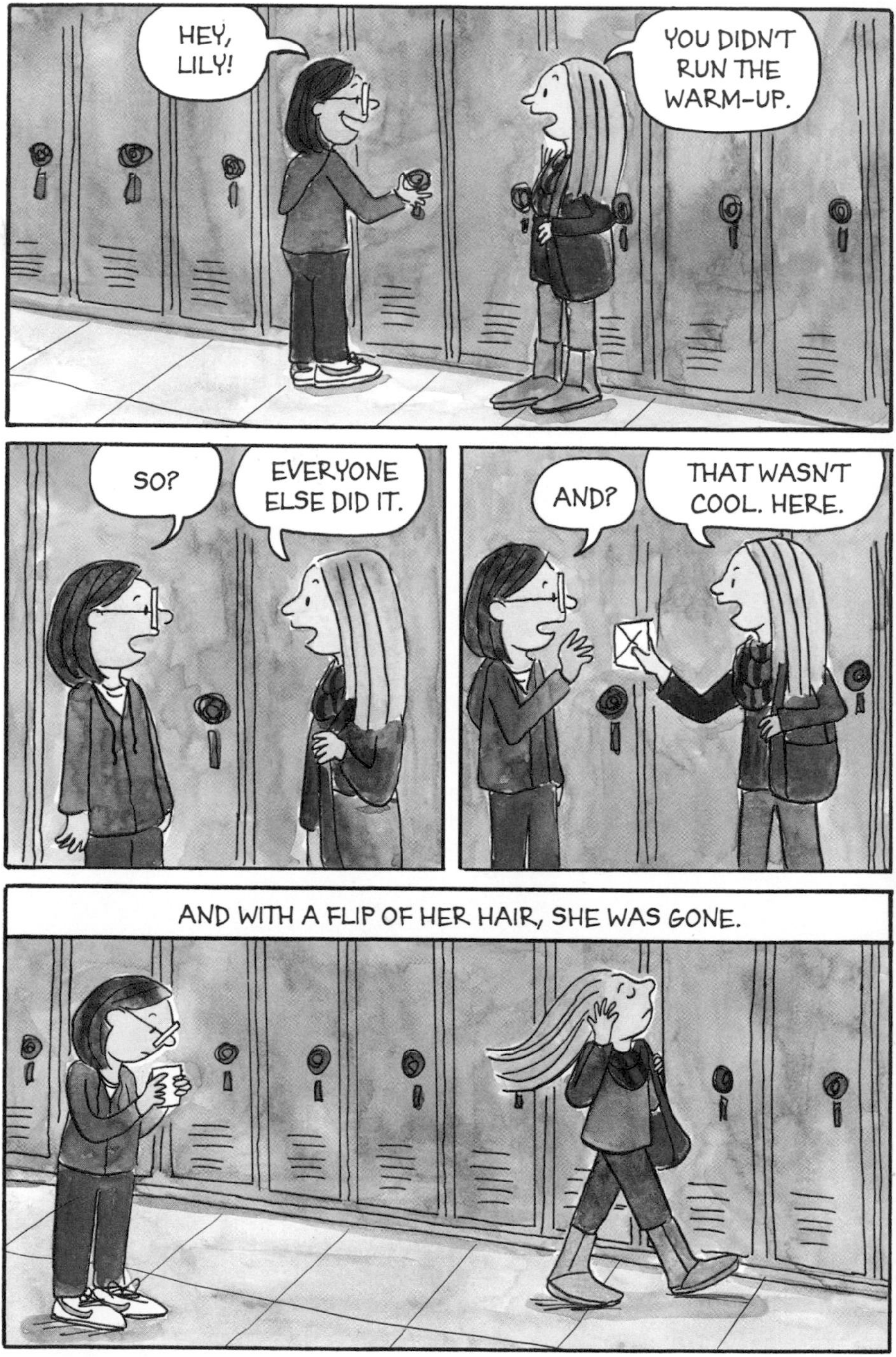
HEY, LILY!
YOU DIDN'T RUN THE WARM-UP.
SO?
EVERYONE ELSE DID IT.
AND?
THAT WASN'T COOL. HERE.
AND WITH A FLIP OF HER HAIR, SHE WAS GONE.

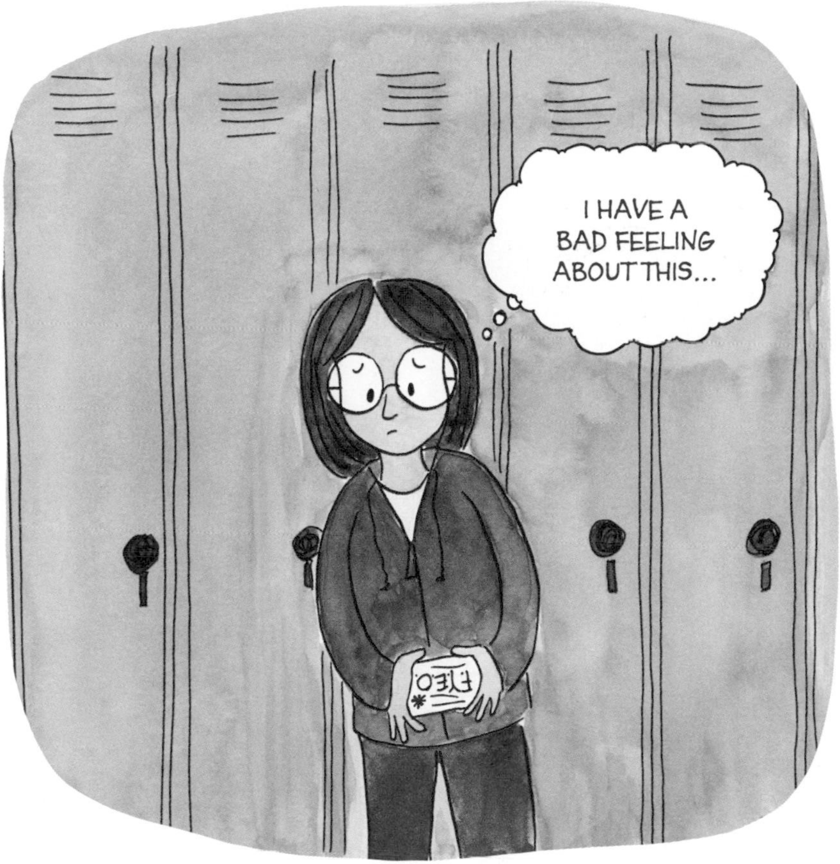
I HAVE A BAD FEELING ABOUT THIS...

* FOR YOUR EYES ONLY

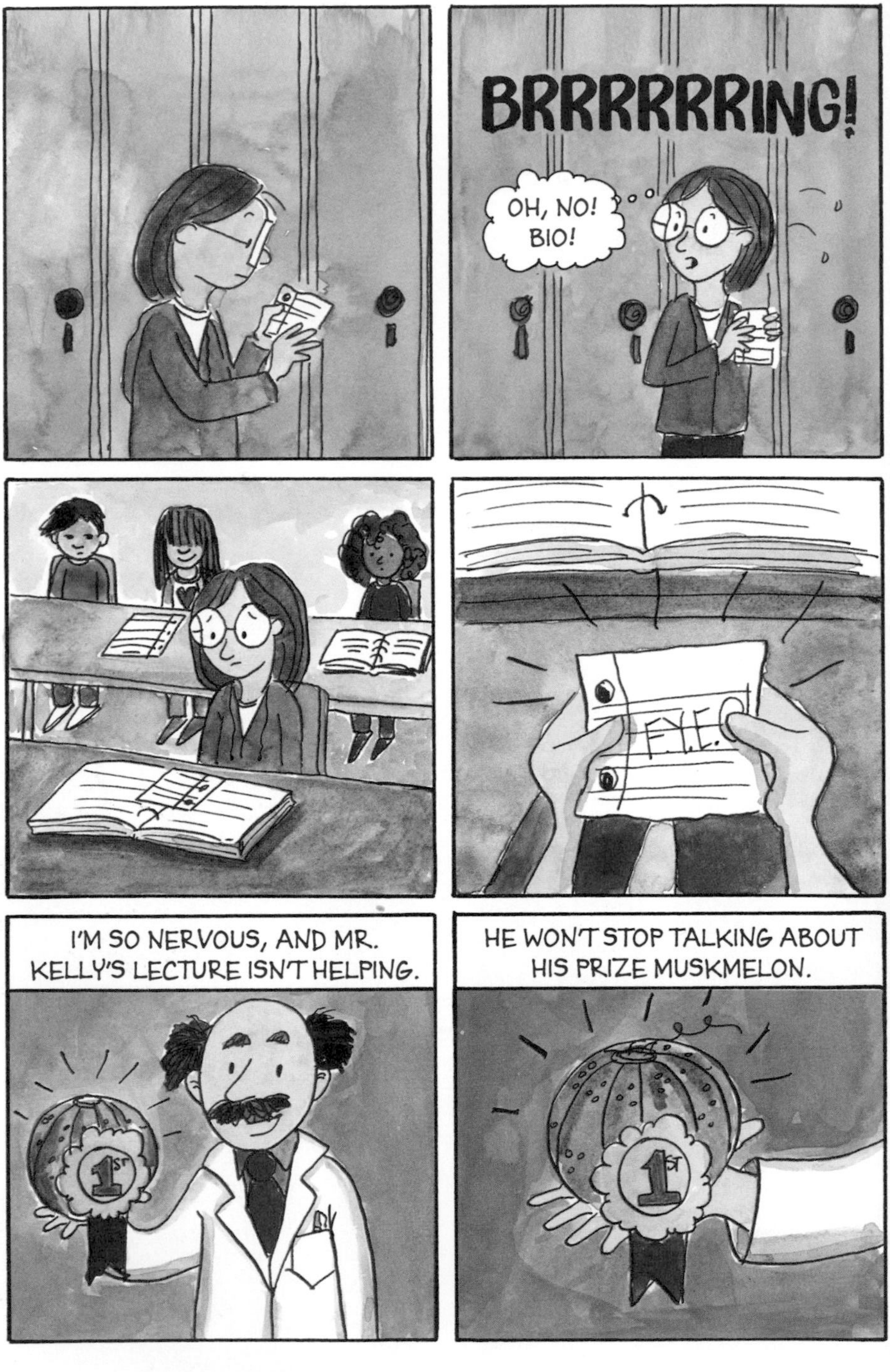
BRRRRRRING!
OH, NO! BIO!
F.Y.E.
I'M SO NERVOUS, AND MR. KELLY'S LECTURE ISN'T HELPING.
HE WON'T STOP TALKING ABOUT HIS PRIZE MUSKMELON.
1ST
1ST

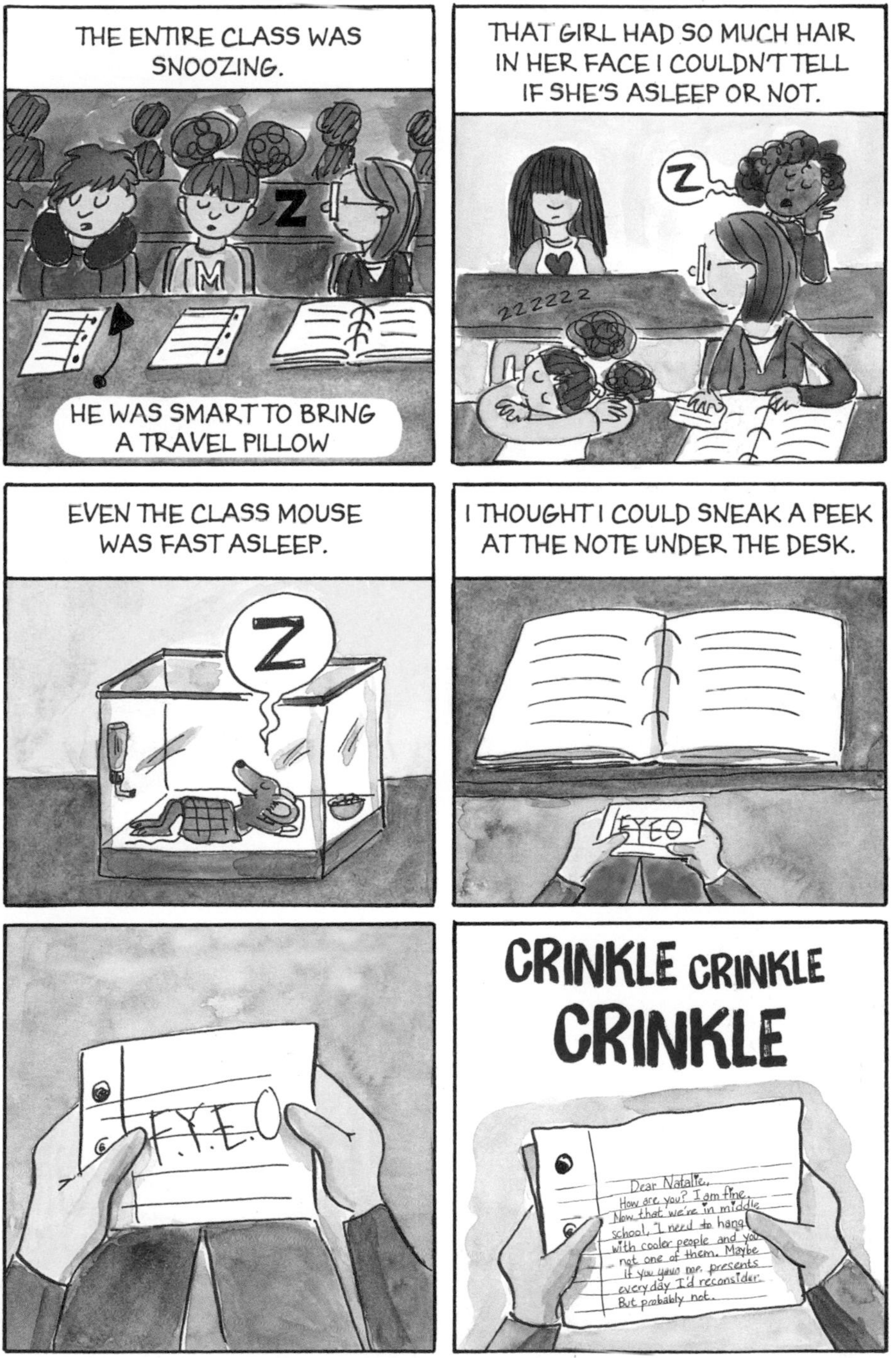
THE ENTIRE CLASS WAS SNOOZING.
Z
HE WAS SMART TO BRING A TRAVEL PILLOW
THAT GIRL HAD SO MUCH HAIR IN HER FACE I COULDN'T TELL IF SHE'S ASLEEP OR NOT.
Z
ZZZZZZ
EVEN THE CLASS MOUSE WAS FAST ASLEEP.
Z
I THOUGHT I COULD SNEAK A PEEK AT THE NOTE UNDER THE DESK.
F.Y.E.O
F.Y.E.O
CRINKLE CRINKLE CRINKLE
Dear Natalie,
How are you? I am fine.
Now that we're in middle
school, I need to hang
with cooler people and you
not one of them. Maybe
if you gave me presents
everyday I'd reconsider.
But probably not.

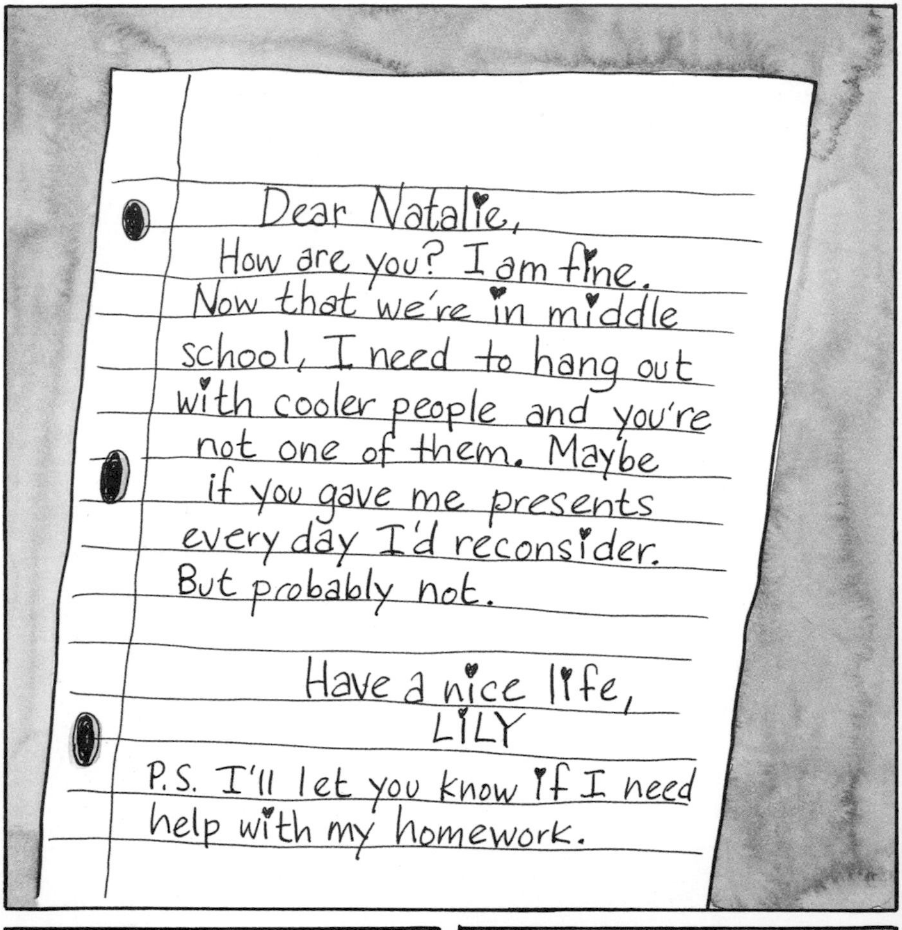
Dear Natalie,
How are you? I am fine. Now that we're in middle school, I need to hang out with cooler people and you're not one of them. Maybe if you gave me presents every day I'd reconsider. But probably not.
Have a nice life,
LILY
P.S. I'll let you know if I need help with my homework.

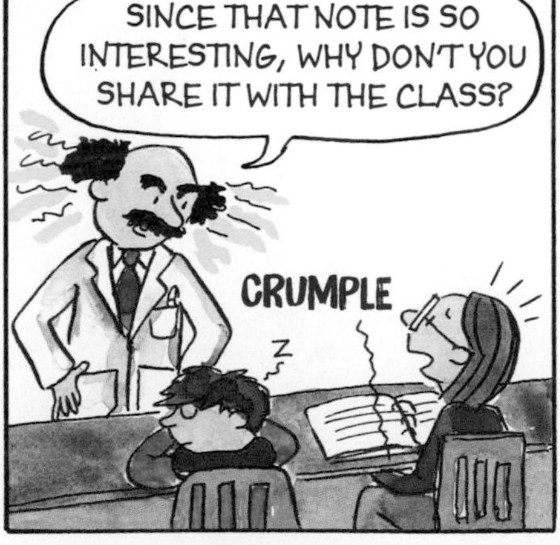
SINCE THAT NOTE IS SO INTERESTING, WHY DON'T YOU SHARE IT WITH THE CLASS?
CRUMPLE
Z

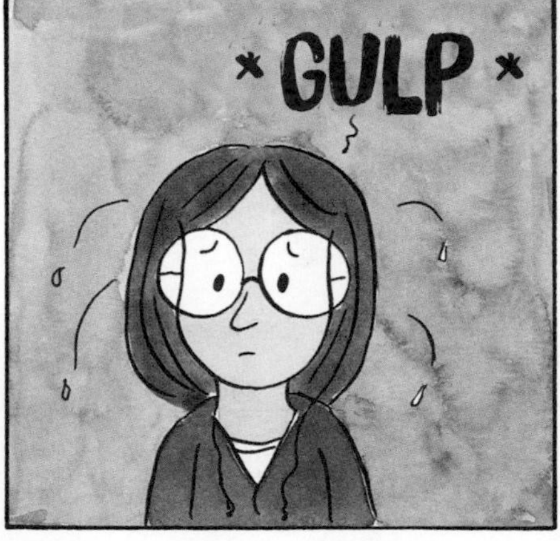
GULP

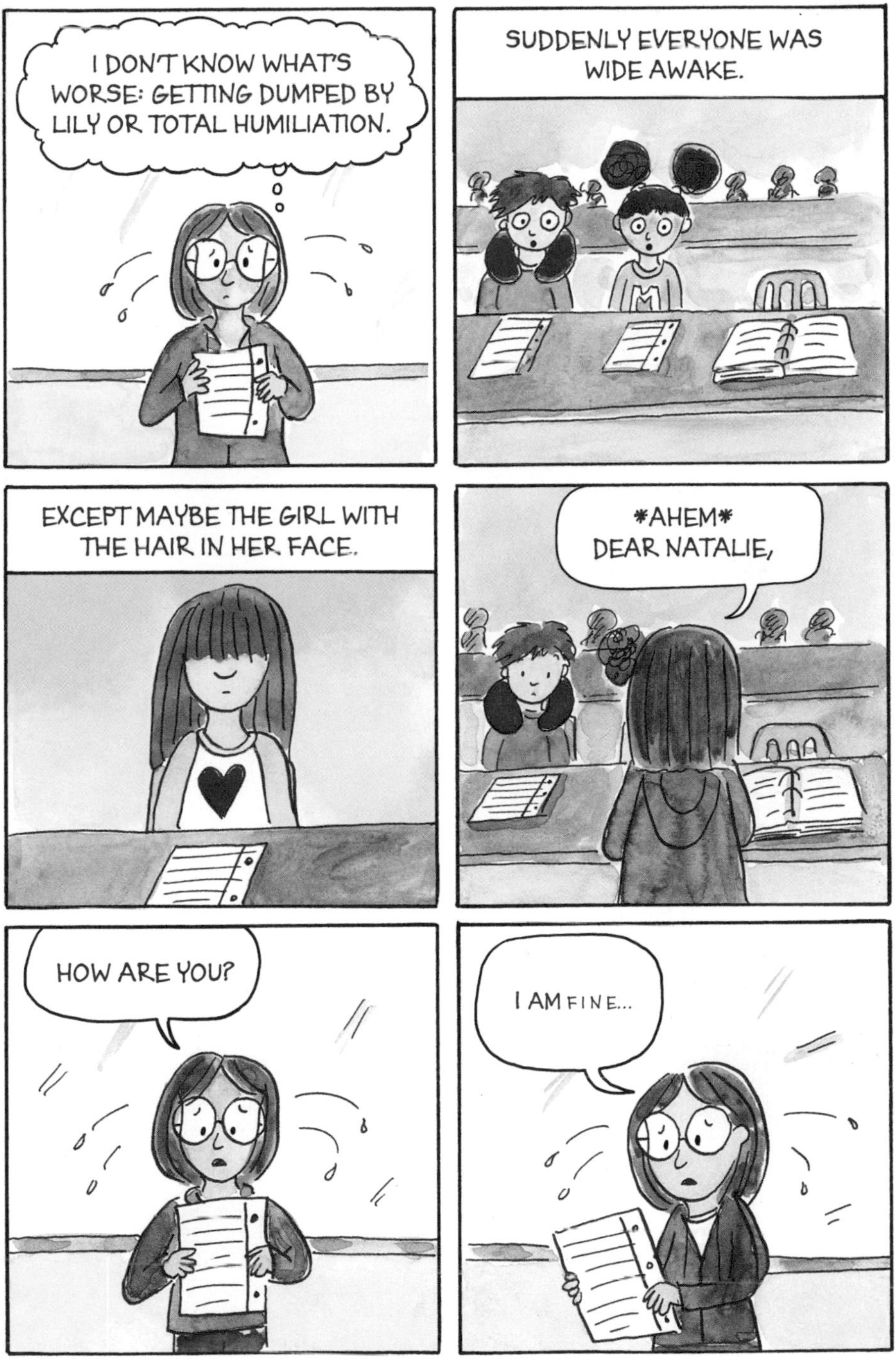
I DON'T KNOW WHAT'S WORSE: GETTING DUMPED BY LILY OR TOTAL HUMILIATION.
SUDDENLY EVERYONE WAS WIDE AWAKE.
EXCEPT MAYBE THE GIRL WITH THE HAIR IN HER FACE.
AHEM DEAR NATALIE,
HOW ARE YOU?
I AM FINE...

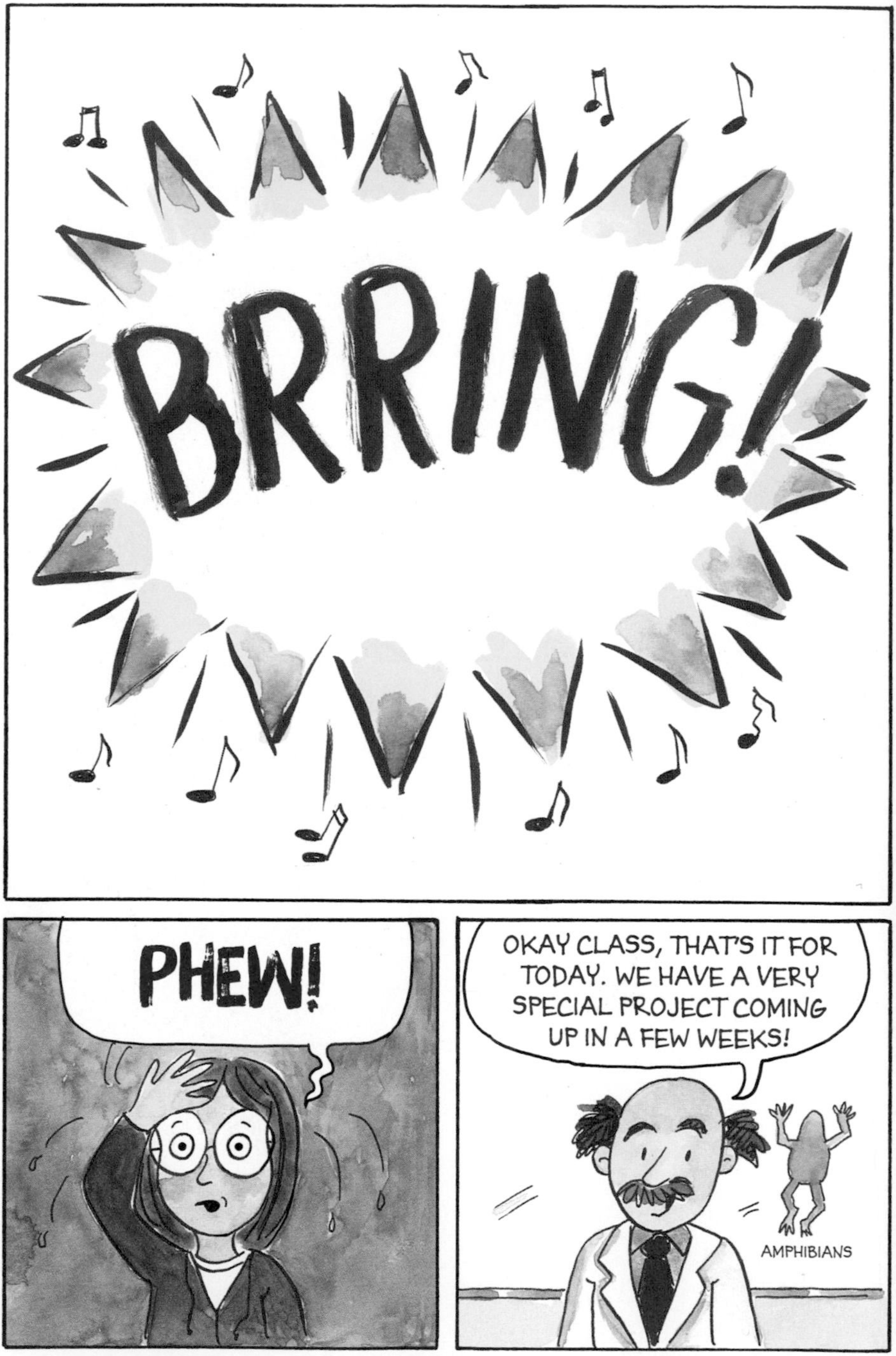
BRRING!
PHEW!
OKAY CLASS, THAT'S IT FOR TODAY. WE HAVE A VERY SPECIAL PROJECT COMING UP IN A FEW WEEKS!
AMPHIBIANS

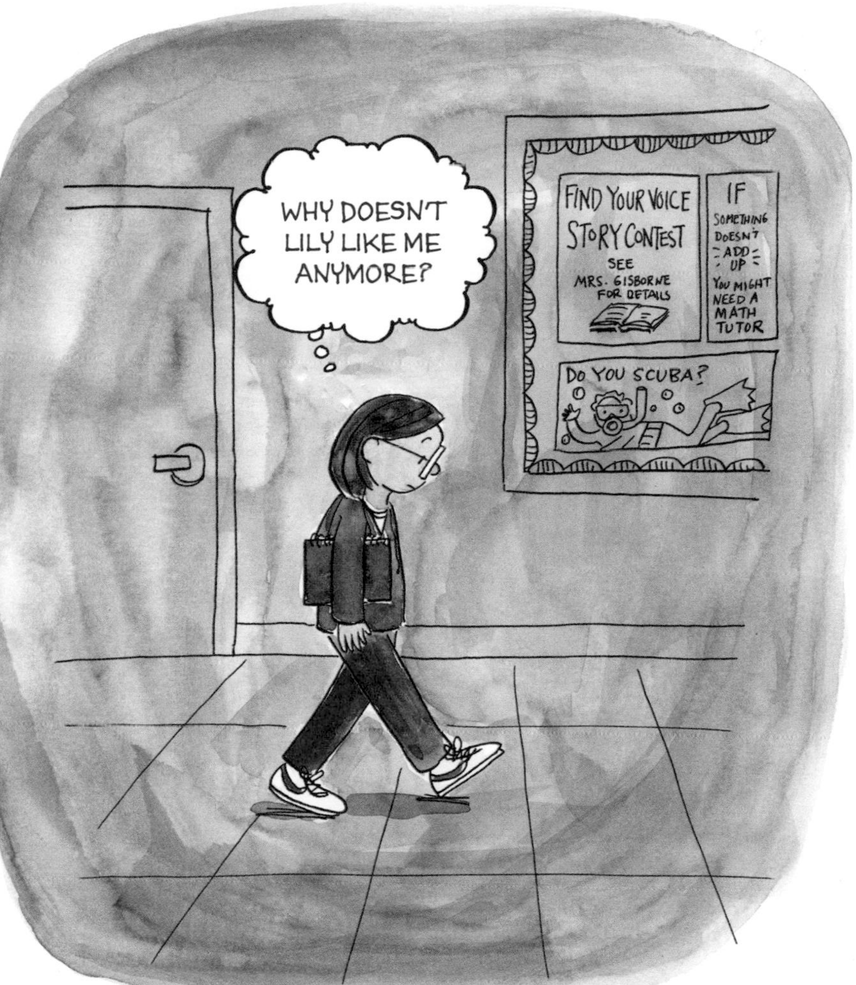
WHY DOESN'T LILY LIKE ME ANYMORE?
FIND YOUR VOICE STORY CONTEST
SEE MRS. GISBORNE FOR DETAILS
IF SOMETHING DOESN'T ADD UP YOU MIGHT NEED A MATH TUTOR
DO YOU SCUBA?

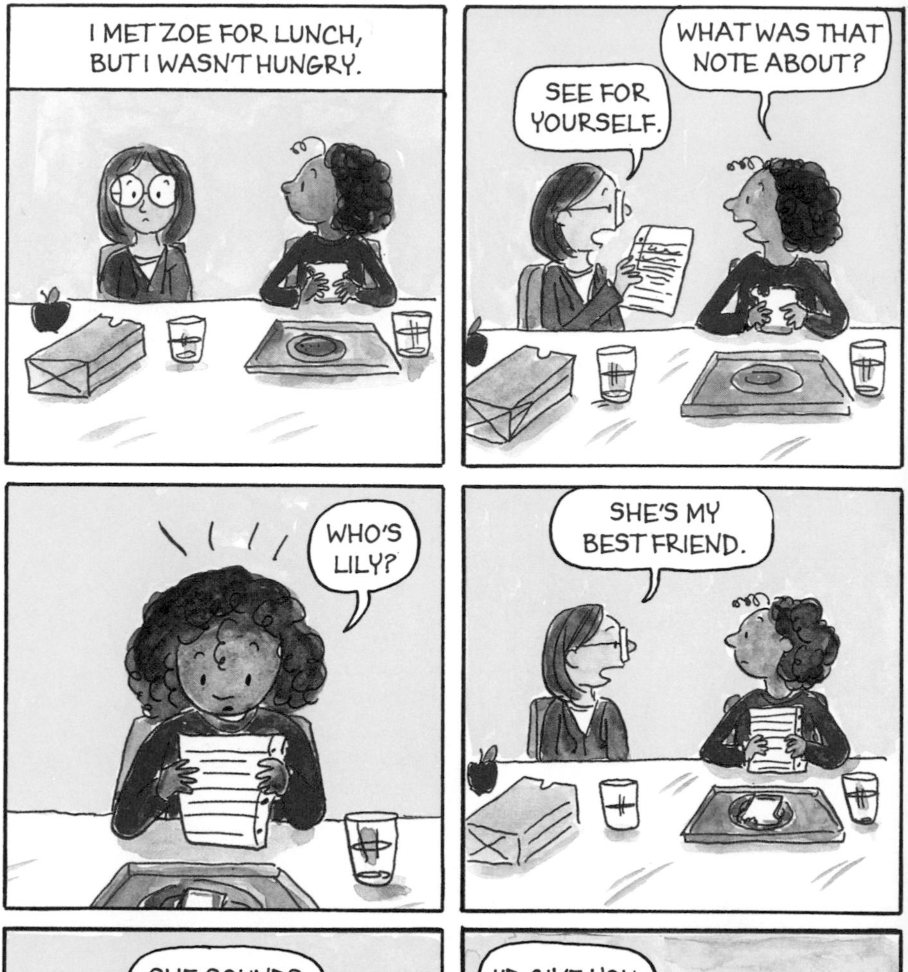
I MET ZOE FOR LUNCH, BUT I WASN'T HUNGRY.
WHAT WAS THAT NOTE ABOUT?
SEE FOR YOURSELF.
WHO'S LILY?
SHE'S MY BEST FRIEND.
SHE SOUNDS LIKE A WORST FRIEND.
I'D GIVE YOU "FRENEMY" AT BEST.

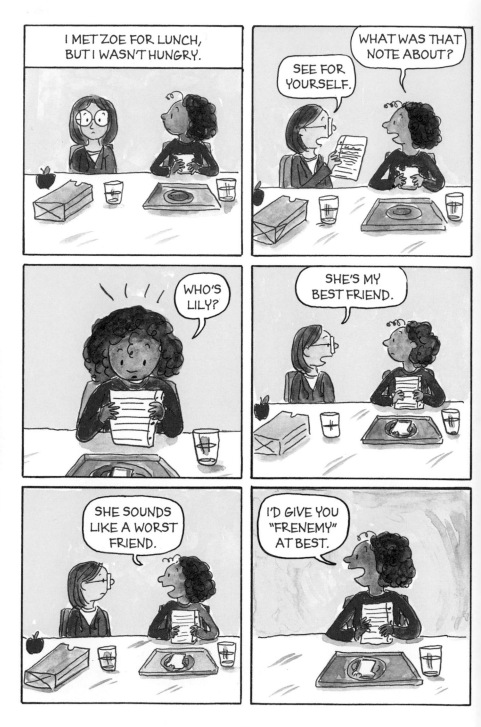

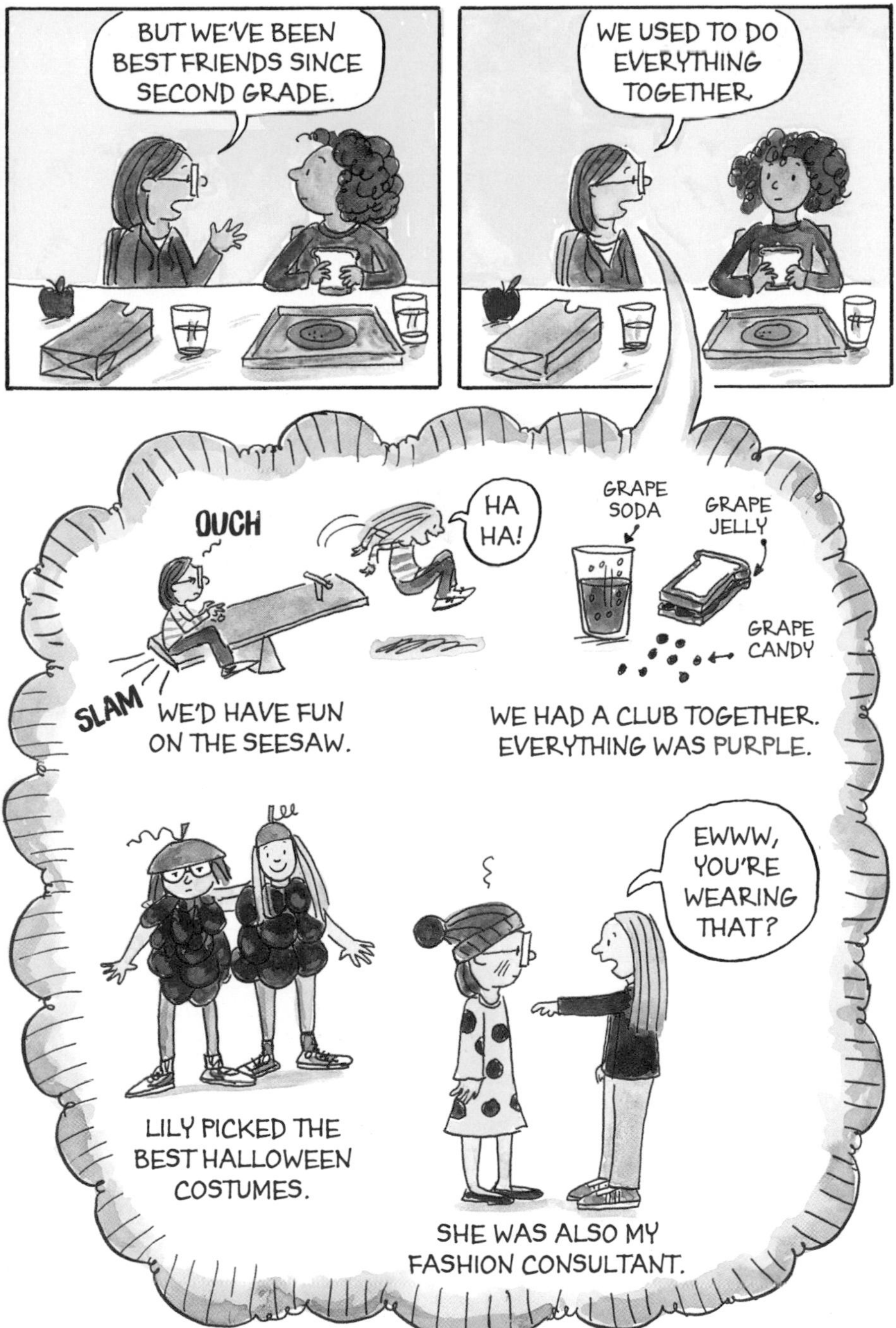
BUT WE'VE BEEN BEST FRIENDS SINCE SECOND GRADE.
WE USED TO DO EVERYTHING TOGETHER.
OUCH
SLAM
HA HA!
WE'D HAVE FUN ON THE SEESAW.
GRAPE SODA
GRAPE JELLY
GRAPE CANDY
WE HAD A CLUB TOGETHER. EVERYTHING WAS PURPLE.
LILY PICKED THE BEST HALLOWEEN COSTUMES.
EWWW, YOU'RE WEARING THAT?
SHE WAS ALSO MY FASHION CONSULTANT.

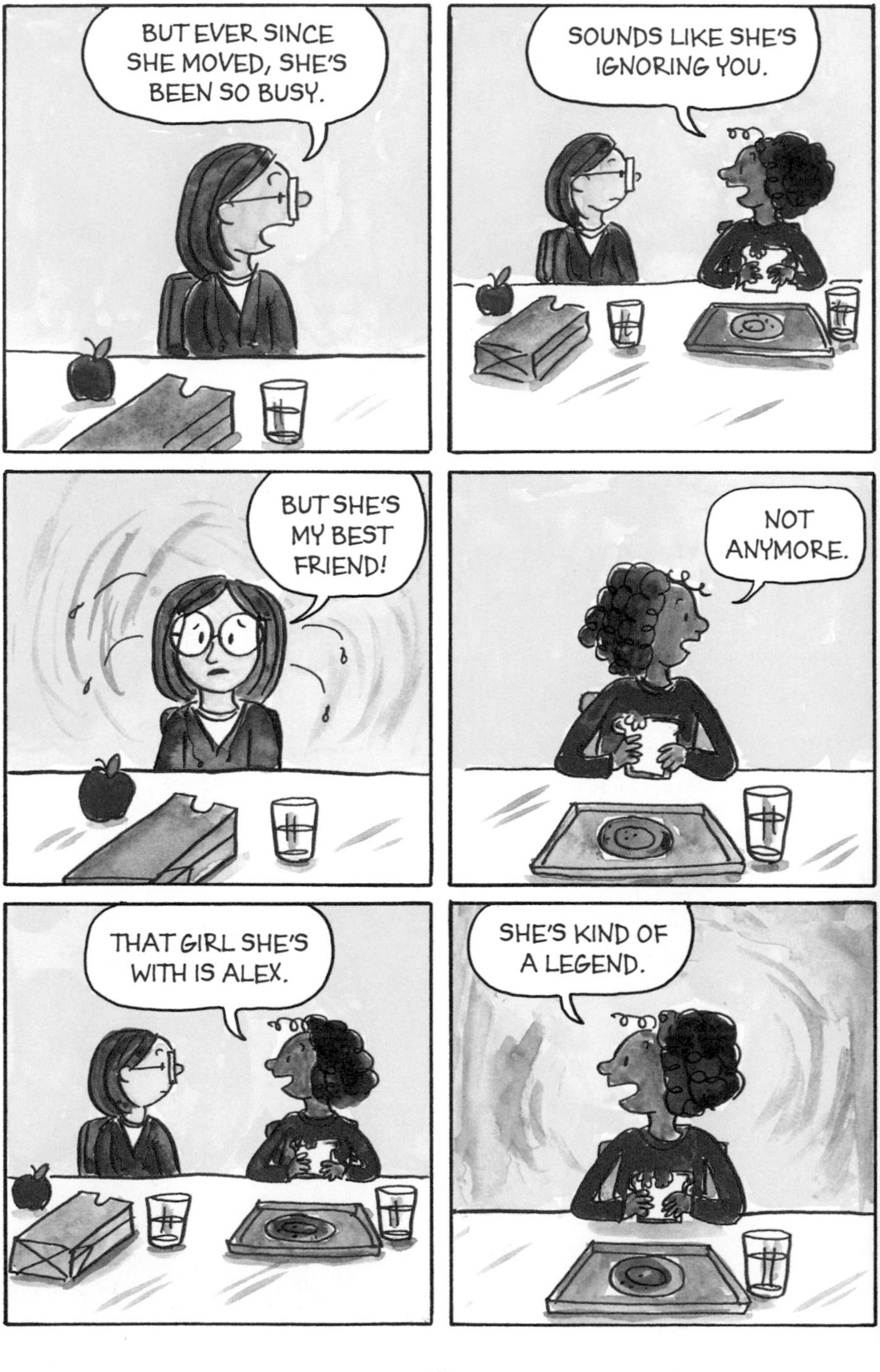
BUT EVER SINCE SHE MOVED, SHE'S BEEN SO BUSY.
SOUNDS LIKE SHE'S IGNORING YOU.
BUT SHE'S MY BEST FRIEND!
NOT ANYMORE.
THAT GIRL SHE'S WITH IS ALEX.
SHE'S KIND OF A LEGEND.

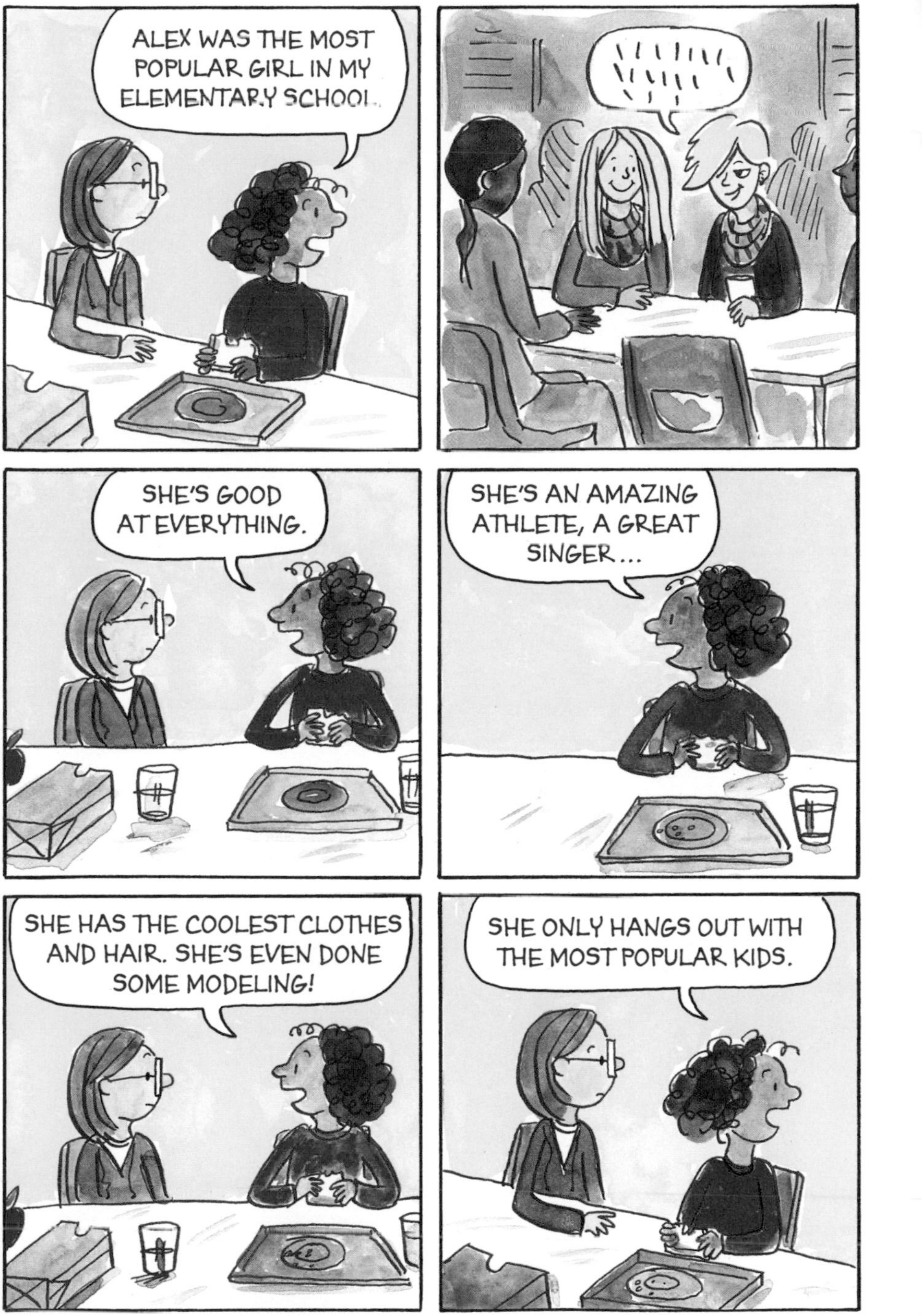
ALEX WAS THE MOST POPULAR GIRL IN MY ELEMENTARY SCHOOL.
SHE'S GOOD AT EVERYTHING.
SHE'S AN AMAZING ATHLETE, A GREAT SINGER...
SHE HAS THE COOLEST CLOTHES AND HAIR. SHE'S EVEN DONE SOME MODELING!
SHE ONLY HANGS OUT WITH THE MOST POPULAR KIDS.

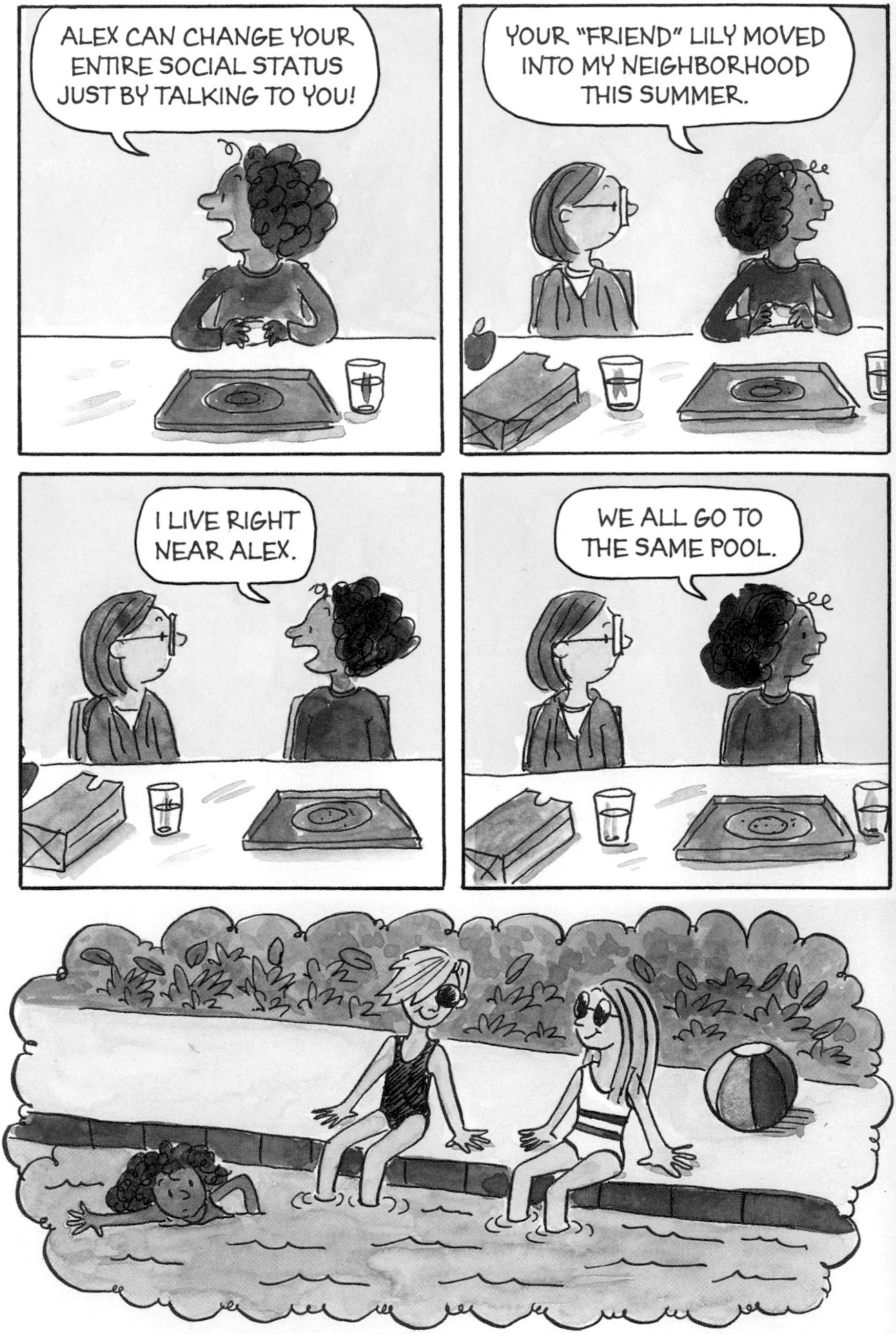
ALEX CAN CHANGE YOUR ENTIRE SOCIAL STATUS JUST BY TALKING TO YOU!
YOUR "FRIEND" LILY MOVED INTO MY NEIGHBORHOOD THIS SUMMER.
I LIVE RIGHT NEAR ALEX.
WE ALL GO TO THE SAME POOL.

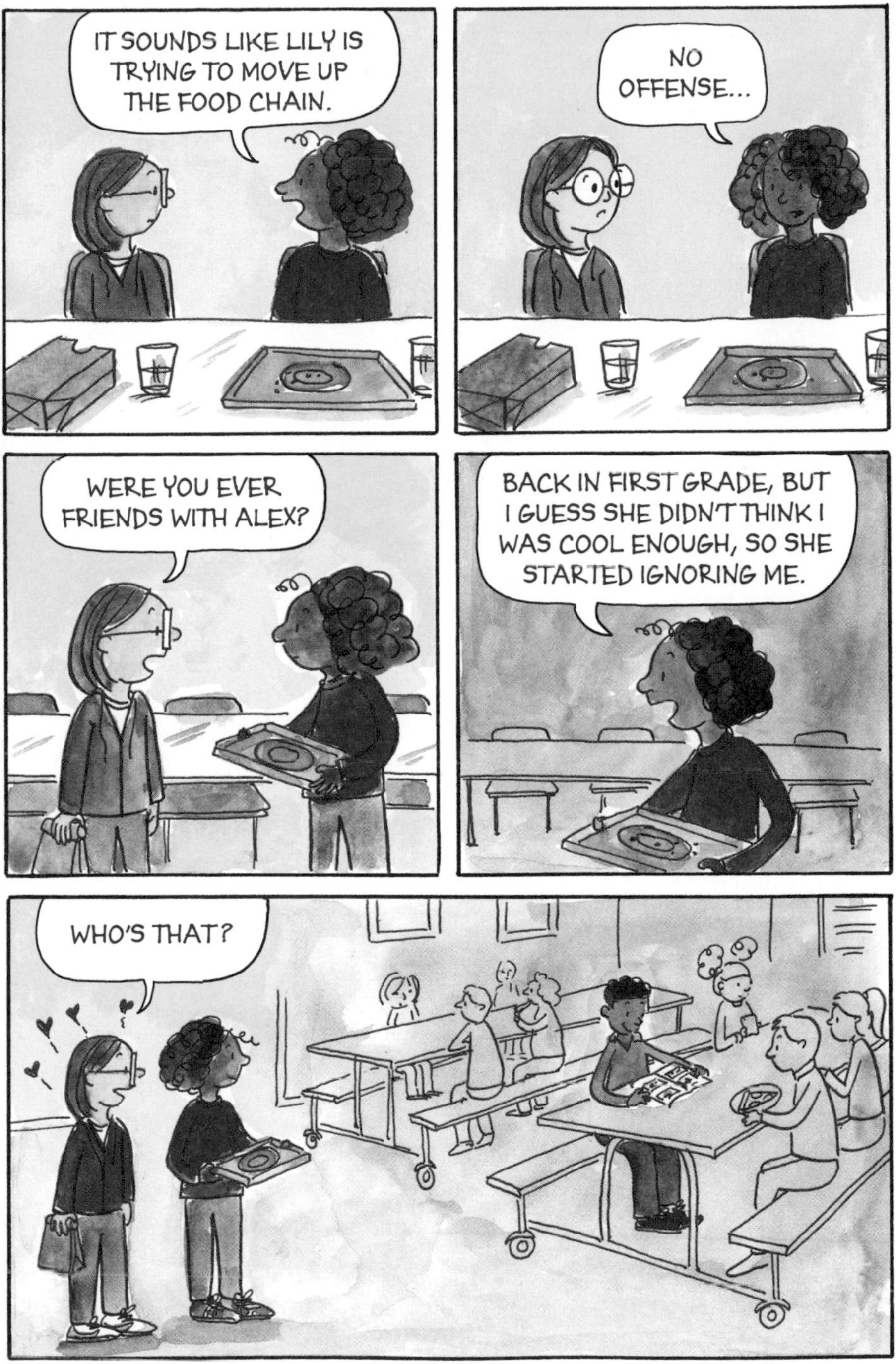
IT SOUNDS LIKE LILY IS TRYING TO MOVE UP THE FOOD CHAIN.
NO OFFENSE...
WERE YOU EVER FRIENDS WITH ALEX?
BACK IN FIRST GRADE, BUT I GUESS SHE DIDN'T THINK I WAS COOL ENOUGH, SO SHE STARTED IGNORING ME.
WHO'S THAT?

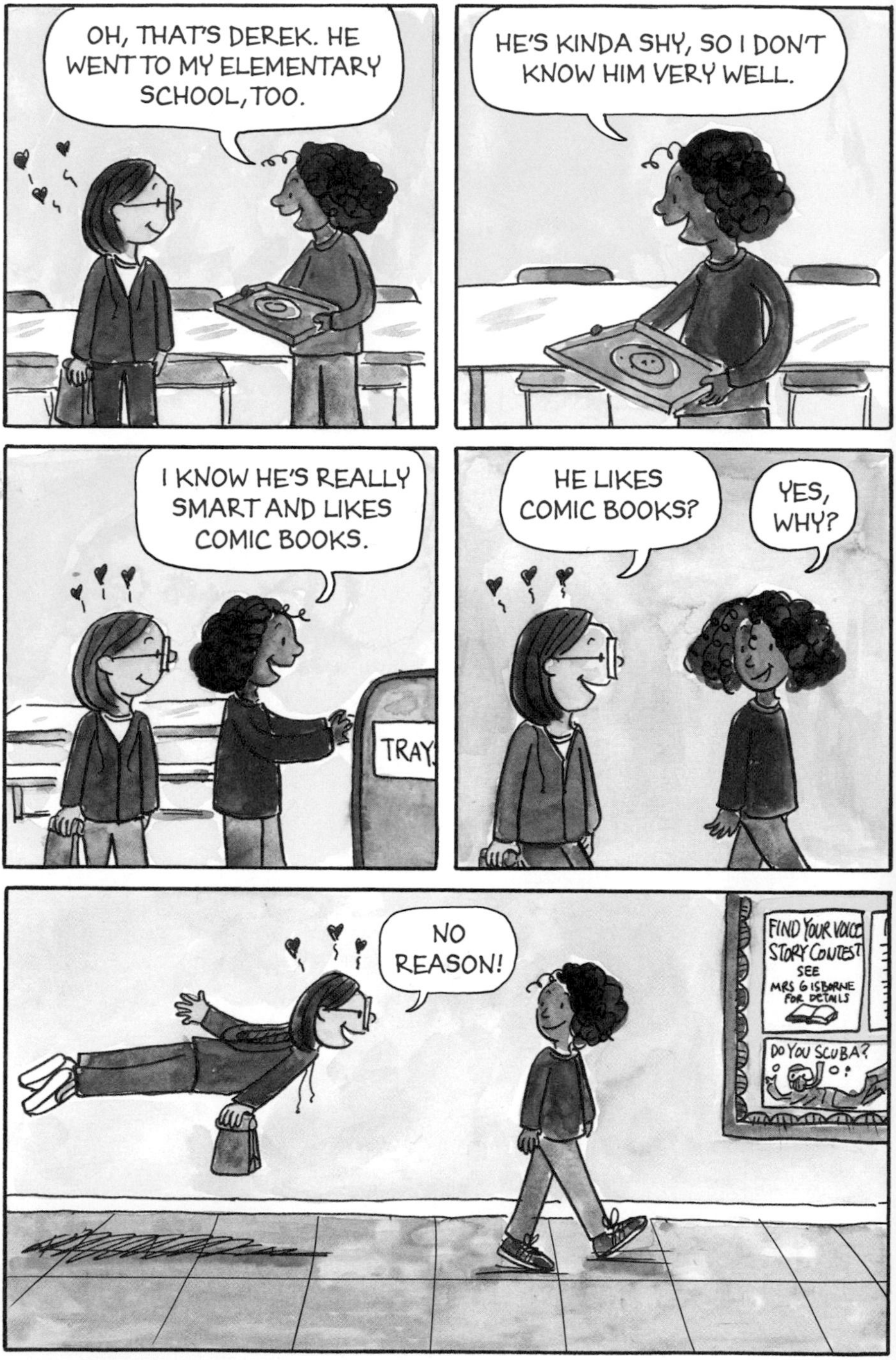
OH, THAT'S DEREK. HE WENT TO MY ELEMENTARY SCHOOL, TOO.
HE'S KINDA SHY, SO I DON'T KNOW HIM VERY WELL.
I KNOW HE'S REALLY SMART AND LIKES COMIC BOOKS.
TRAY
HE LIKES COMIC BOOKS?
YES, WHY?
NO REASON!
FIND YOUR VOICE STORY CONTEST SEE MRS GISBORNE FOR DETAILS
DO YOU SCUBA?

CHAPTER 4
RAINING CATS AND FROGS

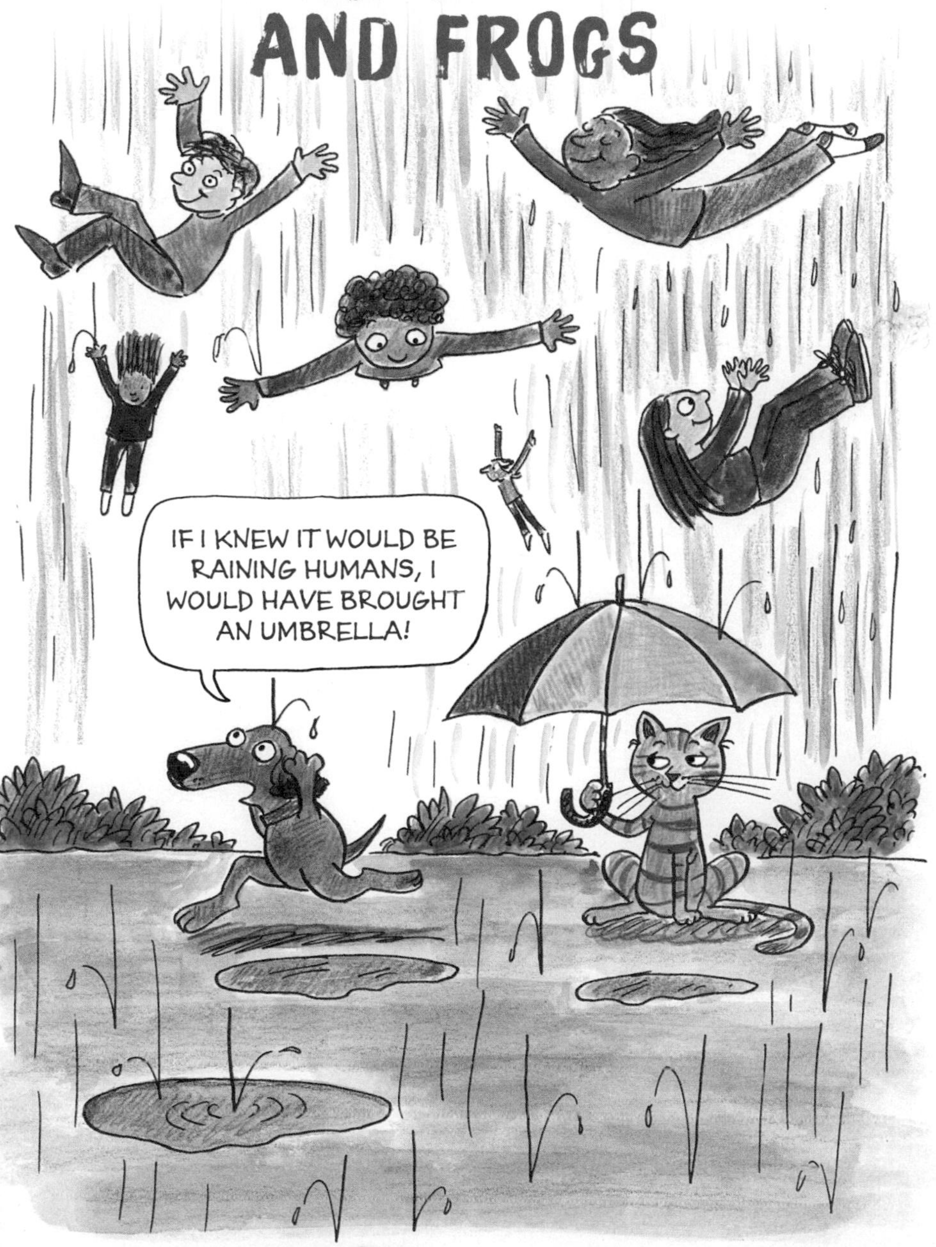
IF I KNEW IT WOULD BE RAINING HUMANS, I WOULD HAVE BROUGHT AN UMBRELLA!

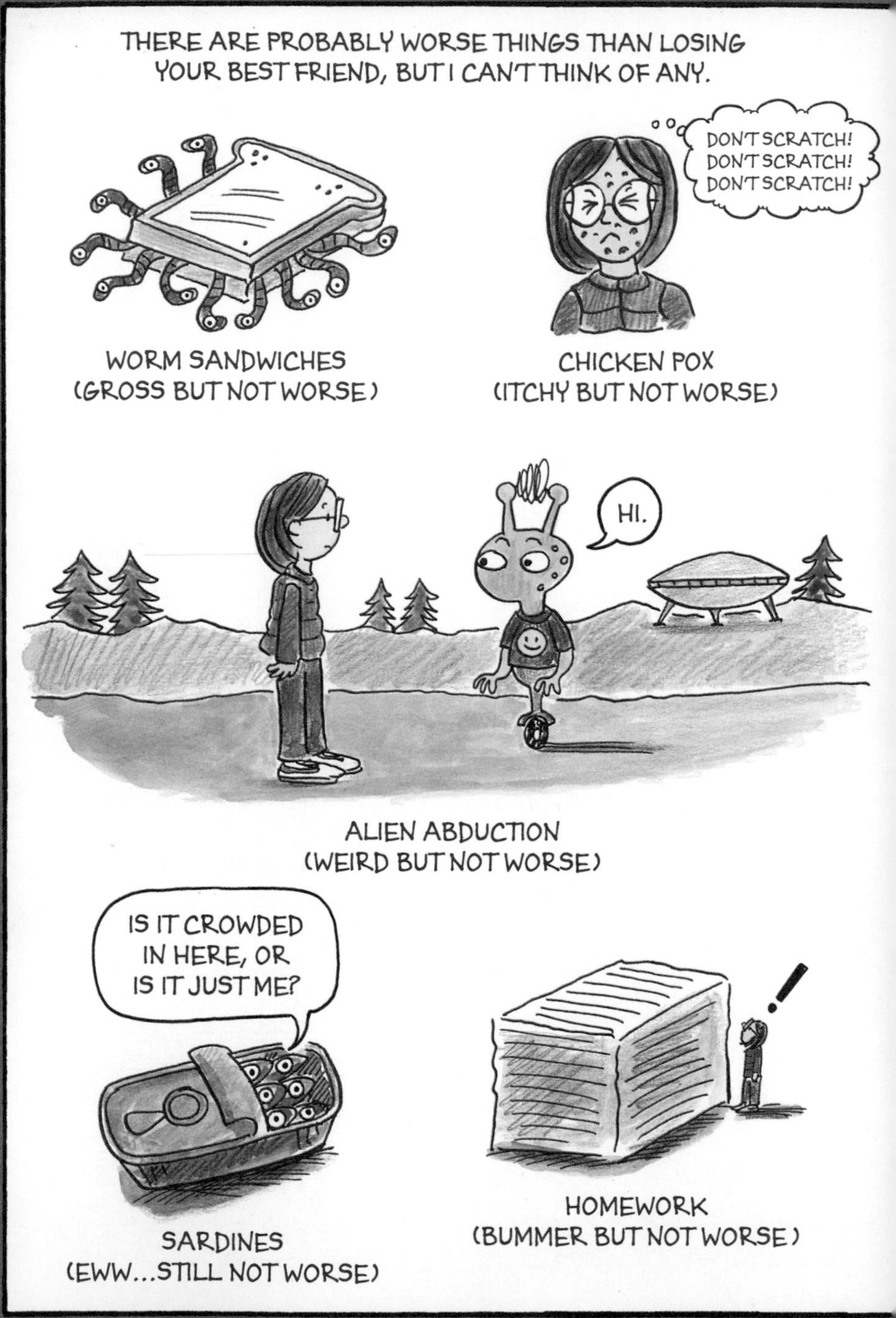
THERE ARE PROBABLY WORSE THINGS THAN LOSING YOUR BEST FRIEND, BUT I CAN'T THINK OF ANY.
DON'T SCRATCH! DON'T SCRATCH! DON'T SCRATCH!
WORM SANDWICHES (GROSS BUT NOT WORSE)
CHICKEN POX (ITCHY BUT NOT WORSE)
HI.
ALIEN ABDUCTION (WEIRD BUT NOT WORSE)
IS IT CROWDED IN HERE, OR IS IT JUST ME?
!
SARDINES (EWW...STILL NOT WORSE)
HOMEWORK (BUMMER BUT NOT WORSE)

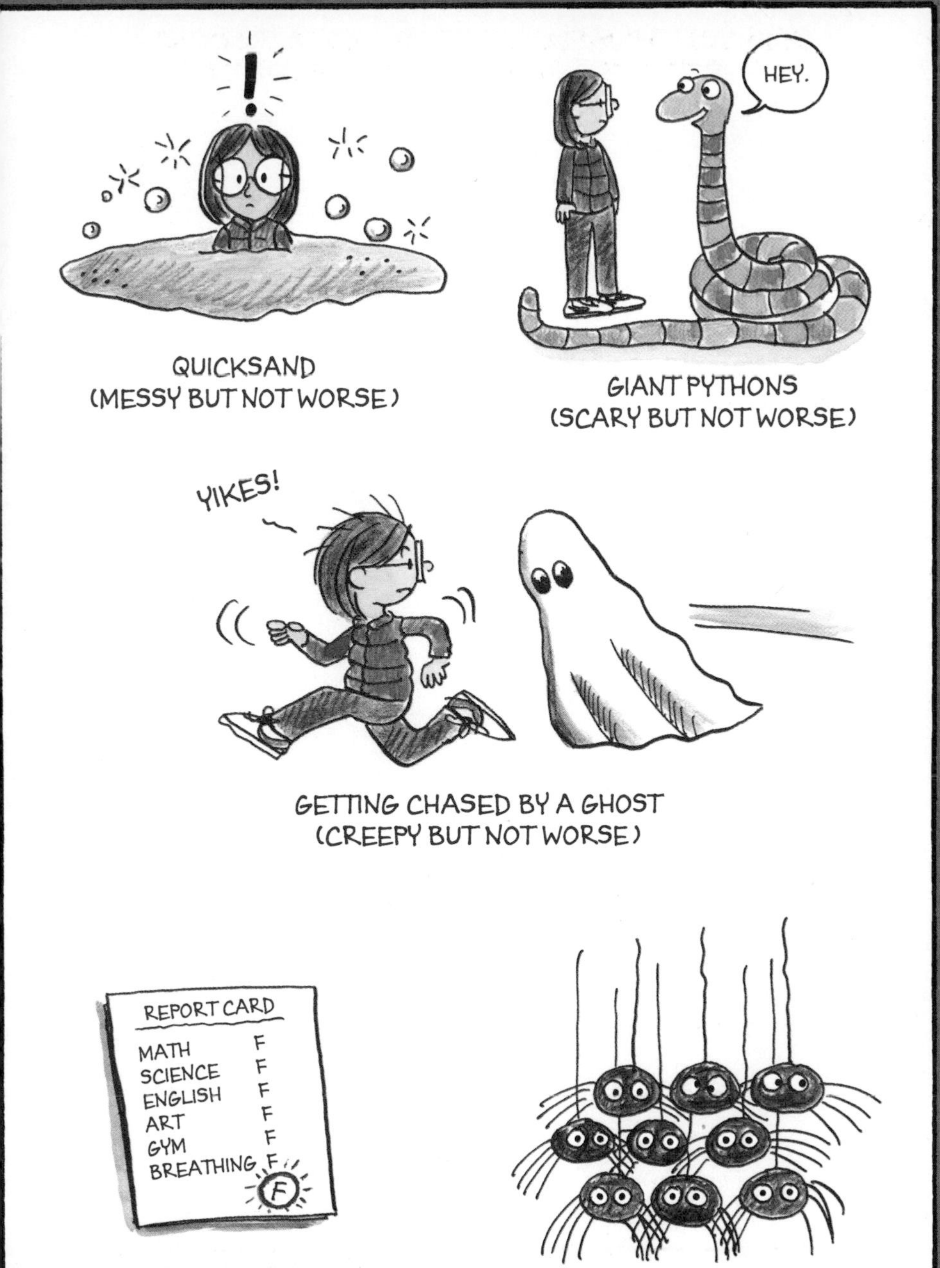

HEY.
QUICKSAND
(MESSY BUT NOT WORSE)
GIANT PYTHONS
(SCARY BUT NOT WORSE)
YIKES!
GETTING CHASED BY A GHOST
(CREEPY BUT NOT WORSE)
REPORT CARD
MATH F
SCIENCE F
ENGLISH F
ART F
GYM F
BREATHING F
F
FAILED REPORT CARD
(BAD BUT NOT WORSE)
LOTS OF SPIDERS
(ALMOST WORSE)

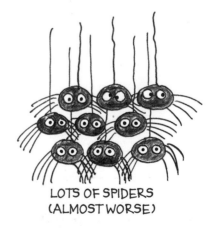

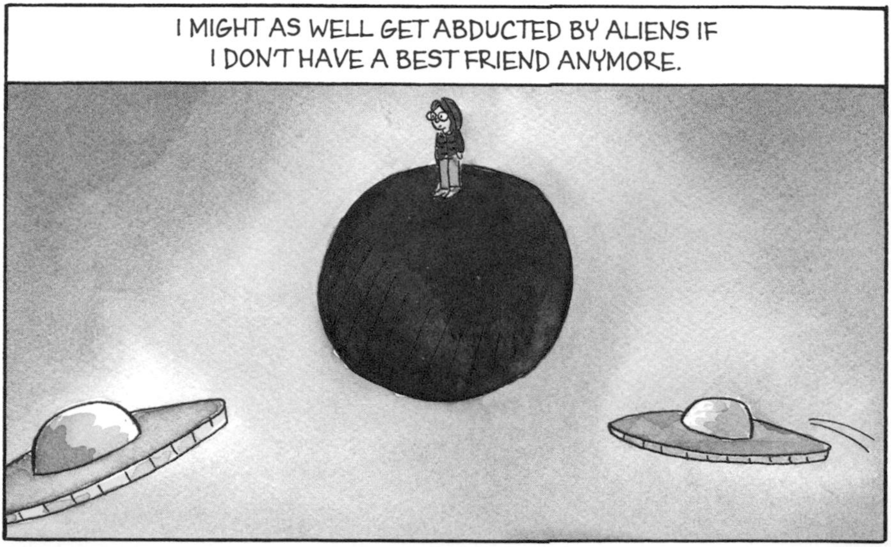
I MIGHT AS WELL GET ABDUCTED BY ALIENS IF I DON'T HAVE A BEST FRIEND ANYMORE.

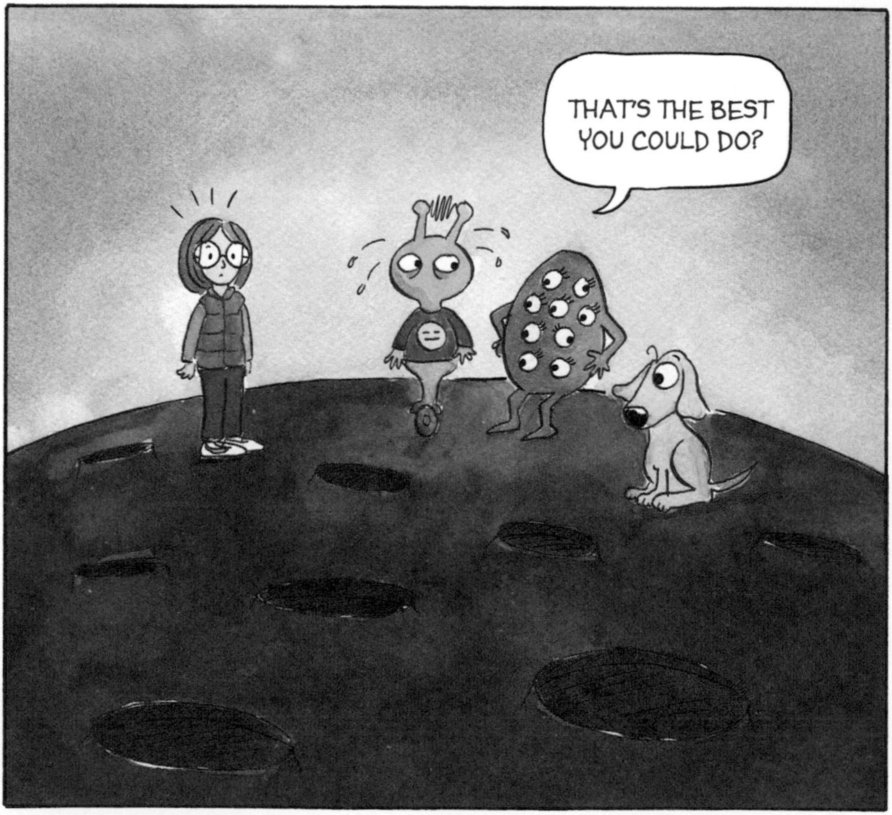
THAT'S THE BEST YOU COULD DO?

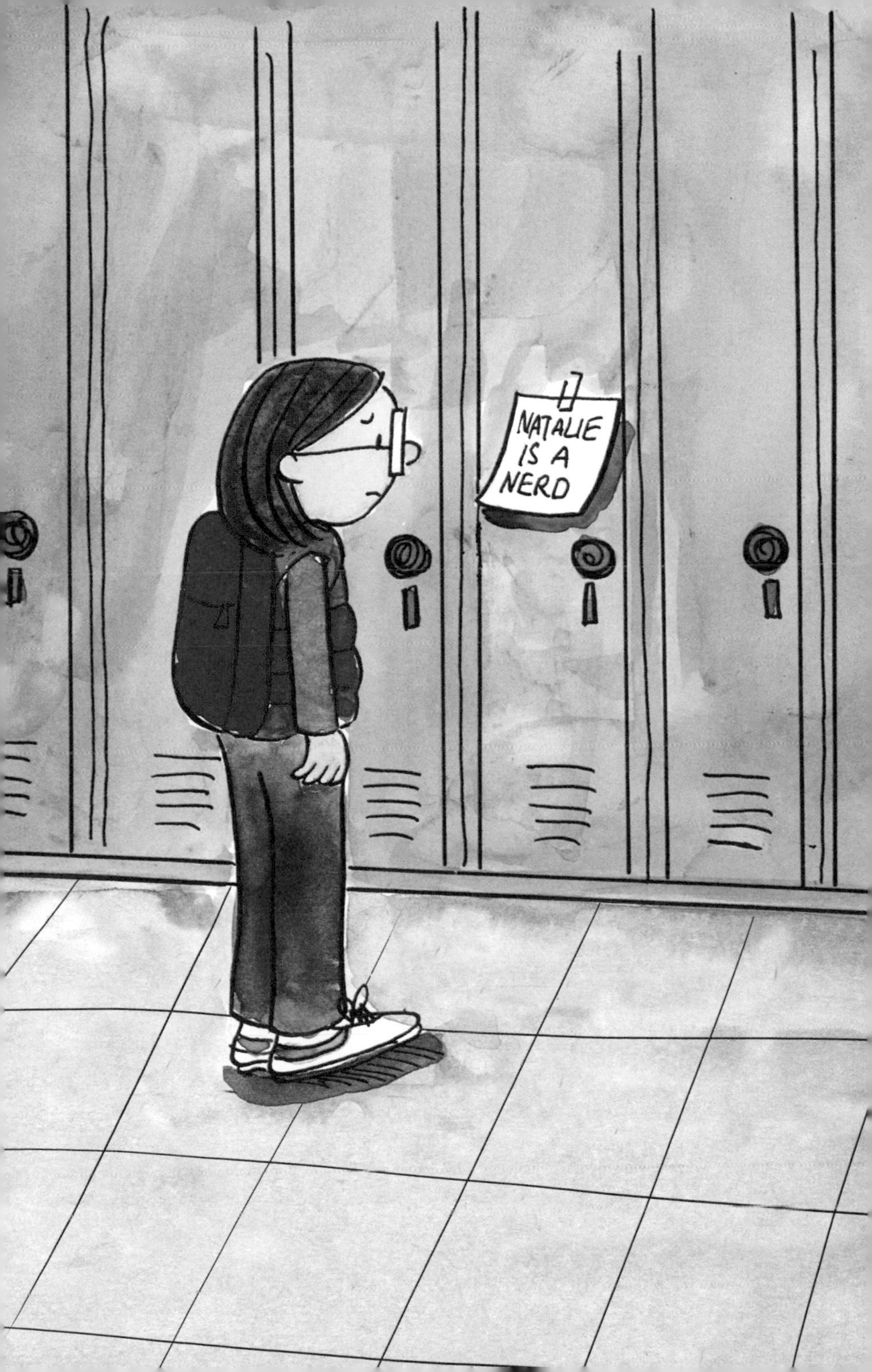
NATALIE IS A NERD

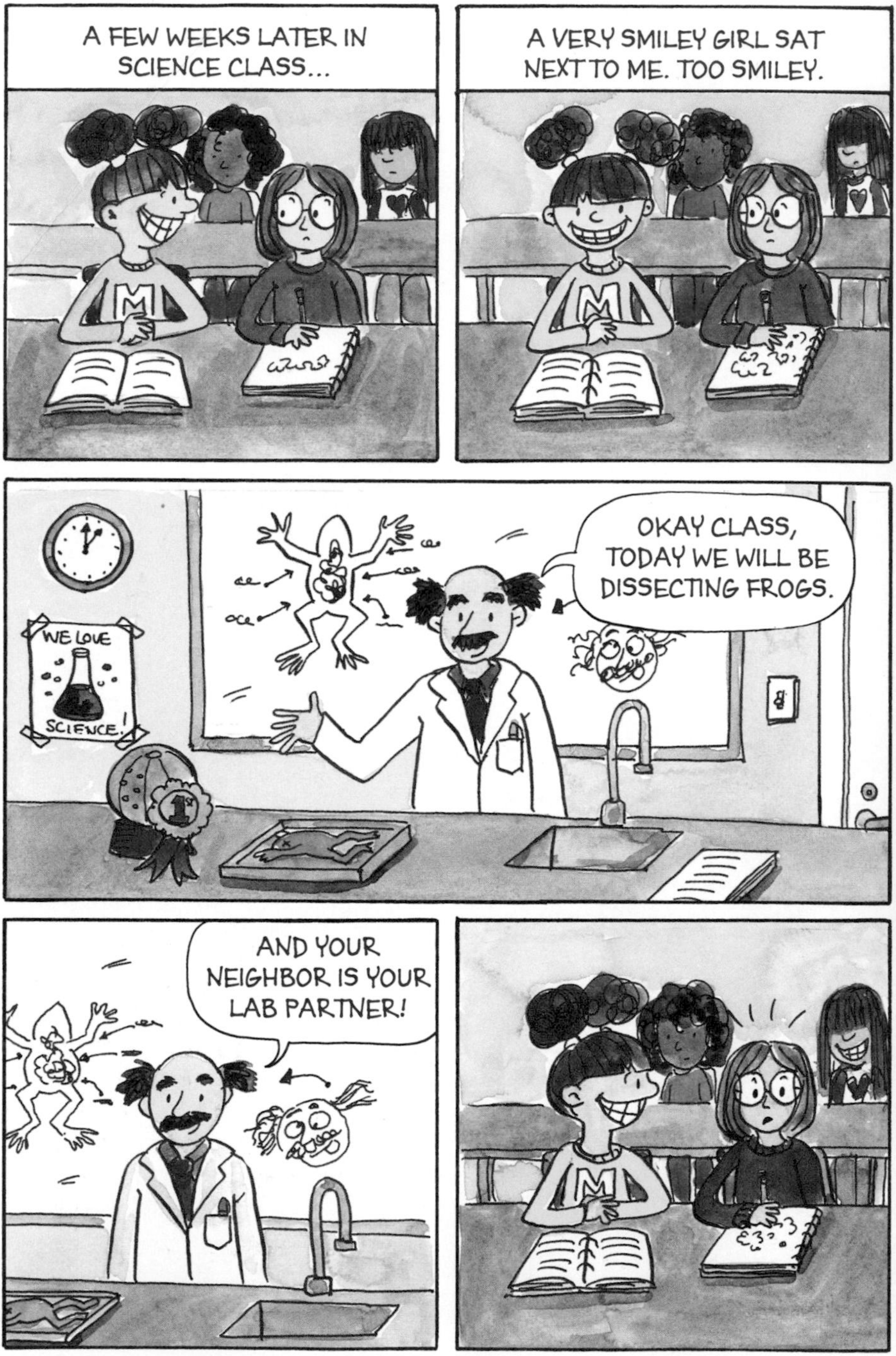
A FEW WEEKS LATER IN SCIENCE CLASS...
A VERY SMILEY GIRL SAT NEXT TO ME. TOO SMILEY.
WE LOVE SCIENCE!
OKAY CLASS, TODAY WE WILL BE DISSECTING FROGS.
AND YOUR NEIGHBOR IS YOUR LAB PARTNER!

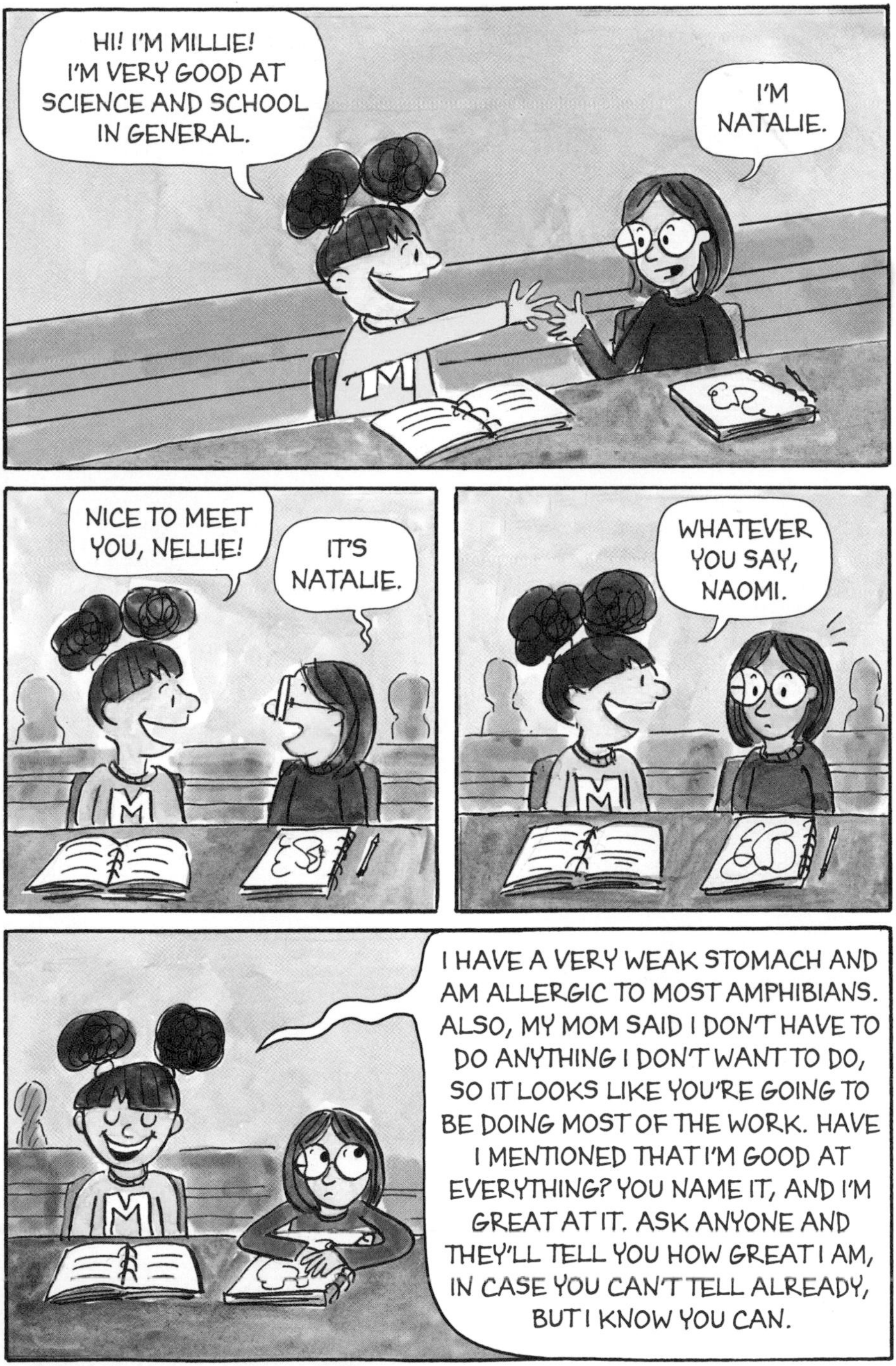
HI! I'M MILLIE! I'M VERY GOOD AT SCIENCE AND SCHOOL IN GENERAL.
I'M NATALIE.
NICE TO MEET YOU, NELLIE!
IT'S NATALIE.
WHATEVER YOU SAY, NAOMI.
I HAVE A VERY WEAK STOMACH AND AM ALLERGIC TO MOST AMPHIBIANS. ALSO, MY MOM SAID I DON'T HAVE TO DO ANYTHING I DON'T WANT TO DO, SO IT LOOKS LIKE YOU'RE GOING TO BE DOING MOST OF THE WORK. HAVE I MENTIONED THAT I'M GOOD AT EVERYTHING? YOU NAME IT, AND I'M GREAT AT IT. ASK ANYONE AND THEY'LL TELL YOU HOW GREAT I AM, IN CASE YOU CAN'T TELL ALREADY, BUT I KNOW YOU CAN.

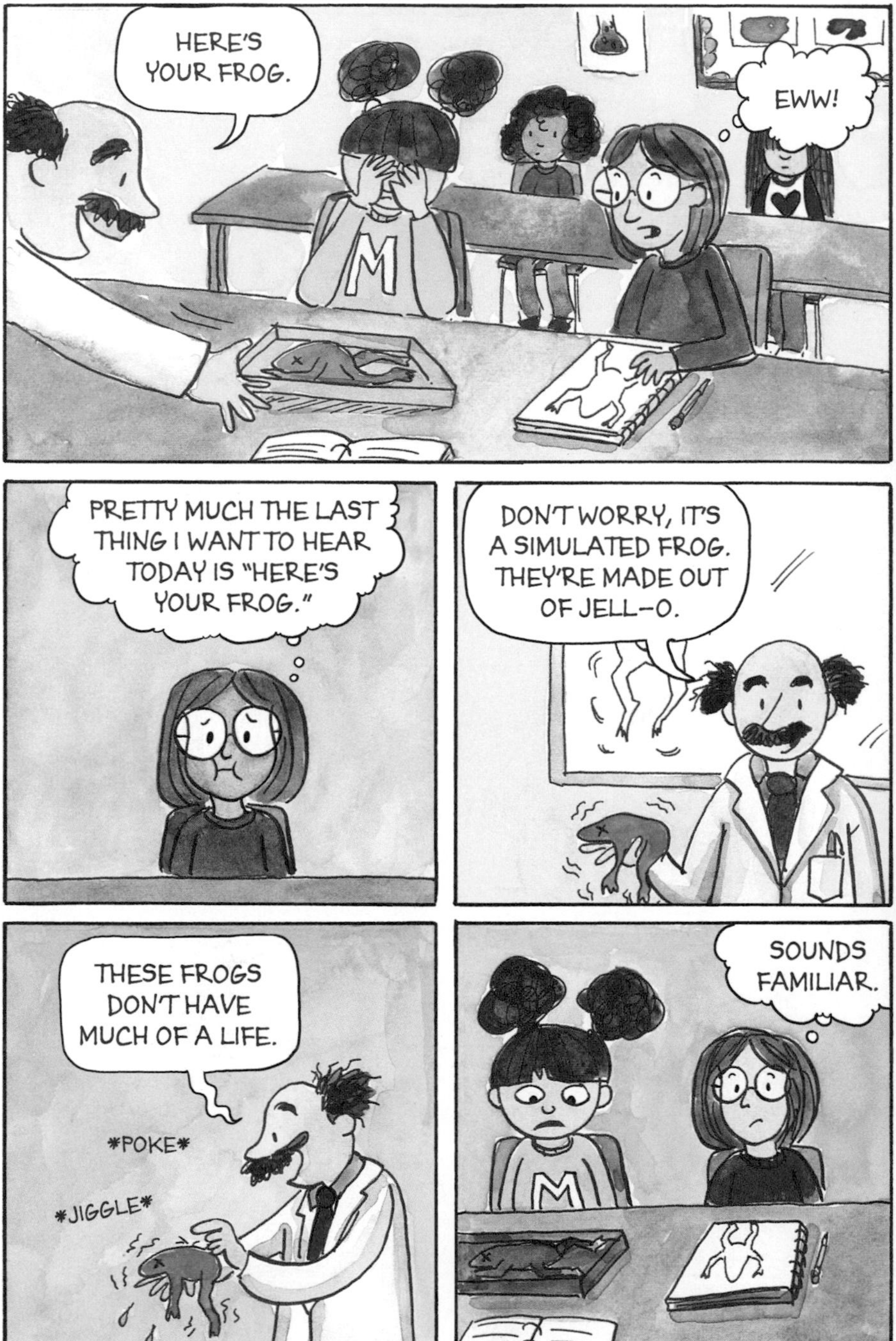
HERE'S YOUR FROG.
EWW!
PRETTY MUCH THE LAST THING I WANT TO HEAR TODAY IS "HERE'S YOUR FROG."
DON'T WORRY, IT'S A SIMULATED FROG. THEY'RE MADE OUT OF JELL-O.
THESE FROGS DON'T HAVE MUCH OF A LIFE.
POKE
JIGGLE
SOUNDS FAMILIAR.

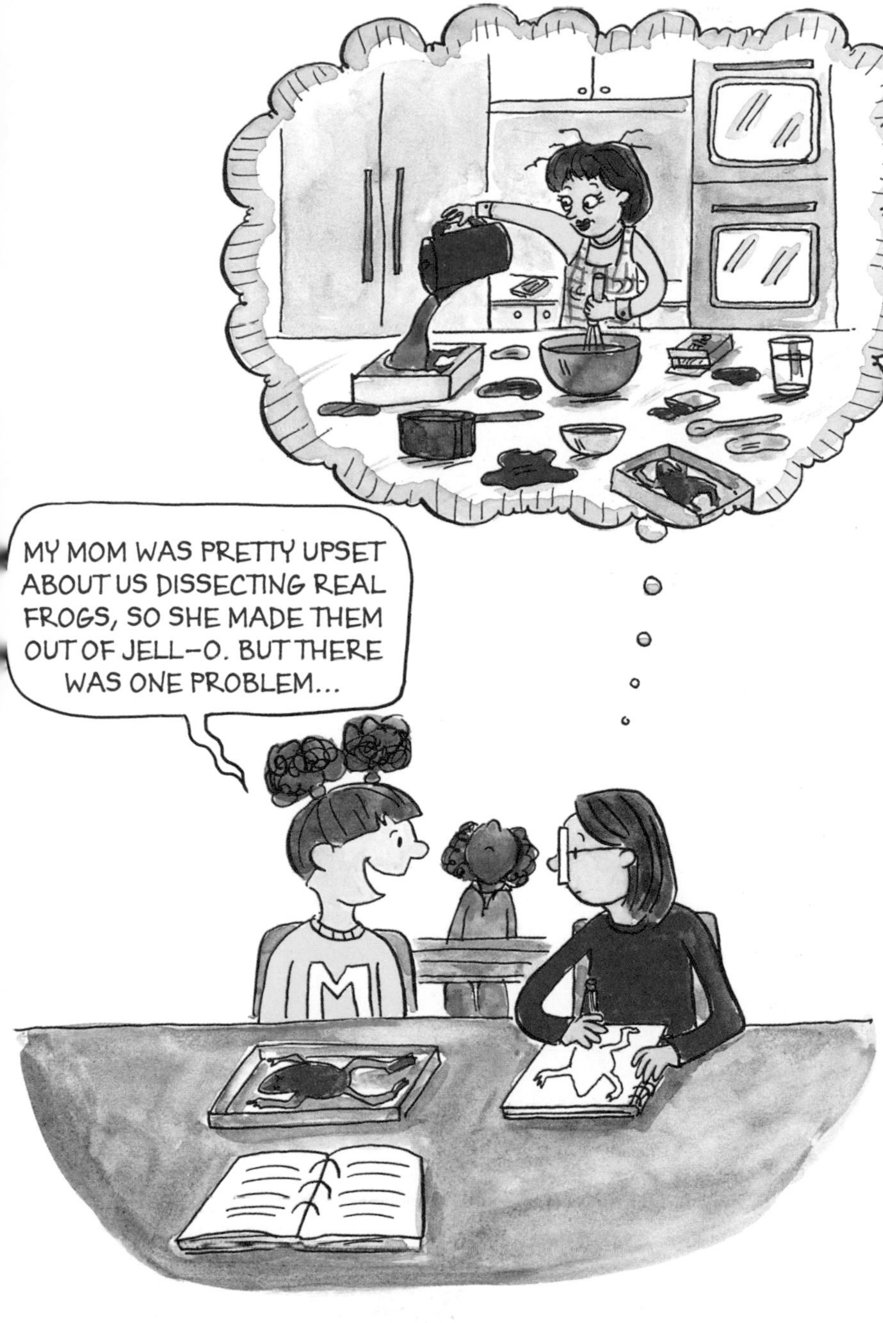
MY MOM WAS PRETTY UPSET ABOUT US DISSECTING REAL FROGS, SO SHE MADE THEM OUT OF JELL-O. BUT THERE WAS ONE PROBLEM...

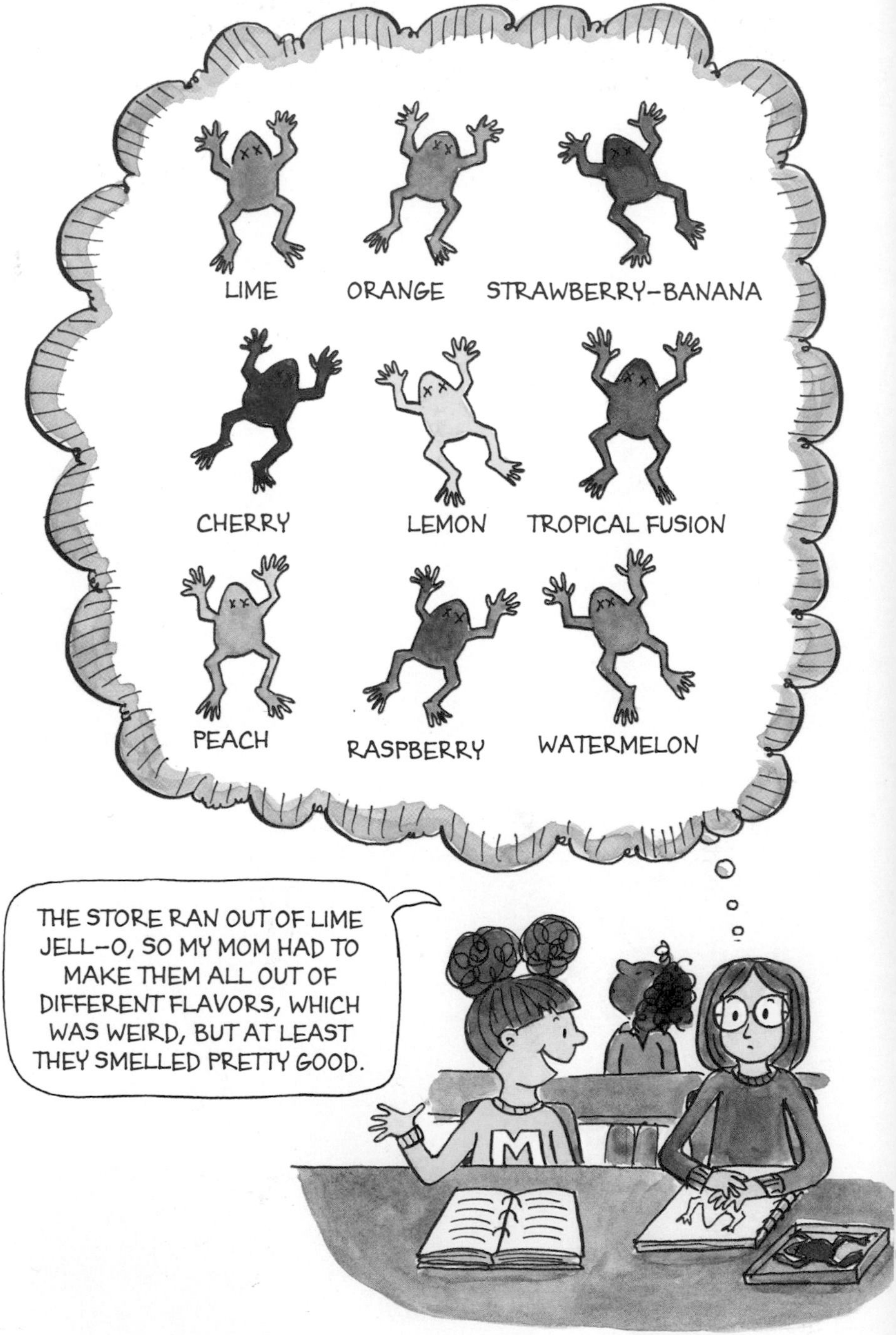
LIME
ORANGE
STRAWBERRY-BANANA
CHERRY
LEMON
TROPICAL FUSION
PEACH
RASPBERRY
WATERMELON
THE STORE RAN OUT OF LIME JELL-O, SO MY MOM HAD TO MAKE THEM ALL OUT OF DIFFERENT FLAVORS, WHICH WAS WEIRD, BUT AT LEAST THEY SMELLED PRETTY GOOD.

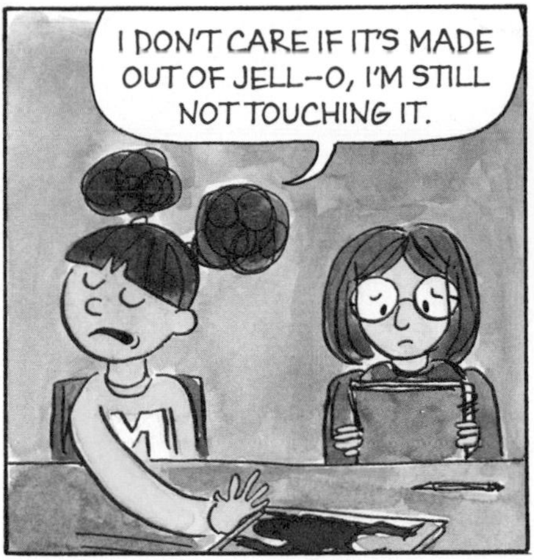
I DON'T CARE IF IT'S MADE OUT OF JELL-O, I'M STILL NOT TOUCHING IT.

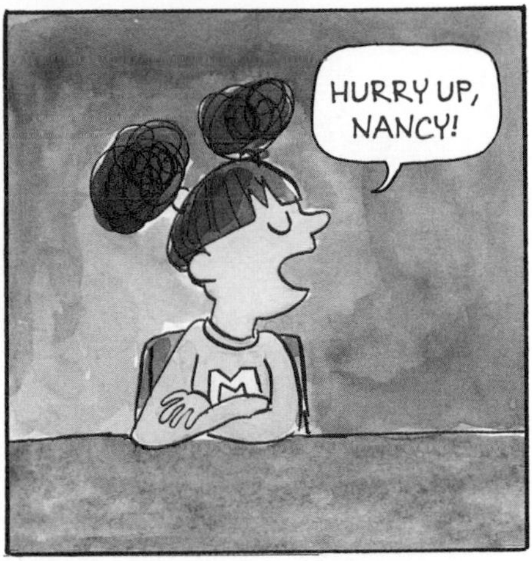
HURRY UP, NANCY!

I WAS TOO BUSY DOODLING TO EVEN THINK ABOUT CUTTING INTO THE FROG, EVEN IF IT WAS MADE OUT OF JELL-O.

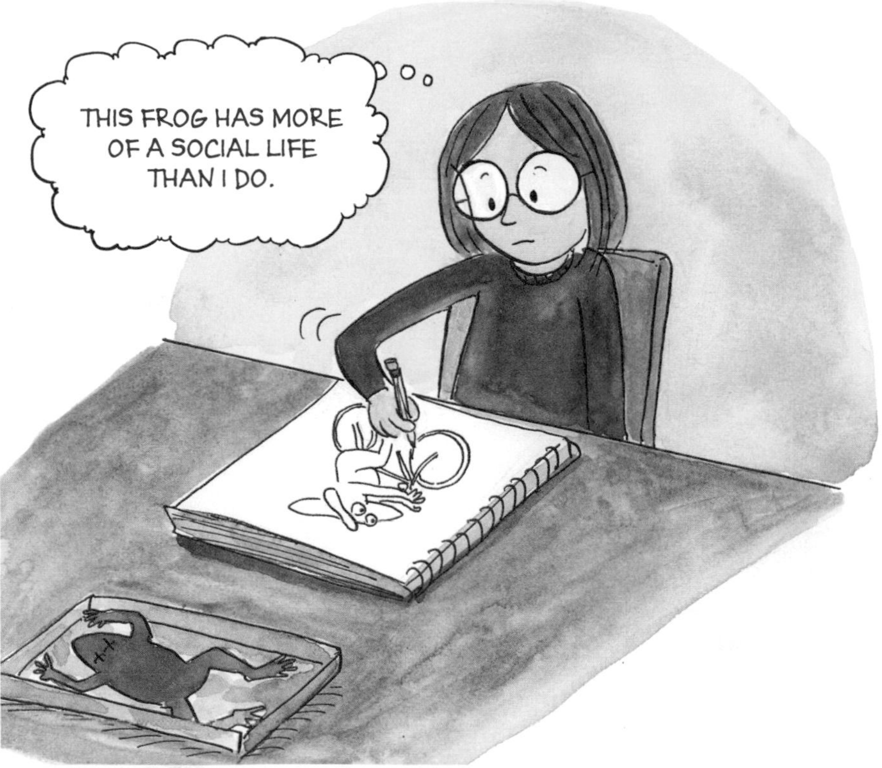
THIS FROG HAS MORE OF A SOCIAL LIFE THAN I DO.

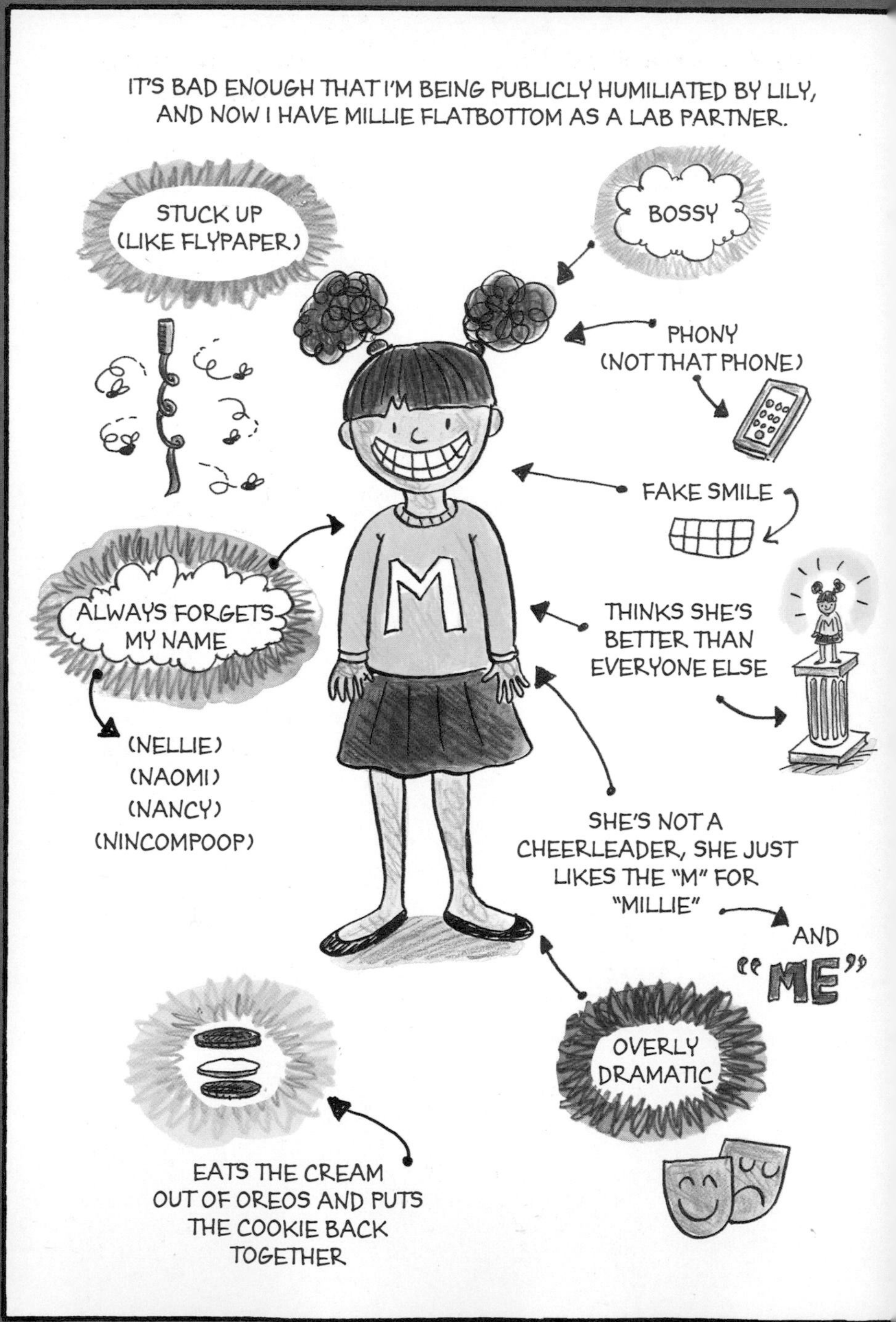
IT'S BAD ENOUGH THAT I'M BEING PUBLICLY HUMILIATED BY LILY, AND NOW I HAVE MILLIE FLATBOTTOM AS A LAB PARTNER.
STUCK UP (LIKE FLYPAPER)
BOSSY
PHONY (NOT THAT PHONE)
FAKE SMILE
M
ALWAYS FORGETS MY NAME
(NELLIE)
(NAOMI)
(NANCY)
(NINCOMPOOP)
THINKS SHE'S BETTER THAN EVERYONE ELSE
SHE'S NOT A CHEERLEADER, SHE JUST LIKES THE "M" FOR "MILLIE"
AND "ME"
OVERLY DRAMATIC
EATS THE CREAM OUT OF OREOS AND PUTS THE COOKIE BACK TOGETHER

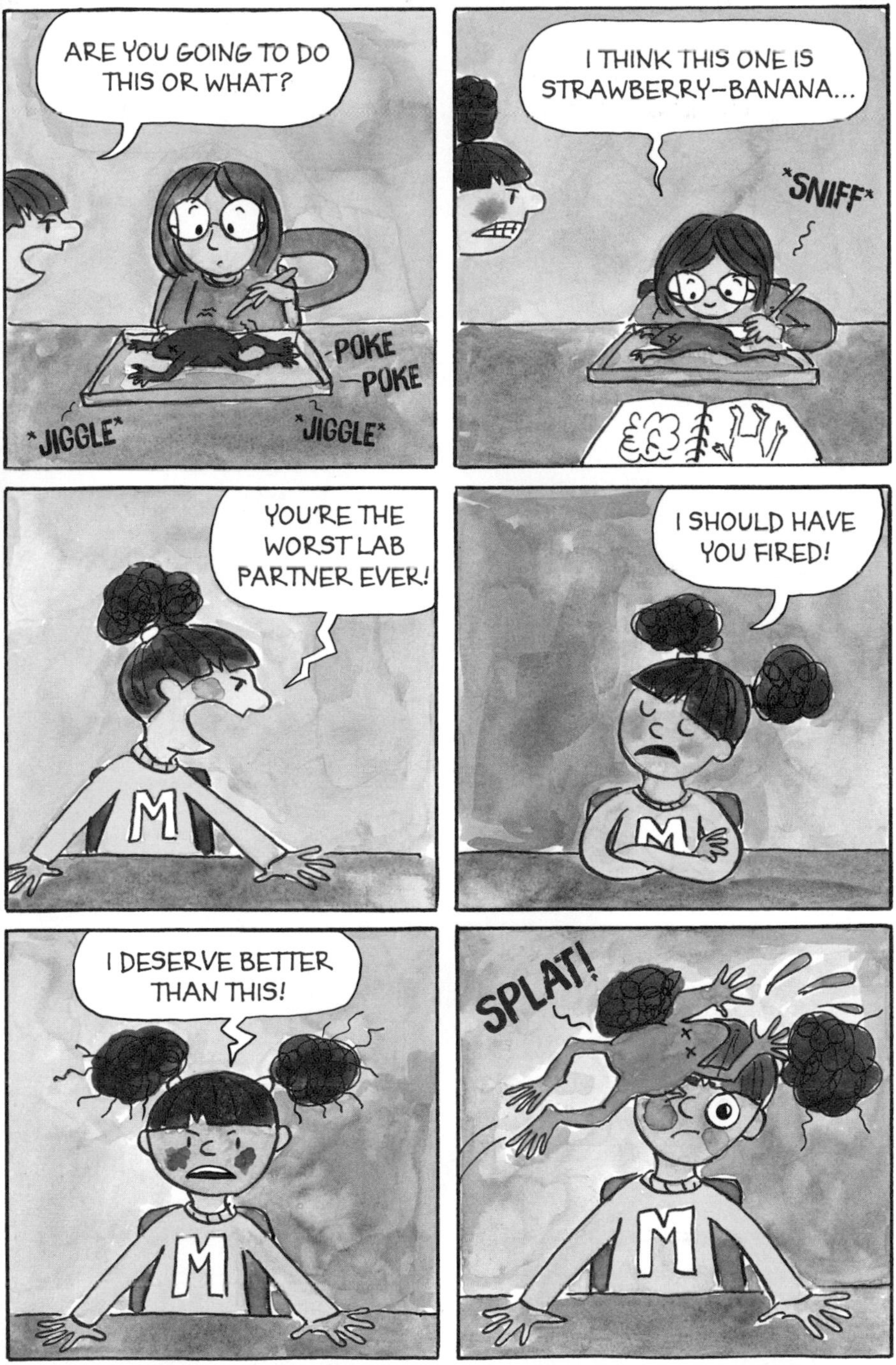
ARE YOU GOING TO DO THIS OR WHAT?
-POKE
-POKE
JIGGLE
JIGGLE
I THINK THIS ONE IS STRAWBERRY-BANANA...
SNIFF
YOU'RE THE WORST LAB PARTNER EVER!
I SHOULD HAVE YOU FIRED!
I DESERVE BETTER THAN THIS!
SPLAT!

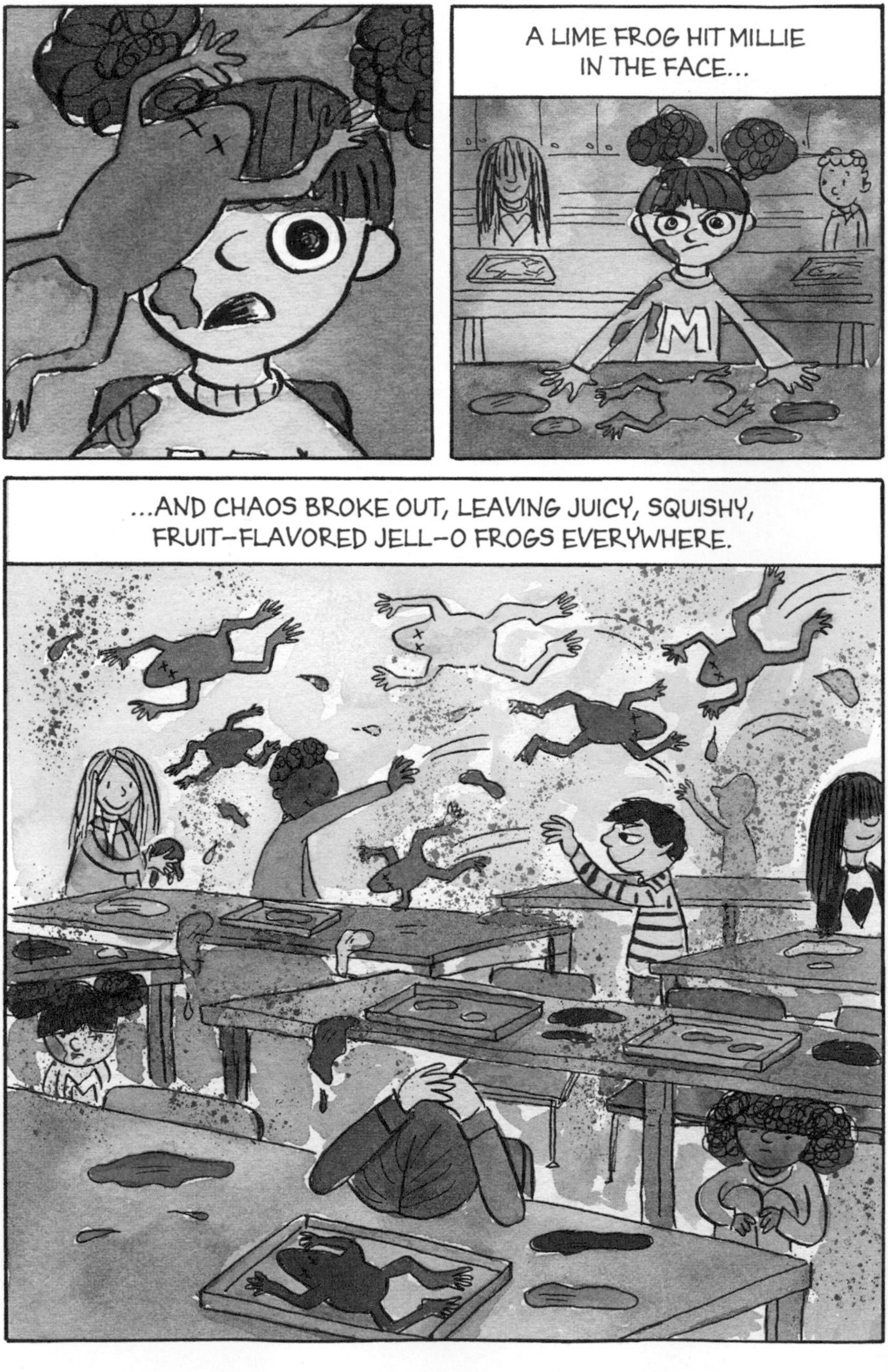
A LIME FROG HIT MILLIE IN THE FACE...
...AND CHAOS BROKE OUT, LEAVING JUICY, SQUISHY, FRUIT-FLAVORED JELL-O FROGS EVERYWHERE.

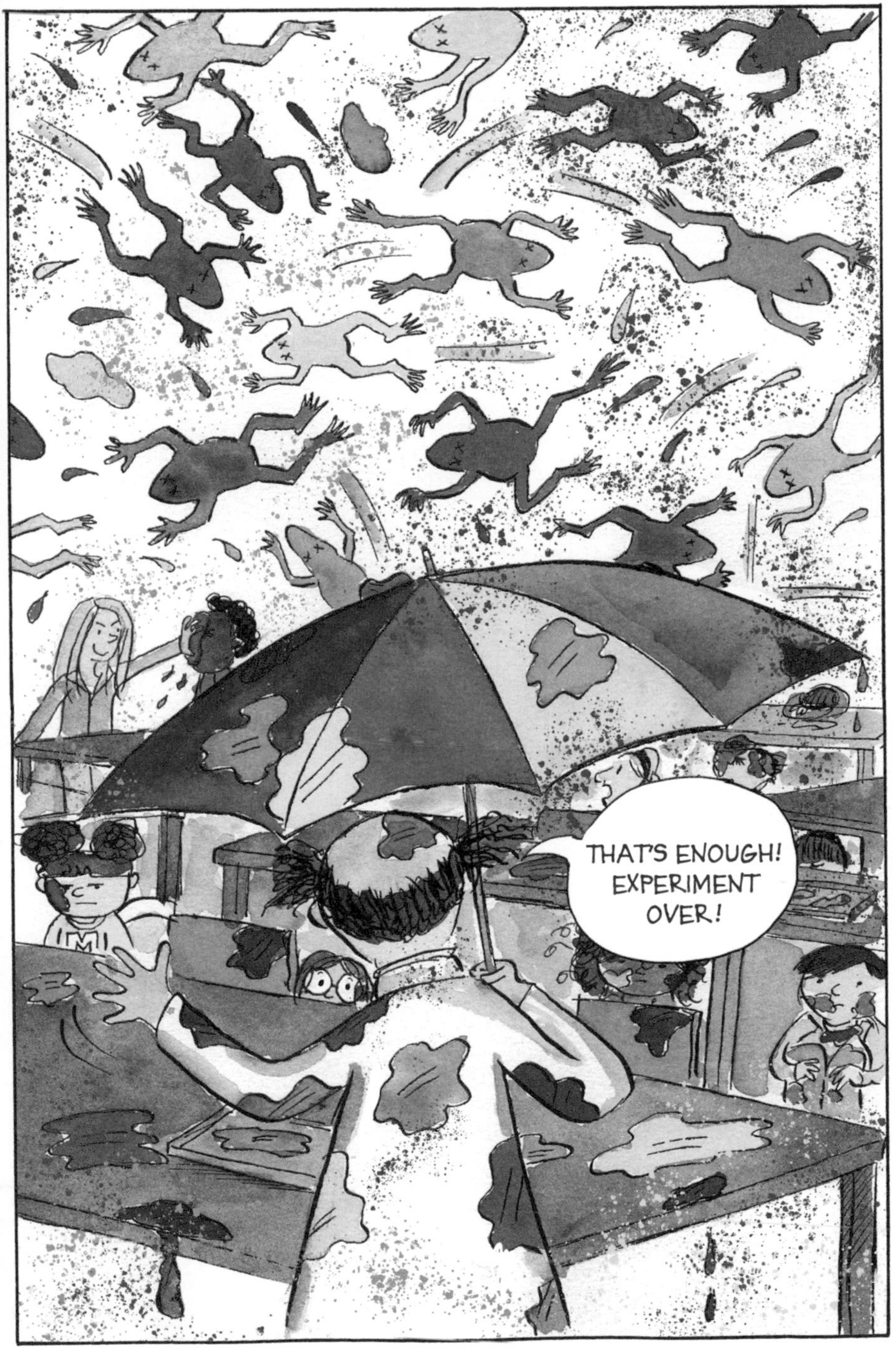
THAT'S ENOUGH! EXPERIMENT OVER!

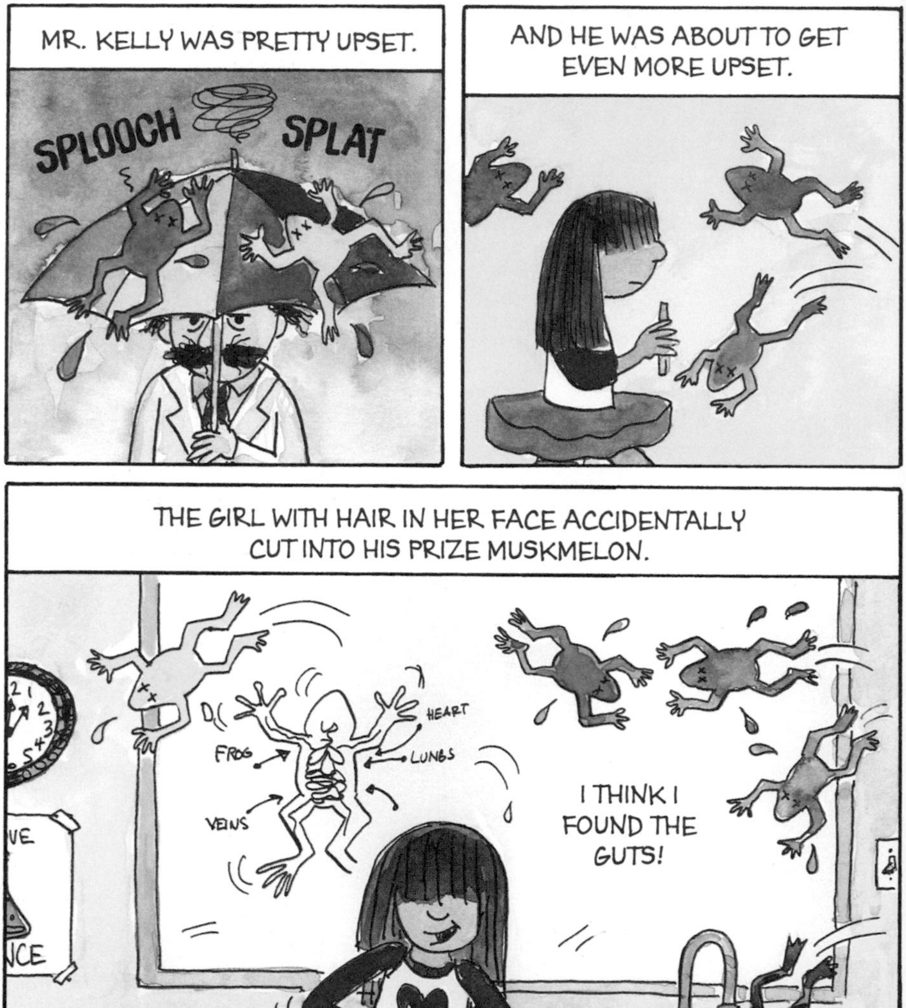
MR. KELLY WAS PRETTY UPSET.
SPLOOCH
SPLAT
AND HE WAS ABOUT TO GET EVEN MORE UPSET.
THE GIRL WITH HAIR IN HER FACE ACCIDENTALLY CUT INTO HIS PRIZE MUSKMELON.
HEART
FROG
LUNGS
VEINS
I THINK I FOUND THE GUTS!

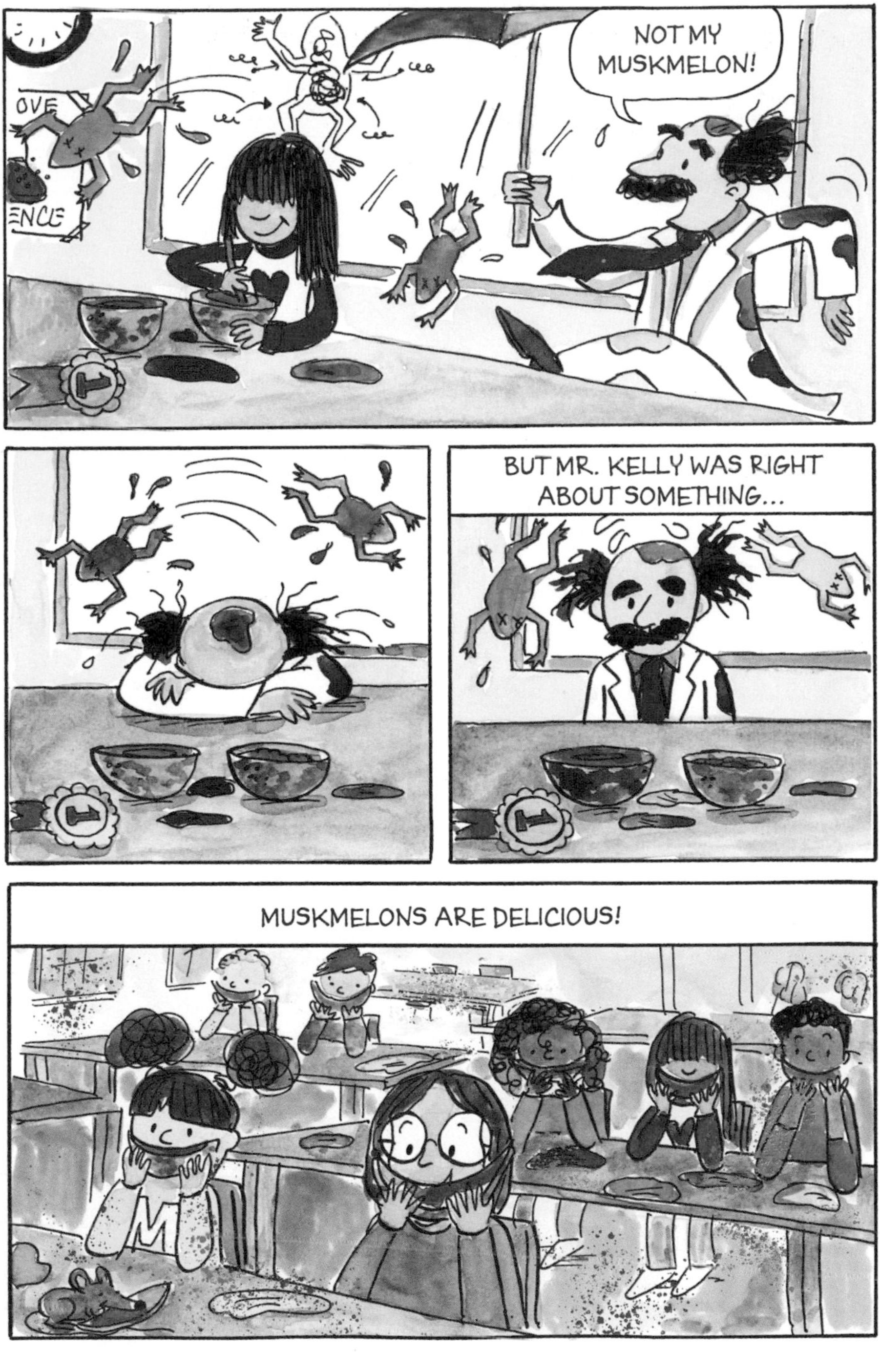
OVE
ENCE
NOT MY MUSKMELON!
BUT MR. KELLY WAS RIGHT ABOUT SOMETHING...
MUSKMELONS ARE DELICIOUS!
M

LILY CONTINUED TO IGNORE ME.

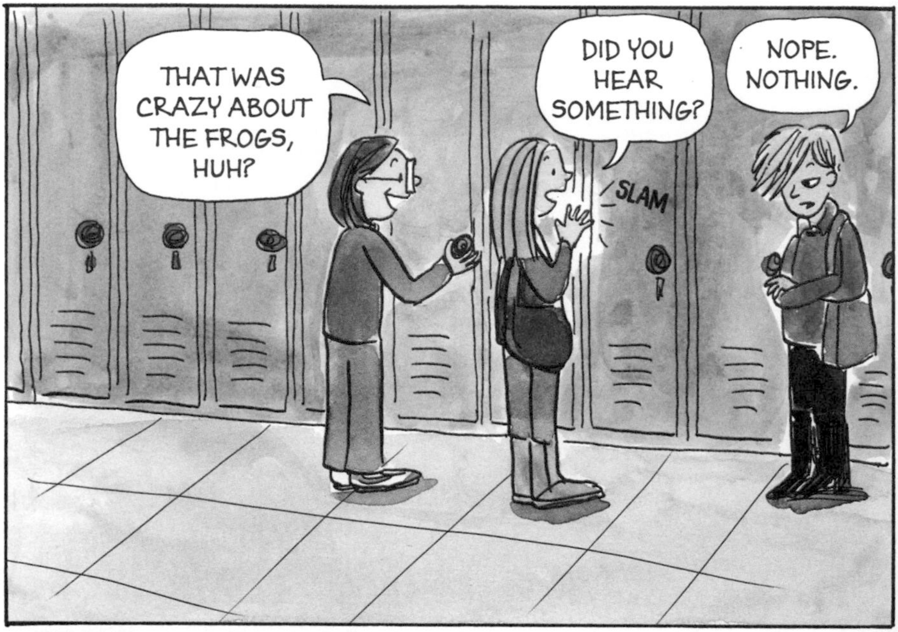
THAT WAS CRAZY ABOUT THE FROGS, HUH?
DID YOU HEAR SOMETHING?
SLAM
NOPE. NOTHING.

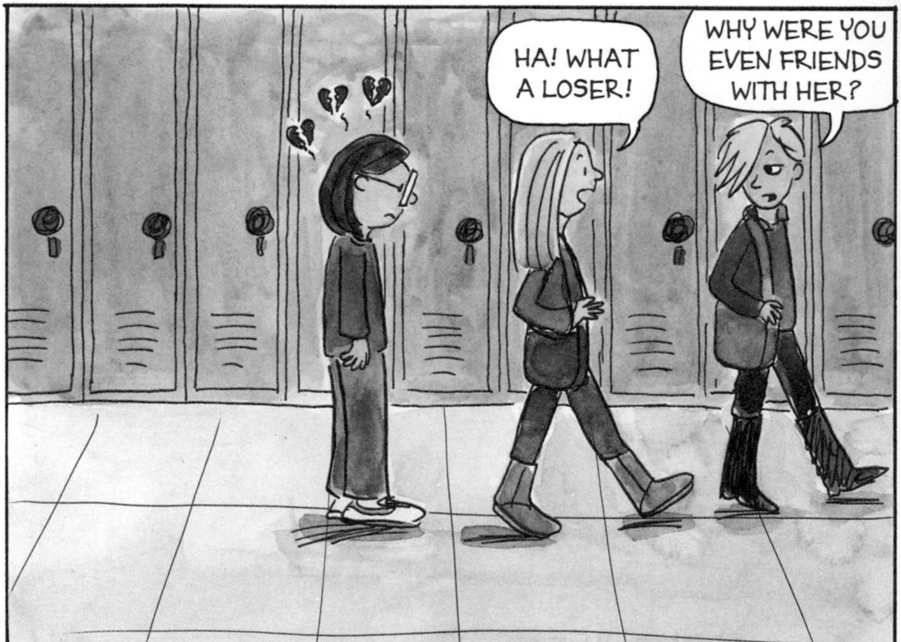
HA! WHAT A LOSER!
WHY WERE YOU EVEN FRIENDS WITH HER?

I AM SO LONELY WITOUT LILY.

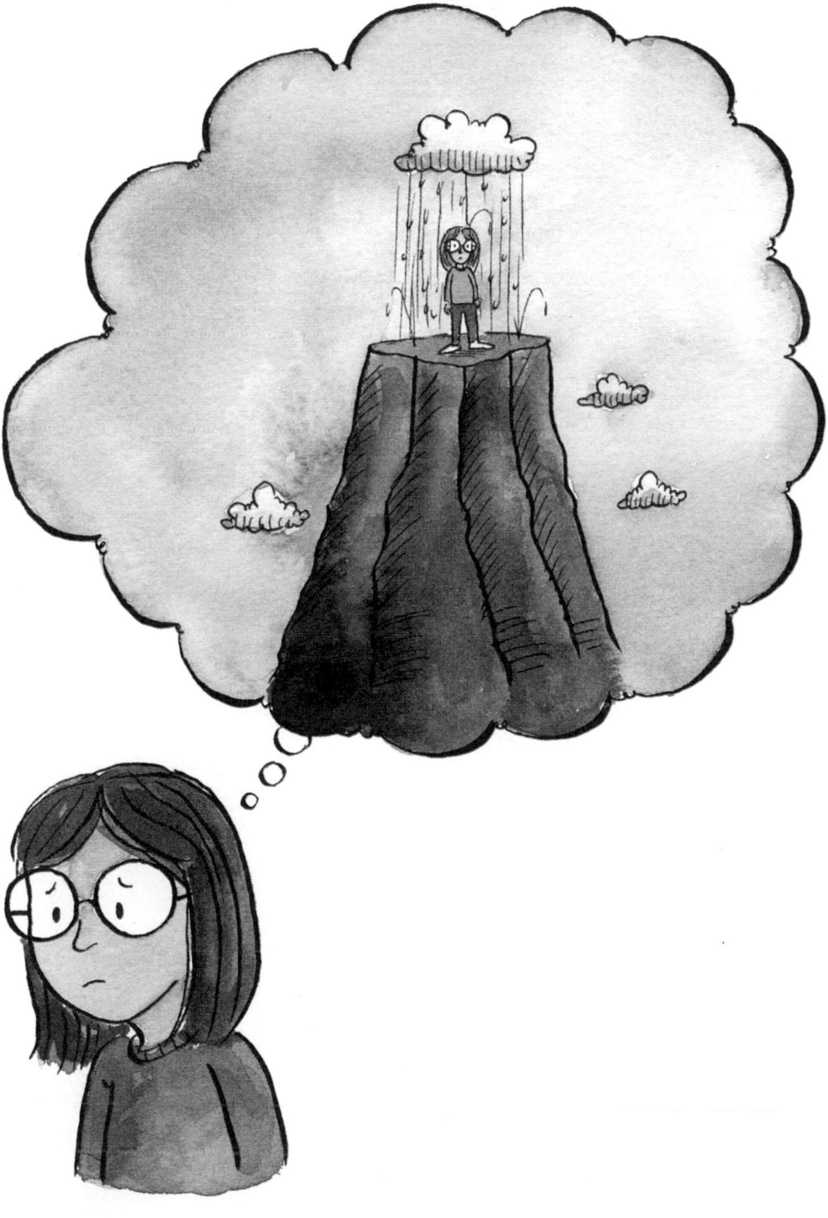

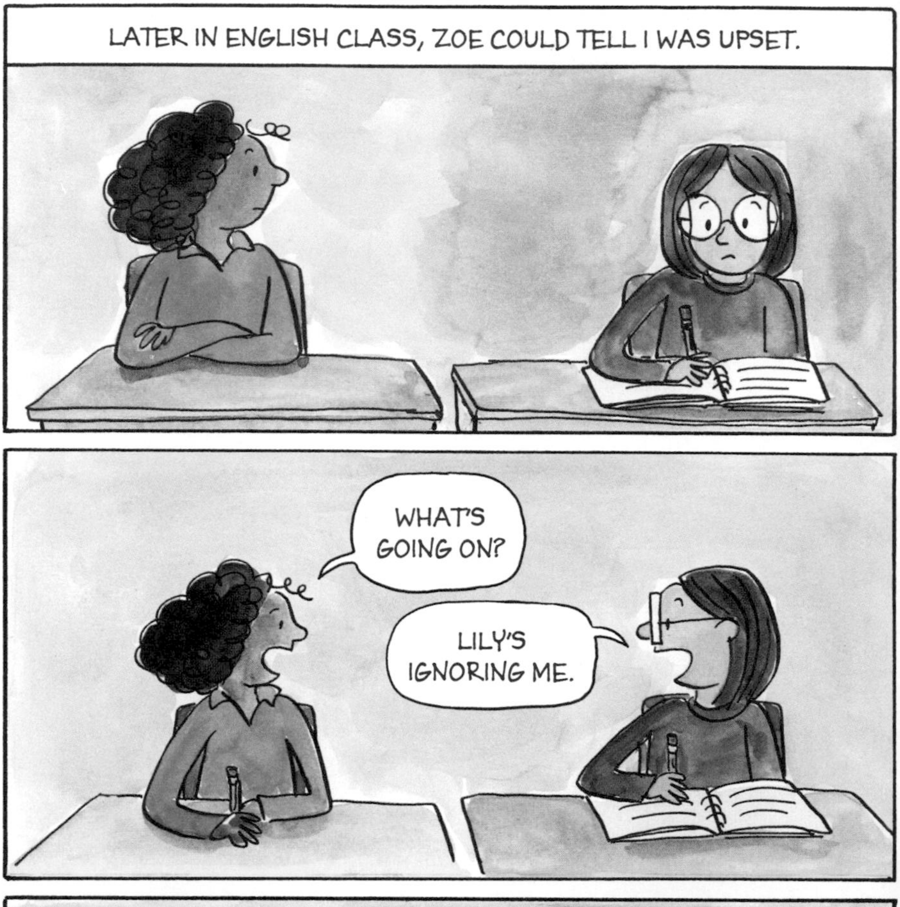
LATER IN ENGLISH CLASS, ZOE COULD TELL I WAS UPSET.
WHAT'S GOING ON?
LILY'S IGNORING ME.
IGNORE HER BACK.
BUT SHE'S MY BEST FRIEND.

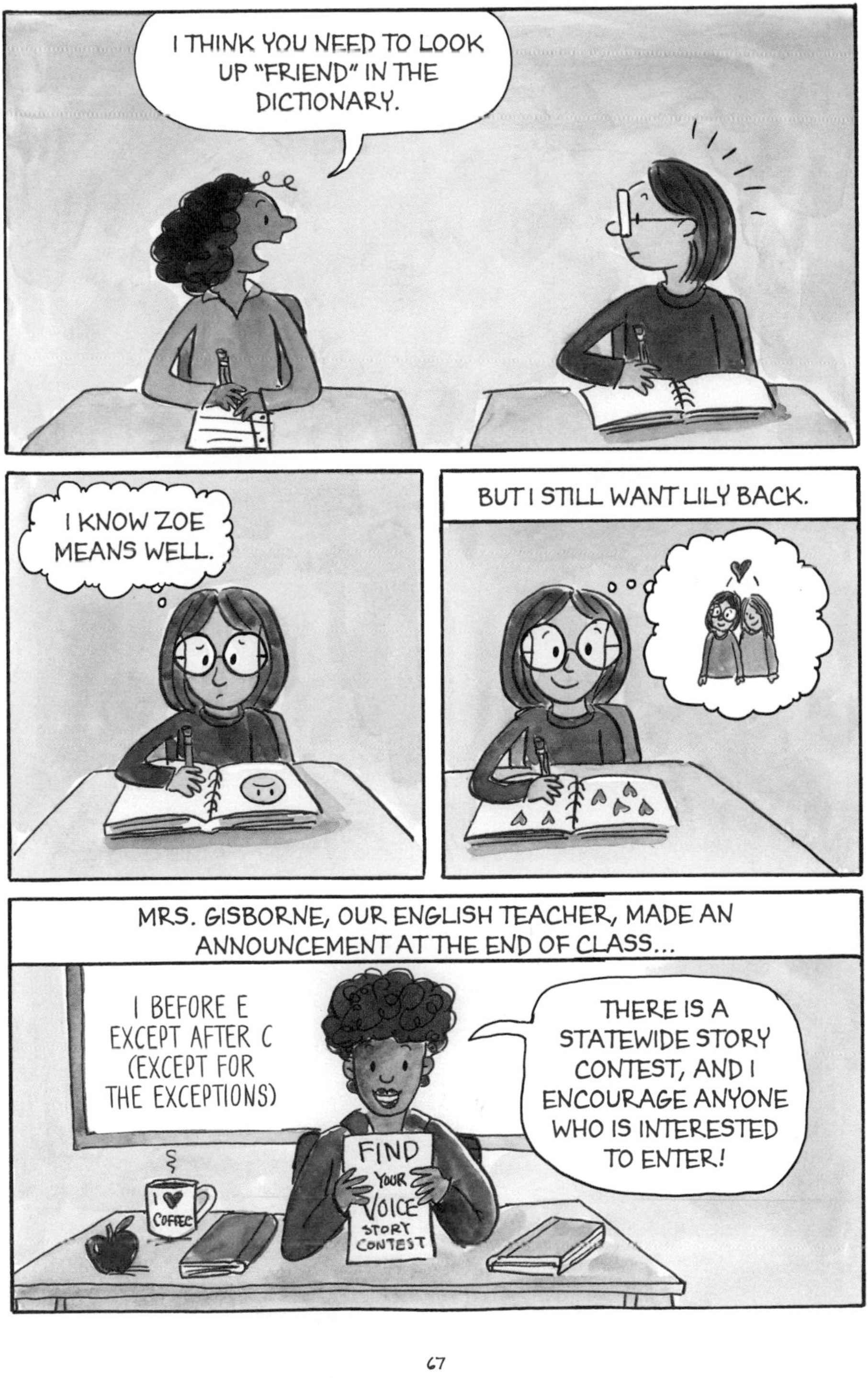
I THINK YOU NEED TO LOOK UP "FRIEND" IN THE DICTIONARY.
I KNOW ZOE MEANS WELL.
BUT I STILL WANT LILY BACK.
MRS. GISBORNE, OUR ENGLISH TEACHER, MADE AN ANNOUNCEMENT AT THE END OF CLASS...
I BEFORE E EXCEPT AFTER C (EXCEPT FOR THE EXCEPTIONS)
THERE IS A STATEWIDE STORY CONTEST, AND I ENCOURAGE ANYONE WHO IS INTERESTED TO ENTER!
FIND YOUR VOICE STORY CONTEST
I ♥ COFFEE

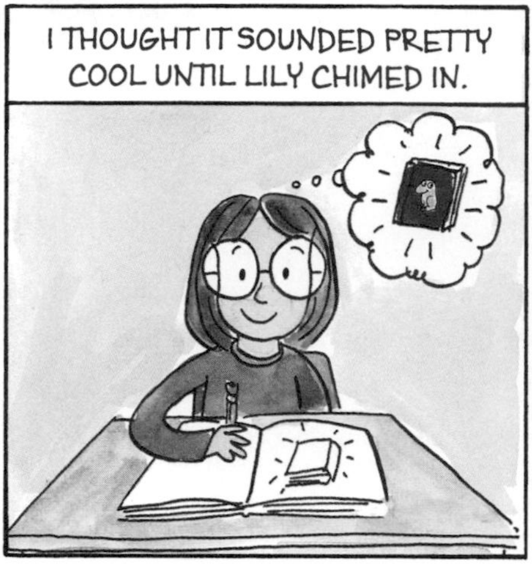
I THOUGHT IT SOUNDED PRETTY COOL UNTIL LILY CHIMED IN.

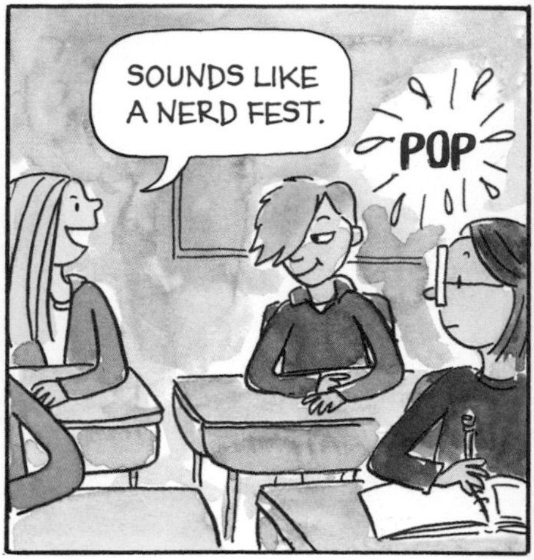
SOUNDS LIKE A NERD FEST.
POP

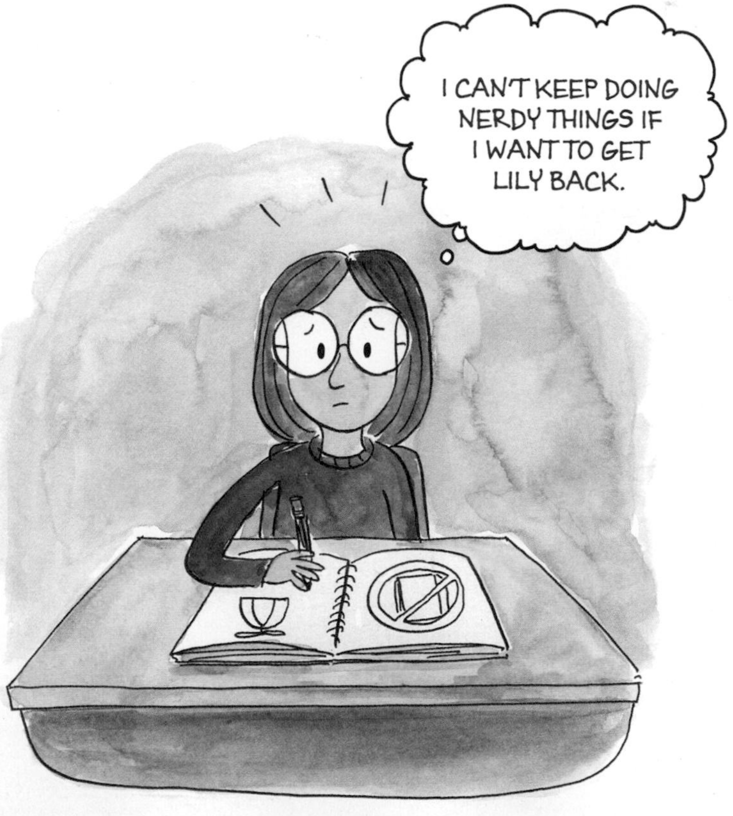
I CAN'T KEEP DOING NERDY THINGS IF I WANT TO GET LILY BACK.

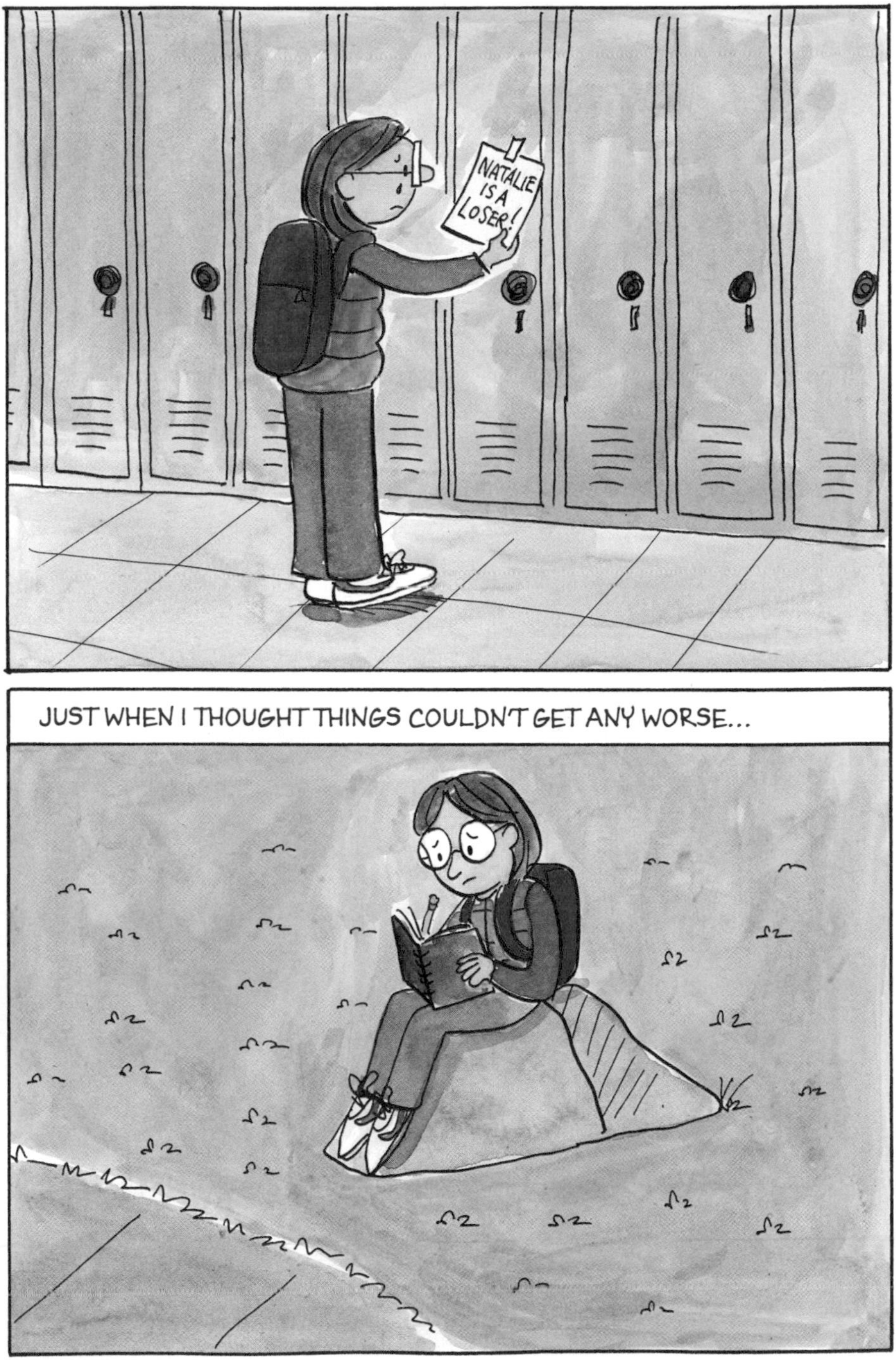
NATALIE IS A LOSER!
JUST WHEN I THOUGHT THINGS COULDN'T GET ANY WORSE...

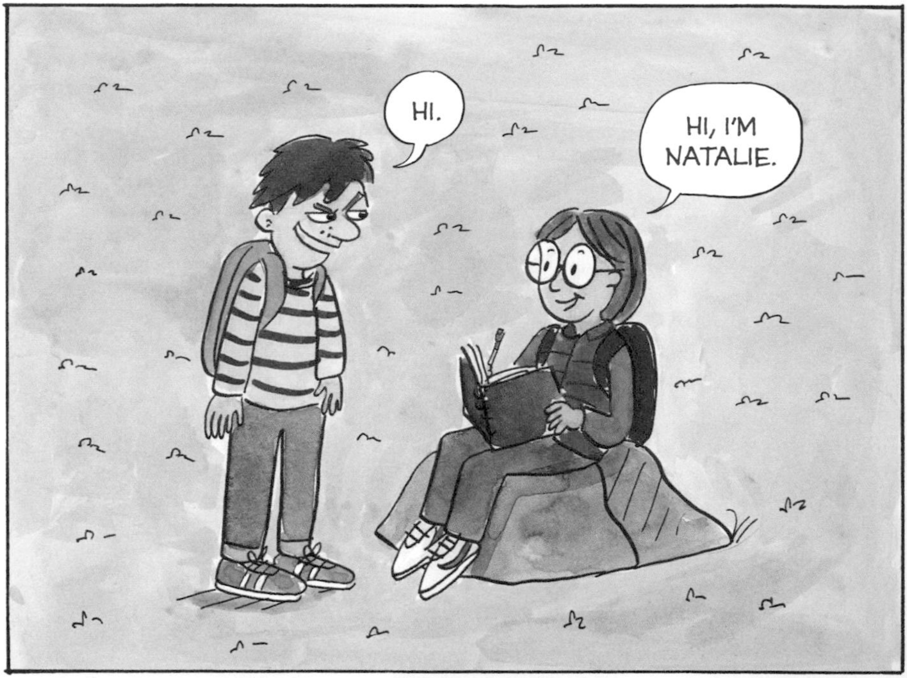
HI.
HI, I'M NATALIE.

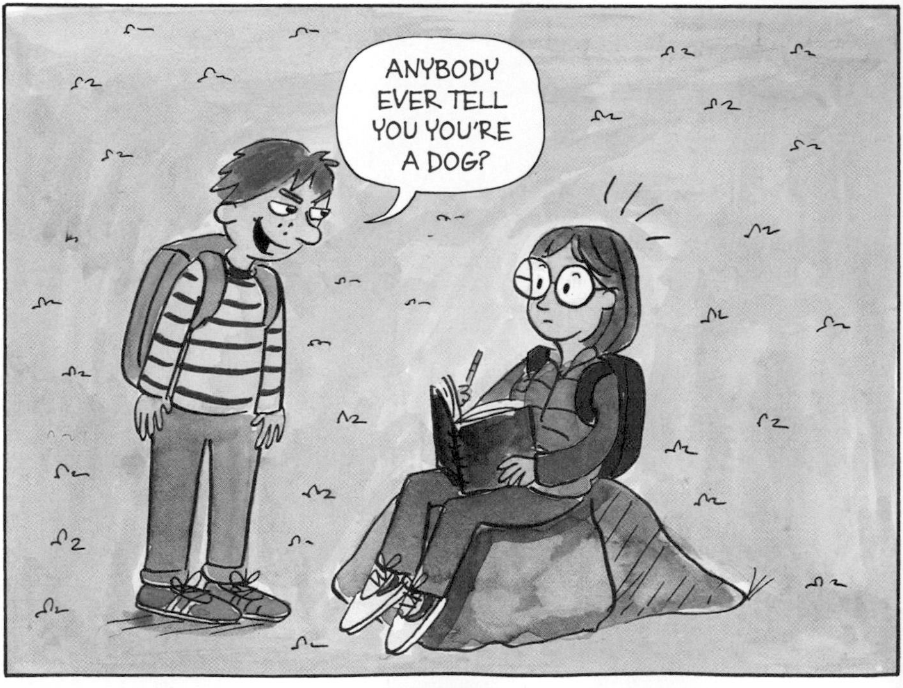
ANYBODY EVER TELL YOU YOU'RE A DOG?

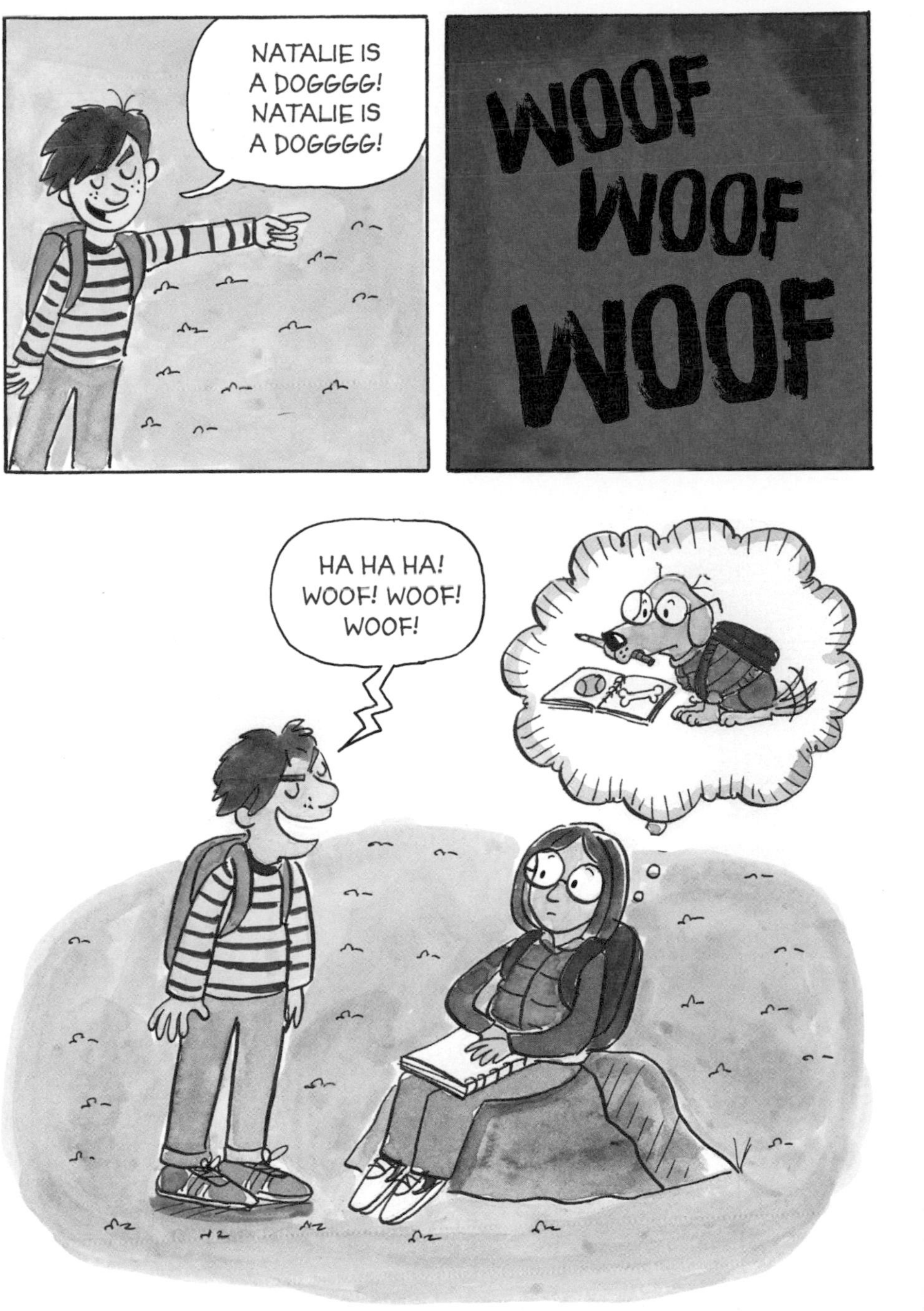
NATALIE IS A DOGGGG! NATALIE IS A DOGGGG!
WOOF WOOF WOOF
HA HA HA! WOOF! WOOF! WOOF!

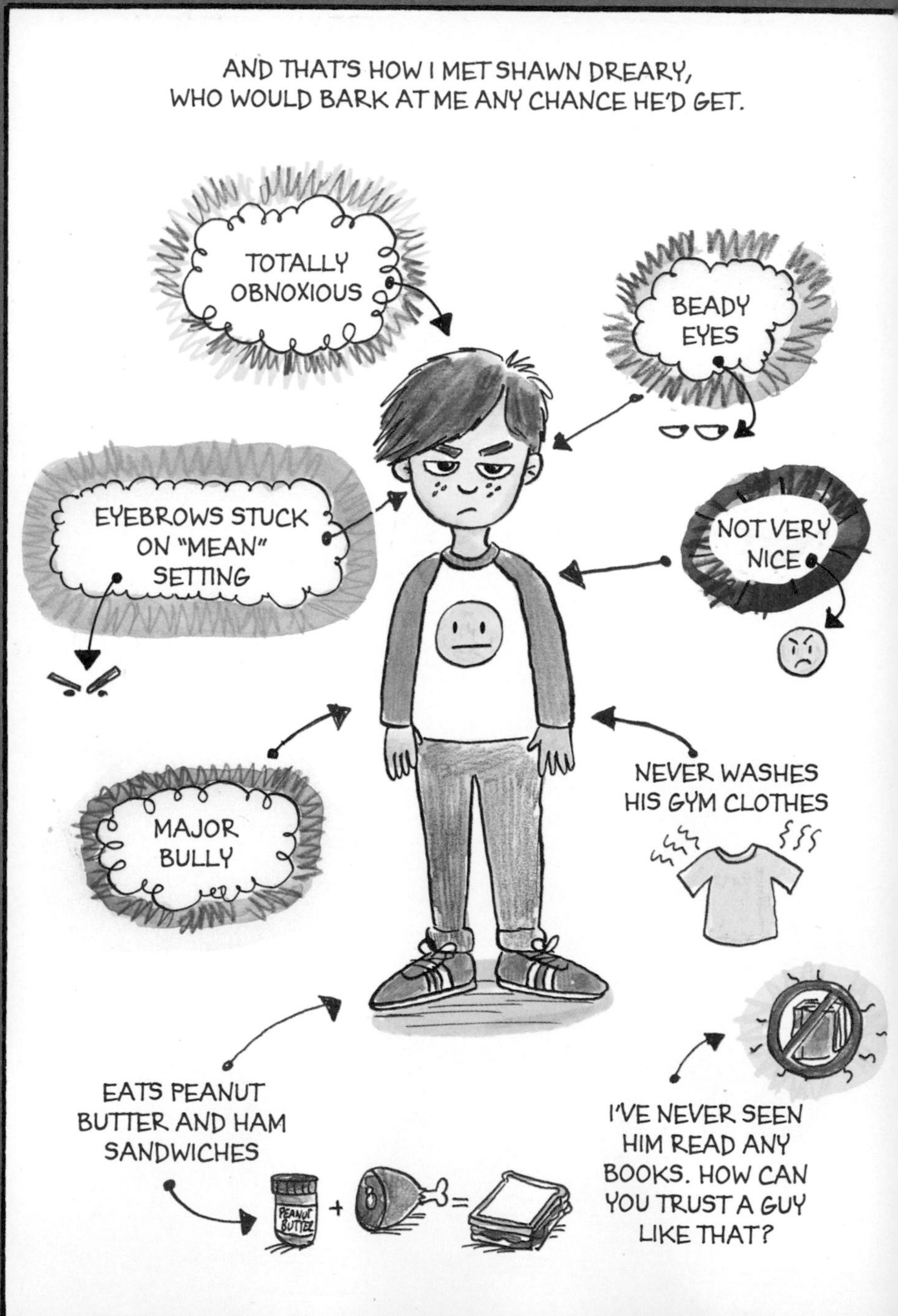
AND THAT'S HOW I MET SHAWN DREARY,
WHO WOULD BARK AT ME ANY CHANCE HE'D GET.
TOTALLY OBNOXIOUS
BEADY EYES
EYEBROWS STUCK ON "MEAN" SETTING
NOT VERY NICE
MAJOR BULLY
NEVER WASHES HIS GYM CLOTHES
EATS PEANUT BUTTER AND HAM SANDWICHES
PEANUT BUTTER
I'VE NEVER SEEN HIM READ ANY BOOKS. HOW CAN YOU TRUST A GUY LIKE THAT?

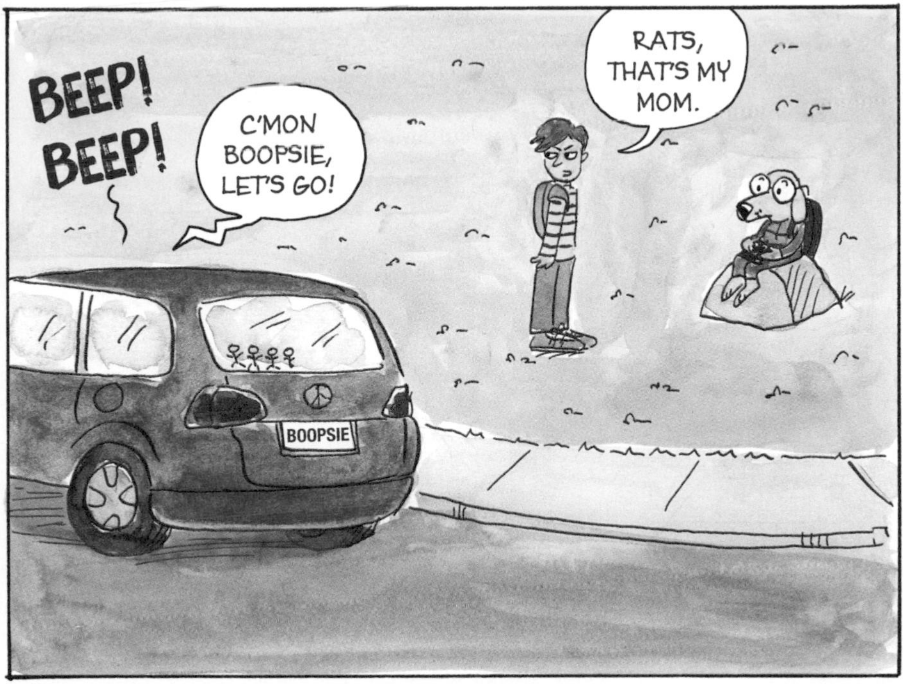
BEEP! BEEP!
C'MON BOOPSIE, LET'S GO!
RATS, THAT'S MY MOM.
BOOPSIE

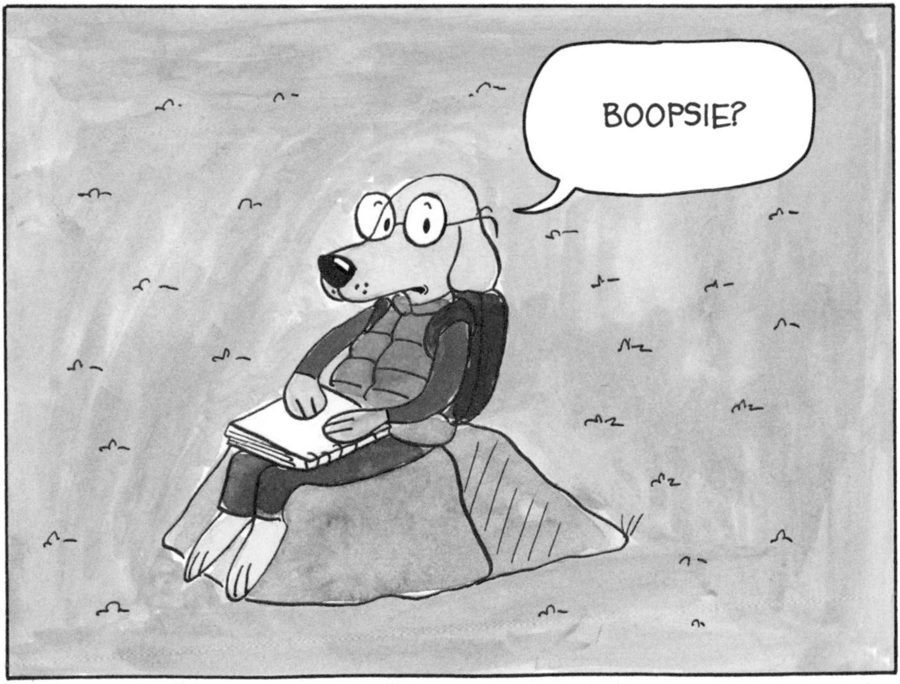
BOOPSIE?

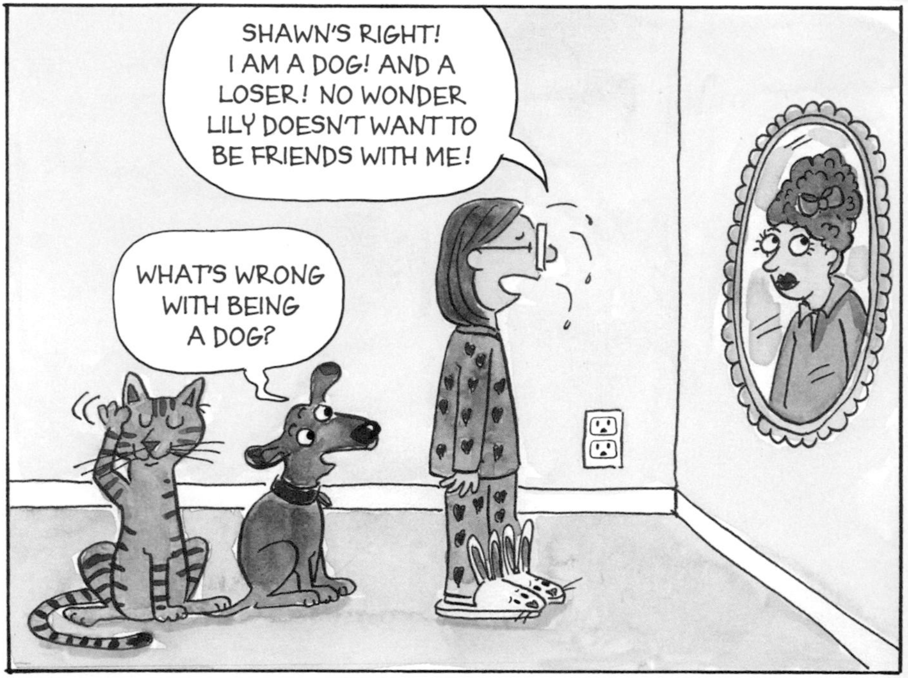
SHAWN'S RIGHT! I AM A DOG! AND A LOSER! NO WONDER LILY DOESN'T WANT TO BE FRIENDS WITH ME!
WHAT'S WRONG WITH BEING A DOG?

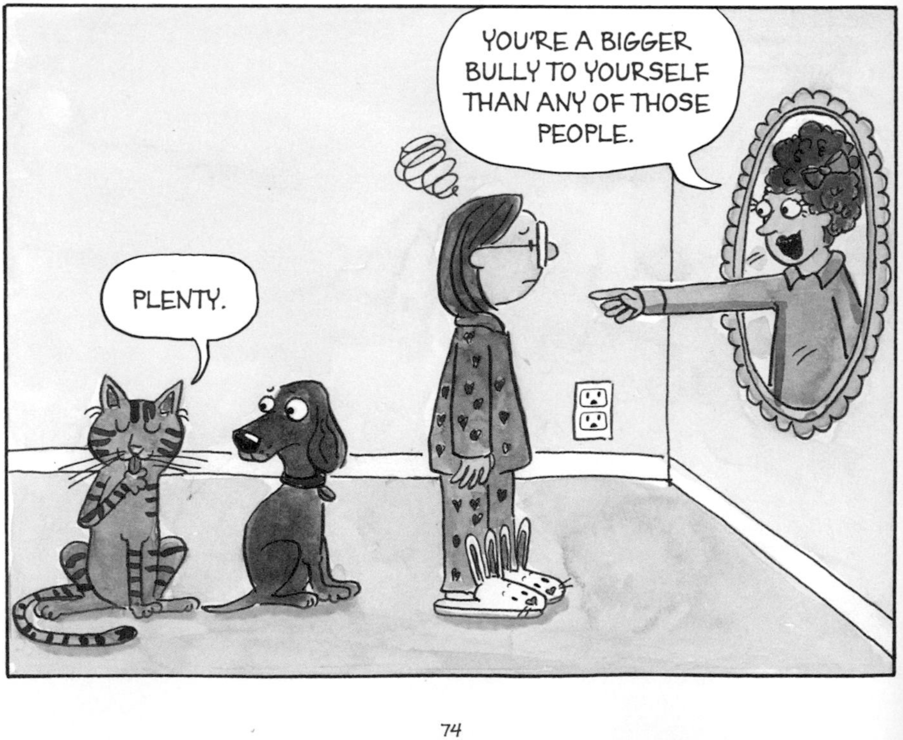
YOU'RE A BIGGER BULLY TO YOURSELF THAN ANY OF THOSE PEOPLE.
PLENTY.

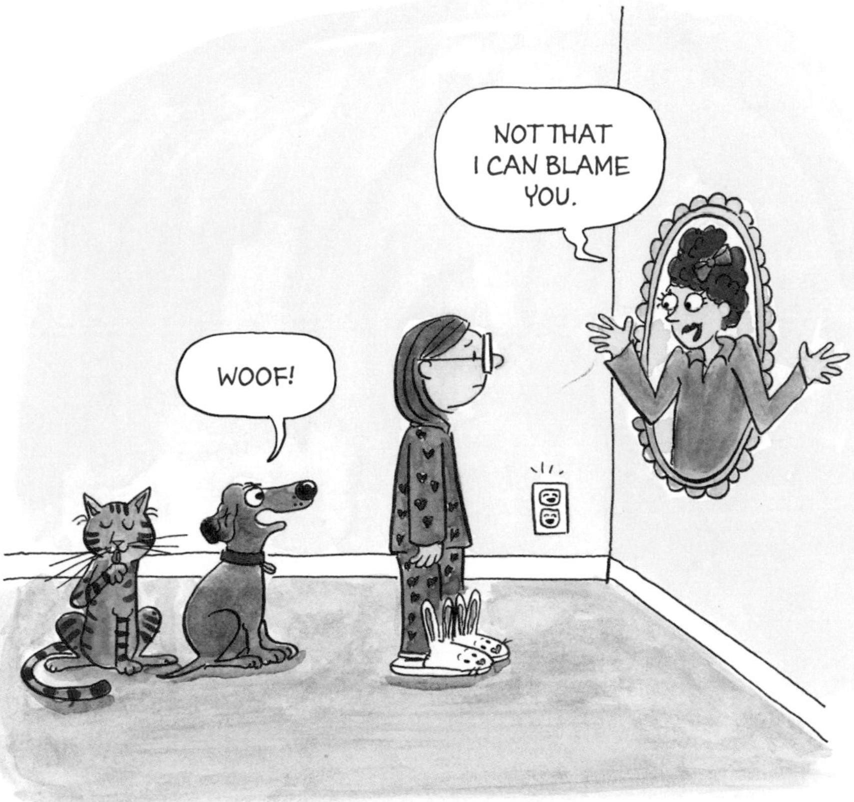
NOT THAT
I CAN BLAME
YOU.
WOOF!

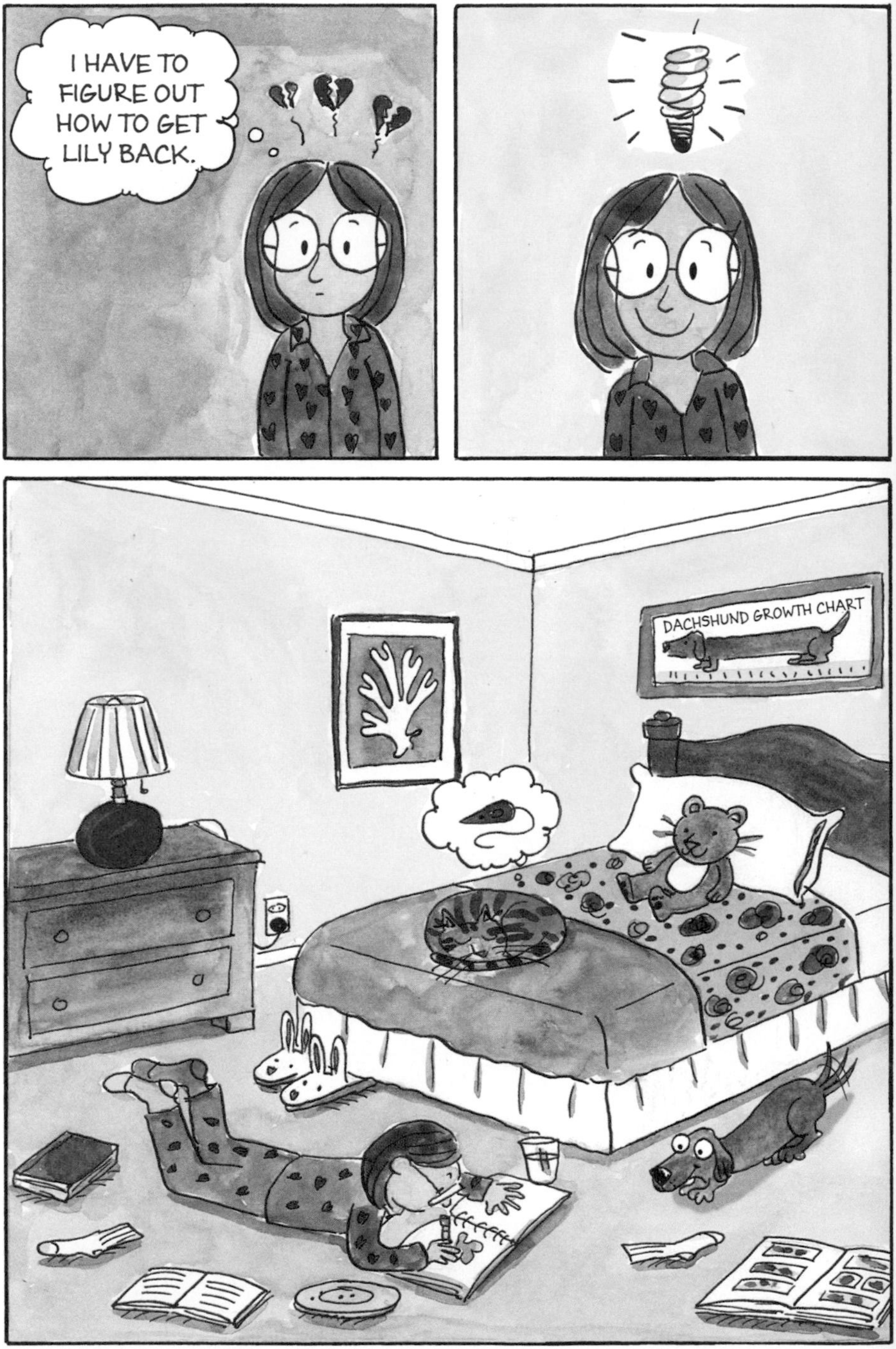
I HAVE TO FIGURE OUT HOW TO GET LILY BACK.
DACHSHUND GROWTH CHART

CHAPTER 5
HATS OFF

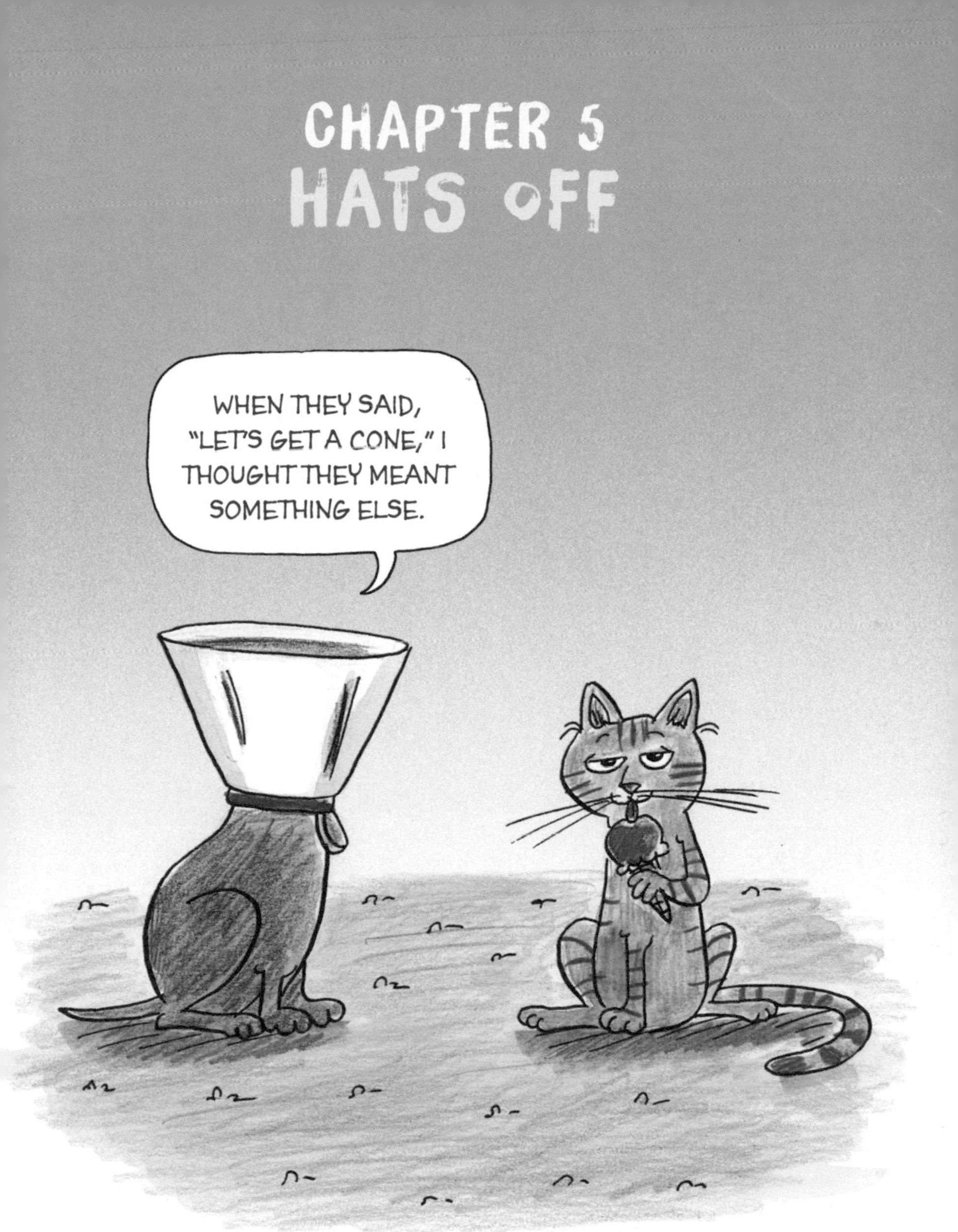
WHEN THEY SAID, "LET'S GET A CONE," I THOUGHT THEY MEANT SOMETHING ELSE.

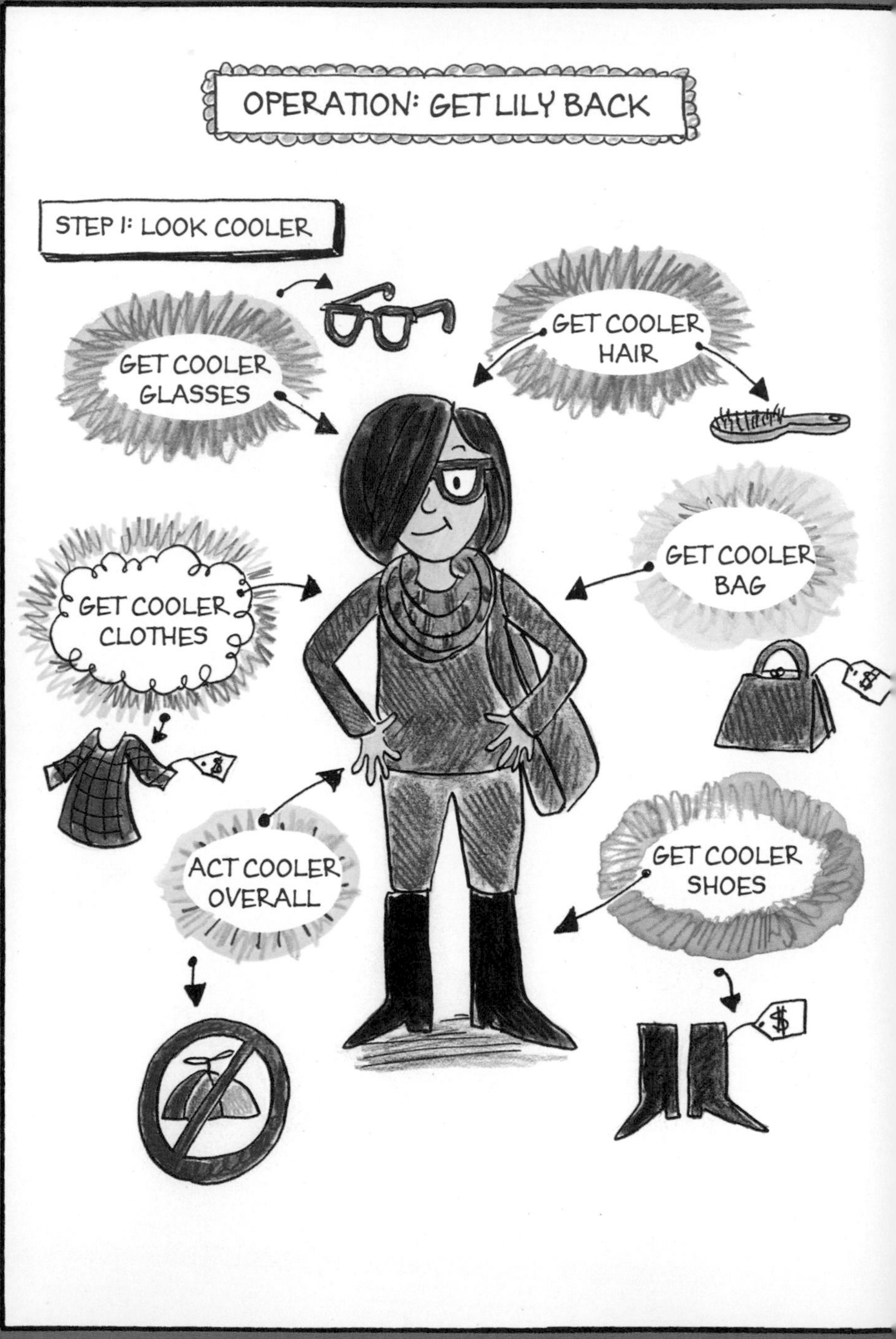
OPERATION: GET LILY BACK
STEP 1: LOOK COOLER
GET COOLER GLASSES
GET COOLER HAIR
GET COOLER CLOTHES
GET COOLER BAG
ACT COOLER OVERALL
GET COOLER SHOES
$
$
$
$

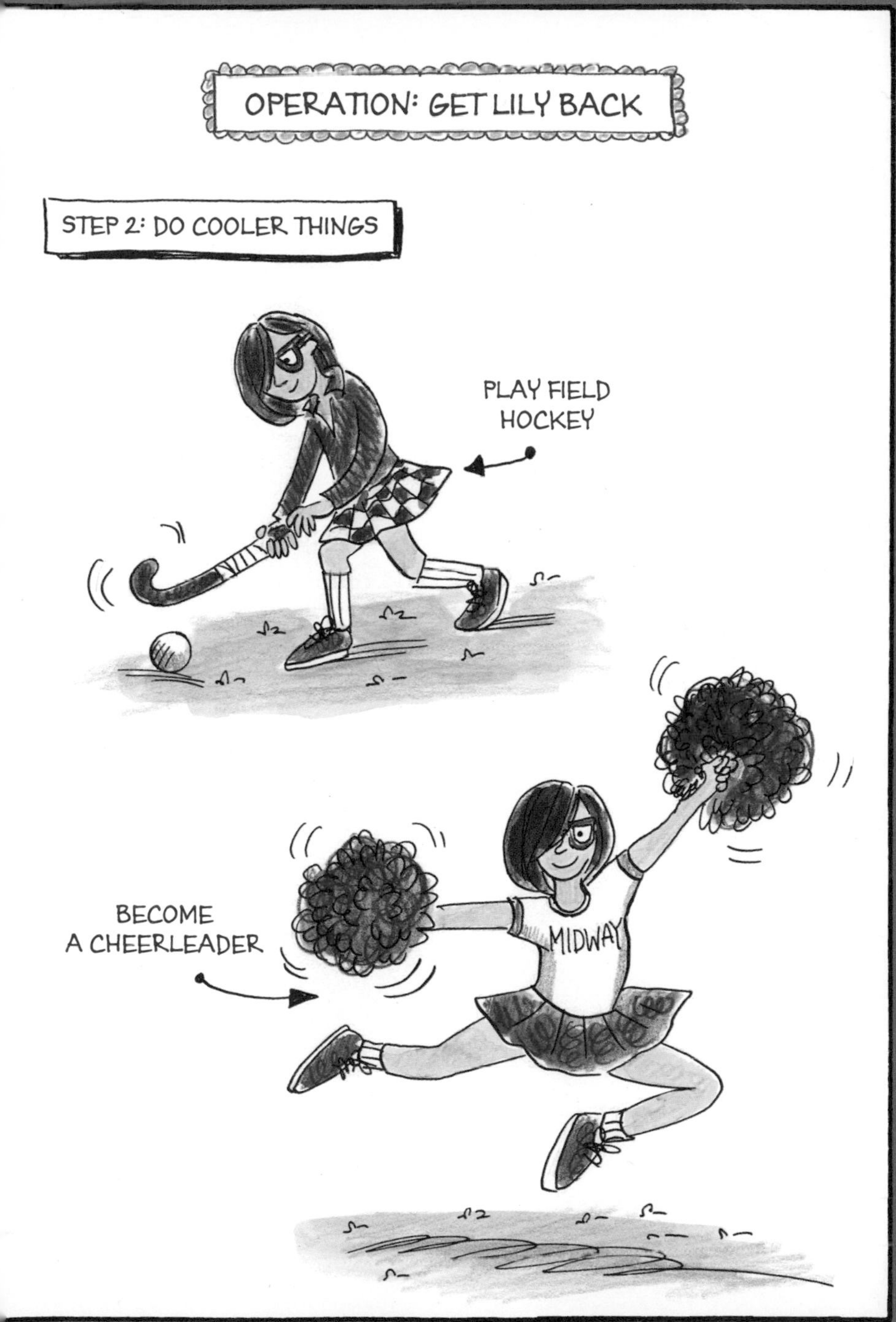
OPERATION: GET LILY BACK
STEP 2: DO COOLER THINGS
PLAY FIELD HOCKEY
BECOME A CHEERLEADER
MIDWAY

OPERATION: GET LILY BACK

STEP 3: HANG OUT WITH COOLER PEOPLE

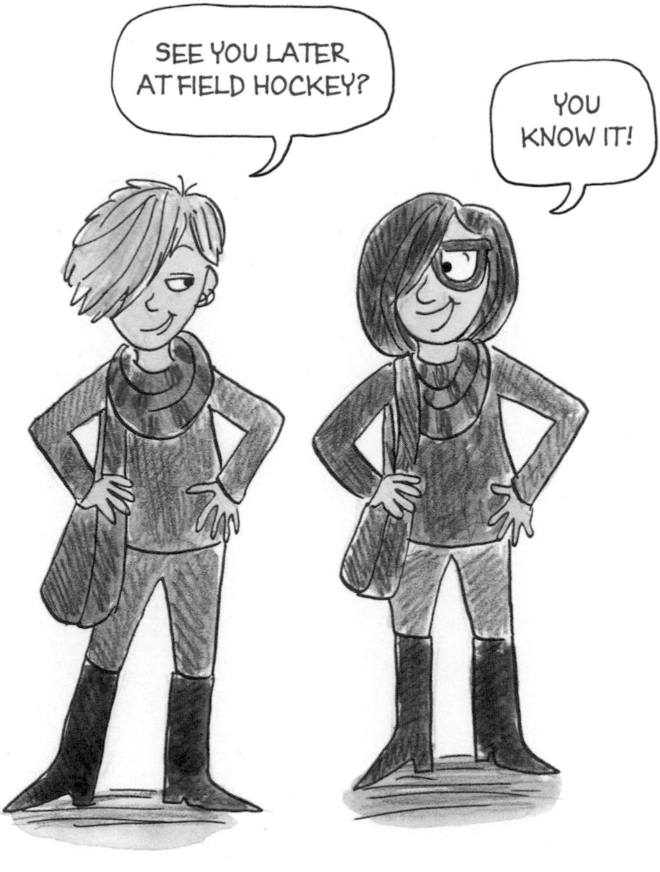

SEE YOU LATER AT FIELD HOCKEY?
YOU KNOW IT!

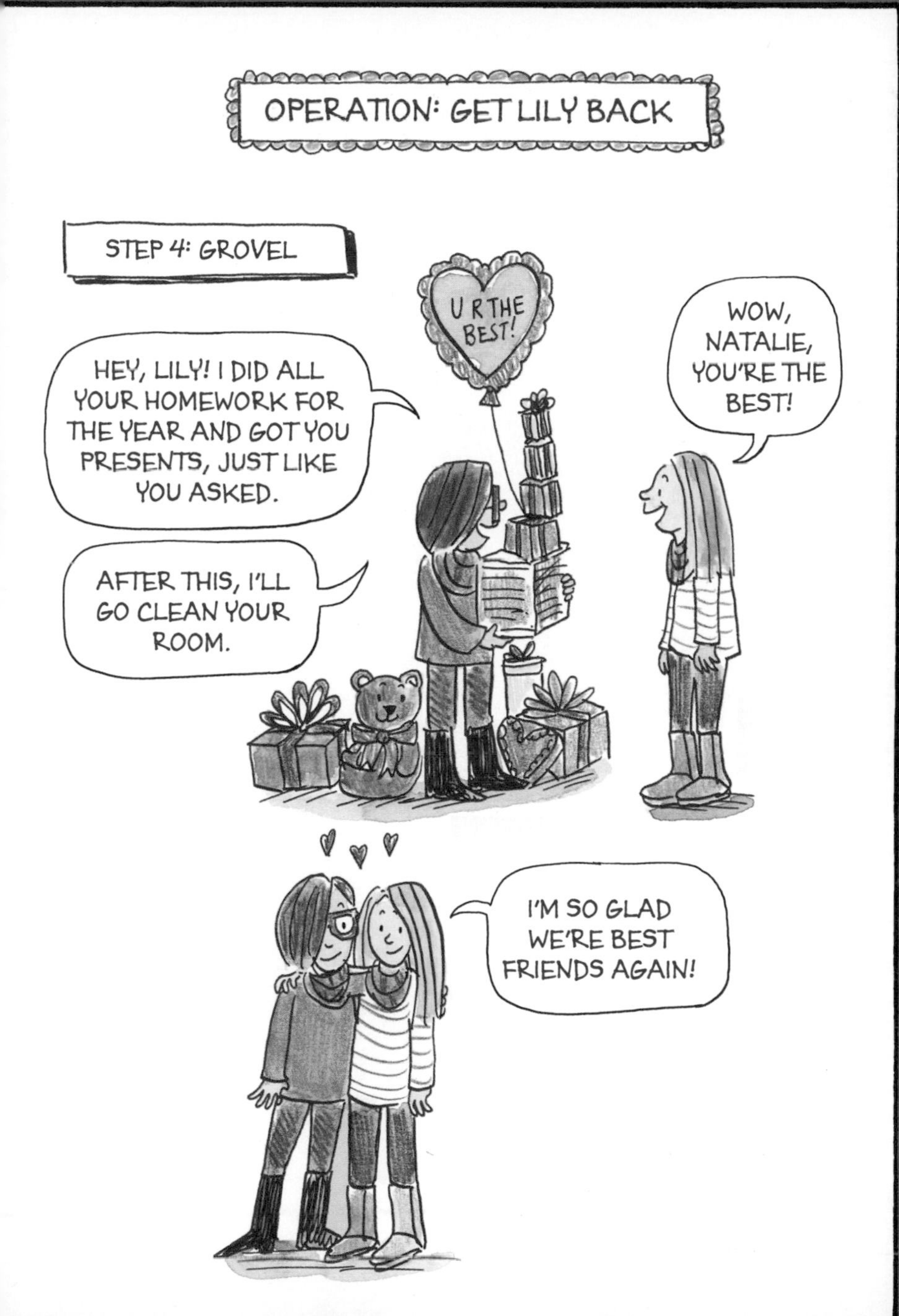
OPERATION: GET LILY BACK
STEP 4: GROVEL
U R THE BEST!
HEY, LILY! I DID ALL YOUR HOMEWORK FOR THE YEAR AND GOT YOU PRESENTS, JUST LIKE YOU ASKED.
WOW, NATALIE, YOU'RE THE BEST!
AFTER THIS, I'LL GO CLEAN YOUR ROOM.
I'M SO GLAD WE'RE BEST FRIENDS AGAIN!

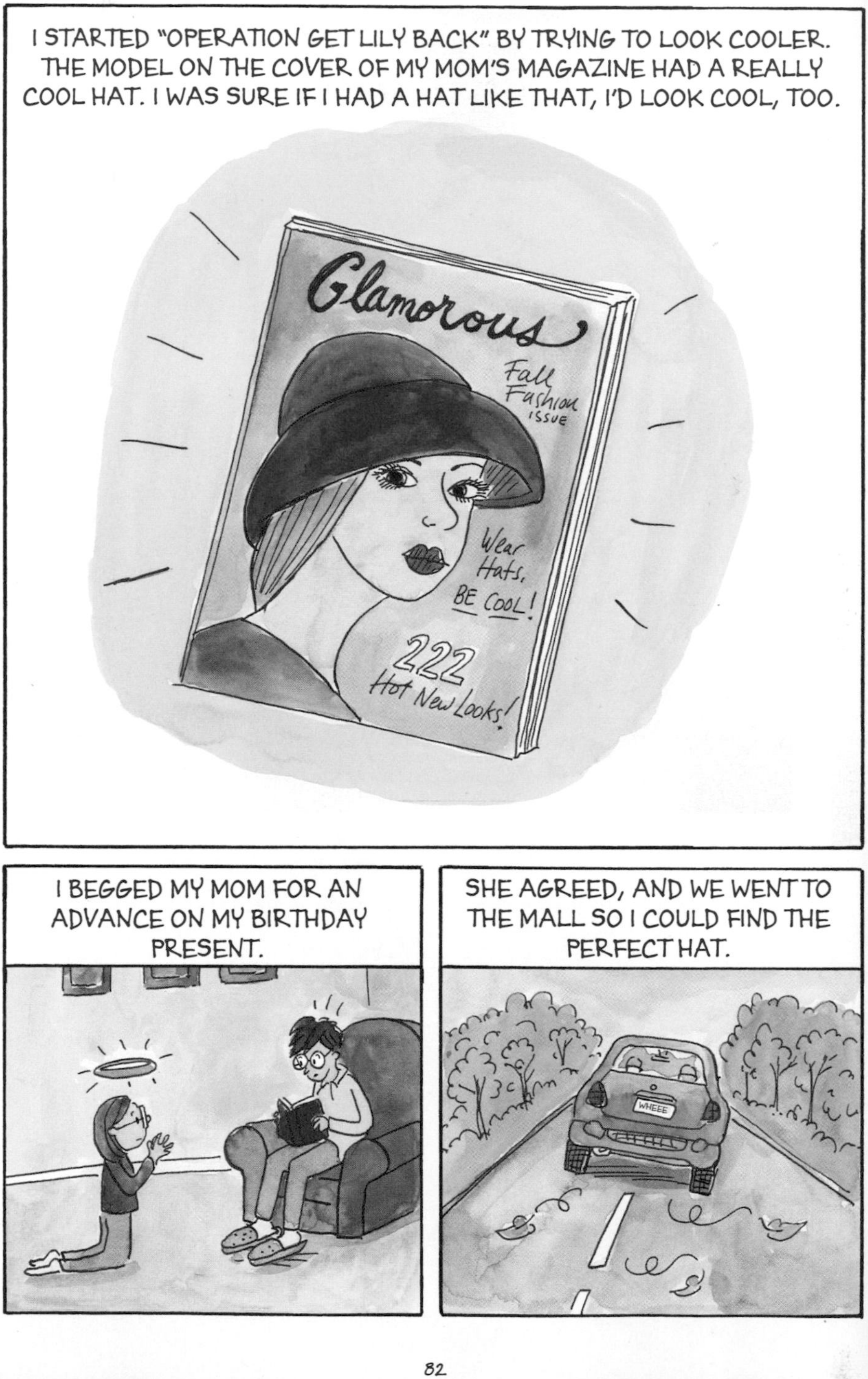
I STARTED "OPERATION GET LILY BACK" BY TRYING TO LOOK COOLER. THE MODEL ON THE COVER OF MY MOM'S MAGAZINE HAD A REALLY COOL HAT. I WAS SURE IF I HAD A HAT LIKE THAT, I'D LOOK COOL, TOO.
Glamorous
Fall Fashion ISSUE
Wear Hats, BE COOL!
222 Hot New Looks!
I BEGGED MY MOM FOR AN ADVANCE ON MY BIRTHDAY PRESENT.
SHE AGREED, AND WE WENT TO THE MALL SO I COULD FIND THE PERFECT HAT.
WHEEE

I TRIED ON ALL KINDS OF HATS.

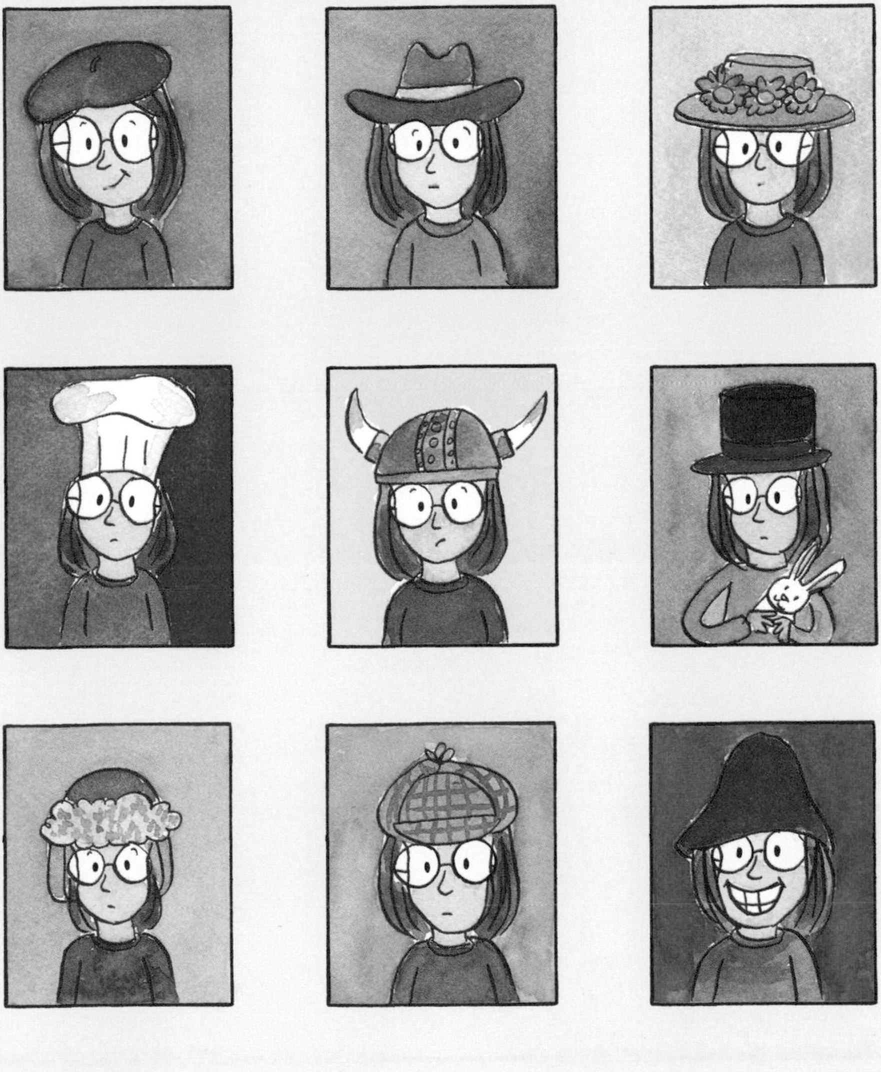

YOU CAN'T GET ANY MORE GLAMOROUS THAN THIS!

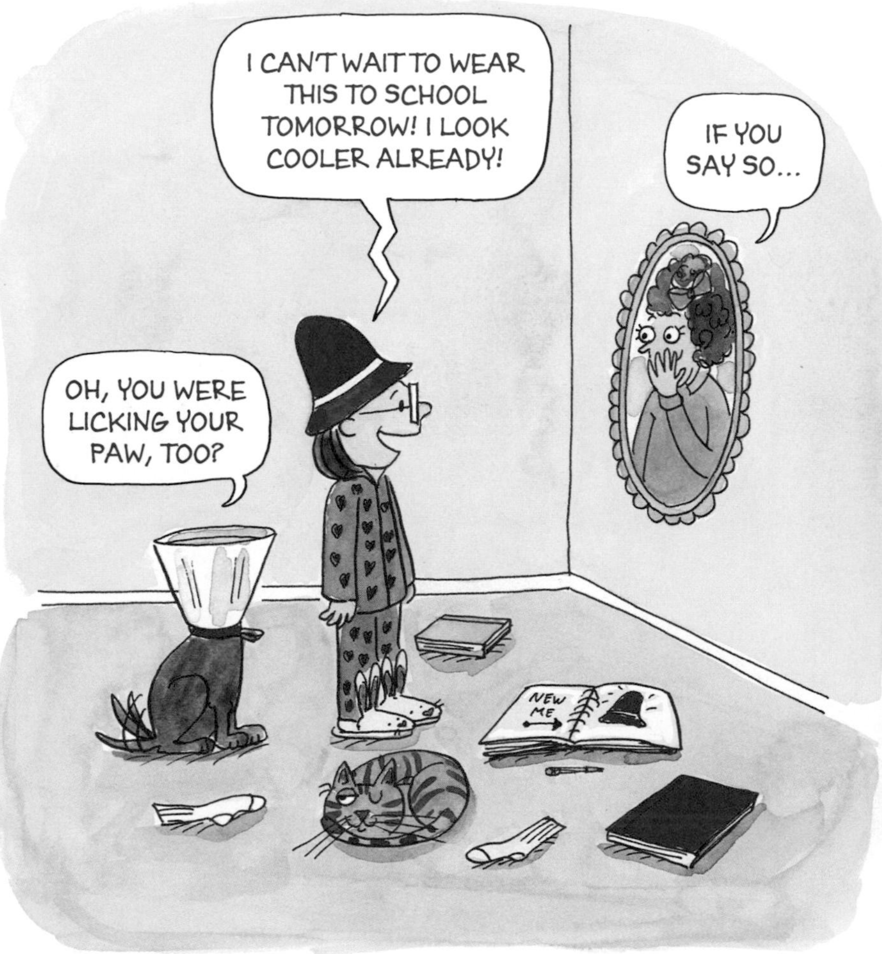
I CAN'T WAIT TO WEAR THIS TO SCHOOL TOMORROW! I LOOK COOLER ALREADY!
IF YOU SAY SO...
OH, YOU WERE LICKING YOUR PAW, TOO?
NEW ME

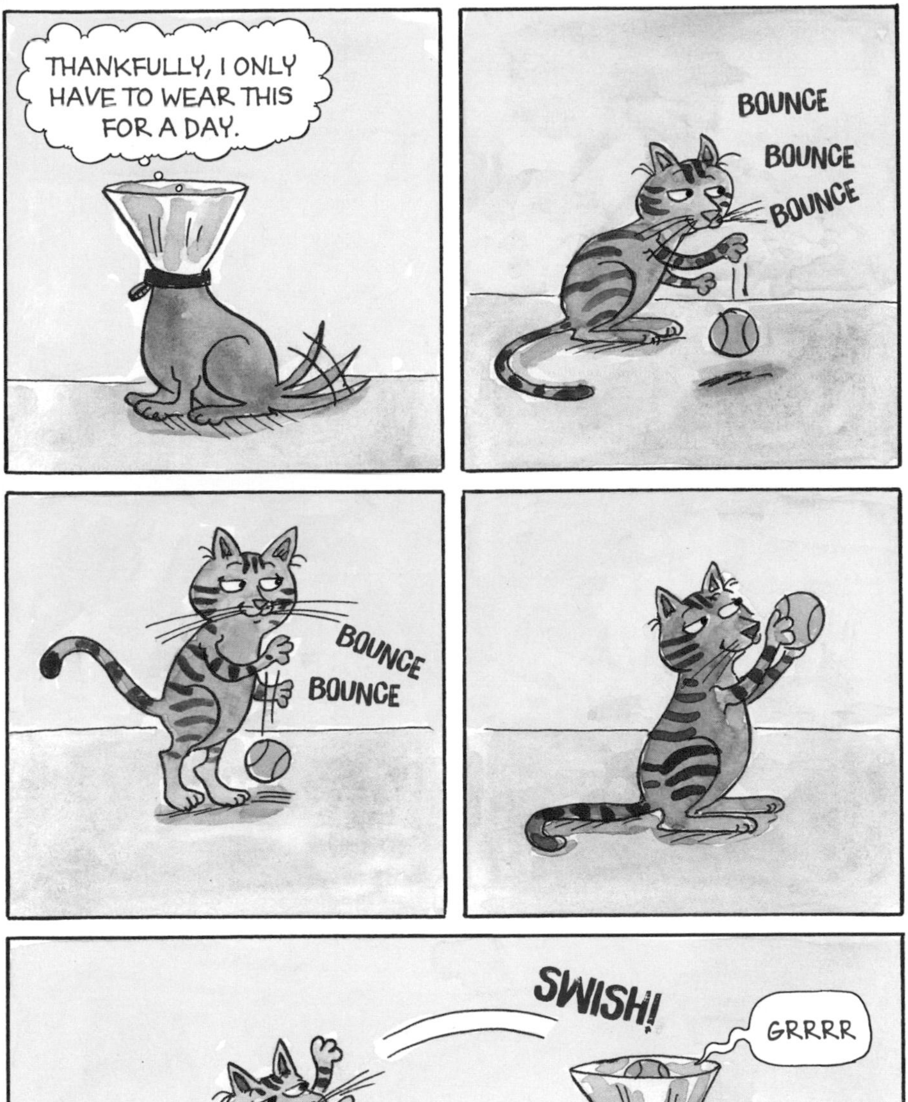
THANKFULLY, I ONLY HAVE TO WEAR THIS FOR A DAY.
BOUNCE
BOUNCE
BOUNCE
BOUNCE
BOUNCE
SWISH!
GRRRR

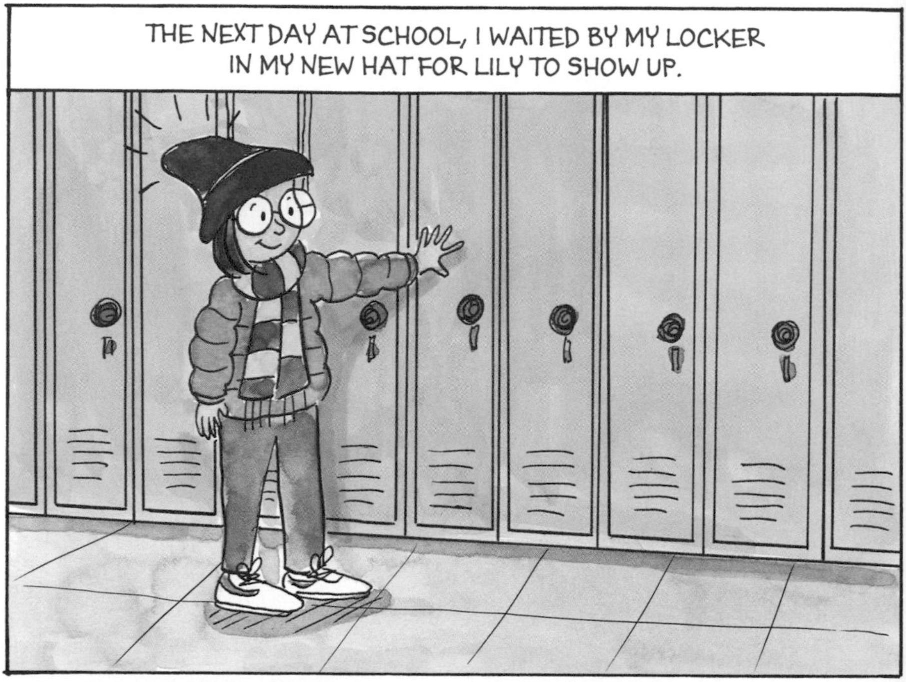
THE NEXT DAY AT SCHOOL, I WAITED BY MY LOCKER IN MY NEW HAT FOR LILY TO SHOW UP.

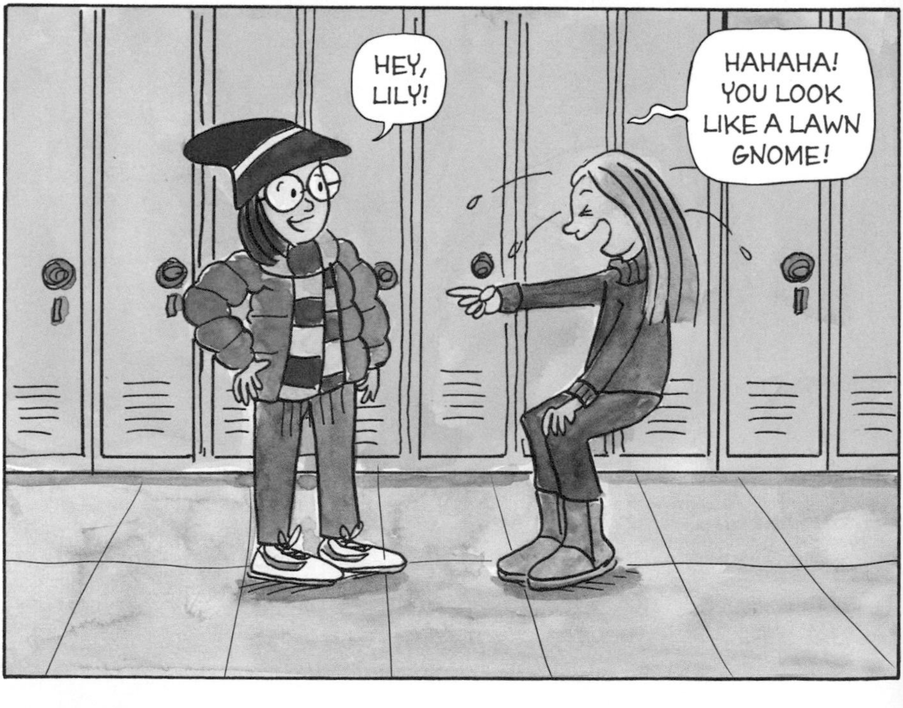
HEY, LILY!
HAHAHA! YOU LOOK LIKE A LAWN GNOME!

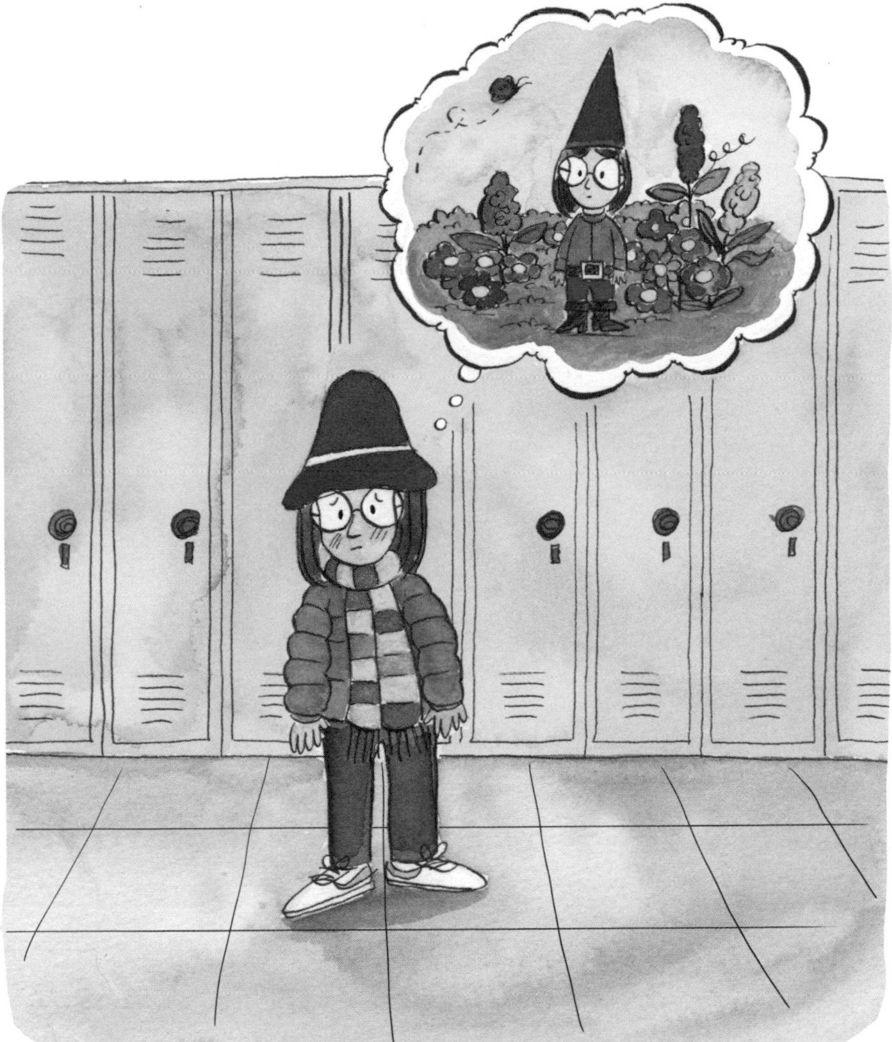

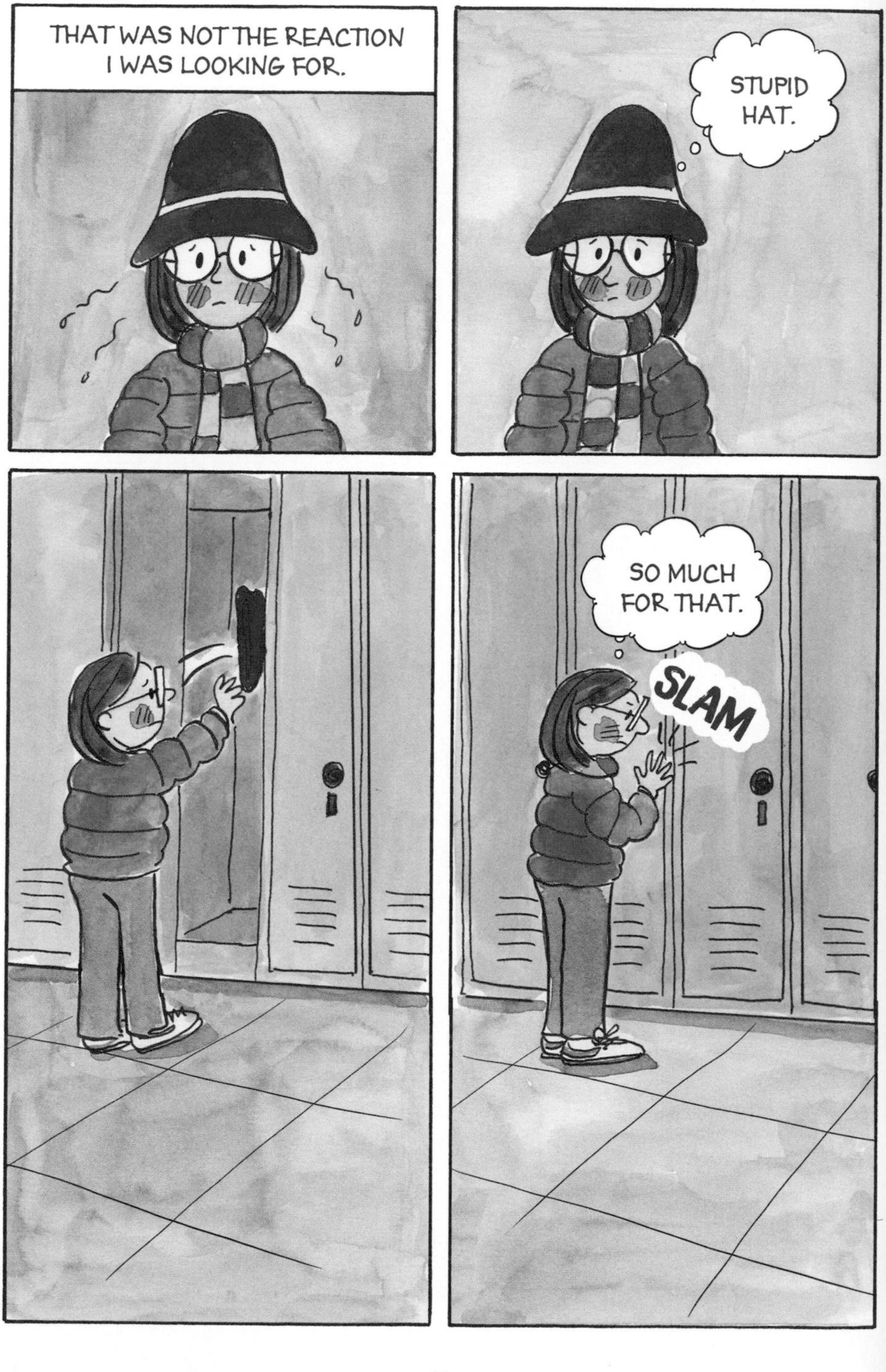
THAT WAS NOT THE REACTION I WAS LOOKING FOR.
STUPID HAT.
SO MUCH FOR THAT.
SLAM

CHAPTER 6
CUPID STRIKES AGAIN

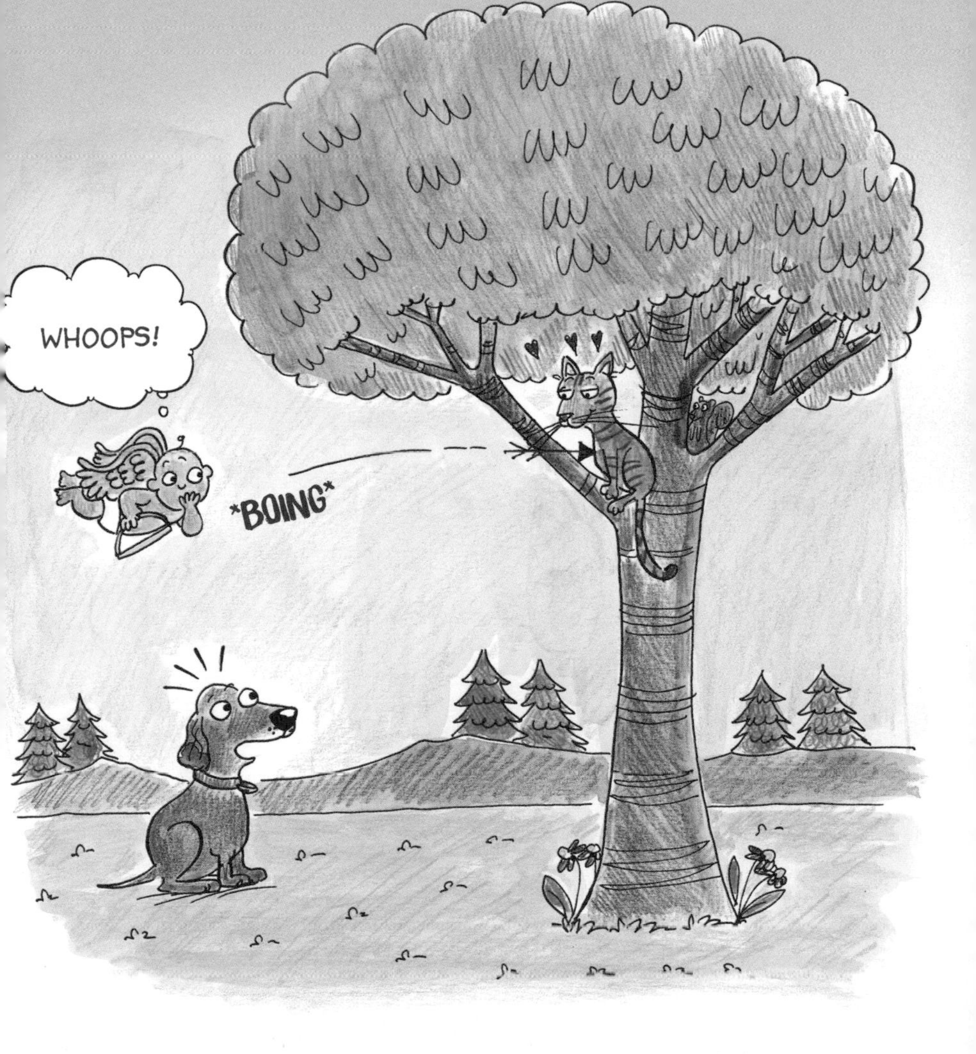

WHOOPS!
BOING

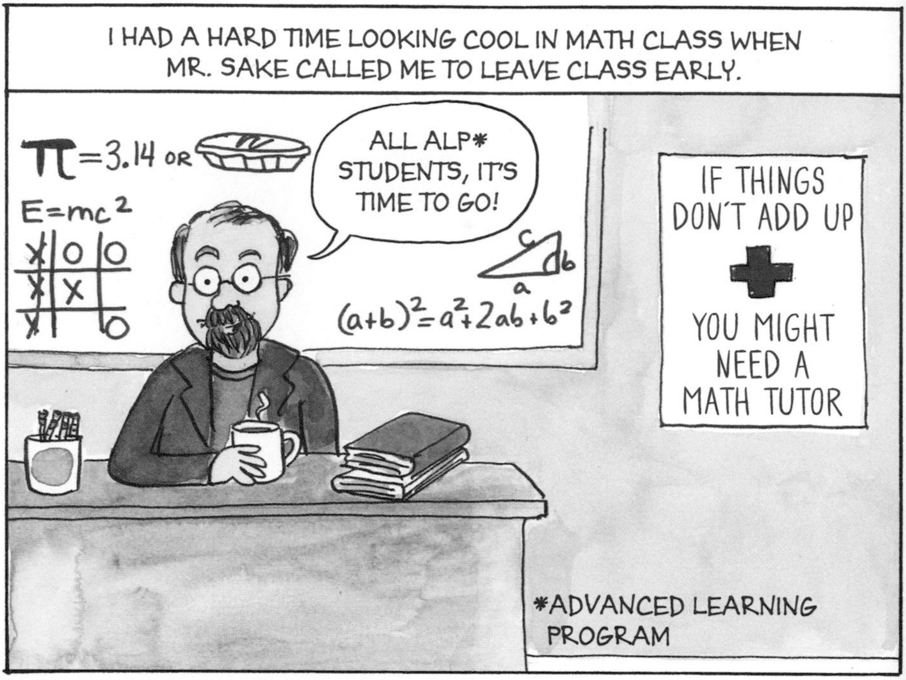
I HAD A HARD TIME LOOKING COOL IN MATH CLASS WHEN MR. SAKE CALLED ME TO LEAVE CLASS EARLY.
ALL ALP* STUDENTS, IT'S TIME TO GO!
π=3.14 OR
E=mc²
(a+b)²=a²+2ab+b²
c
b
a
IF THINGS DON'T ADD UP + YOU MIGHT NEED A MATH TUTOR
*ADVANCED LEARNING PROGRAM

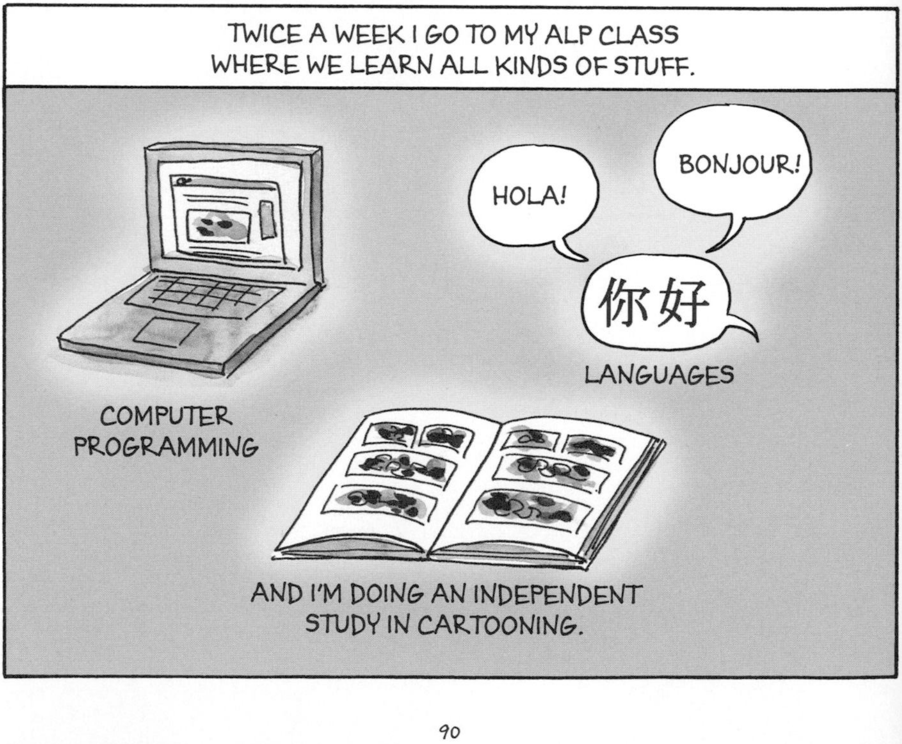
TWICE A WEEK I GO TO MY ALP CLASS WHERE WE LEARN ALL KINDS OF STUFF.
HOLA!
BONJOUR!
你好
LANGUAGES
COMPUTER PROGRAMMING
AND I'M DOING AN INDEPENDENT STUDY IN CARTOONING.

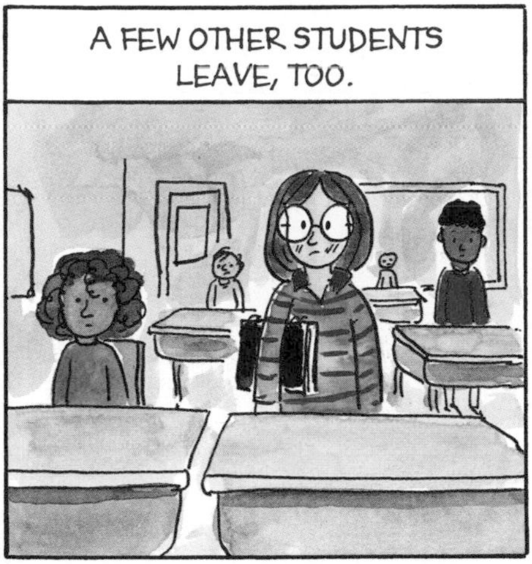
A FEW OTHER STUDENTS LEAVE, TOO.

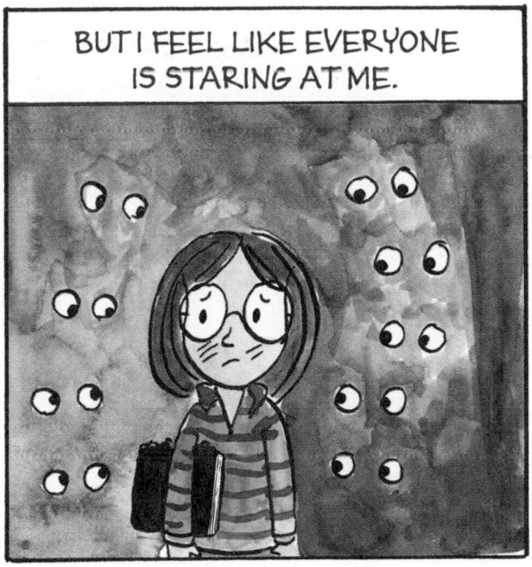
BUT I FEEL LIKE EVERYONE IS STARING AT ME.

LILY DOESN'T THINK IT'S COOL...

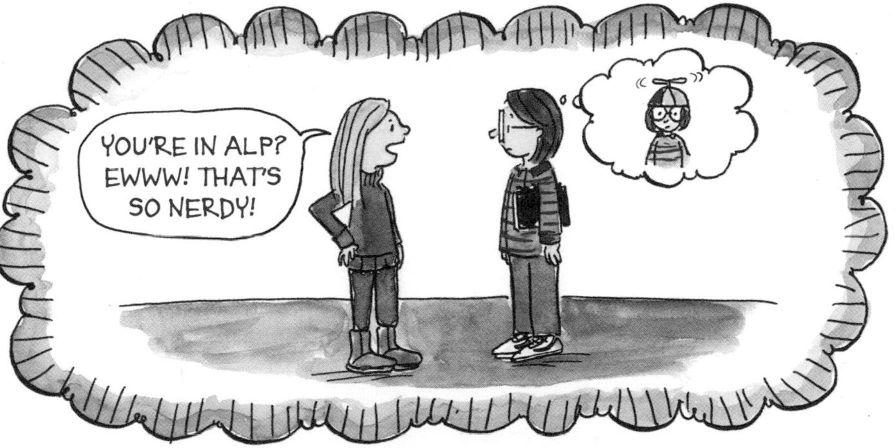
YOU'RE IN ALP? EWWW! THAT'S SO NERDY!

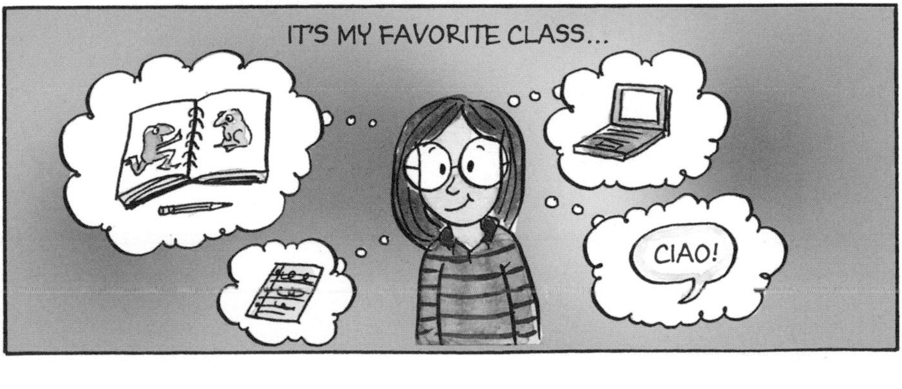
IT'S MY FAVORITE CLASS...
CIAO!

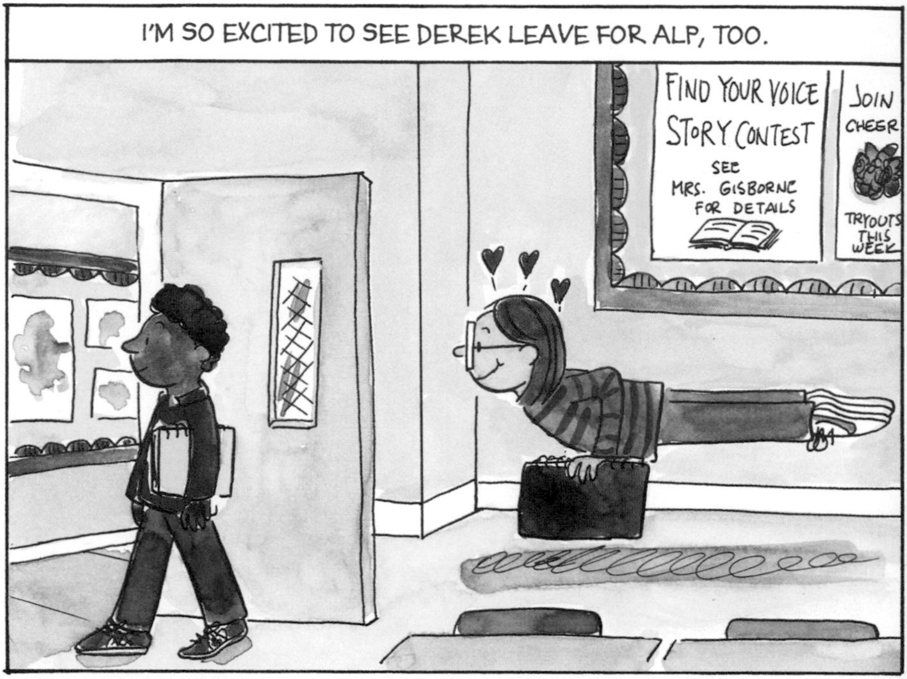
I'M SO EXCITED TO SEE DEREK LEAVE FOR ALP, TOO.
FIND YOUR VOICE STORY CONTEST
SEE MRS. GISBORNE FOR DETAILS
JOIN CHEER
TRYOUTS THIS WEEK

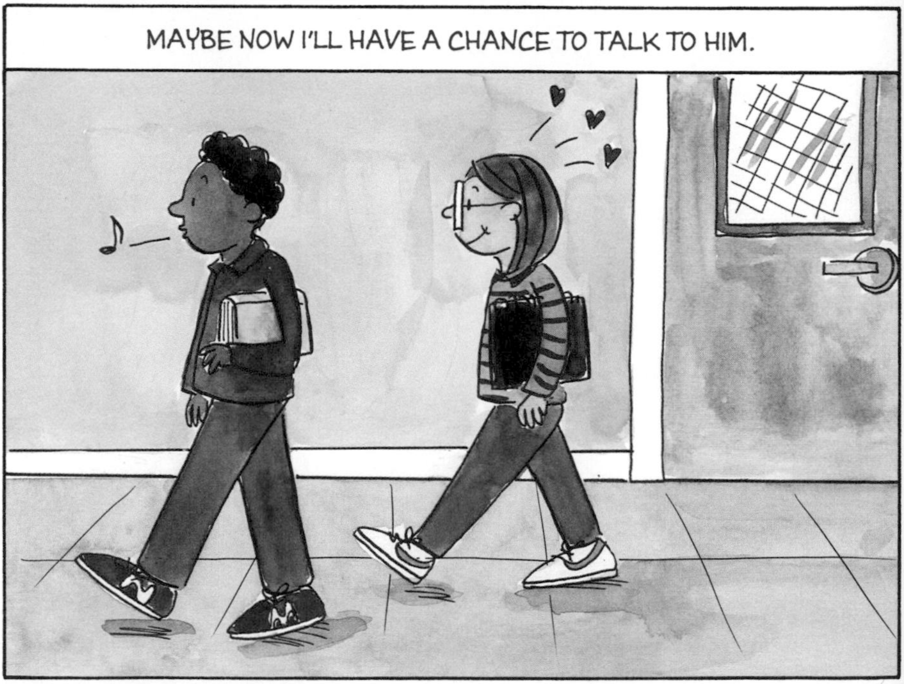
MAYBE NOW I'LL HAVE A CHANCE TO TALK TO HIM.

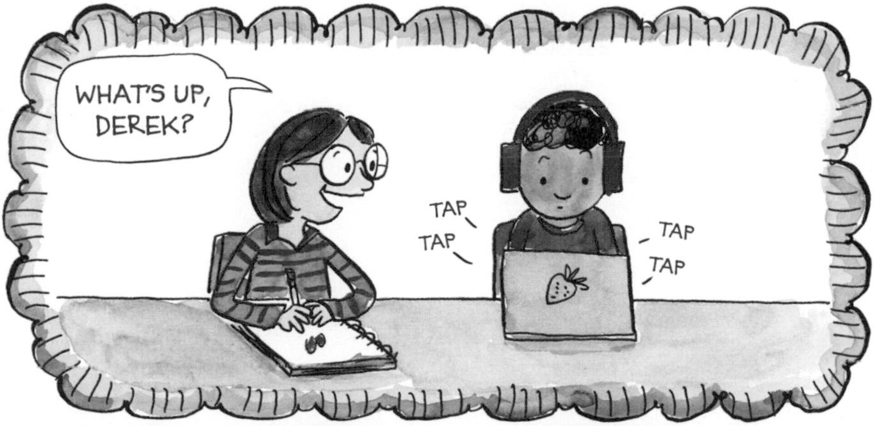
WHAT'S UP, DEREK?
TAP TAP
TAP TAP

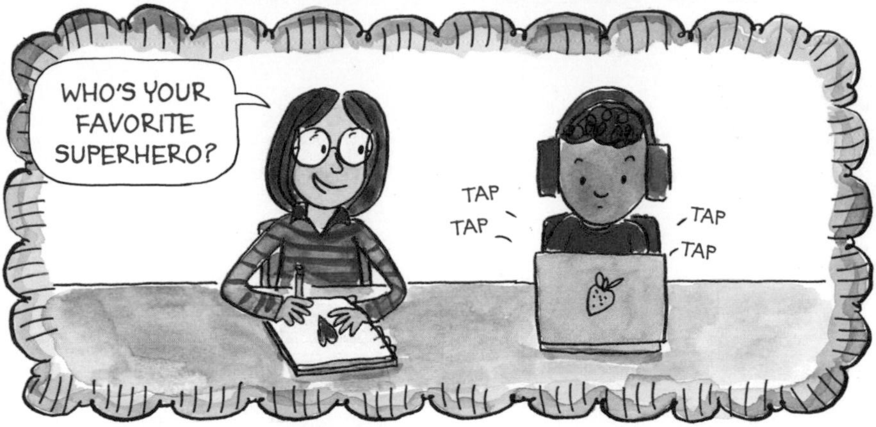
WHO'S YOUR FAVORITE SUPERHERO?
TAP TAP
TAP TAP

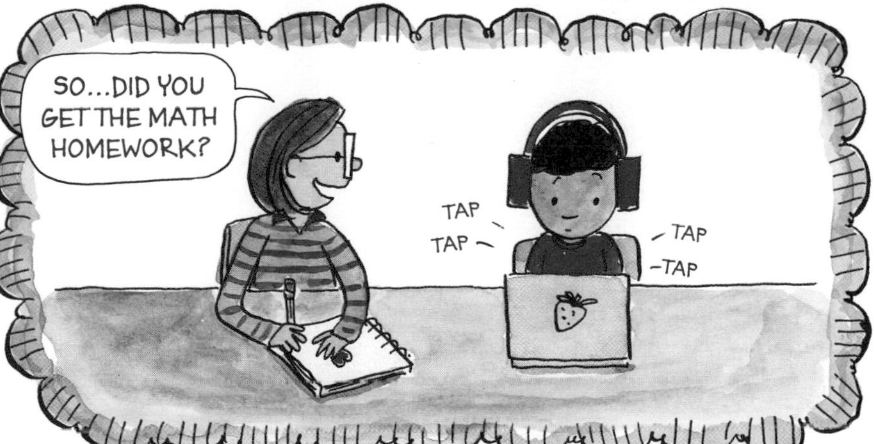
SO...DID YOU GET THE MATH HOMEWORK?
TAP TAP
TAP TAP

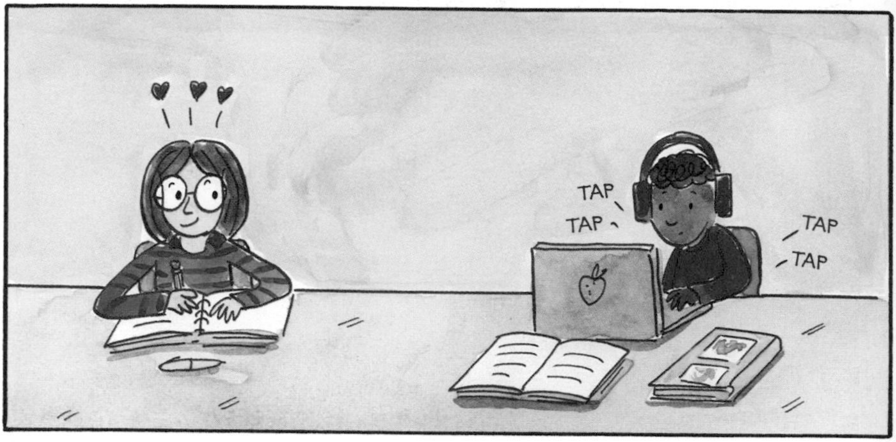
TAP
TAP
TAP
TAP

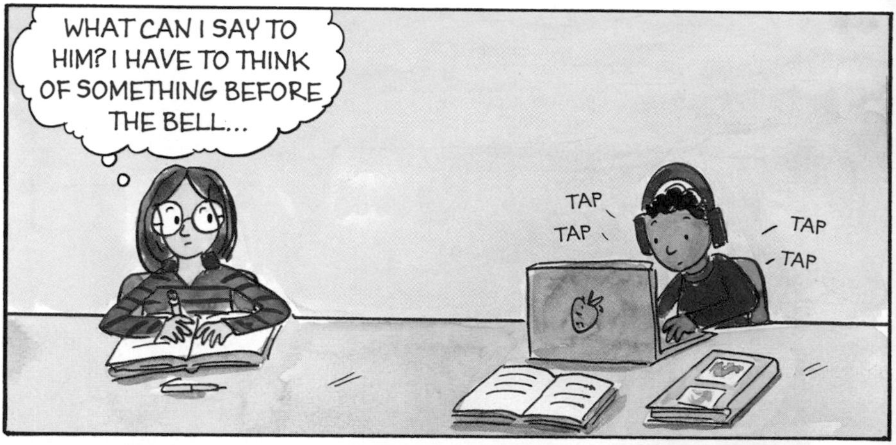
WHAT CAN I SAY TO HIM? I HAVE TO THINK OF SOMETHING BEFORE THE BELL...
TAP
TAP
TAP
TAP

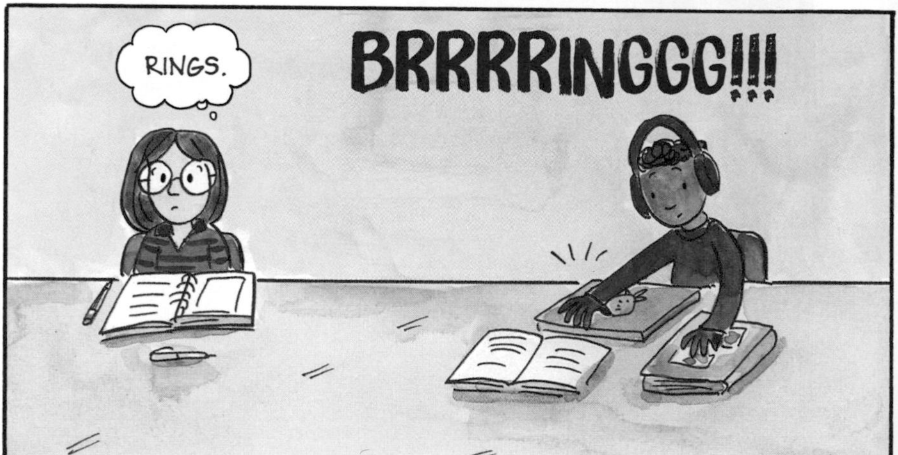
RINGS.
BRRRRINGGG!!!

THE MORE I GET TO KNOW DEREK, THE BIGGER MY CRUSH GETS...

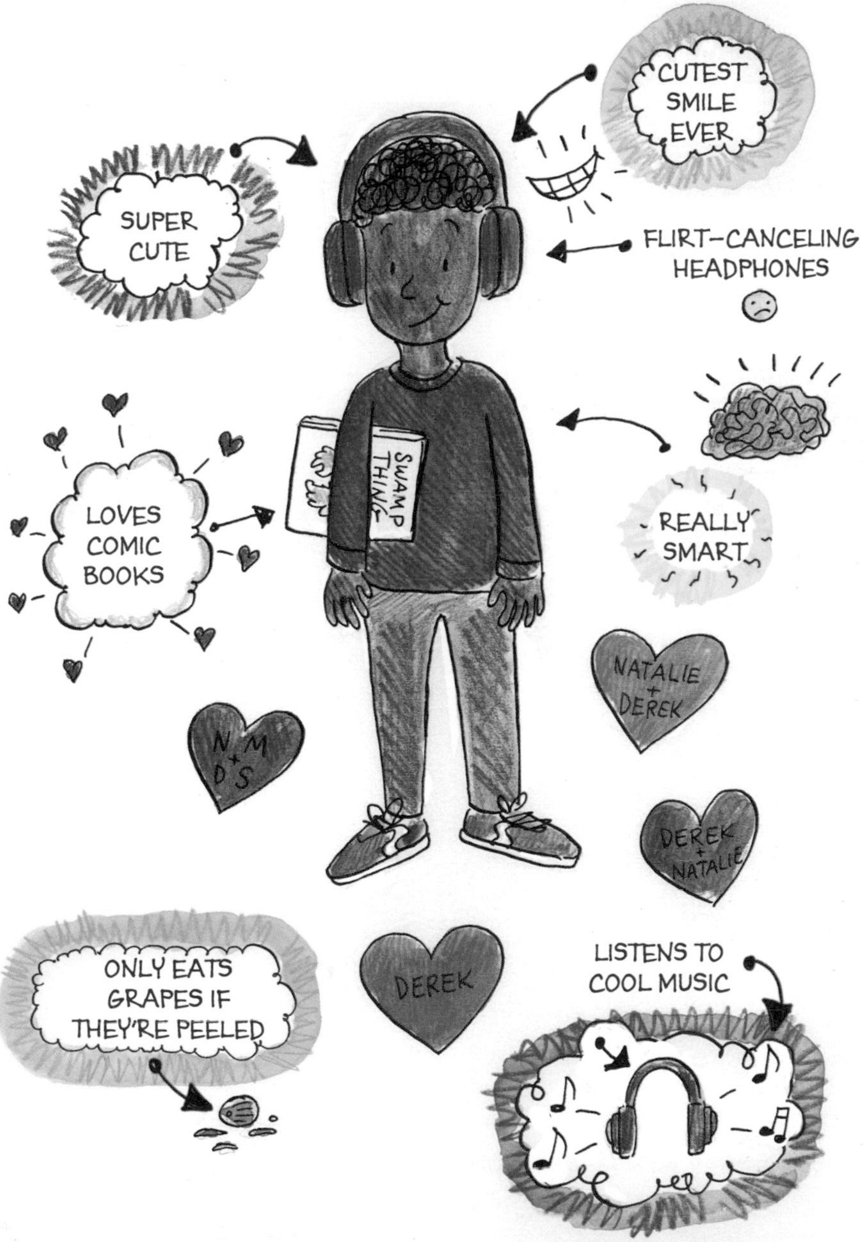

SUPER CUTE
CUTEST SMILE EVER
FLIRT-CANCELING HEADPHONES
SWAMP THING
LOVES COMIC BOOKS
REALLY SMART
NATALIE + DEREK
N + M
D S
DEREK + NATALIE
DEREK
ONLY EATS GRAPES IF THEY'RE PEELED
LISTENS TO COOL MUSIC

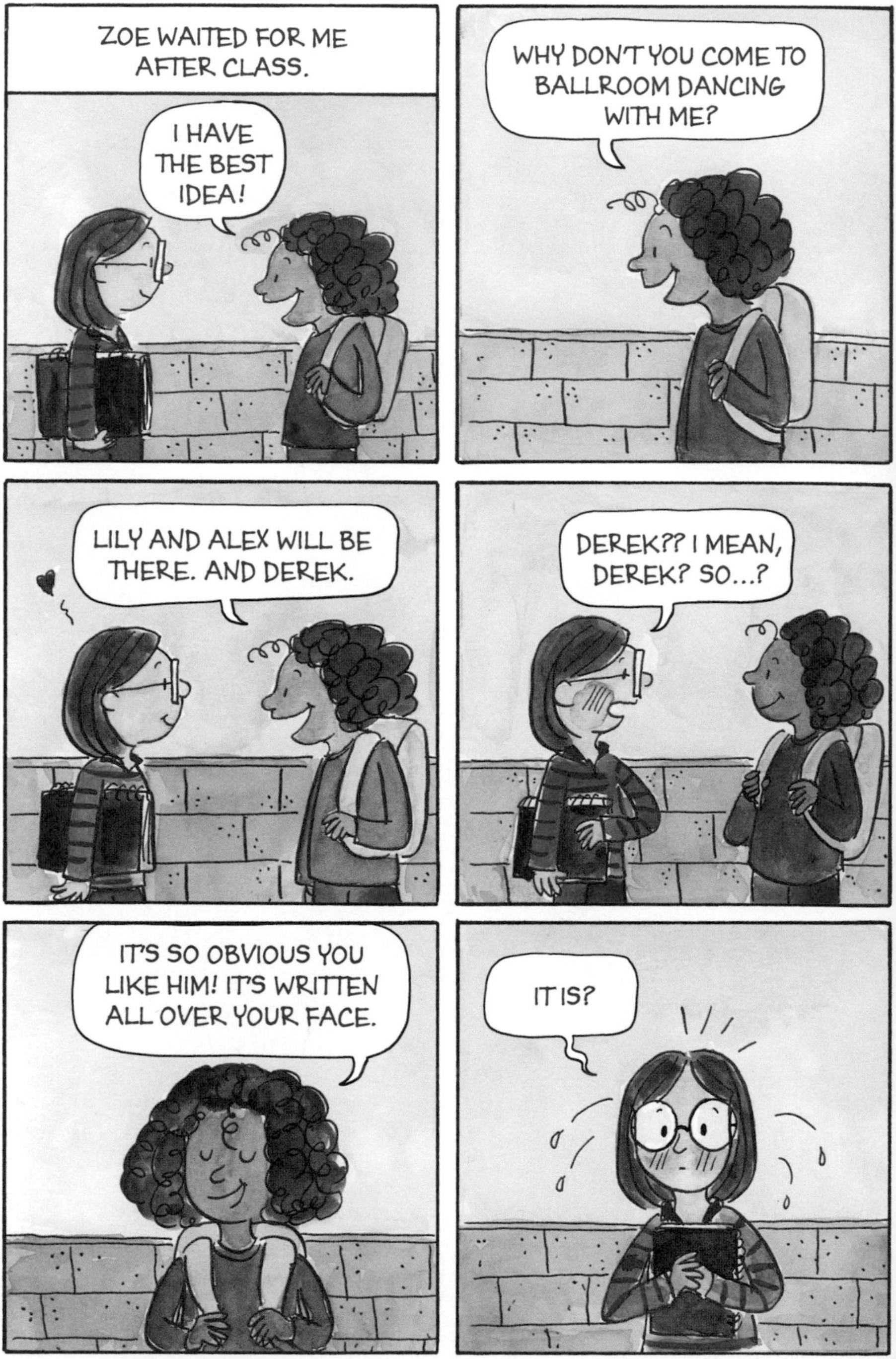
ZOE WAITED FOR ME AFTER CLASS.
I HAVE THE BEST IDEA!
WHY DON'T YOU COME TO BALLROOM DANCING WITH ME?
LILY AND ALEX WILL BE THERE. AND DEREK.
DEREK?? I MEAN, DEREK? SO...?
IT'S SO OBVIOUS YOU LIKE HIM! IT'S WRITTEN ALL OVER YOUR FACE.
IT IS?

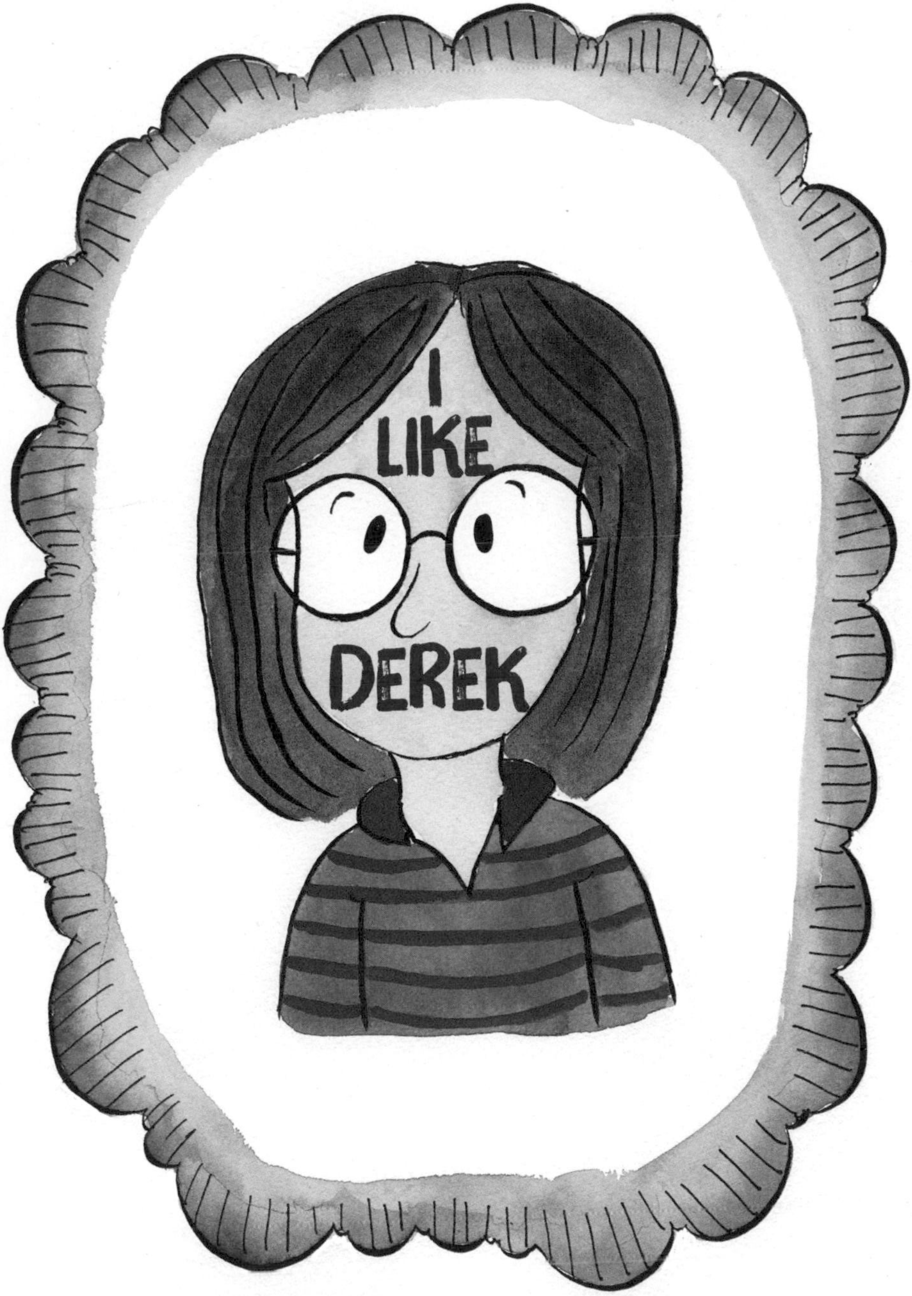
I LIKE DEREK

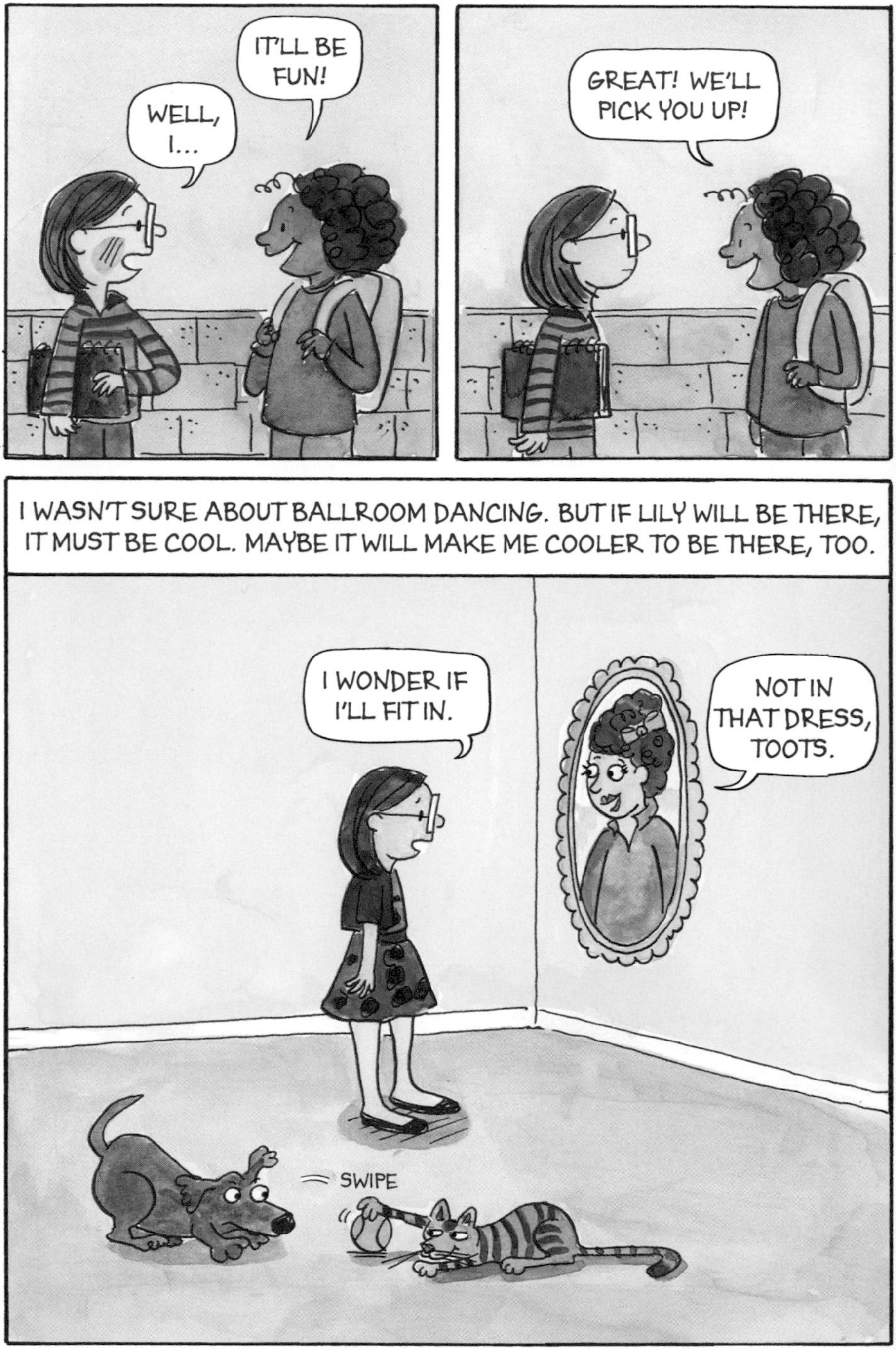

IT'LL BE FUN!
WELL, I...
GREAT! WE'LL PICK YOU UP!
I WASN'T SURE ABOUT BALLROOM DANCING. BUT IF LILY WILL BE THERE, IT MUST BE COOL. MAYBE IT WILL MAKE ME COOLER TO BE THERE, TOO.
I WONDER IF I'LL FIT IN.
NOT IN THAT DRESS, TOOTS.
SWIPE

CHAPTER 7
DANCE
(BUT EVERYONE IS WATCHING)

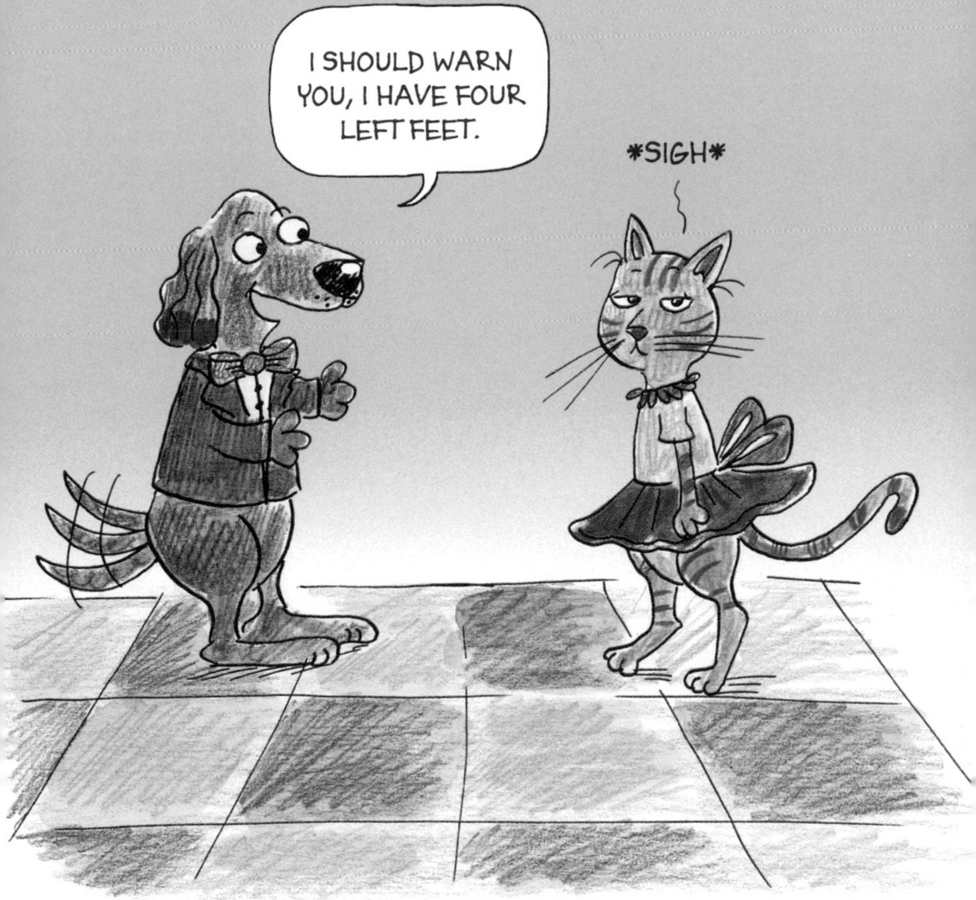
I SHOULD WARN YOU, I HAVE FOUR LEFT FEET.
SIGH

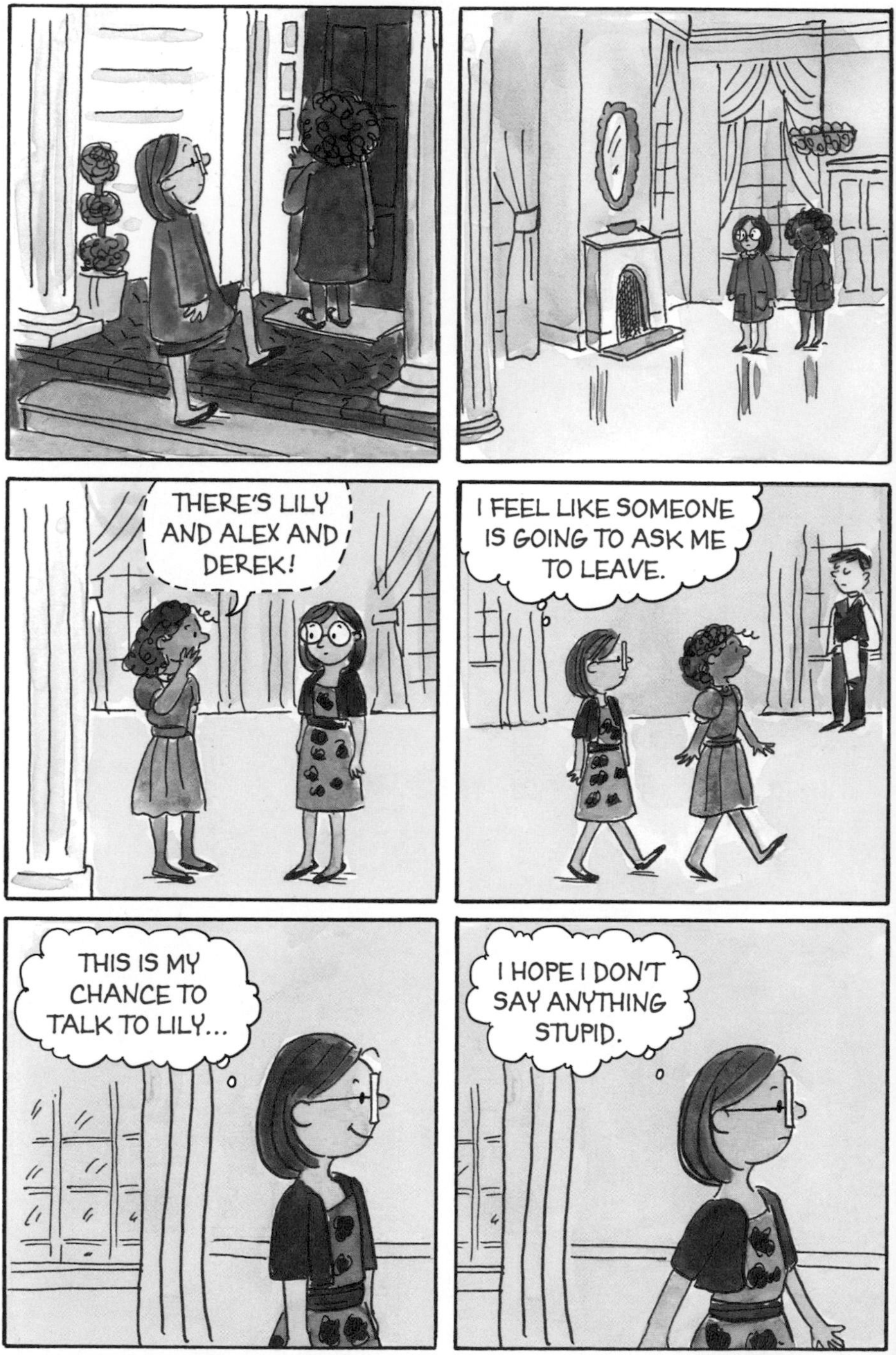
THERE'S LILY AND ALEX AND DEREK!
I FEEL LIKE SOMEONE IS GOING TO ASK ME TO LEAVE.
THIS IS MY CHANCE TO TALK TO LILY...
I HOPE I DON'T SAY ANYTHING STUPID.

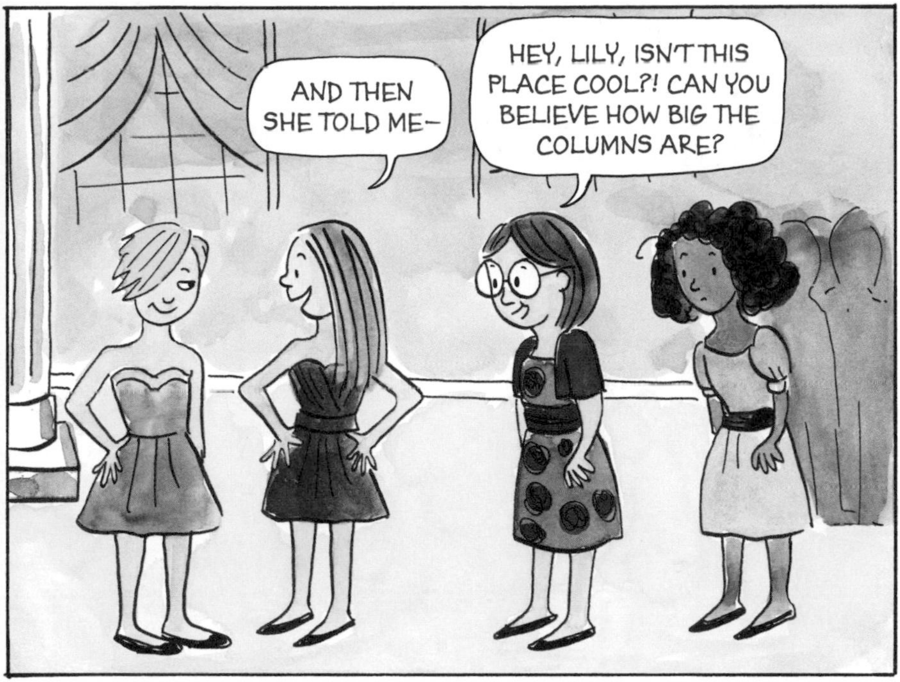
AND THEN SHE TOLD ME–
HEY, LILY, ISN'T THIS PLACE COOL?! CAN YOU BELIEVE HOW BIG THE COLUMNS ARE?

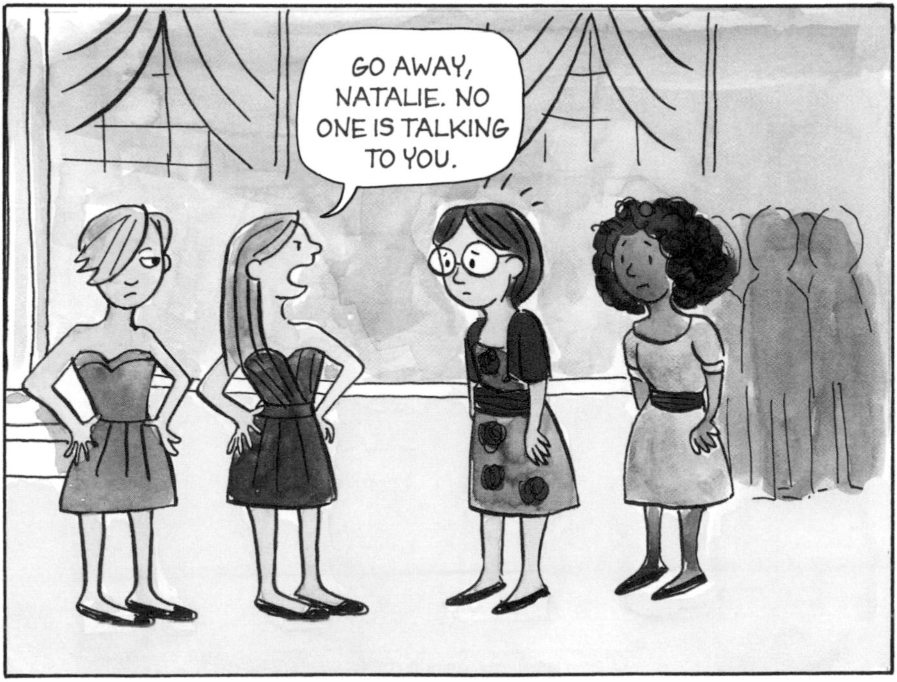
GO AWAY, NATALIE. NO ONE IS TALKING TO YOU.

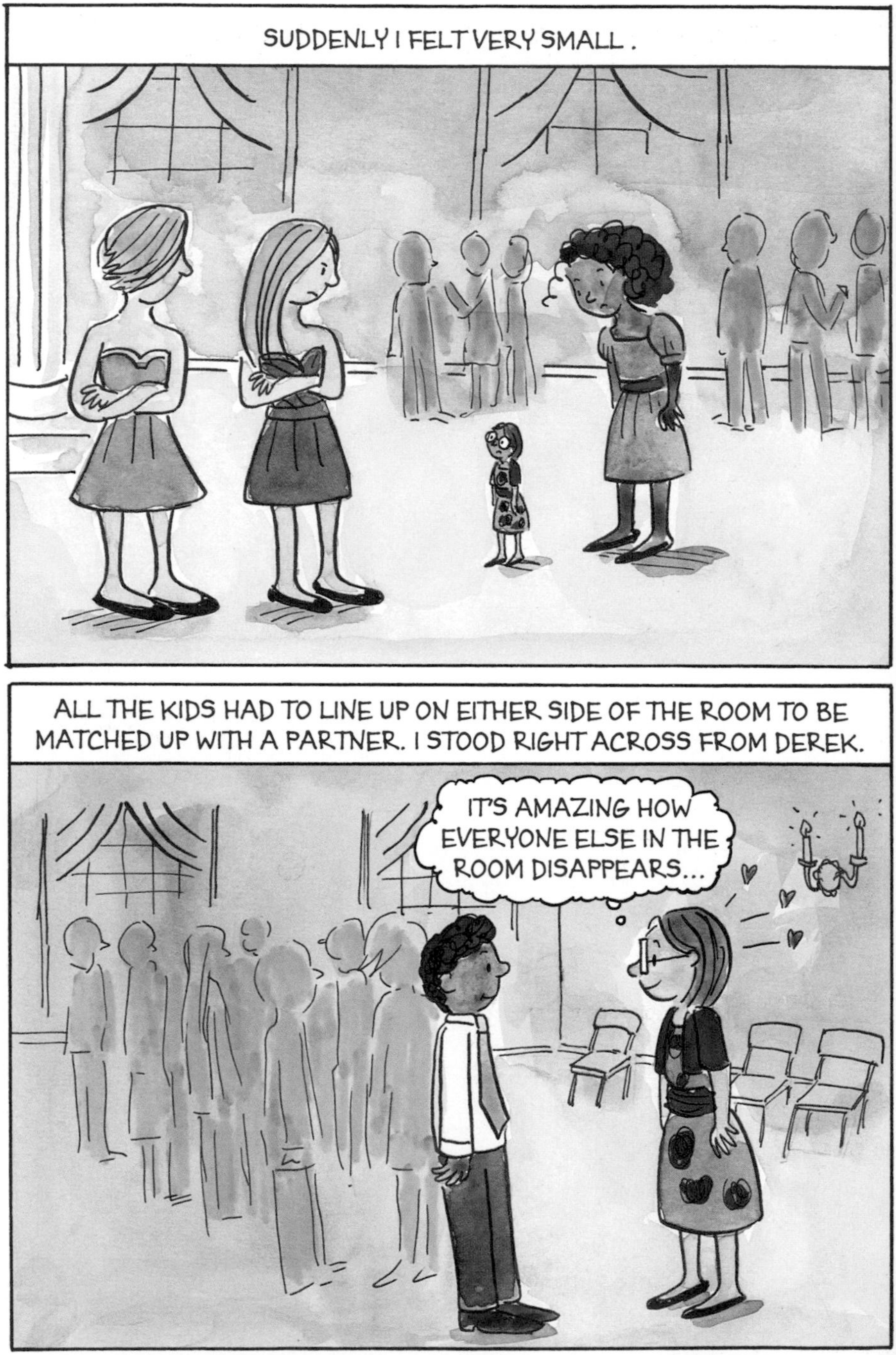
SUDDENLY I FELT VERY SMALL.
ALL THE KIDS HAD TO LINE UP ON EITHER SIDE OF THE ROOM TO BE MATCHED UP WITH A PARTNER. I STOOD RIGHT ACROSS FROM DEREK.
IT'S AMAZING HOW EVERYONE ELSE IN THE ROOM DISAPPEARS...

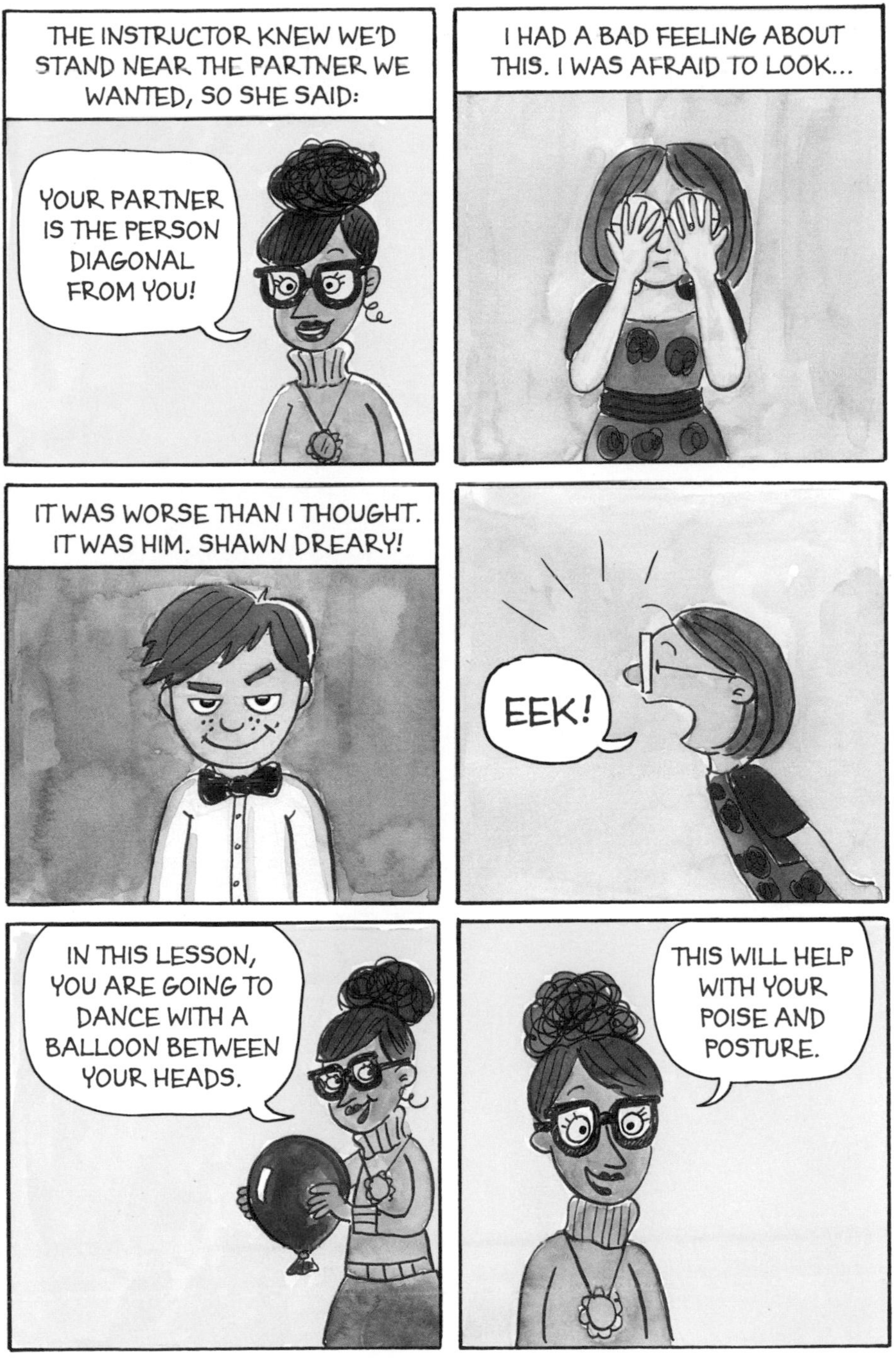
THE INSTRUCTOR KNEW WE'D STAND NEAR THE PARTNER WE WANTED, SO SHE SAID:
YOUR PARTNER IS THE PERSON DIAGONAL FROM YOU!
I HAD A BAD FEELING ABOUT THIS. I WAS AFRAID TO LOOK...
IT WAS WORSE THAN I THOUGHT. IT WAS HIM. SHAWN DREARY!
EEK!
IN THIS LESSON, YOU ARE GOING TO DANCE WITH A BALLOON BETWEEN YOUR HEADS.
THIS WILL HELP WITH YOUR POISE AND POSTURE.

I DON'T KNOW WHICH WAS WORSE: GETTING IGNORED BY LILY OR HAVING TO DANCE WITH SHAWN. I THINK IT'S A TIE.

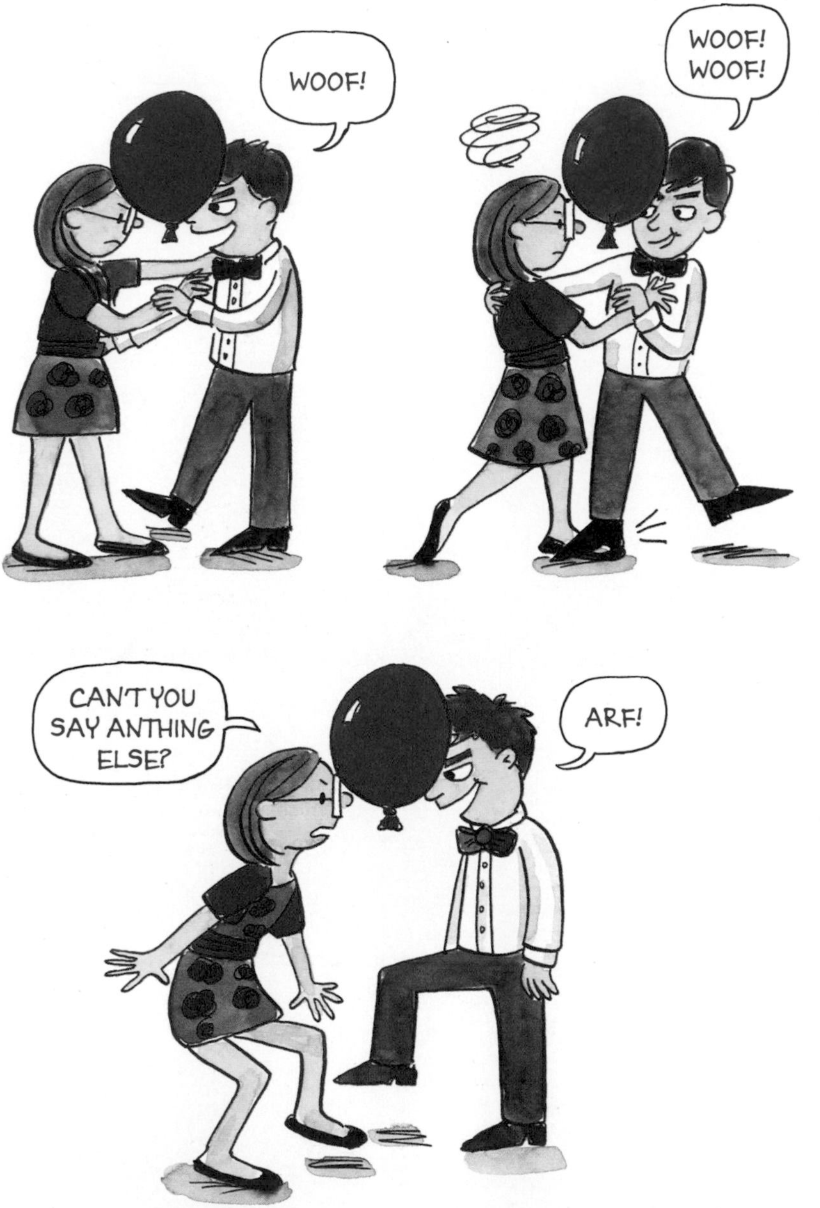
WOOF!
WOOF! WOOF!
CAN'T YOU SAY ANTHING ELSE?
ARF!

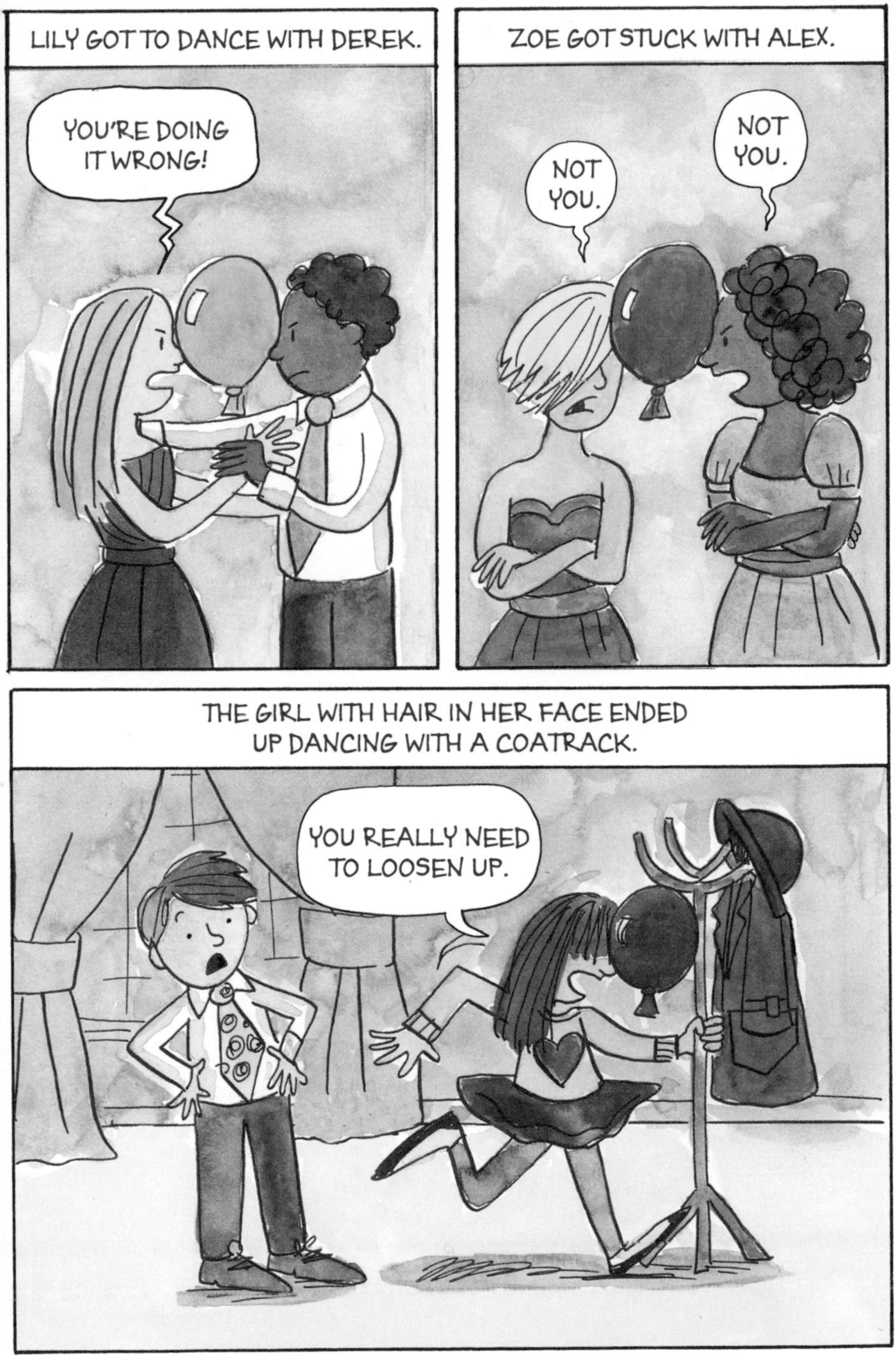
LILY GOT TO DANCE WITH DEREK.
YOU'RE DOING IT WRONG!
ZOE GOT STUCK WITH ALEX.
NOT YOU.
NOT YOU.
THE GIRL WITH HAIR IN HER FACE ENDED UP DANCING WITH A COATRACK.
YOU REALLY NEED TO LOOSEN UP.

BALLROOM DANCING WASN'T FUN...FOR ANYONE. AND I'M PRETTY SURE I DIDN'T GET ANY CLOSER TO GETTING LILY BACK.

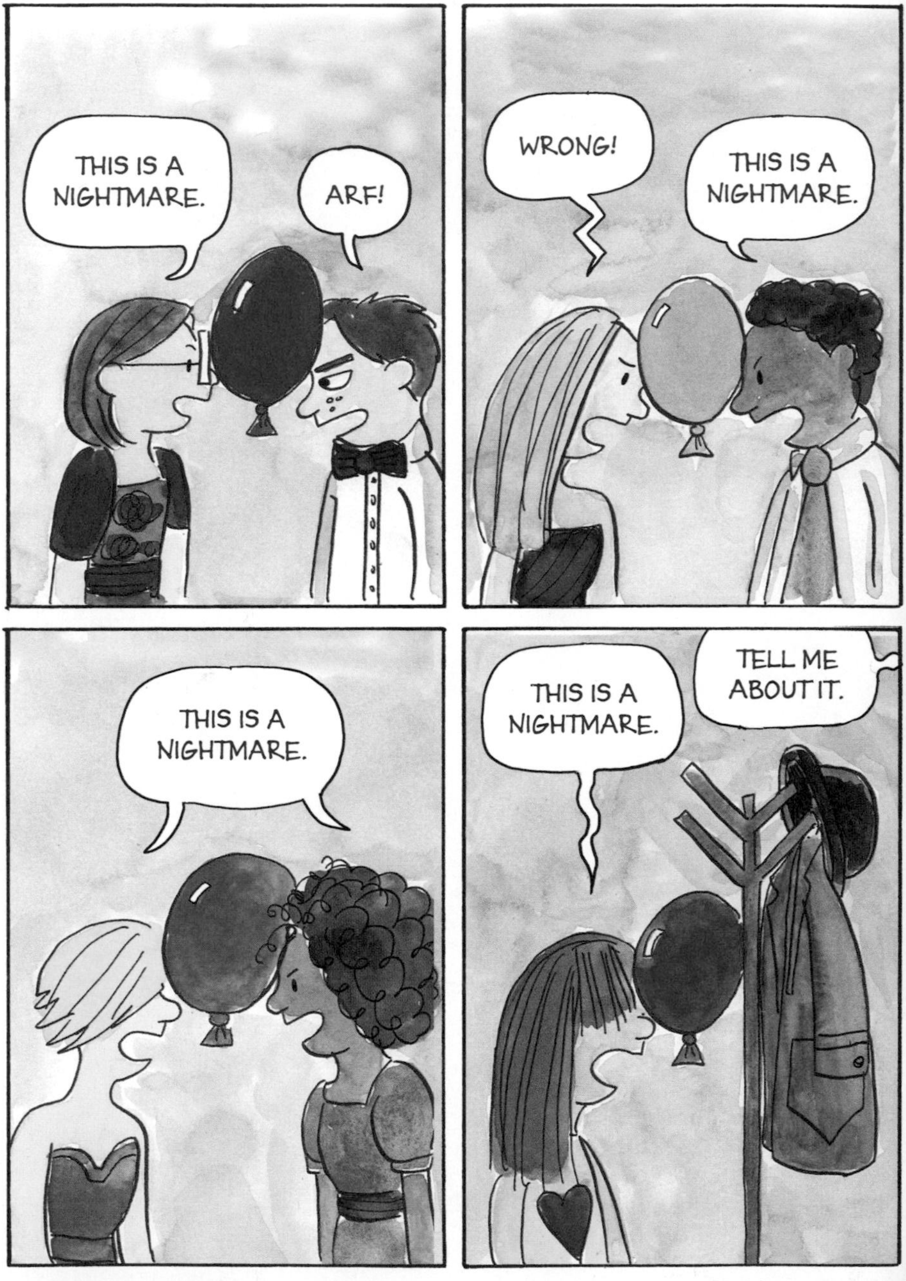
THIS IS A NIGHTMARE.
ARF!
WRONG!
THIS IS A NIGHTMARE.
THIS IS A NIGHTMARE.
THIS IS A NIGHTMARE.
TELL ME ABOUT IT.

CHAPTER 8
SING LIKE NO ONE CAN HEAR YOU

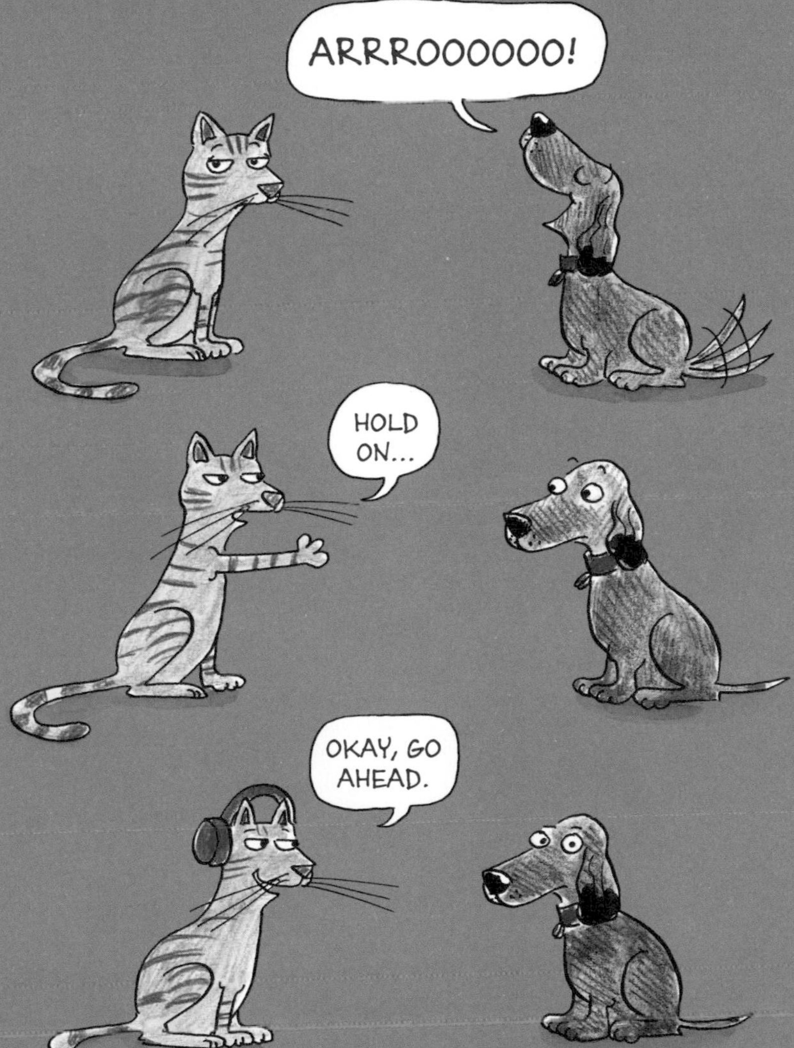
ARRROOOOOO!
HOLD ON...
OKAY, GO AHEAD.

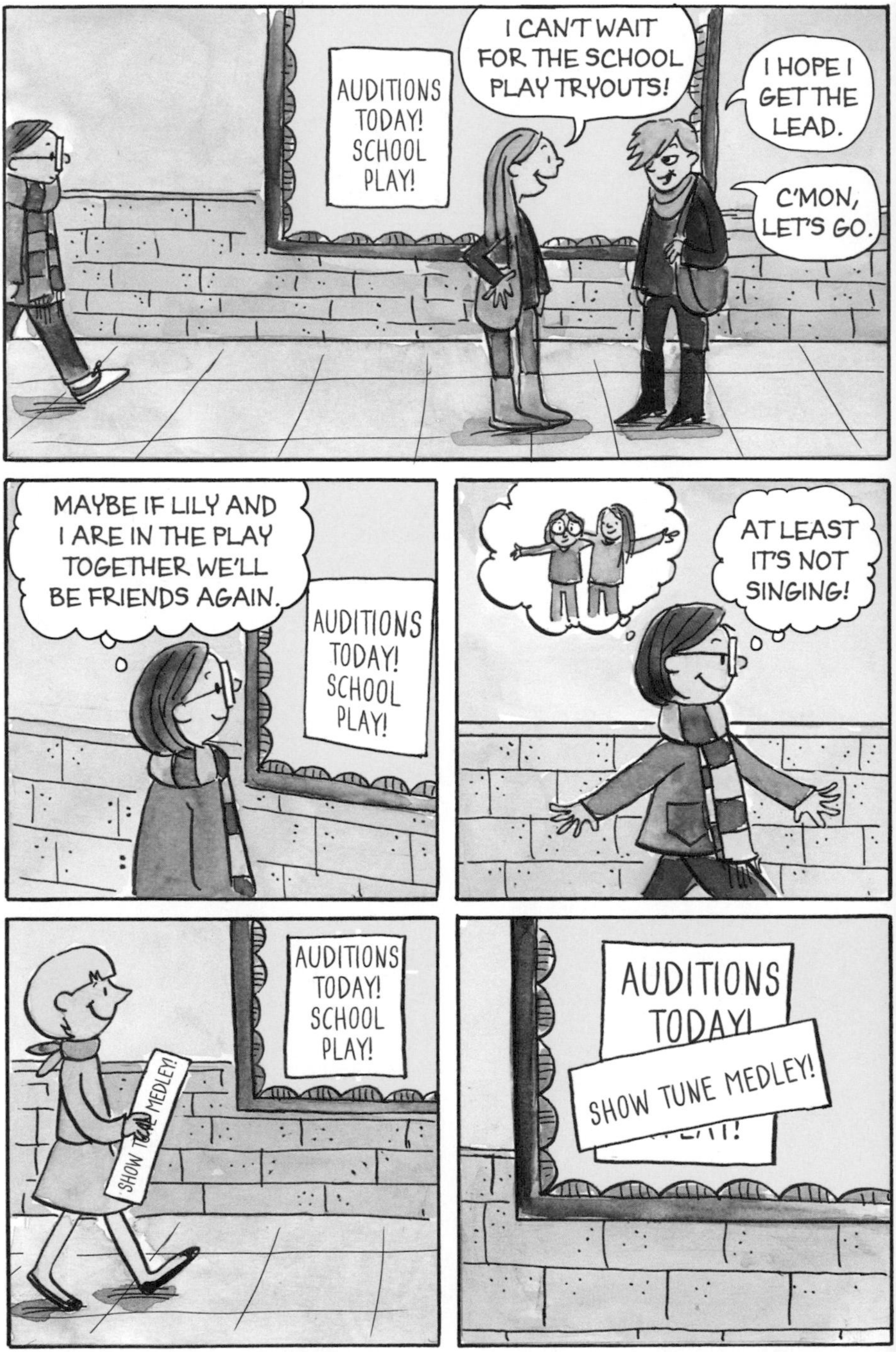
AUDITIONS TODAY! SCHOOL PLAY!
I CAN'T WAIT FOR THE SCHOOL PLAY TRYOUTS!
I HOPE I GET THE LEAD.
C'MON, LET'S GO.
MAYBE IF LILY AND I ARE IN THE PLAY TOGETHER WE'LL BE FRIENDS AGAIN.
AUDITIONS TODAY! SCHOOL PLAY!
AT LEAST IT'S NOT SINGING!
AUDITIONS TODAY! SCHOOL PLAY!
SHOW TUNE MEDLEY!
AUDITIONS TODAY!
SHOW TUNE MEDLEY!

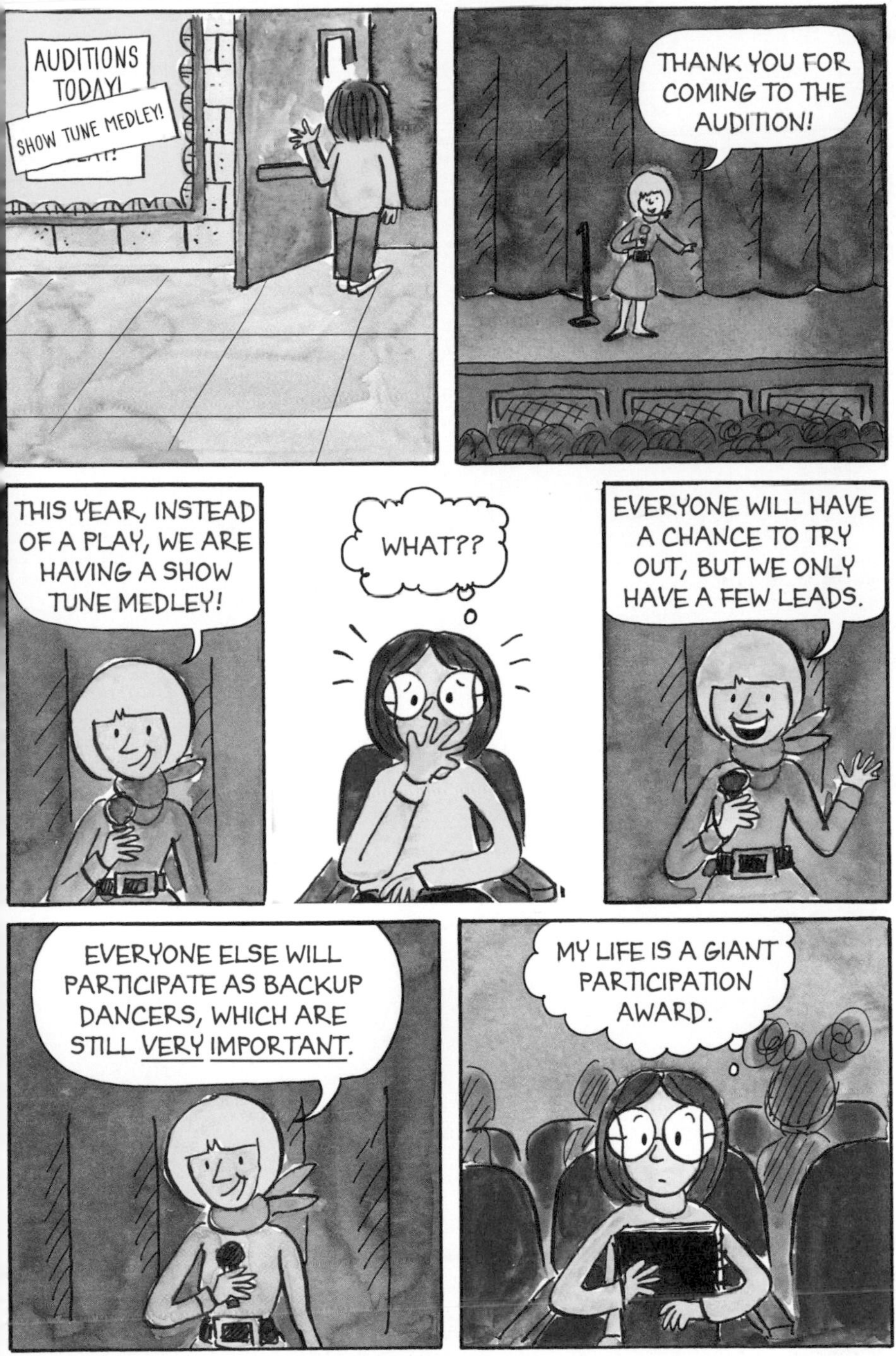
AUDITIONS TODAY!
SHOW TUNE MEDLEY!
THANK YOU FOR COMING TO THE AUDITION!
THIS YEAR, INSTEAD OF A PLAY, WE ARE HAVING A SHOW TUNE MEDLEY!
WHAT??
EVERYONE WILL HAVE A CHANCE TO TRY OUT, BUT WE ONLY HAVE A FEW LEADS.
EVERYONE ELSE WILL PARTICIPATE AS BACKUP DANCERS, WHICH ARE STILL VERY IMPORTANT.
MY LIFE IS A GIANT PARTICIPATION AWARD.

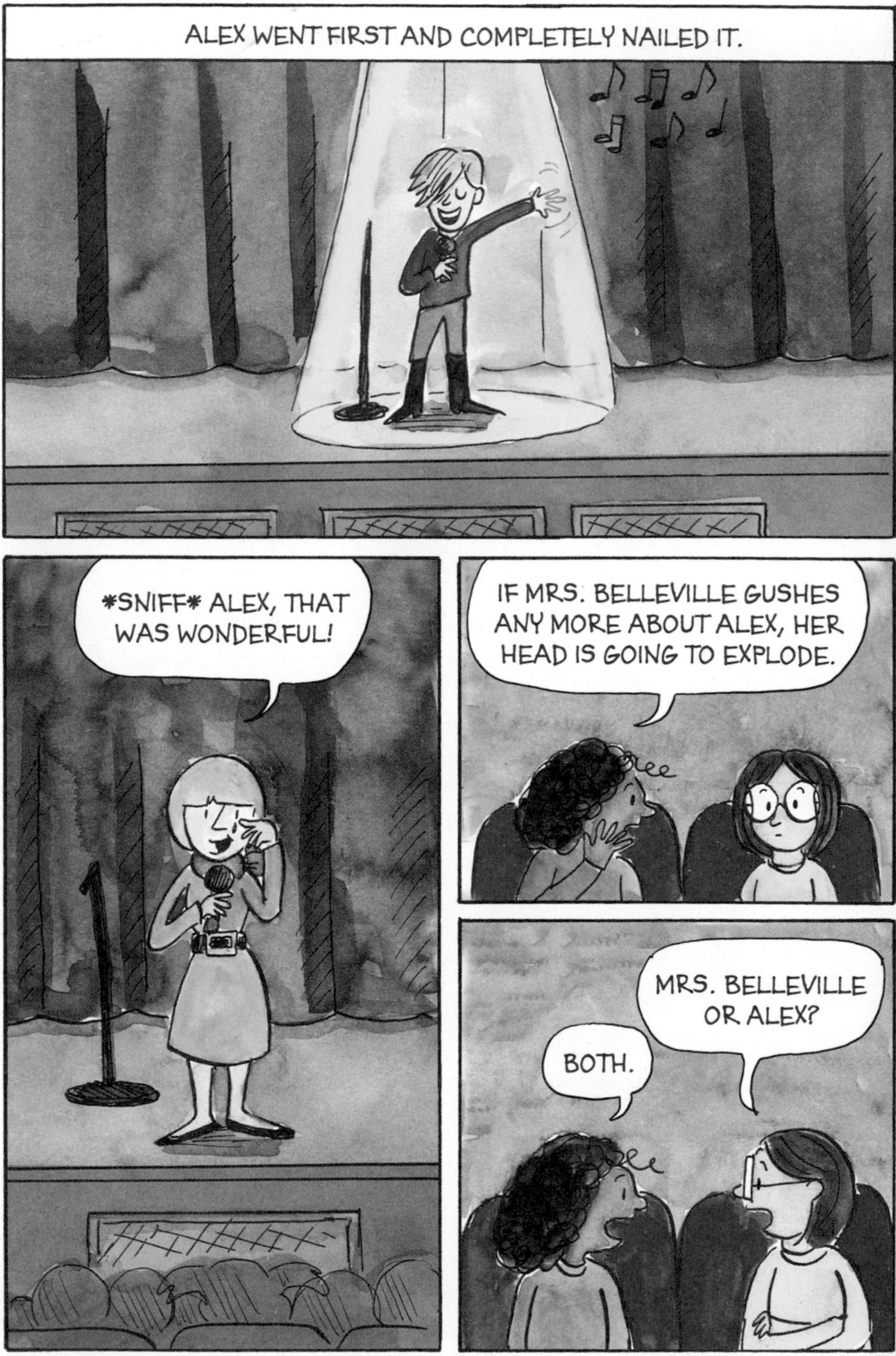
ALEX WENT FIRST AND COMPLETELY NAILED IT.
SNIFF ALEX, THAT WAS WONDERFUL!
IF MRS. BELLEVILLE GUSHES ANY MORE ABOUT ALEX, HER HEAD IS GOING TO EXPLODE.
MRS. BELLEVILLE OR ALEX?
BOTH.

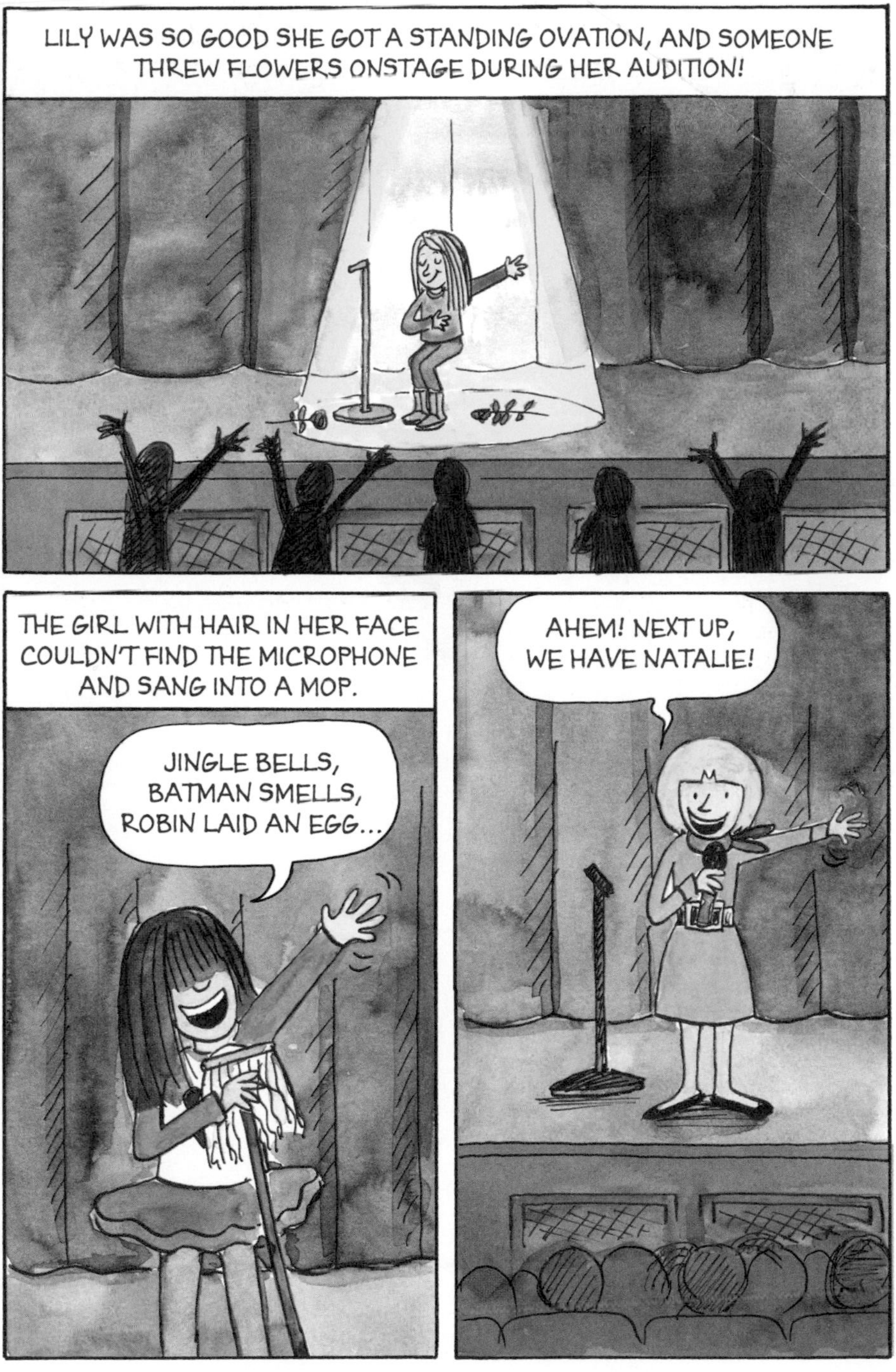
LILY WAS SO GOOD SHE GOT A STANDING OVATION, AND SOMEONE THREW FLOWERS ONSTAGE DURING HER AUDITION!
THE GIRL WITH HAIR IN HER FACE COULDN'T FIND THE MICROPHONE AND SANG INTO A MOP.
JINGLE BELLS, BATMAN SMELLS, ROBIN LAID AN EGG...
AHEM! NEXT UP, WE HAVE NATALIE!

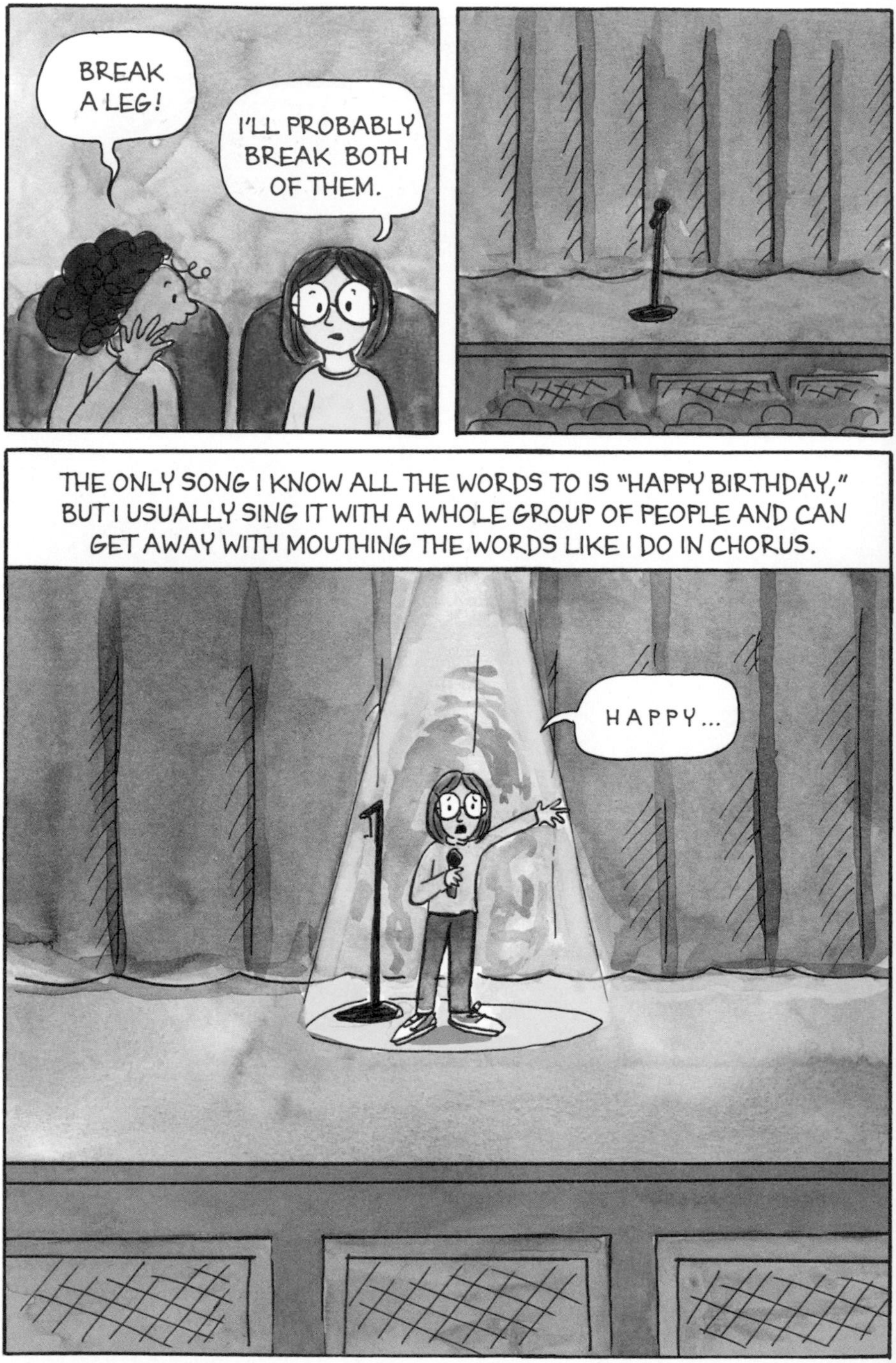
BREAK A LEG!
I'LL PROBABLY BREAK BOTH OF THEM.
THE ONLY SONG I KNOW ALL THE WORDS TO IS "HAPPY BIRTHDAY," BUT I USUALLY SING IT WITH A WHOLE GROUP OF PEOPLE AND CAN GET AWAY WITH MOUTHING THE WORDS LIKE I DO IN CHORUS.
HAPPY...

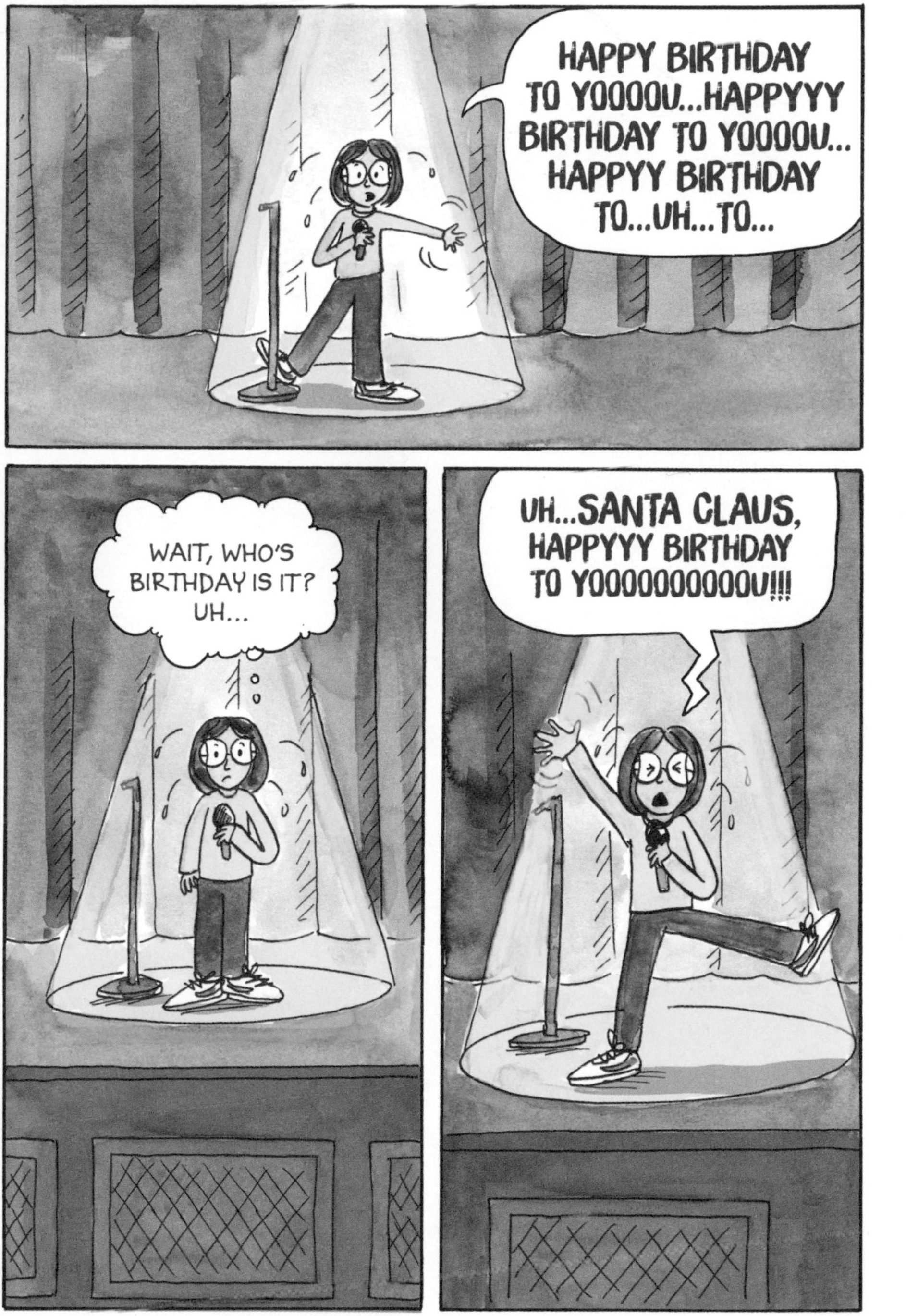
HAPPY BIRTHDAY TO YOOOOU...HAPPYYY BIRTHDAY TO YOOOOU... HAPPYY BIRTHDAY TO...UH...TO...
WAIT, WHO'S BIRTHDAY IS IT? UH...
UH...SANTA CLAUS, HAPPYYY BIRTHDAY TO YOOOOOOOOOOOU!!!

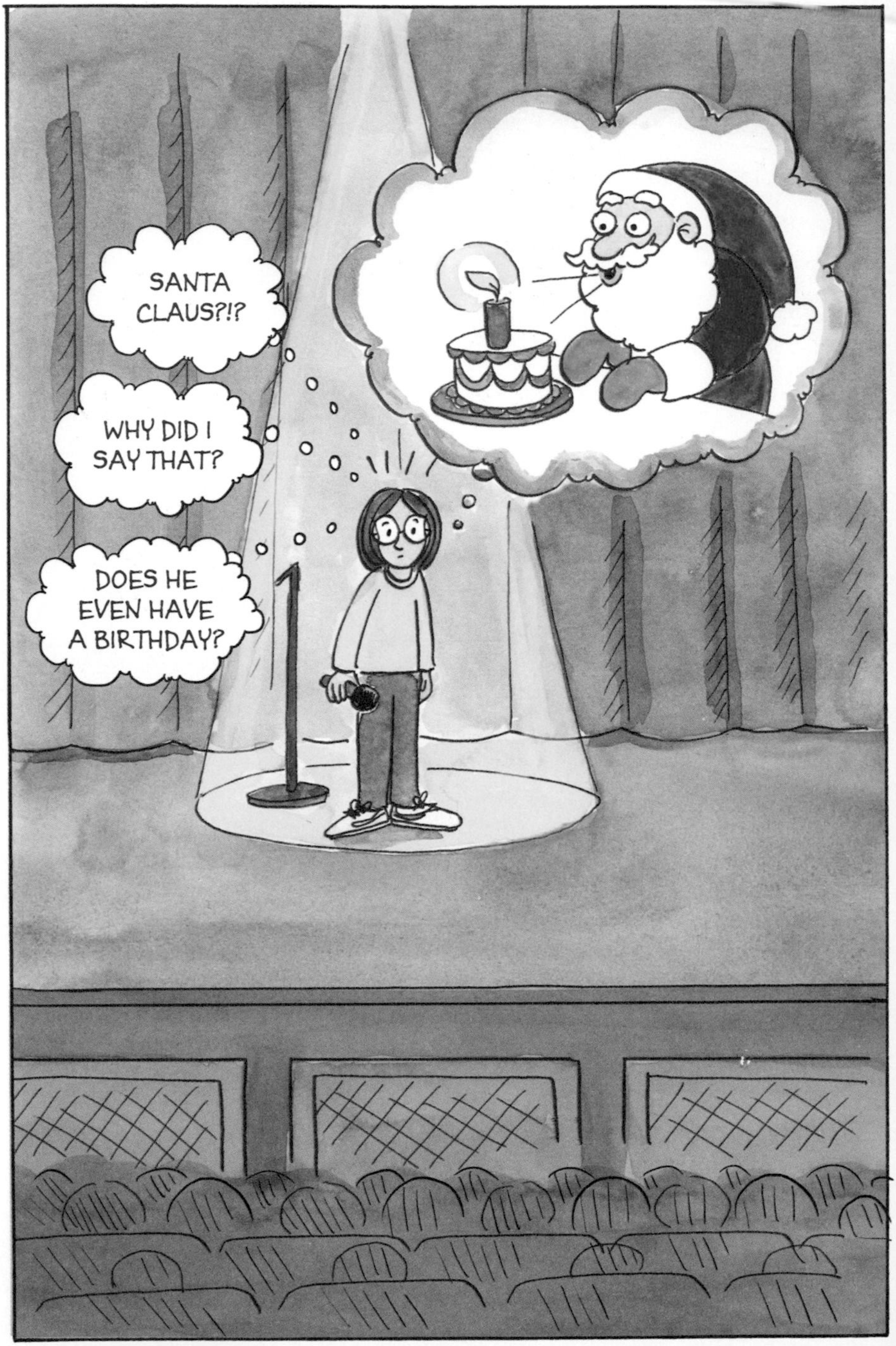
SANTA CLAUS?!?
WHY DID I SAY THAT?
DOES HE EVEN HAVE A BIRTHDAY?

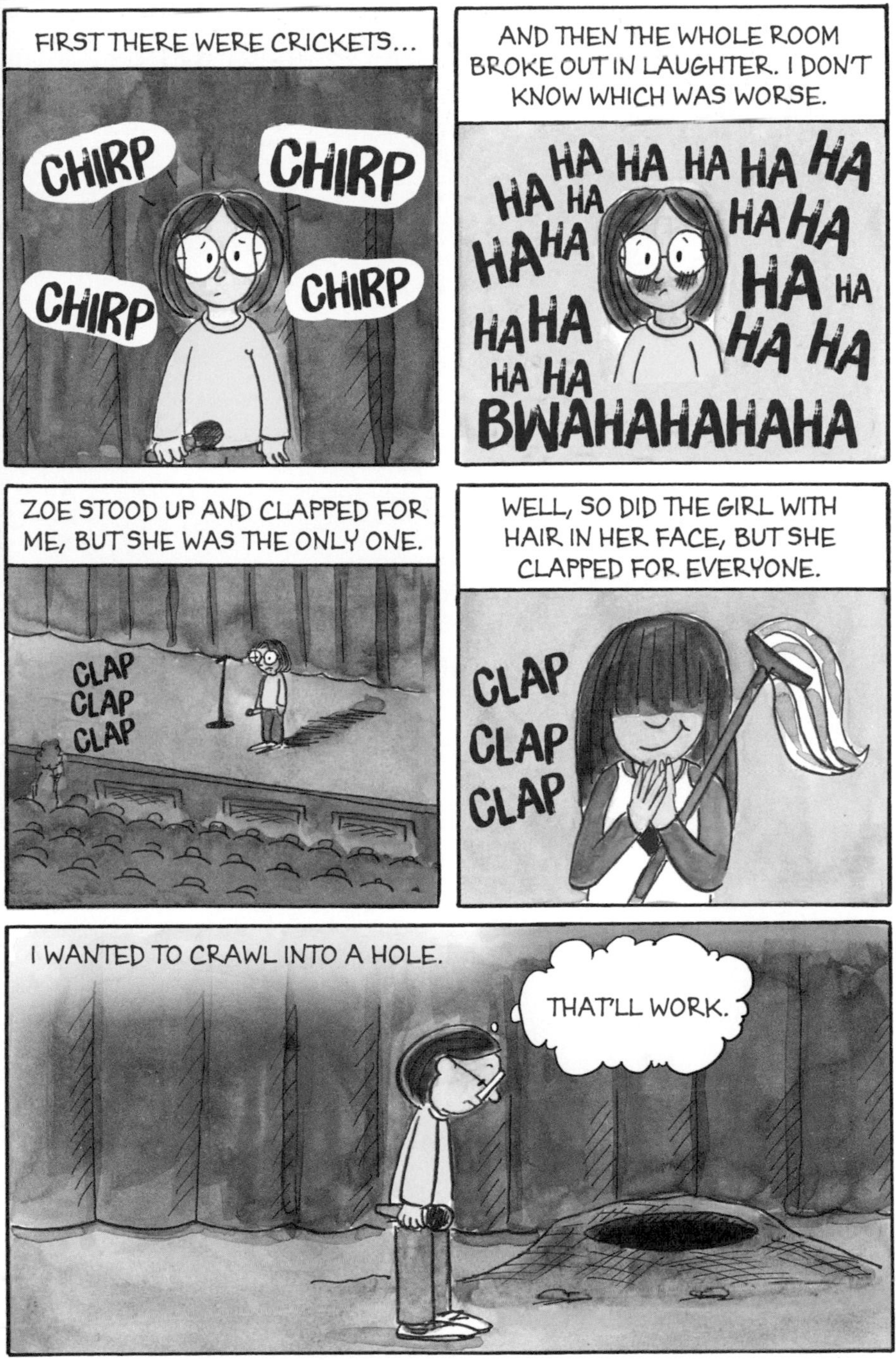
FIRST THERE WERE CRICKETS...
CHIRP
CHIRP
CHIRP
CHIRP
AND THEN THE WHOLE ROOM BROKE OUT IN LAUGHTER. I DON'T KNOW WHICH WAS WORSE.
HA HA HA HA HA HA HA HA HA HA HA HA HA HA HA HA HA HA HA HA HA HA HA
BWAHAHAHAHAHA
ZOE STOOD UP AND CLAPPED FOR ME, BUT SHE WAS THE ONLY ONE.
CLAP CLAP CLAP
WELL, SO DID THE GIRL WITH HAIR IN HER FACE, BUT SHE CLAPPED FOR EVERYONE.
CLAP CLAP CLAP
I WANTED TO CRAWL INTO A HOLE.
THAT'LL WORK.

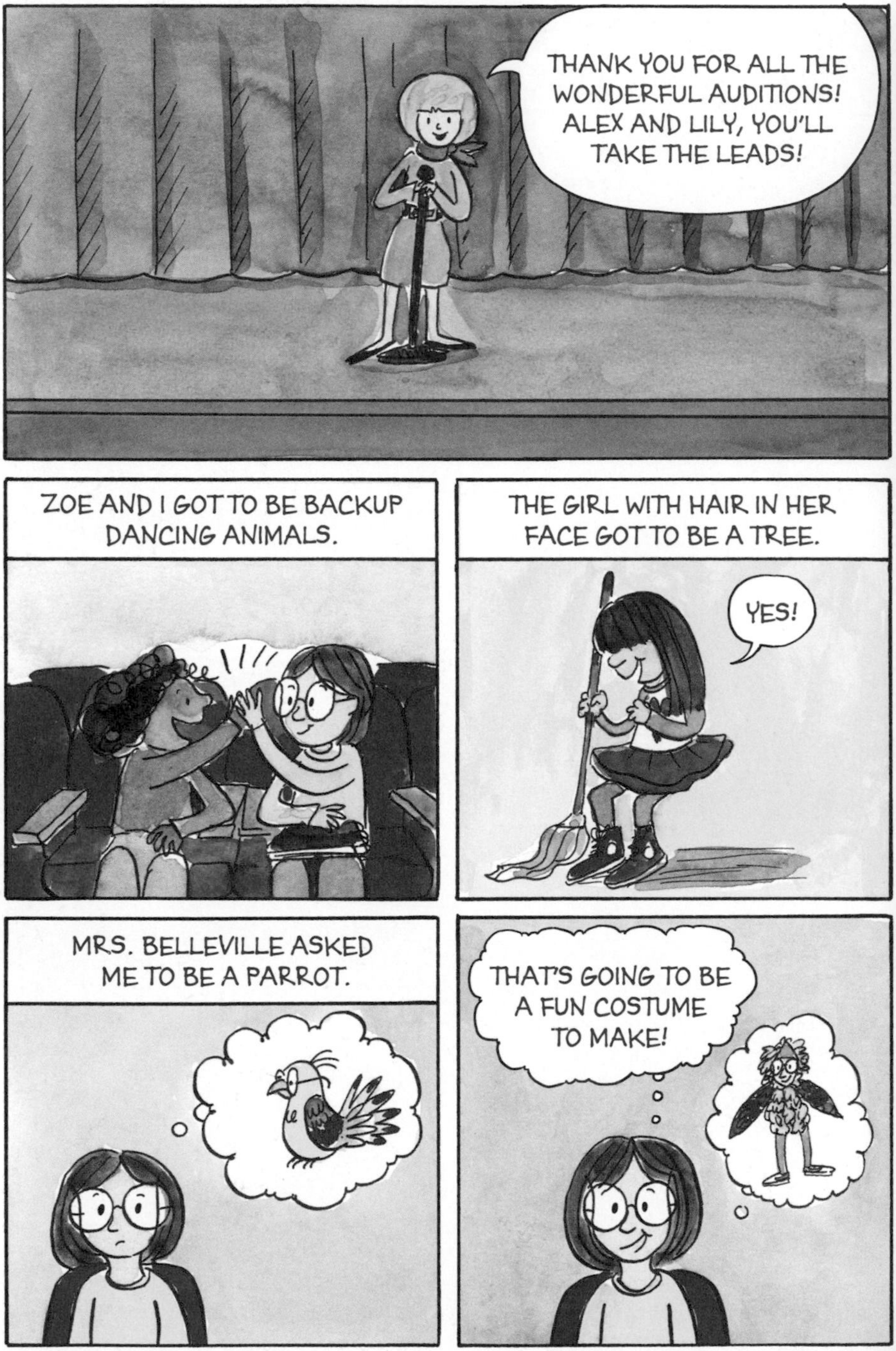
THANK YOU FOR ALL THE WONDERFUL AUDITIONS! ALEX AND LILY, YOU'LL TAKE THE LEADS!
ZOE AND I GOT TO BE BACKUP DANCING ANIMALS.
THE GIRL WITH HAIR IN HER FACE GOT TO BE A TREE.
YES!
MRS. BELLEVILLE ASKED ME TO BE A PARROT.
THAT'S GOING TO BE A FUN COSTUME TO MAKE!

CHAPTER 9
COSTUMES, PLEASE

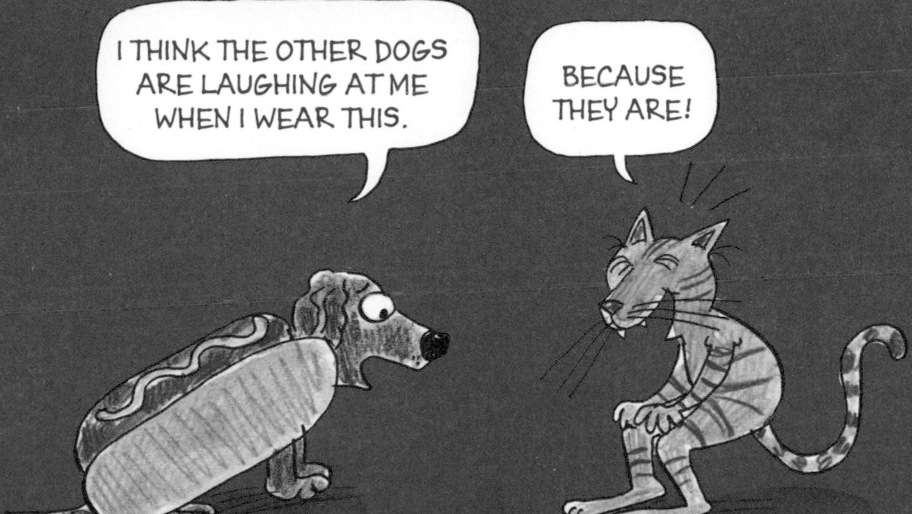
I THINK THE OTHER DOGS ARE LAUGHING AT ME WHEN I WEAR THIS.
BECAUSE THEY ARE!

I WAS SO EXCITED TO DESIGN MY PARROT COSTUME!

BLUE, RED, AND YELLOW FEATHERS SEWN ON TO A BLACK LEOTARD,
HAT WITH DETACHABLE BEAK, ORANGE TIGHTS, AND SNEAKERS

I HELPED ZOE DESIGN HER PENGUIN COSTUME, TOO.

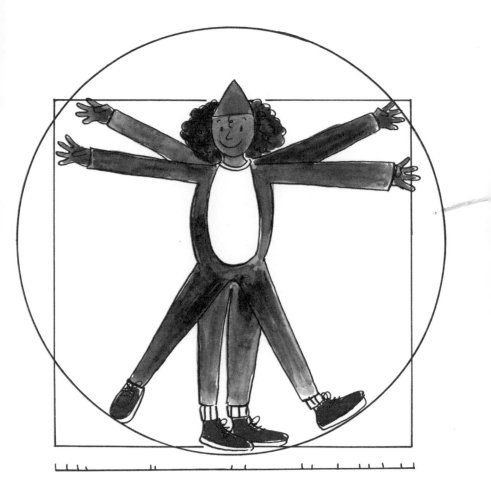

BLACK PANTS, BLACK SHIRT, WHITE BIB,
WHITE HAT, ORANGE BEAK, AND SNEAKERS

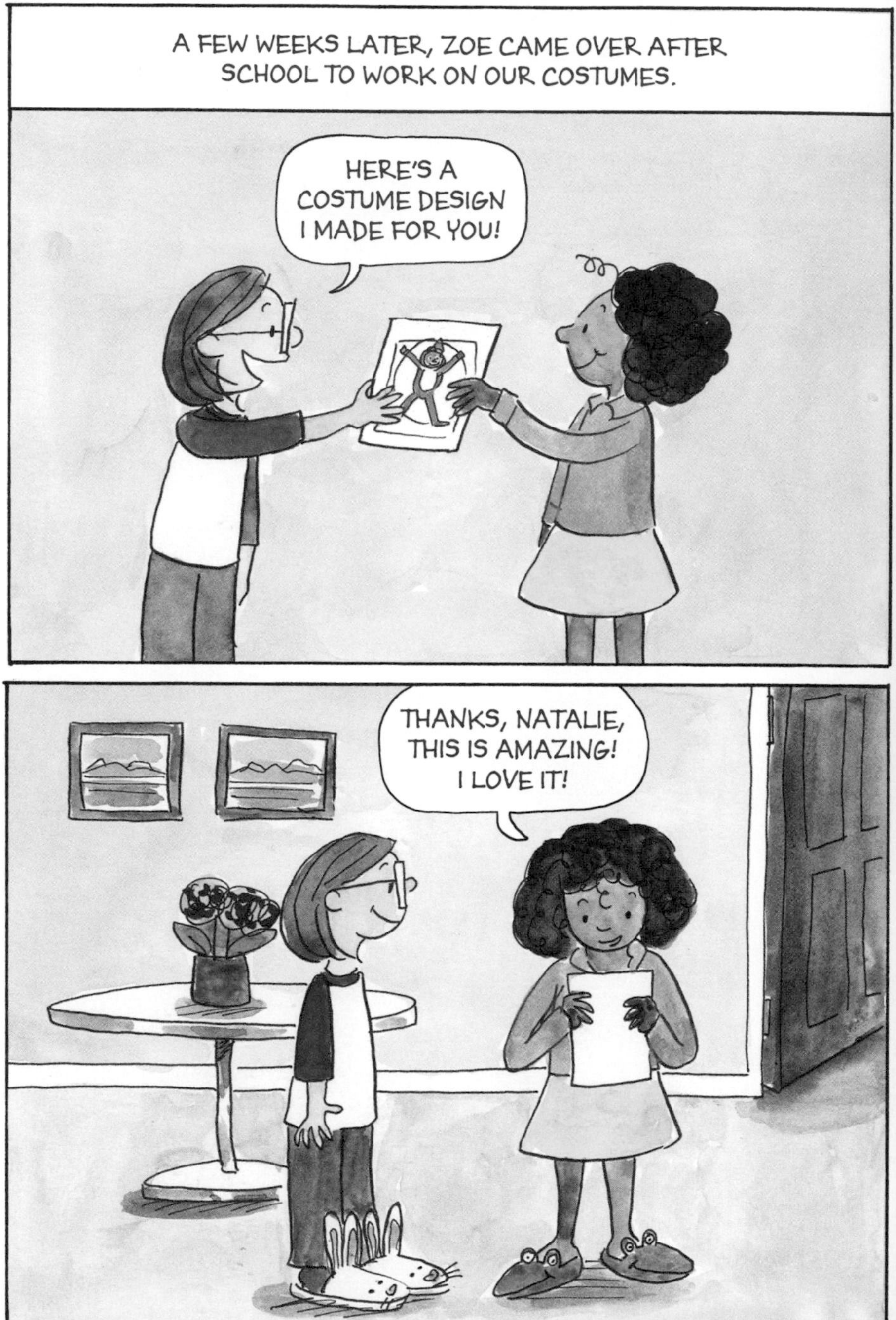
A FEW WEEKS LATER, ZOE CAME OVER AFTER SCHOOL TO WORK ON OUR COSTUMES.
HERE'S A COSTUME DESIGN I MADE FOR YOU!
THANKS, NATALIE, THIS IS AMAZING! I LOVE IT!

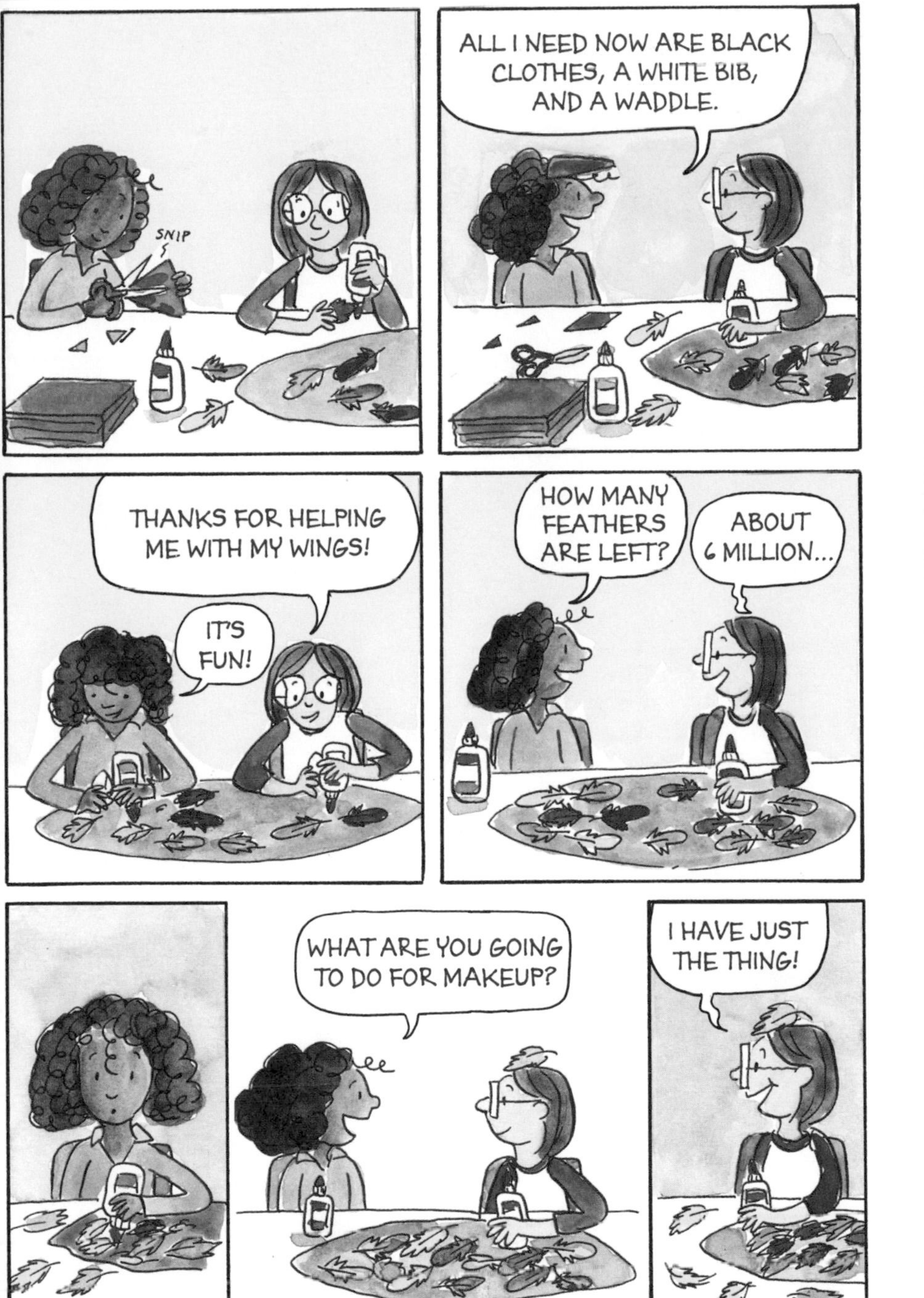
SNIP
ALL I NEED NOW ARE BLACK CLOTHES, A WHITE BIB, AND A WADDLE.
THANKS FOR HELPING ME WITH MY WINGS!
IT'S FUN!
HOW MANY FEATHERS ARE LEFT?
ABOUT 6 MILLION...
WHAT ARE YOU GOING TO DO FOR MAKEUP?
I HAVE JUST THE THING!

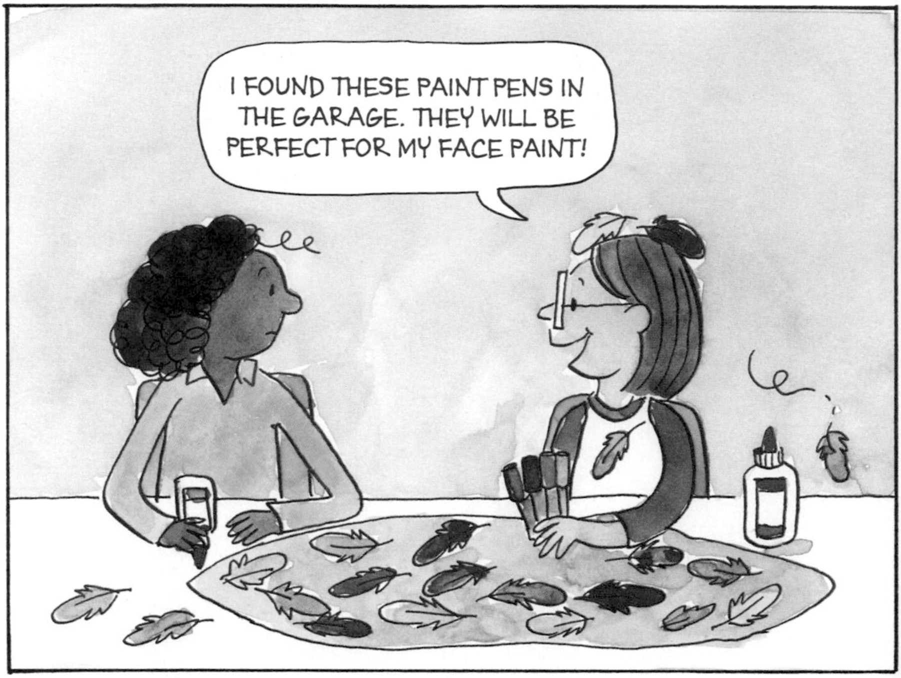
I FOUND THESE PAINT PENS IN THE GARAGE. THEY WILL BE PERFECT FOR MY FACE PAINT!

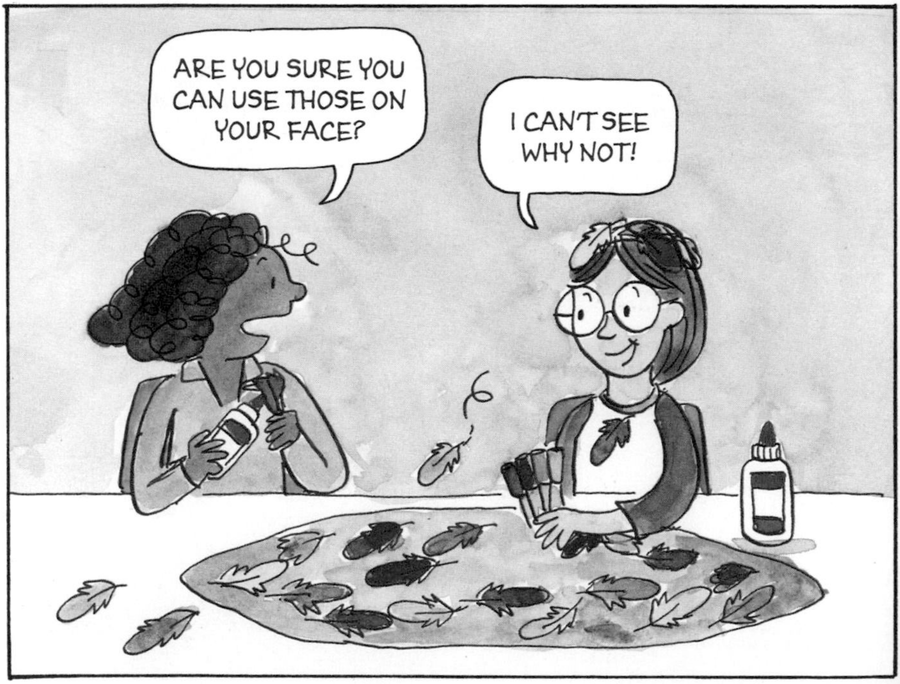
ARE YOU SURE YOU CAN USE THOSE ON YOUR FACE?
I CAN'T SEE WHY NOT!

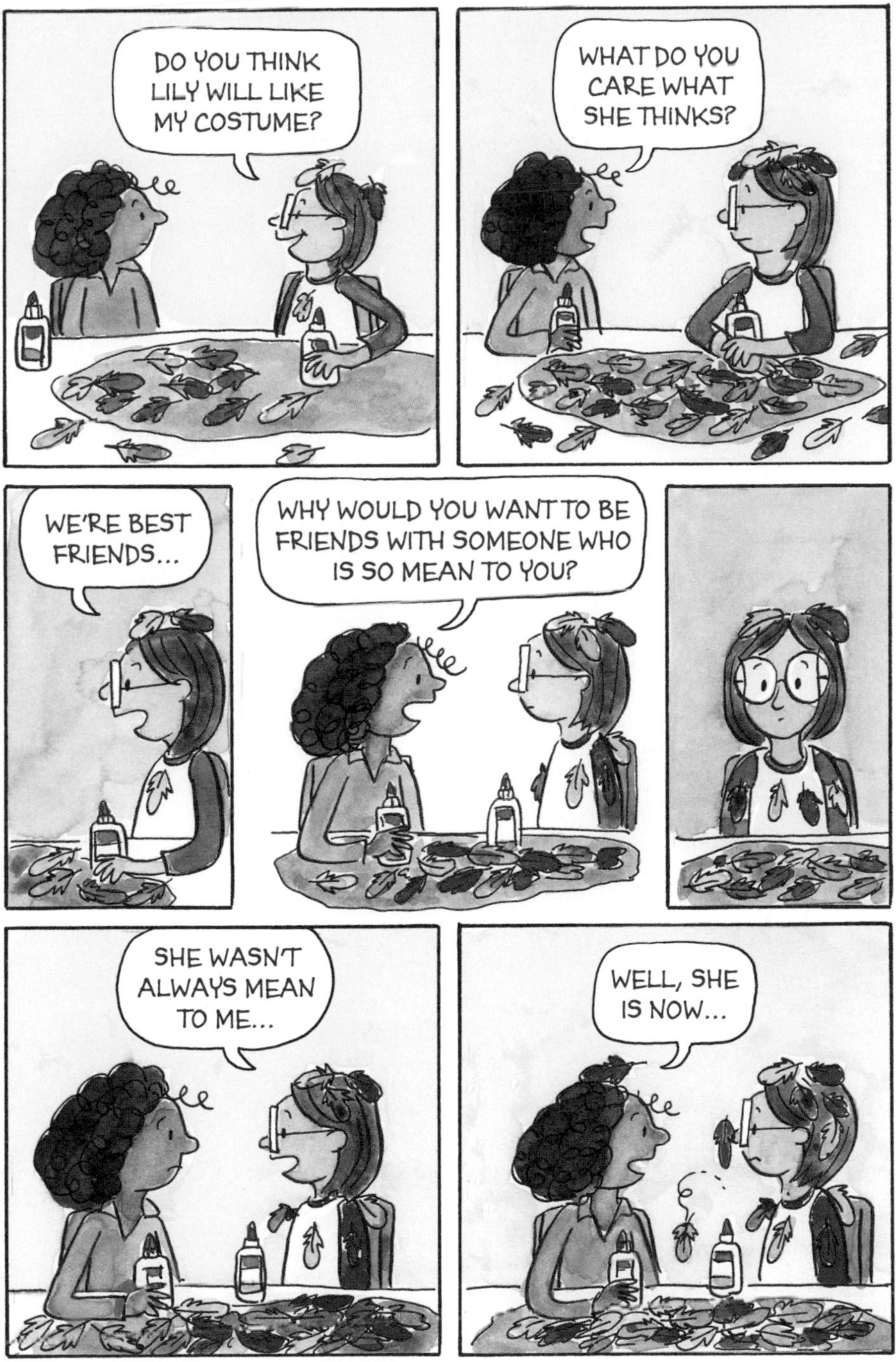
DO YOU THINK LILY WILL LIKE MY COSTUME?
WHAT DO YOU CARE WHAT SHE THINKS?
WE'RE BEST FRIENDS...
WHY WOULD YOU WANT TO BE FRIENDS WITH SOMEONE WHO IS SO MEAN TO YOU?
SHE WASN'T ALWAYS MEAN TO ME...
WELL, SHE IS NOW...

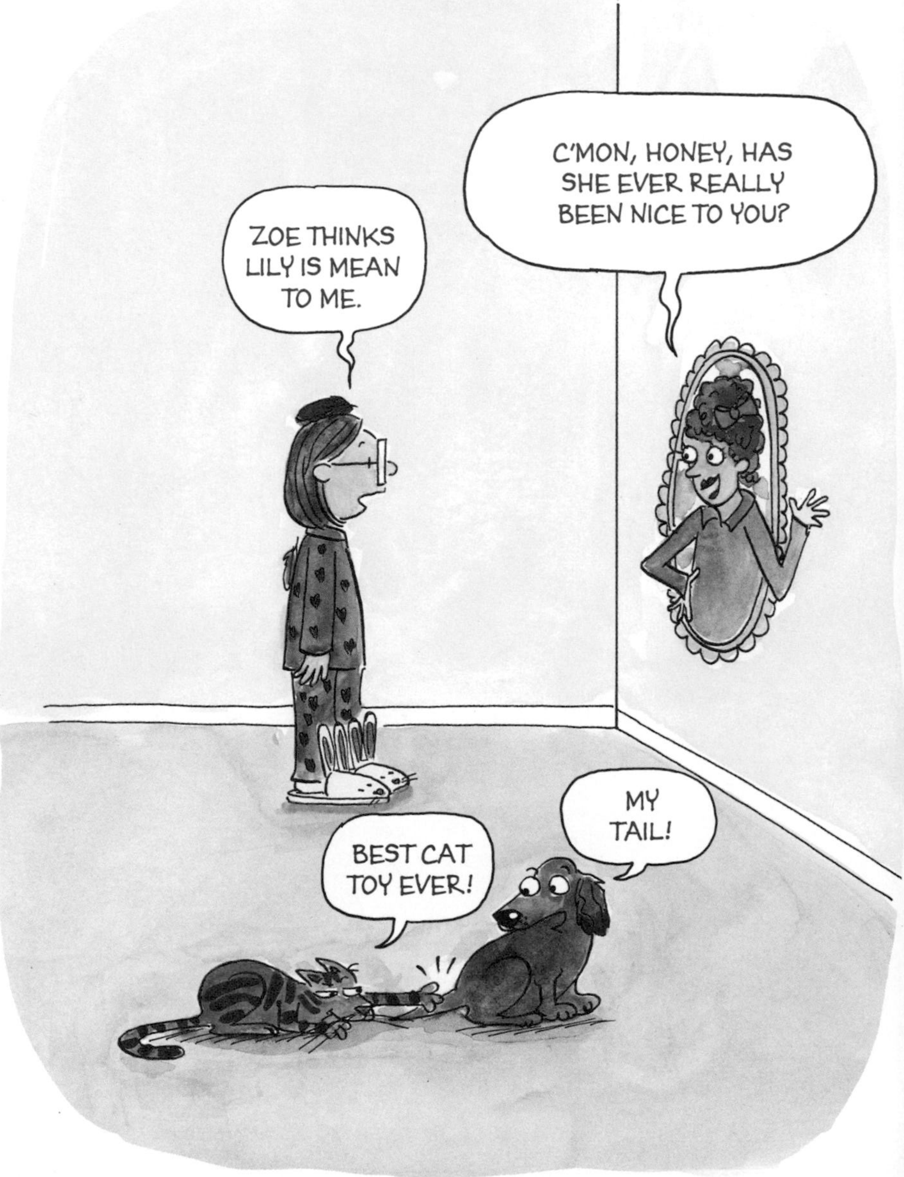
ZOE THINKS LILY IS MEAN TO ME.
C'MON, HONEY, HAS SHE EVER REALLY BEEN NICE TO YOU?
MY TAIL!
BEST CAT TOY EVER!

CHAPTER 10
SHOWSTOPPER

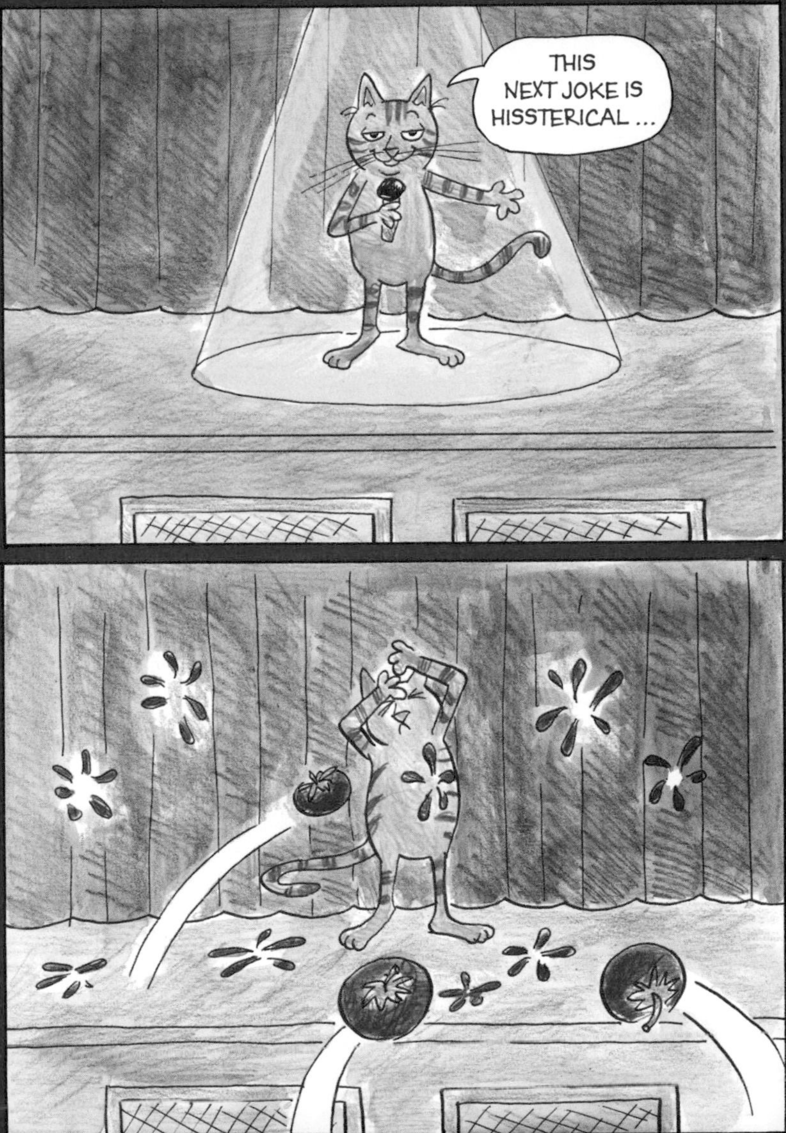
THIS NEXT JOKE IS HISSTERICAL …

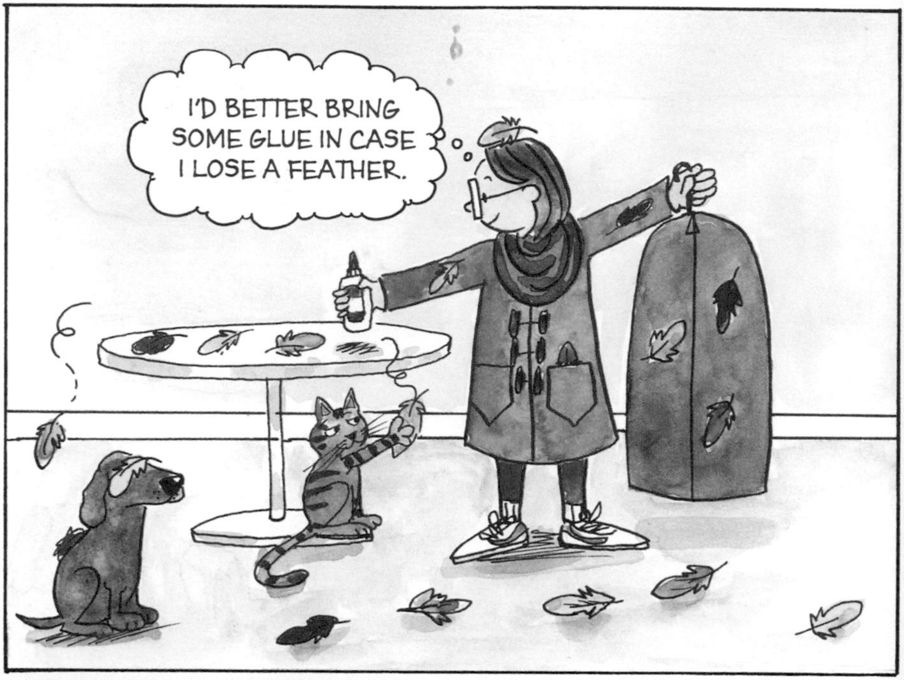
I'D BETTER BRING SOME GLUE IN CASE I LOSE A FEATHER.

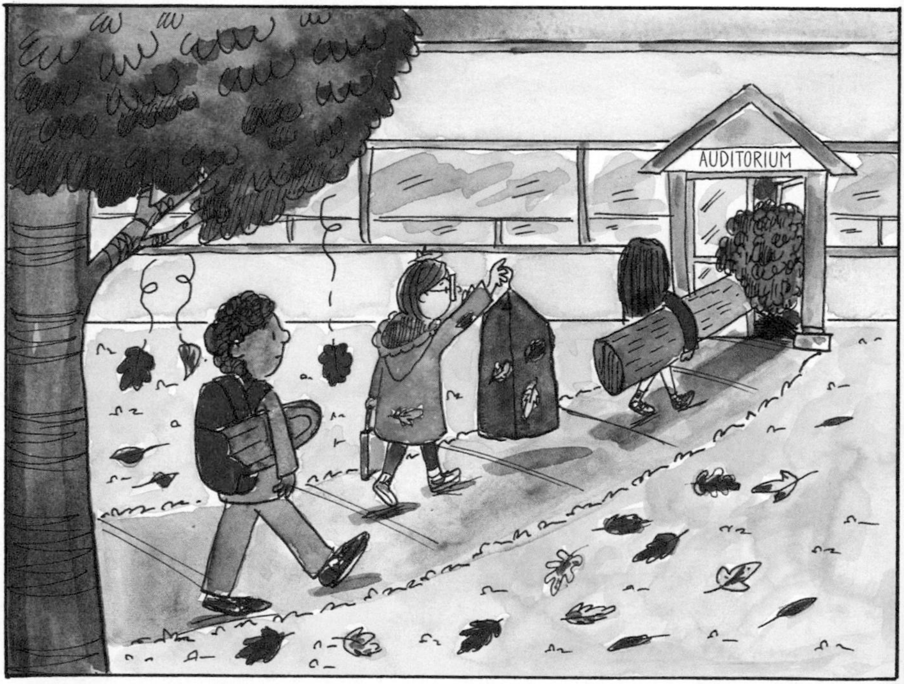
AUDITORIUM

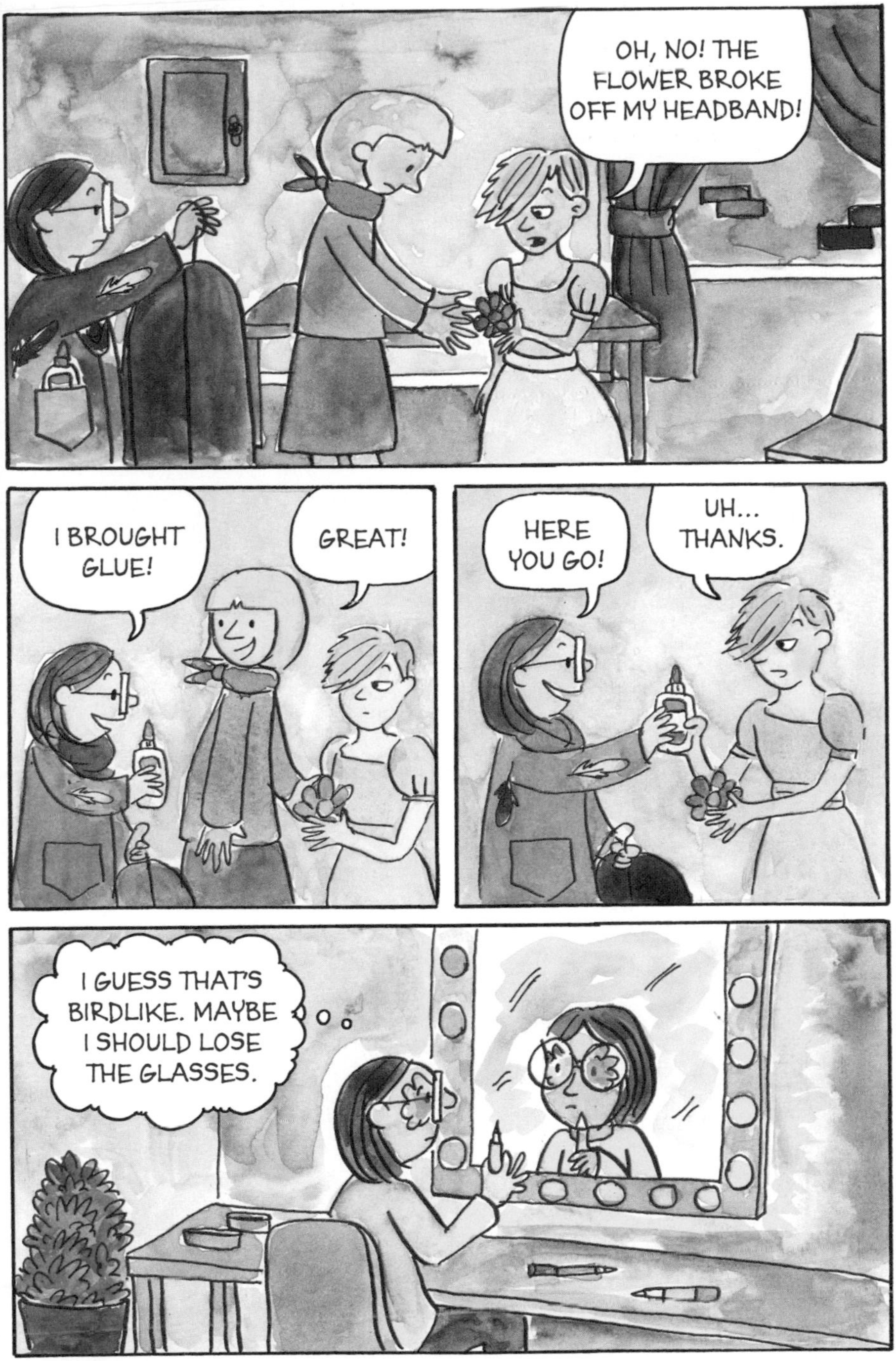
OH, NO! THE FLOWER BROKE OFF MY HEADBAND!
I BROUGHT GLUE!
GREAT!
HERE YOU GO!
UH... THANKS.
I GUESS THAT'S BIRDLIKE. MAYBE I SHOULD LOSE THE GLASSES.

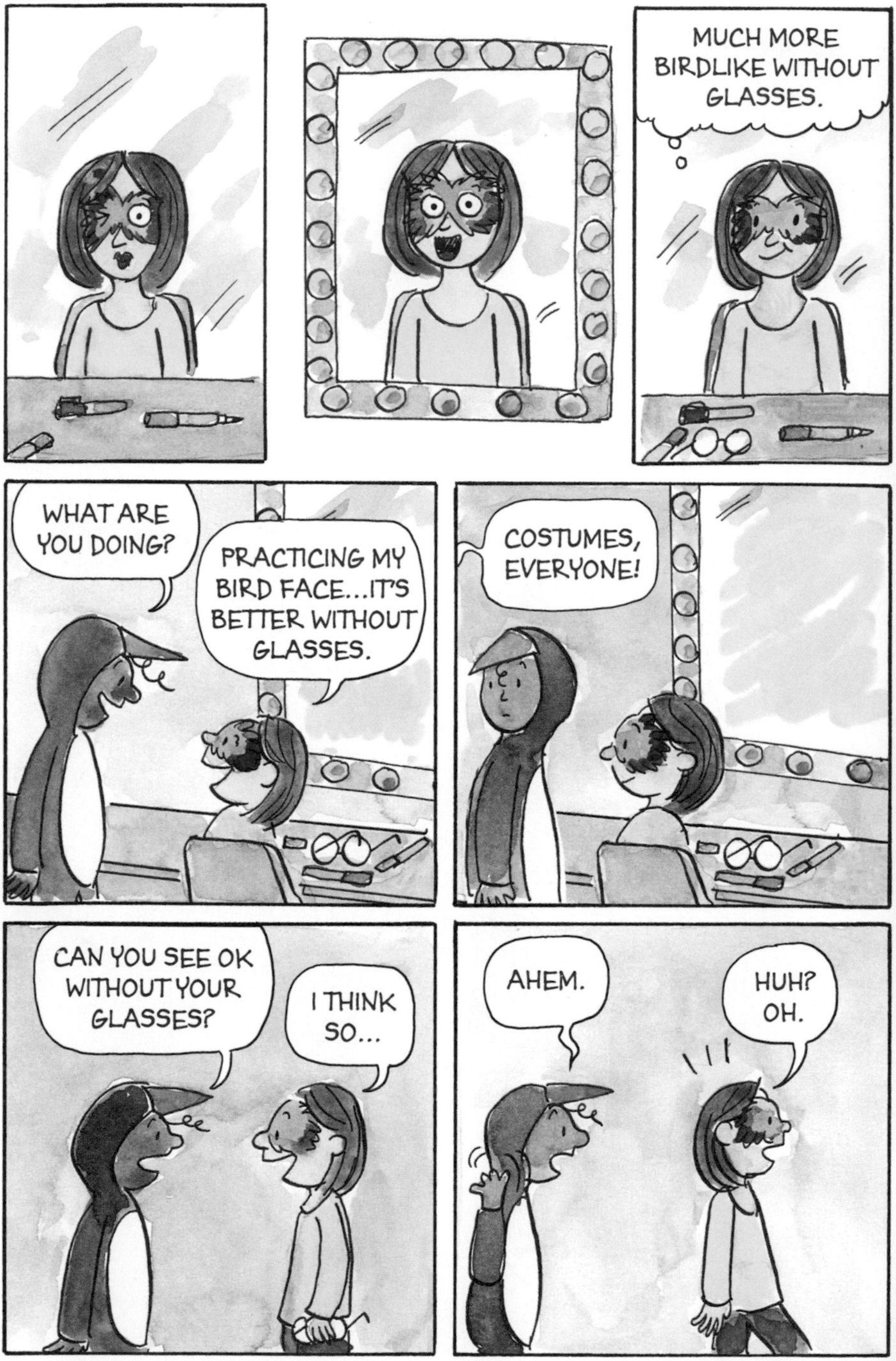
MUCH MORE BIRDLIKE WITHOUT GLASSES.
WHAT ARE YOU DOING?
PRACTICING MY BIRD FACE...IT'S BETTER WITHOUT GLASSES.
COSTUMES, EVERYONE!
CAN YOU SEE OK WITHOUT YOUR GLASSES?
I THINK SO...
AHEM.
HUH? OH.

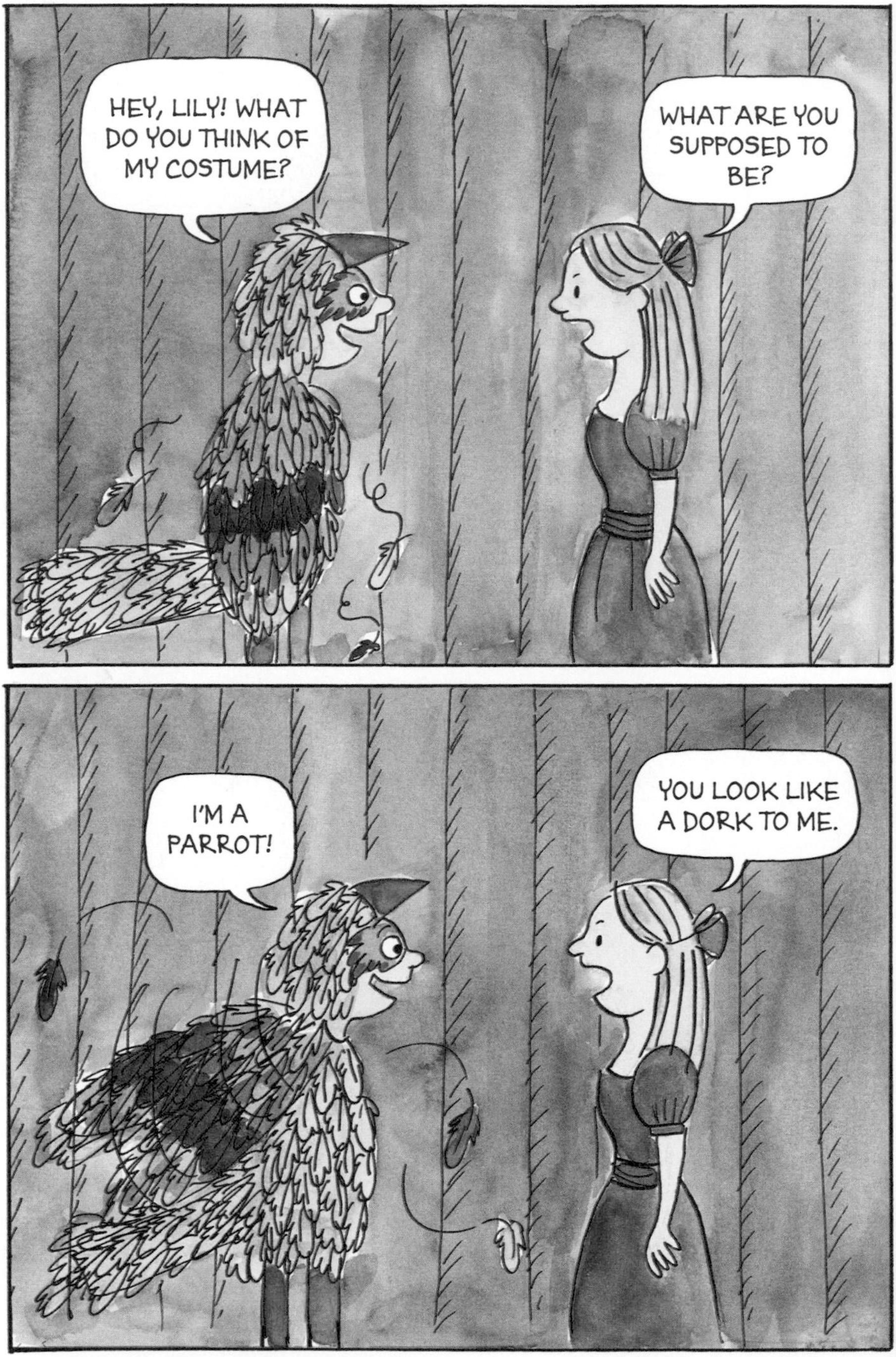
HEY, LILY! WHAT DO YOU THINK OF MY COSTUME?
WHAT ARE YOU SUPPOSED TO BE?
I'M A PARROT!
YOU LOOK LIKE A DORK TO ME.

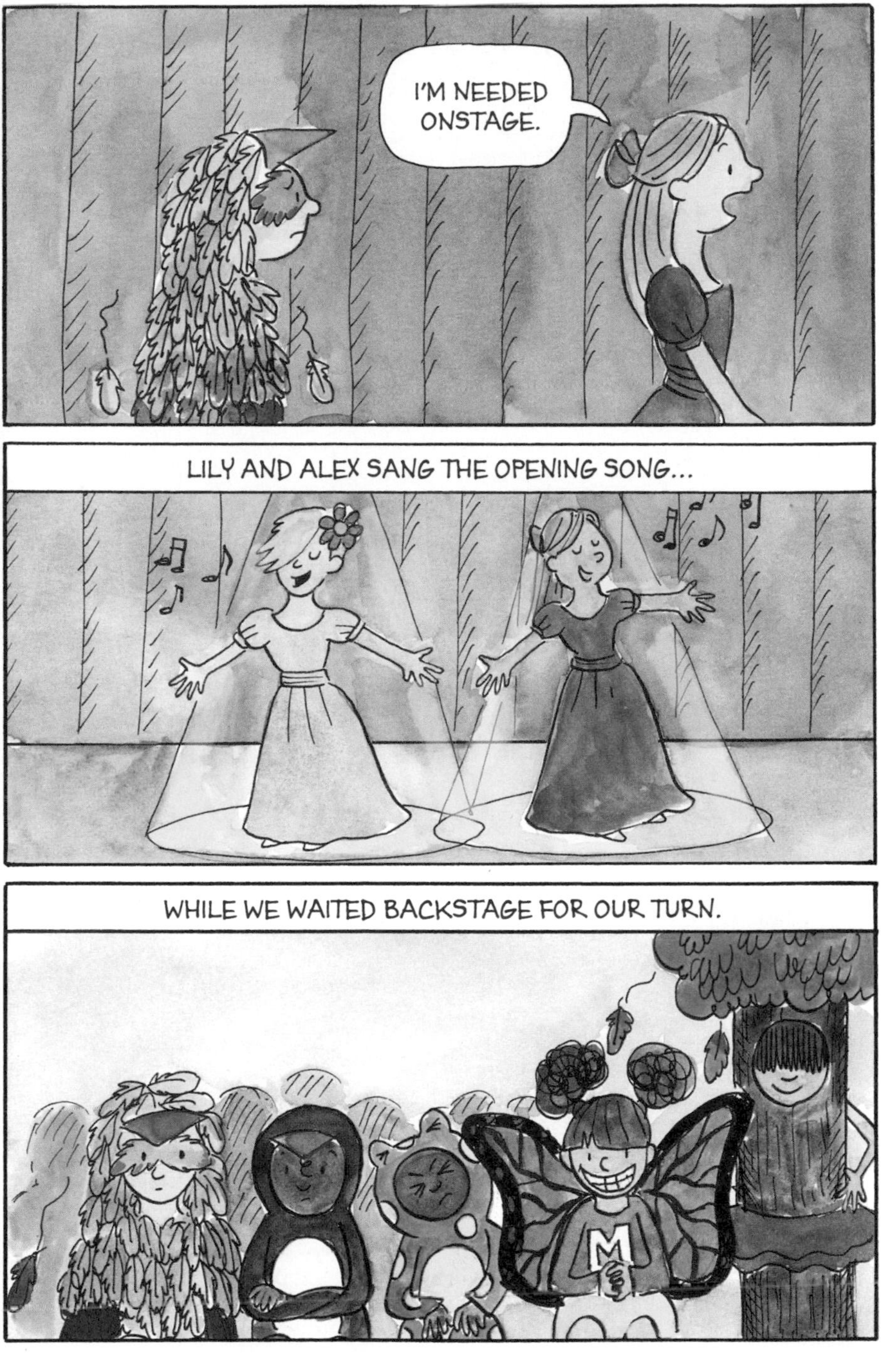
I'M NEEDED ONSTAGE.
LILY AND ALEX SANG THE OPENING SONG...
WHILE WE WAITED BACKSTAGE FOR OUR TURN.
M

AND THE GIRL WITH HAIR IN HER FACE HAD A HARD TIME MOVING AROUND AS A TREE.

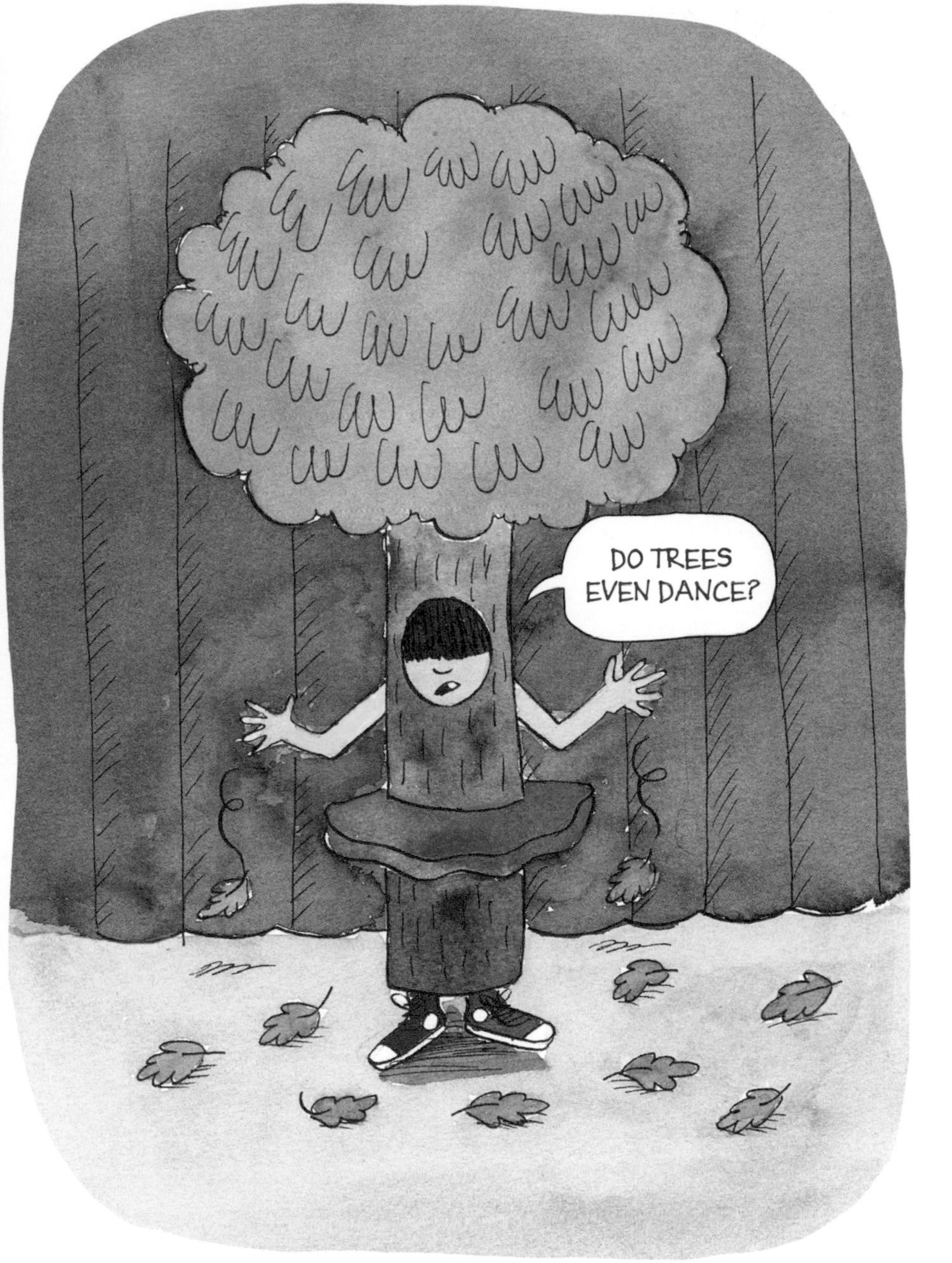
DO TREES EVEN DANCE?

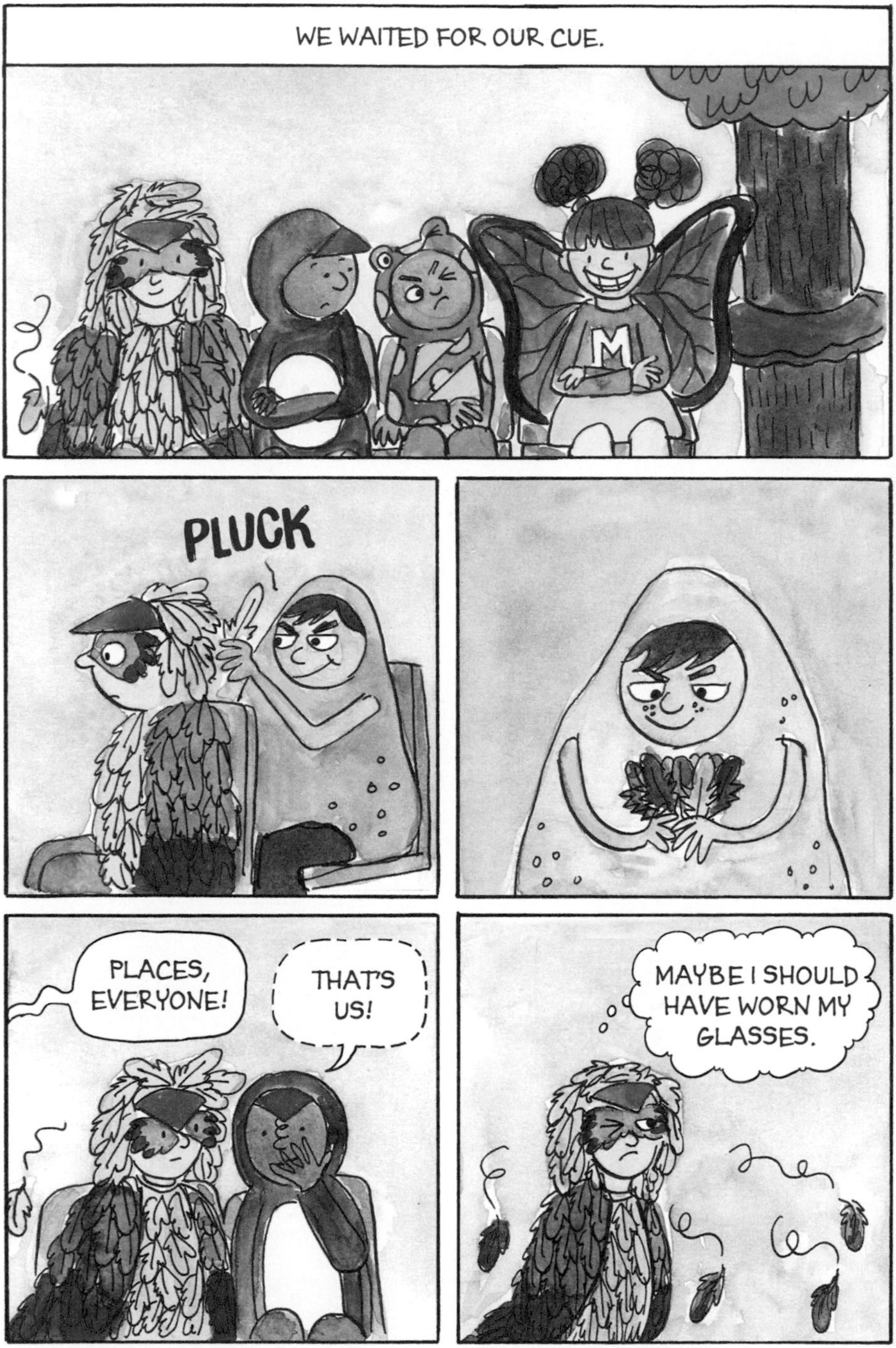
WE WAITED FOR OUR CUE.
PLUCK
PLACES, EVERYONE!
THAT'S US!
MAYBE I SHOULD HAVE WORN MY GLASSES.

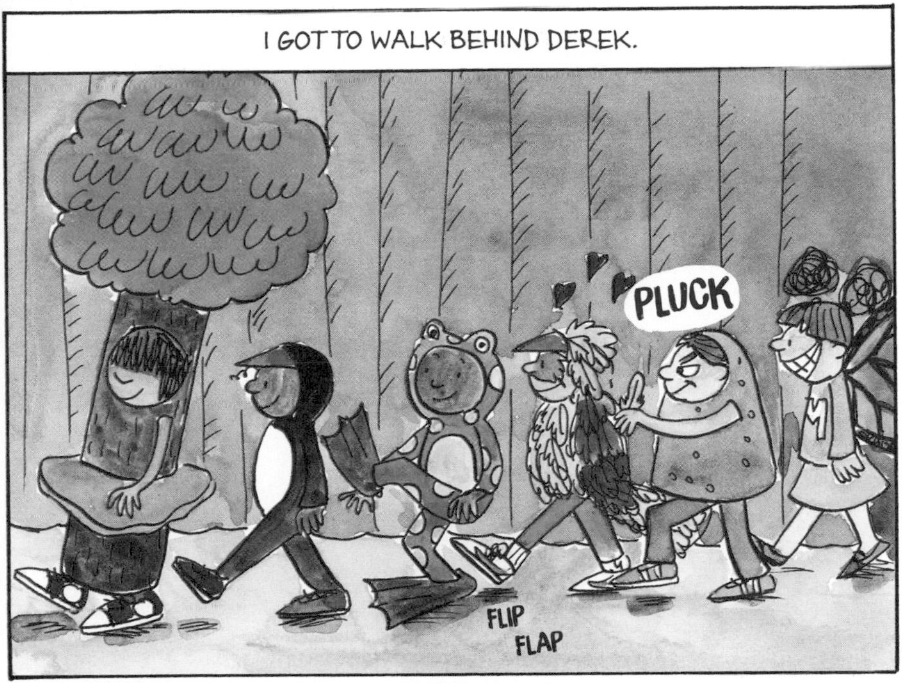
I GOT TO WALK BEHIND DEREK.
PLUCK
FLIP
FLAP

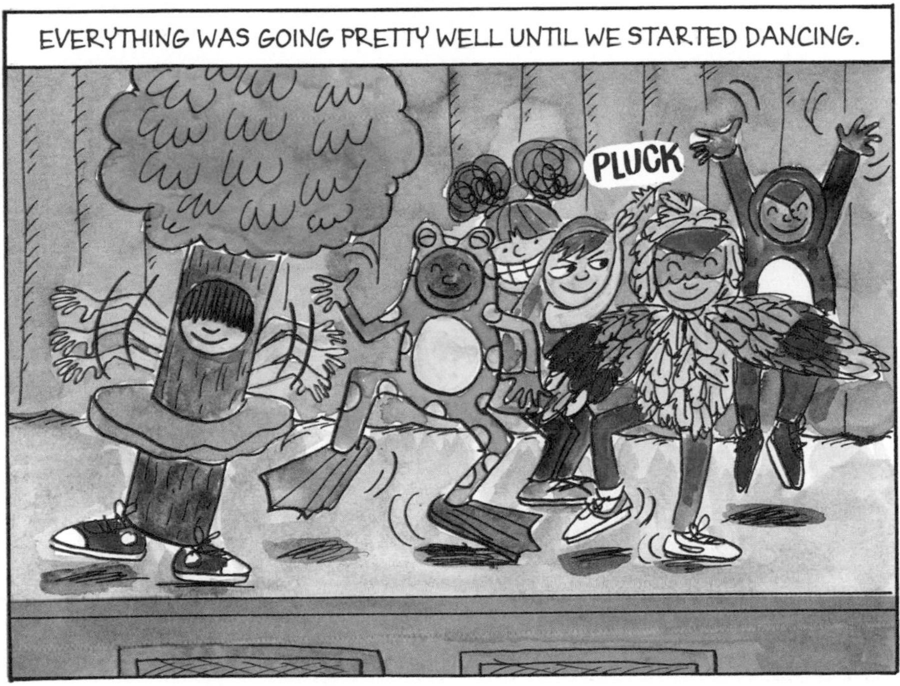
EVERYTHING WAS GOING PRETTY WELL UNTIL WE STARTED DANCING.
PLUCK

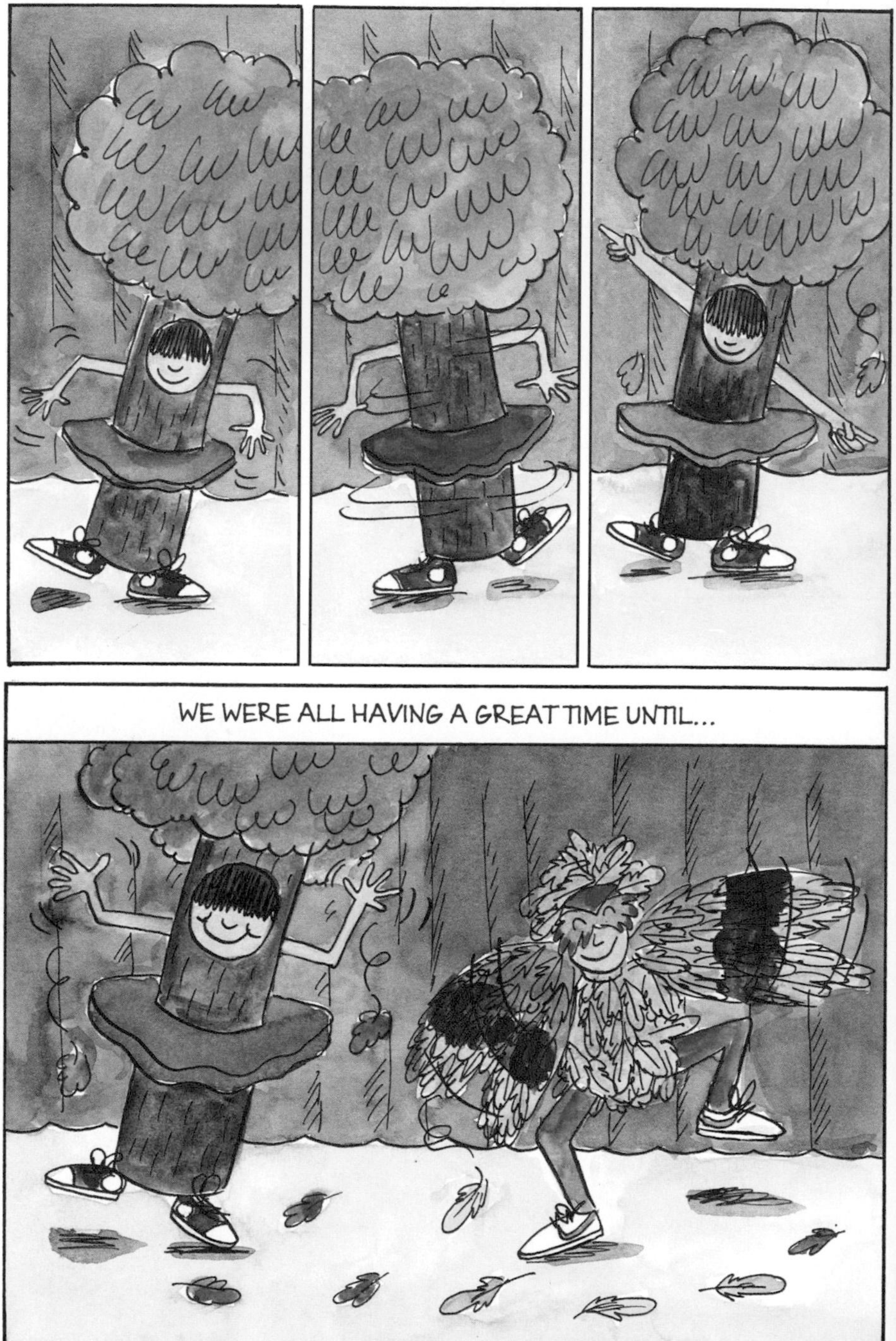
WE WERE ALL HAVING A GREAT TIME UNTIL...

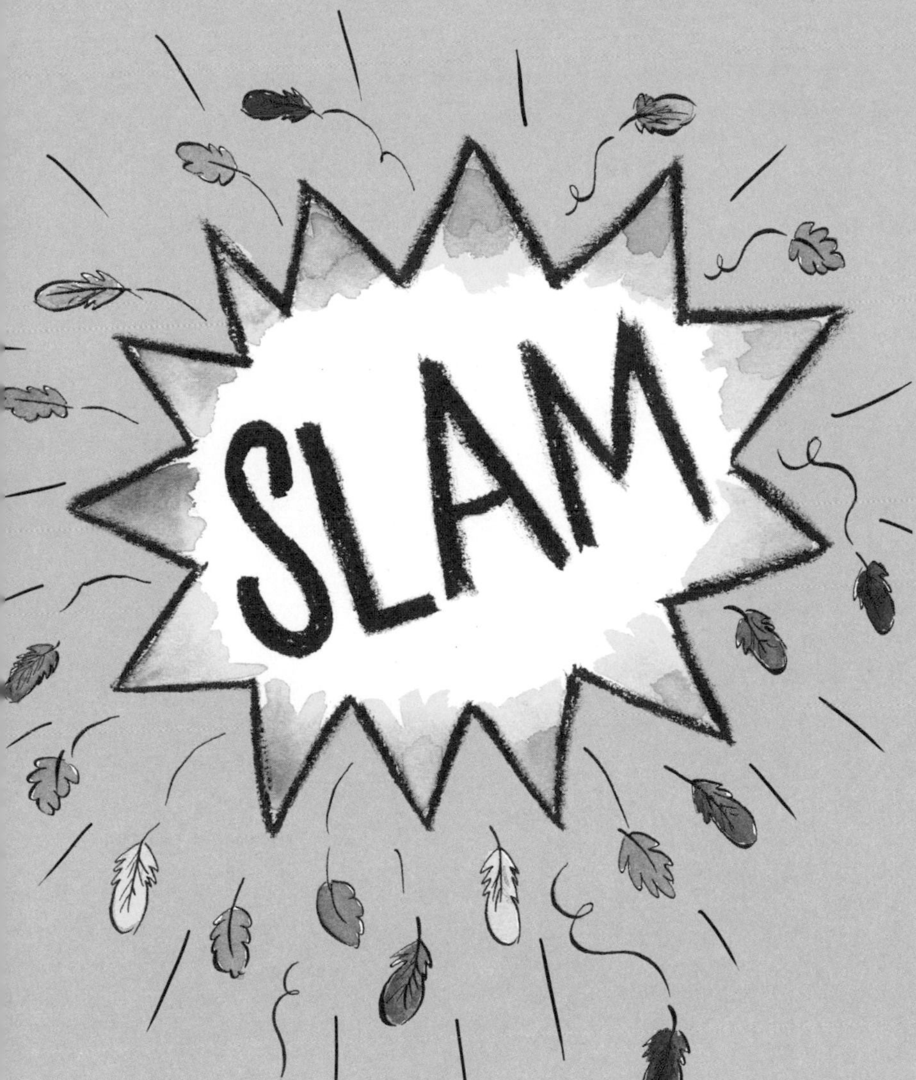
SLAM

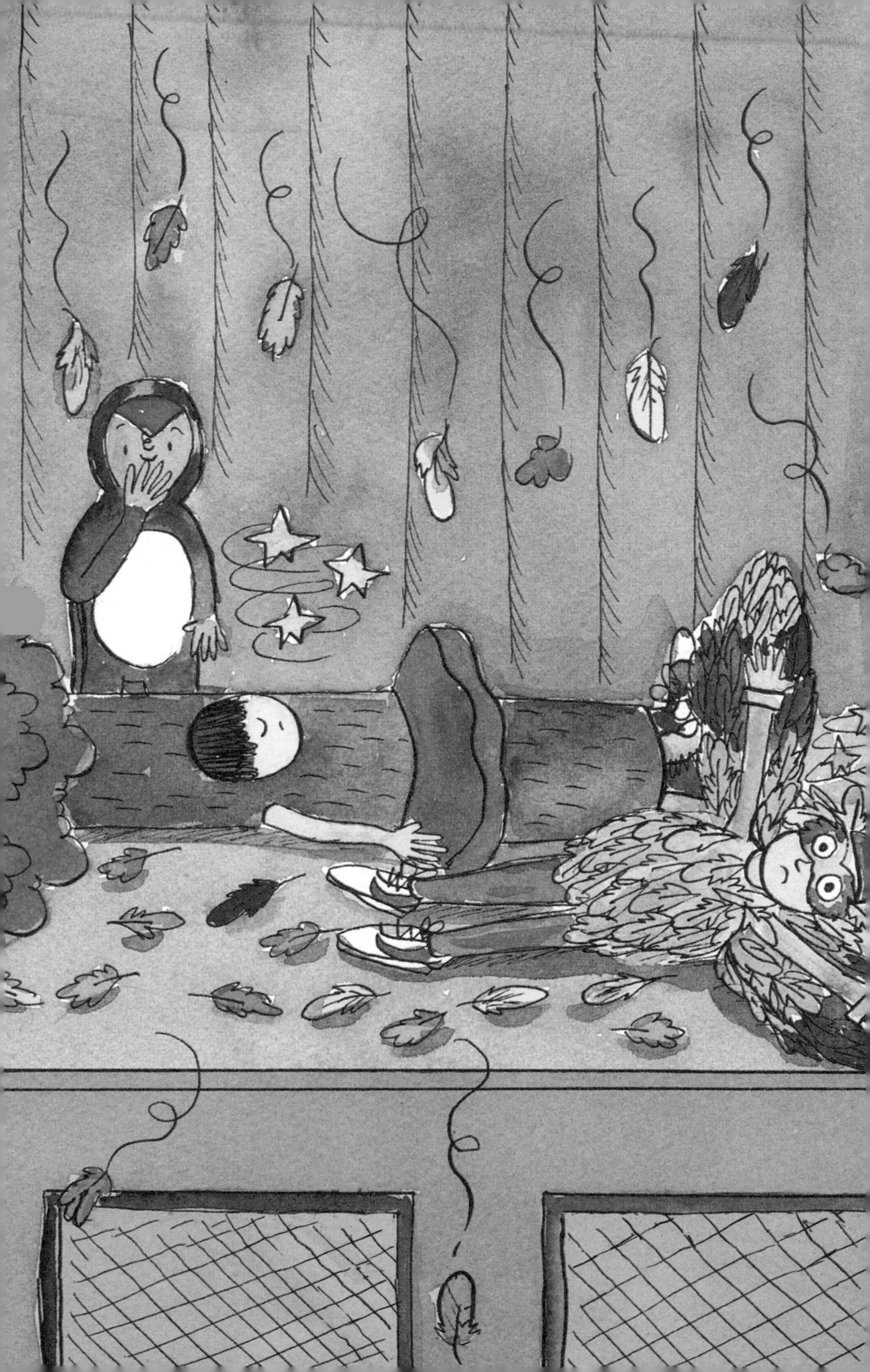

AND THAT'S HOW I MET "THE GIRL WITH HAIR IN HER FACE," ALSO KNOWN AS FLO.

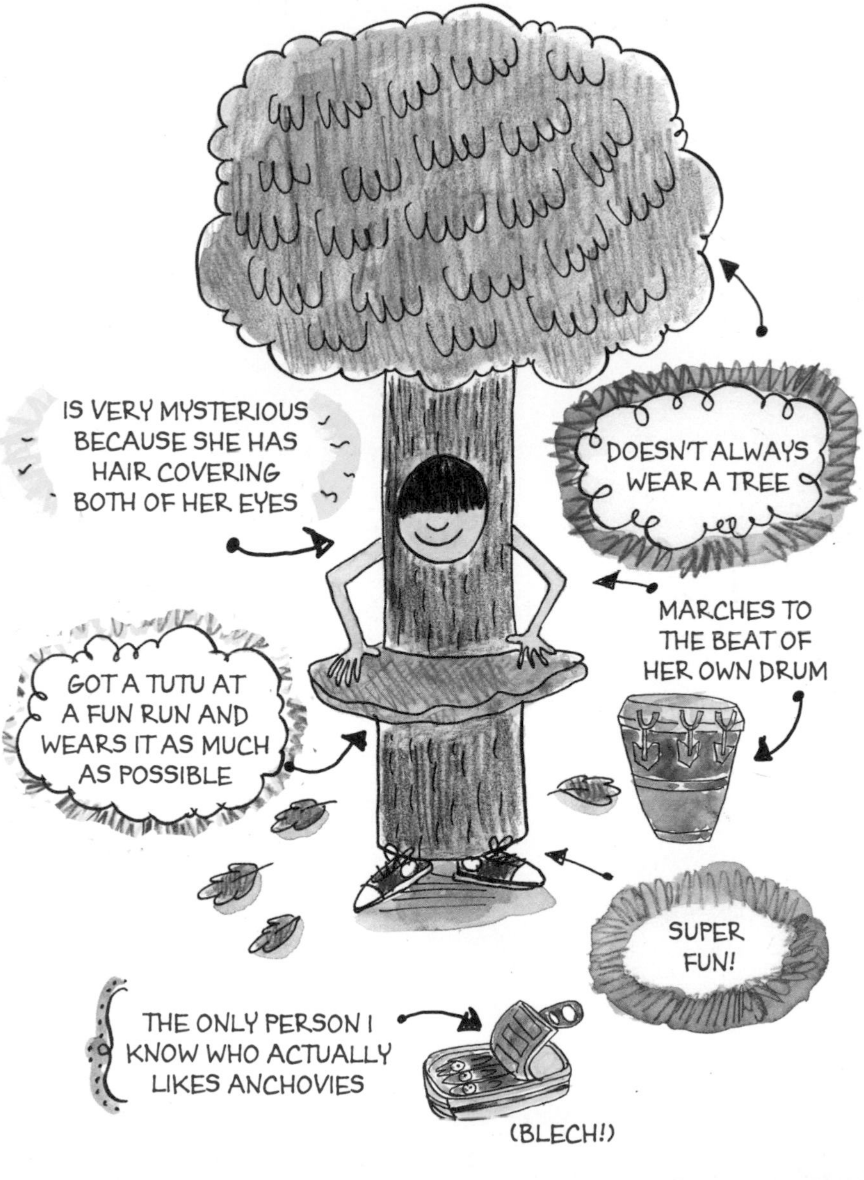
IS VERY MYSTERIOUS BECAUSE SHE HAS HAIR COVERING BOTH OF HER EYES
DOESN'T ALWAYS WEAR A TREE
MARCHES TO THE BEAT OF HER OWN DRUM
GOT A TUTU AT A FUN RUN AND WEARS IT AS MUCH AS POSSIBLE
SUPER FUN!
THE ONLY PERSON I KNOW WHO ACTUALLY LIKES ANCHOVIES
(BLECH!)

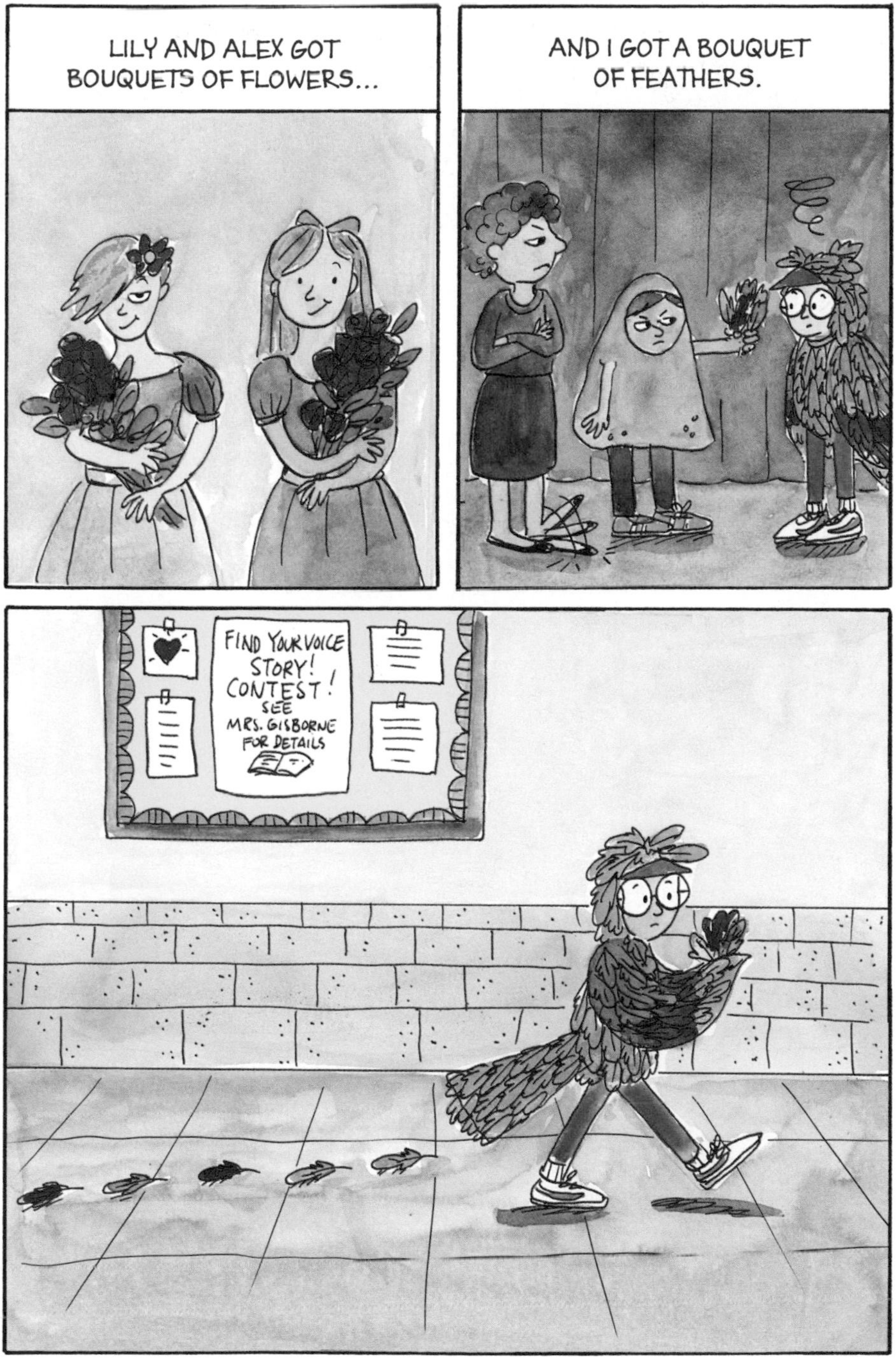
LILY AND ALEX GOT BOUQUETS OF FLOWERS...
AND I GOT A BOUQUET OF FEATHERS.
FIND YOUR VOICE STORY! CONTEST!
SEE MRS. GISBORNE FOR DETAILS

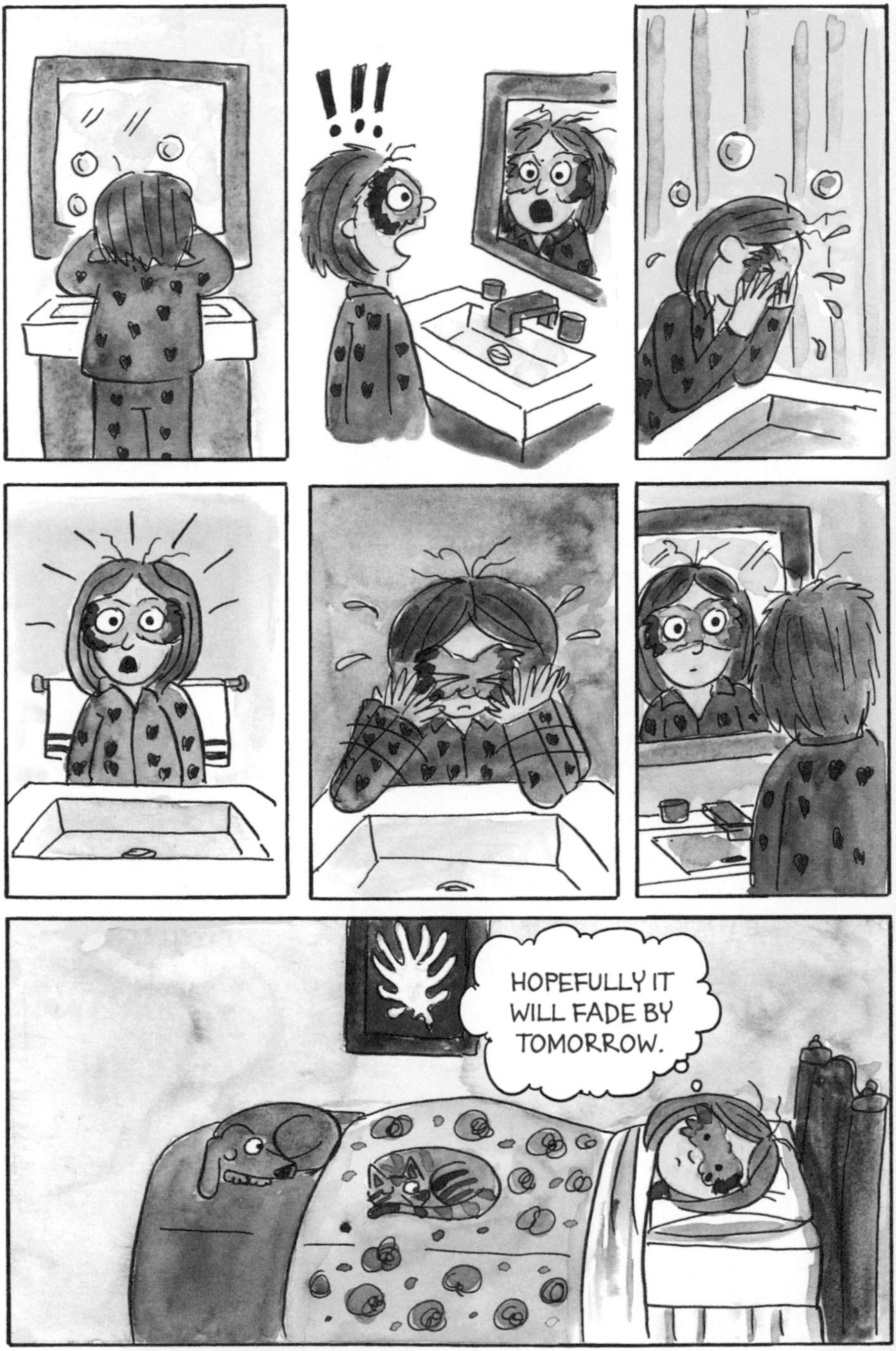
!!!
HOPEFULLY IT WILL FADE BY TOMORROW.

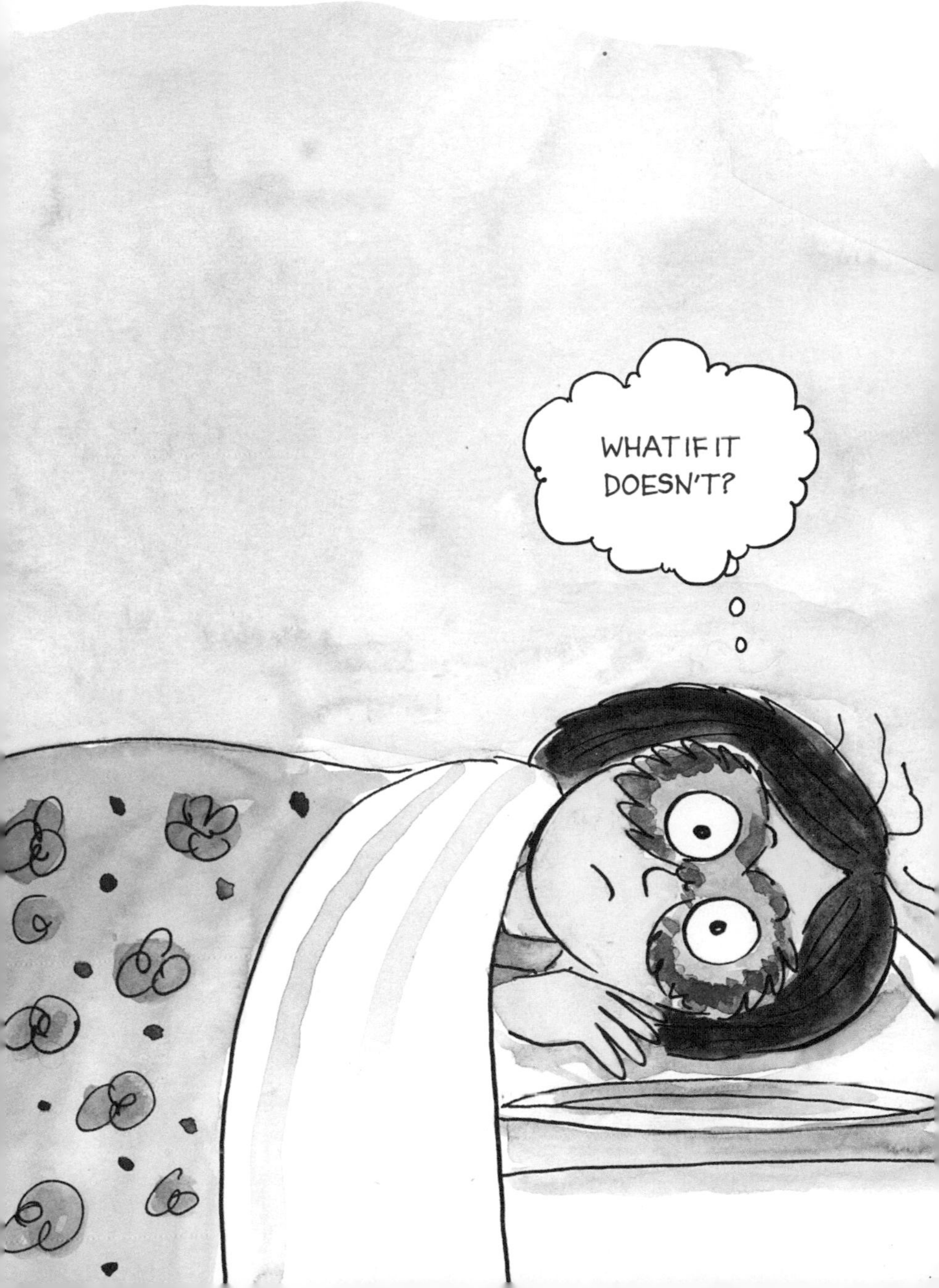
WHAT IF IT DOESN'T?

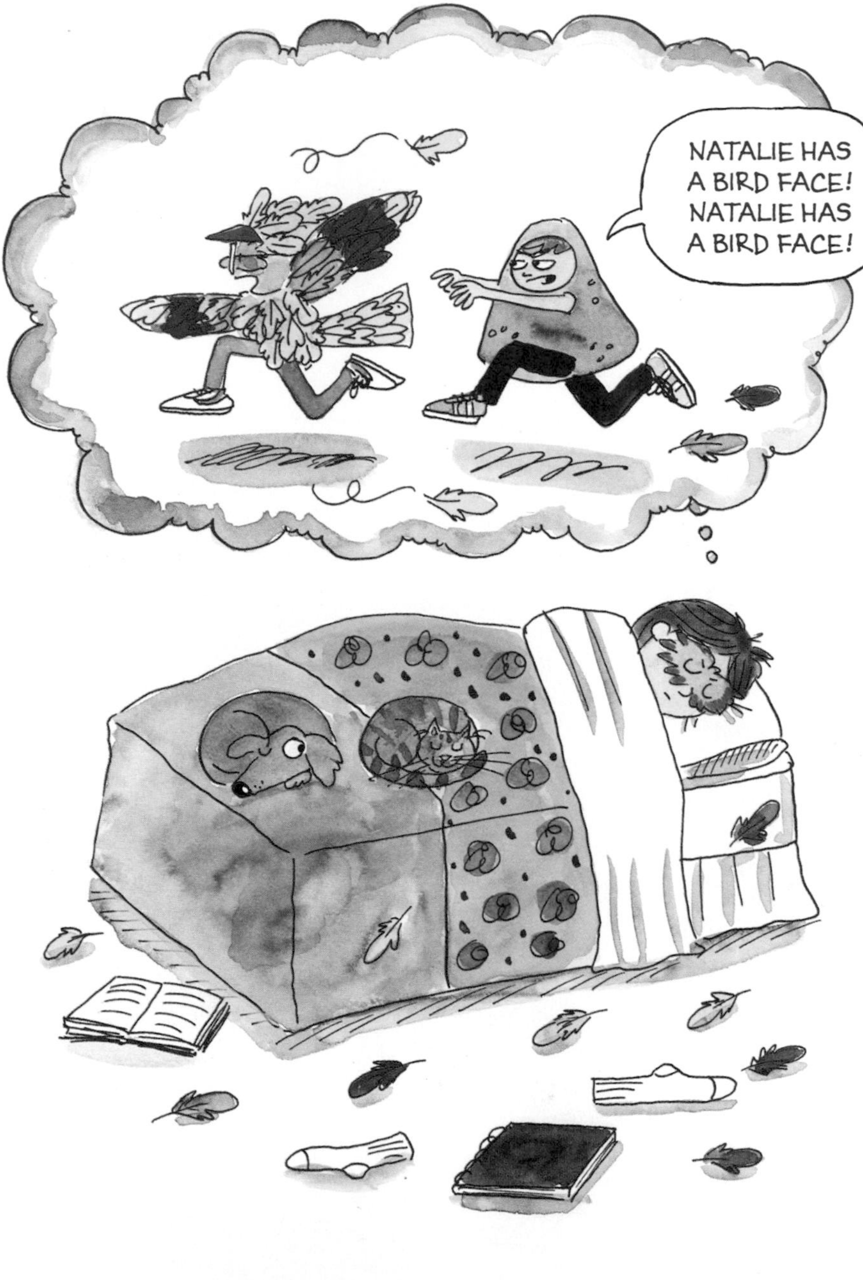
NATALIE HAS A BIRD FACE! NATALIE HAS A BIRD FACE!

CHAPTER 11
SMOKE AND MIRRORS

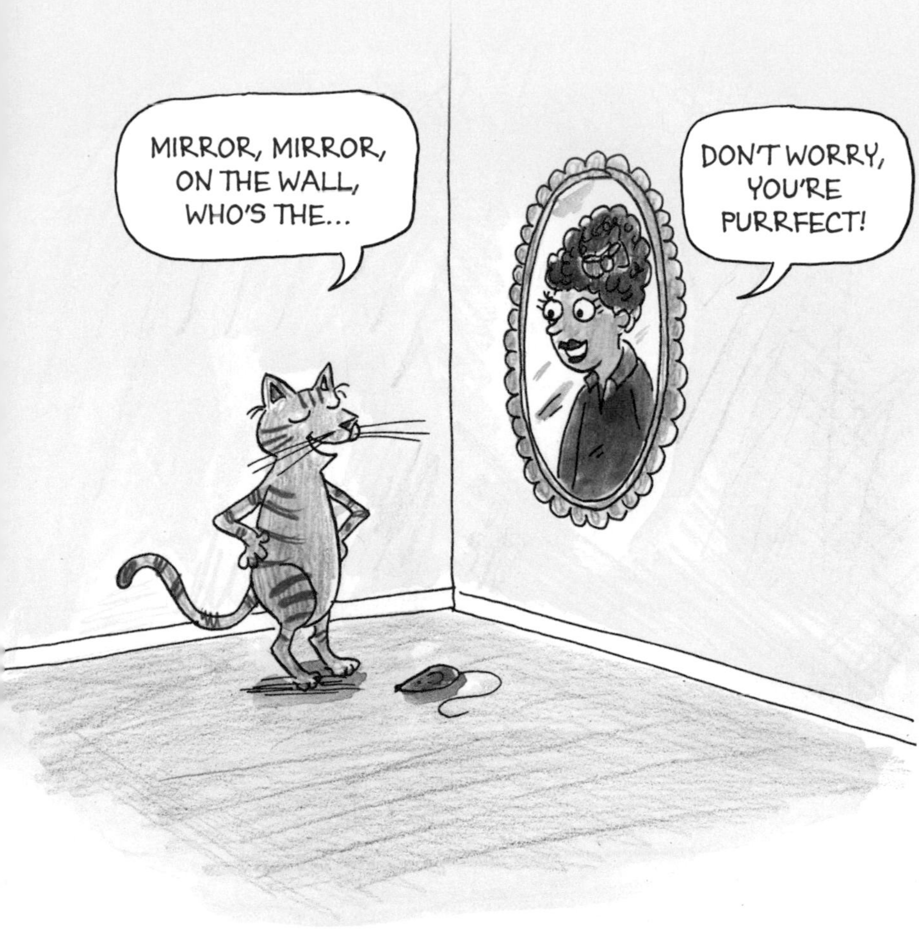
MIRROR, MIRROR, ON THE WALL, WHO'S THE...
DON'T WORRY, YOU'RE PURRFECT!

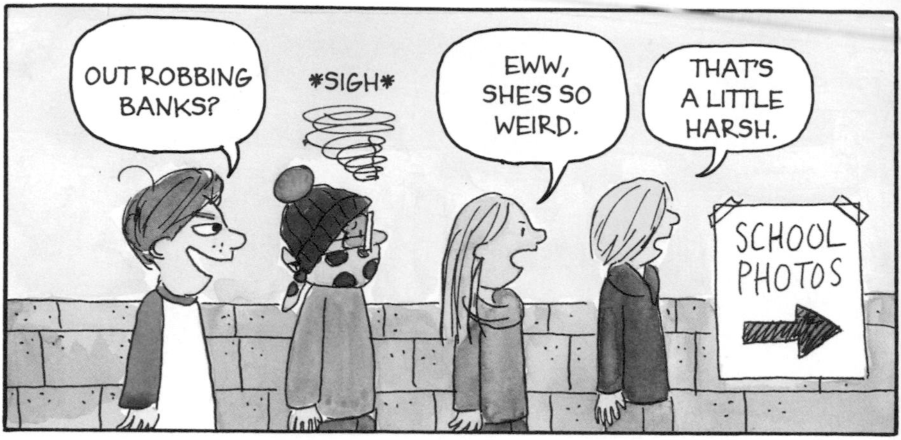
OUT ROBBING BANKS?
SIGH
EWW, SHE'S SO WEIRD.
THAT'S A LITTLE HARSH.
SCHOOL PHOTOS

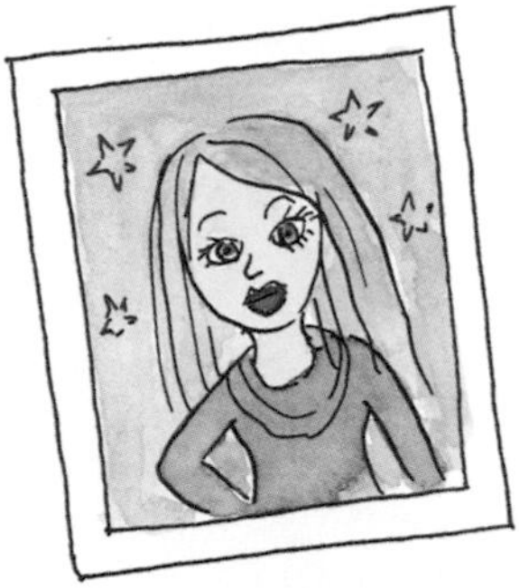
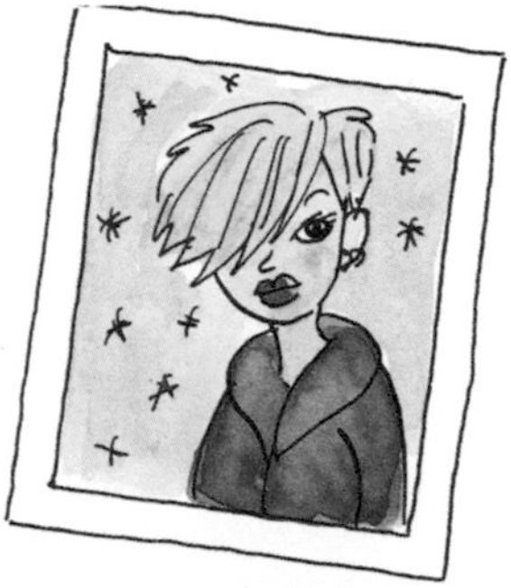

LILY AND ALEX LOOKED LIKE SUPERMODELS.

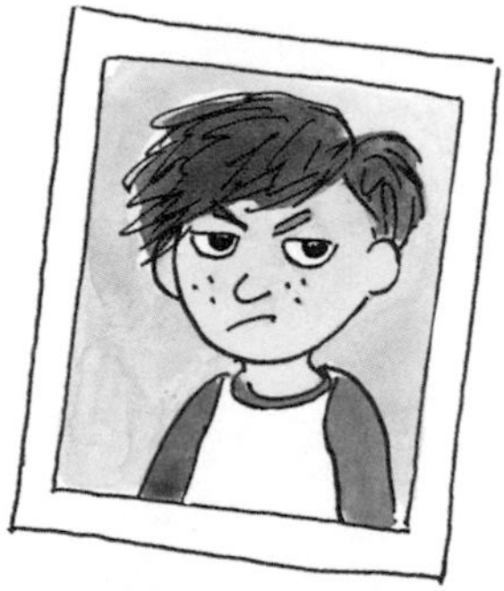

SHAWN LOOKED MEAN.

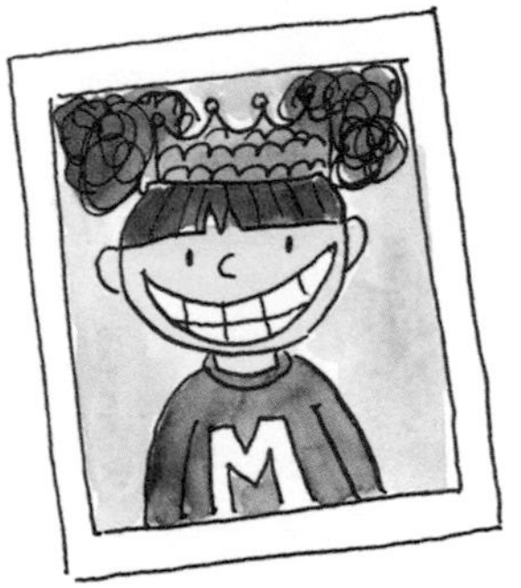

MILLIE WORE A TIARA.

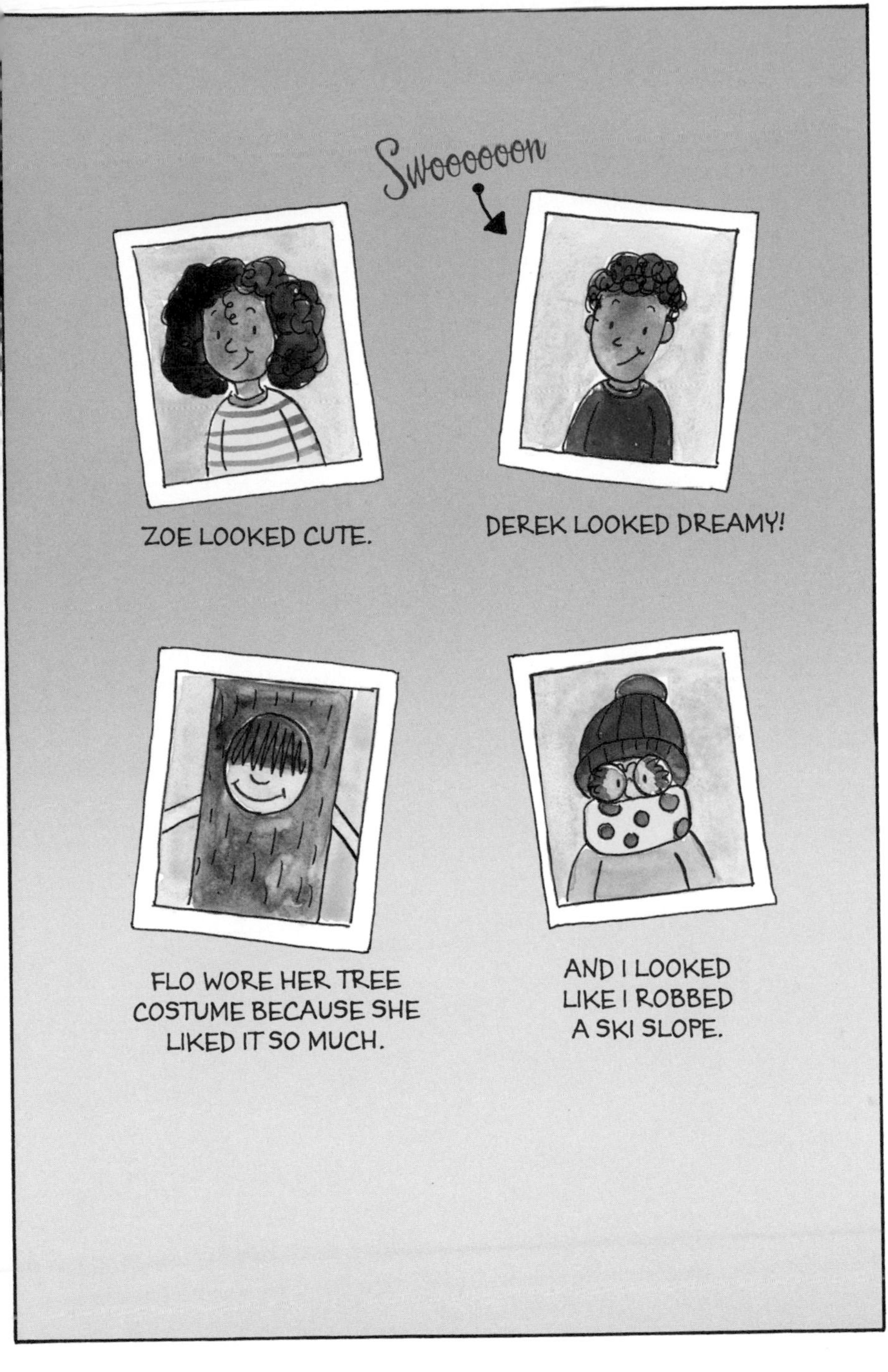
Swoooooon
ZOE LOOKED CUTE.
DEREK LOOKED DREAMY!
FLO WORE HER TREE COSTUME BECAUSE SHE LIKED IT SO MUCH.
AND I LOOKED LIKE I ROBBED A SKI SLOPE.

153

CHAPTER 12
A DAY IN THE LIFE

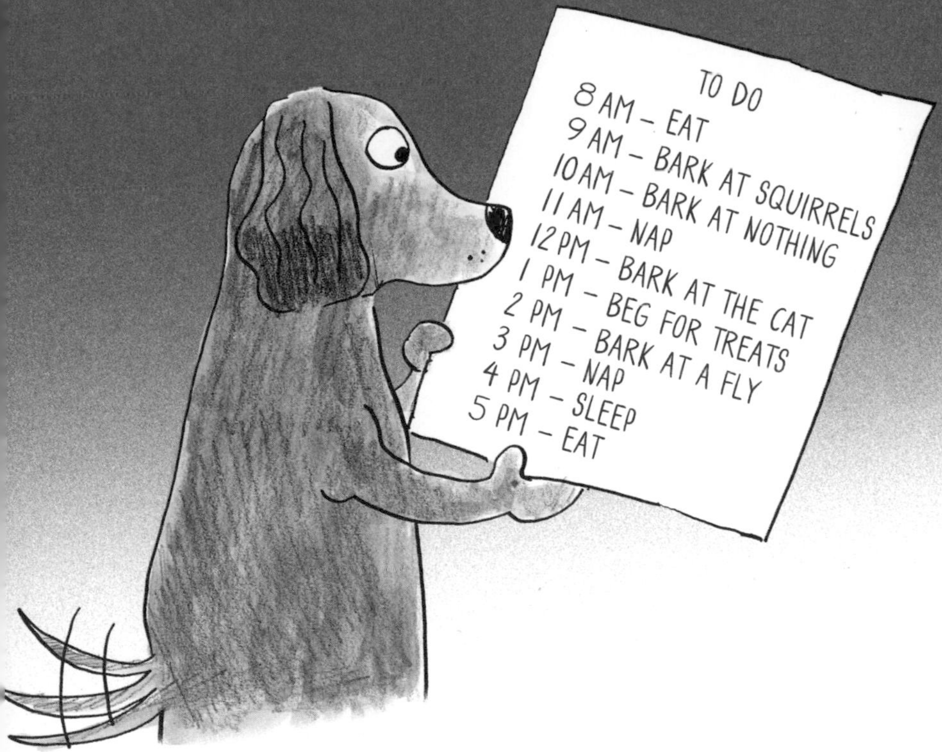
TO DO
8 AM – EAT
9 AM – BARK AT SQUIRRELS
10 AM – BARK AT NOTHING
11 AM – NAP
12 PM – BARK AT THE CAT
1 PM – BEG FOR TREATS
2 PM – BARK AT A FLY
3 PM – NAP
4 PM – SLEEP
5 PM – EAT

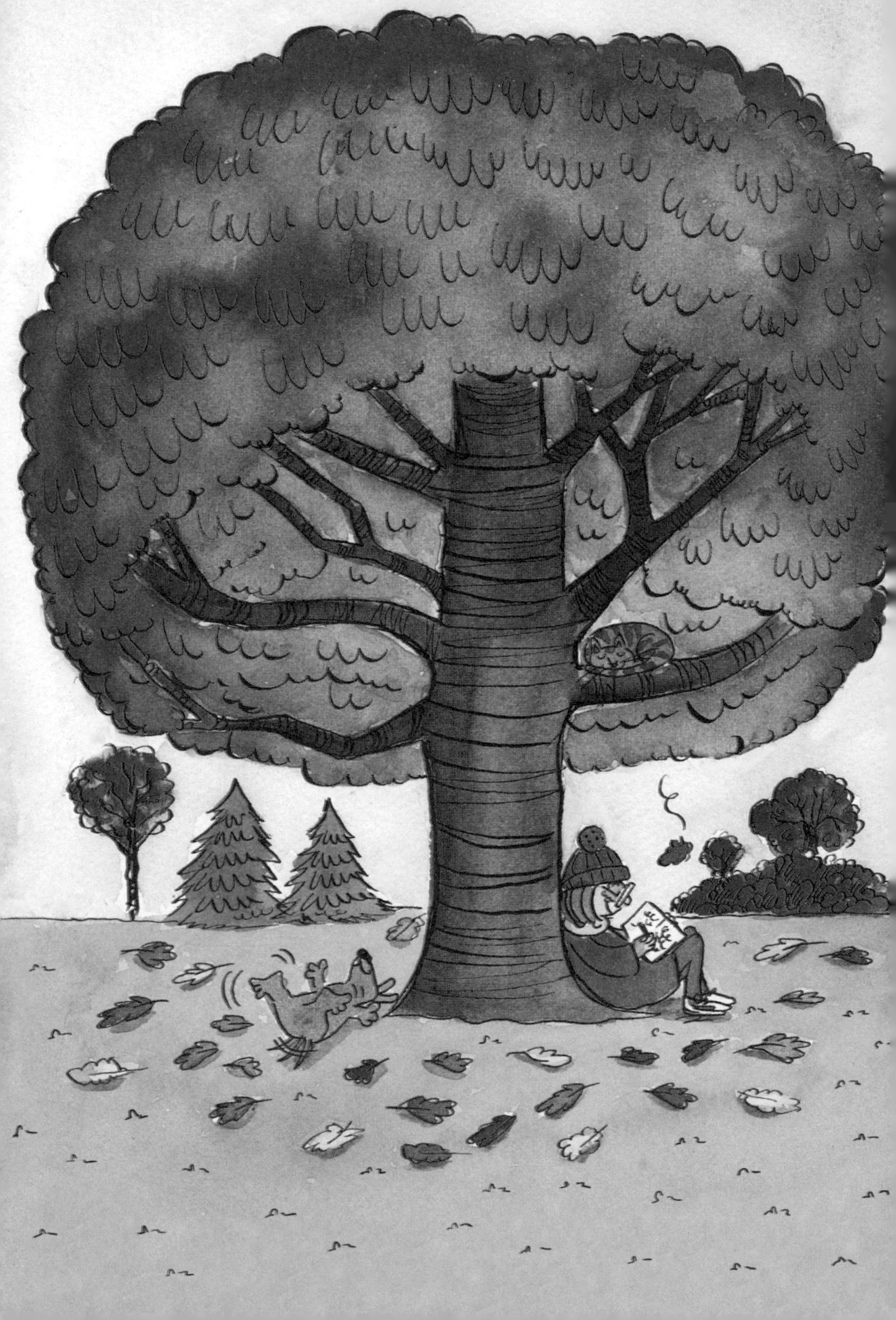

CHAPTER 13
ABOUT TIME

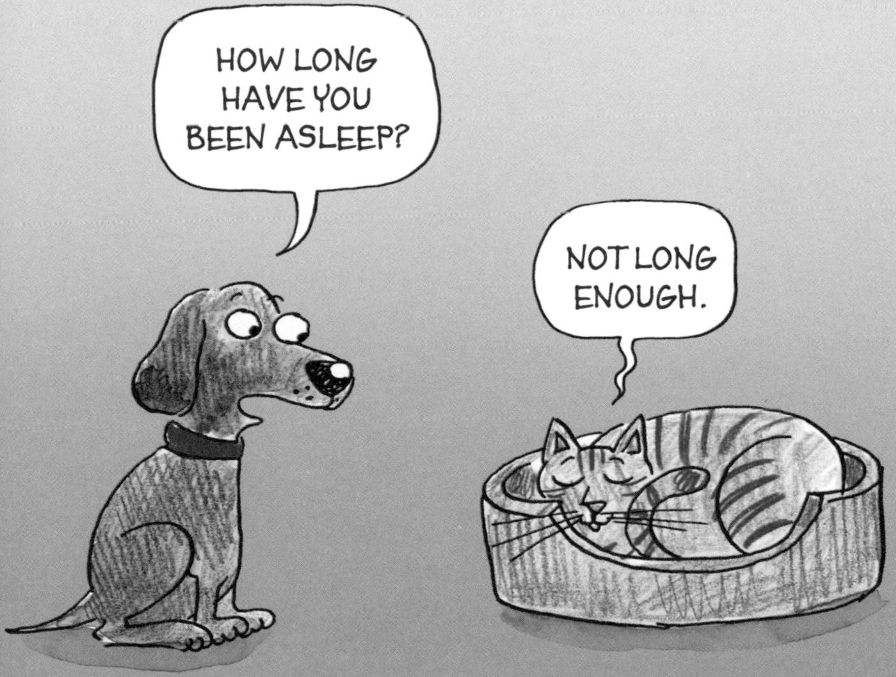
HOW LONG HAVE YOU BEEN ASLEEP?
NOT LONG ENOUGH.

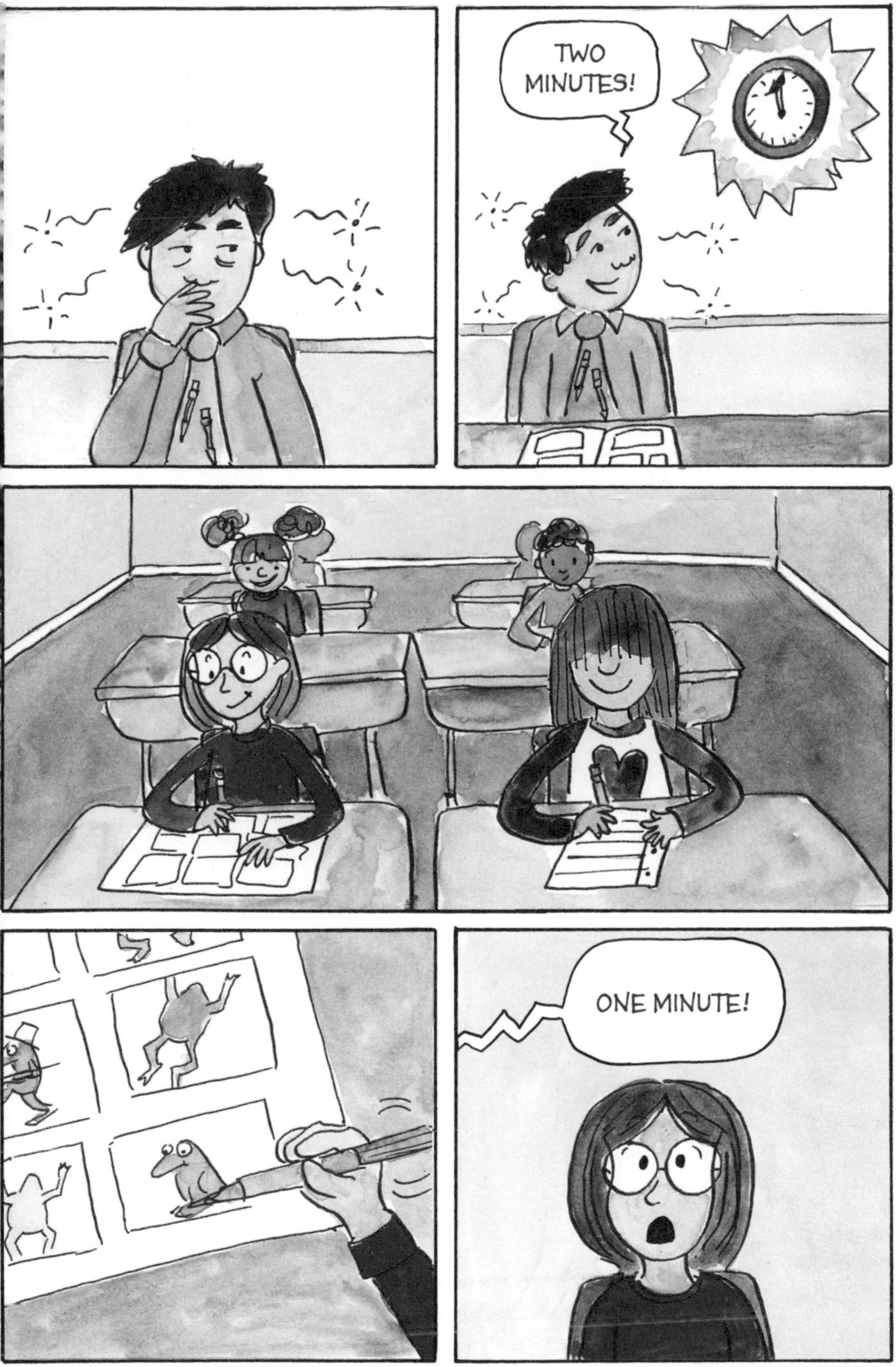
TWO MINUTES!
ONE MINUTE!

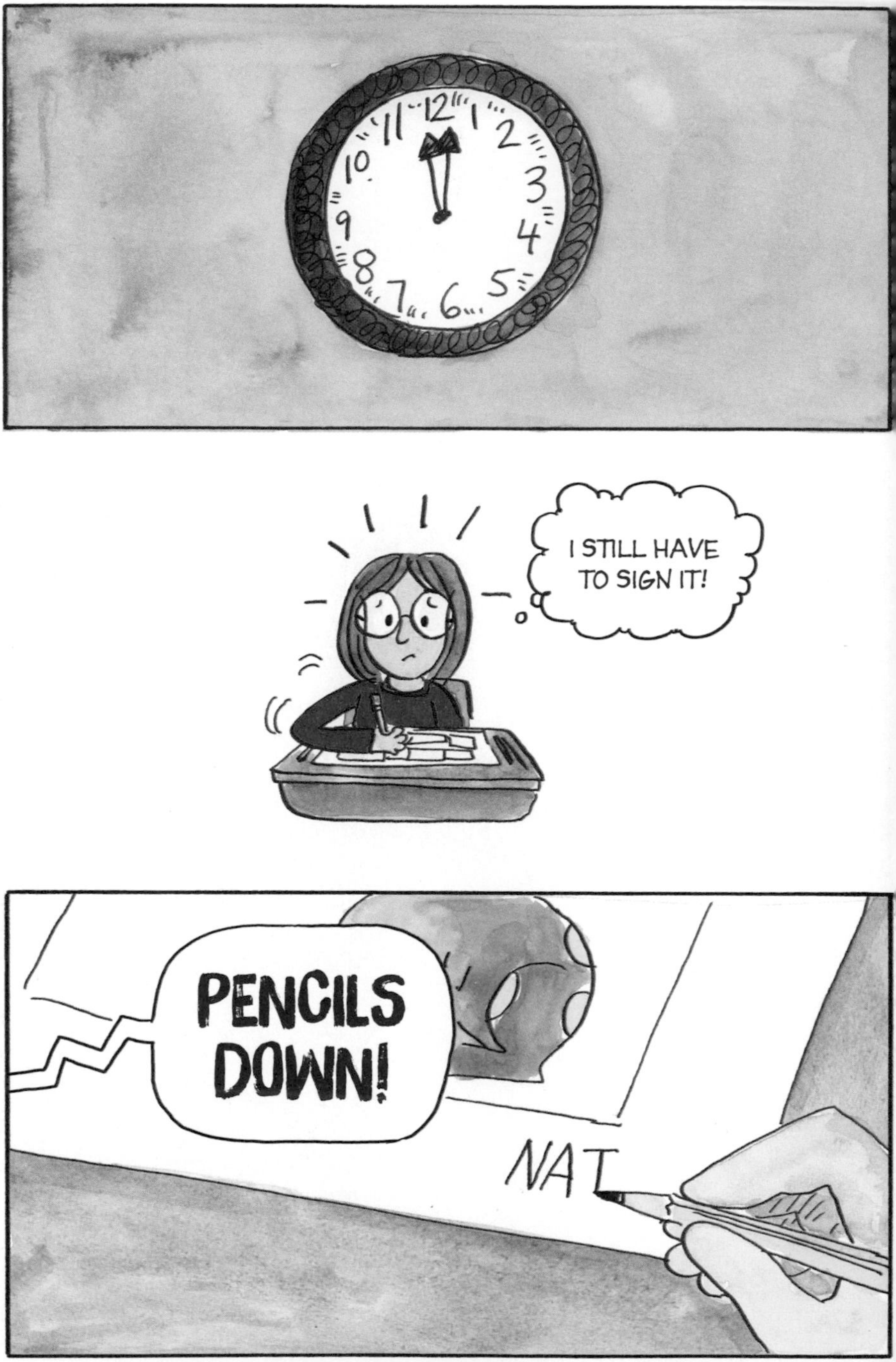
I STILL HAVE TO SIGN IT!
PENCILS DOWN!
NAT

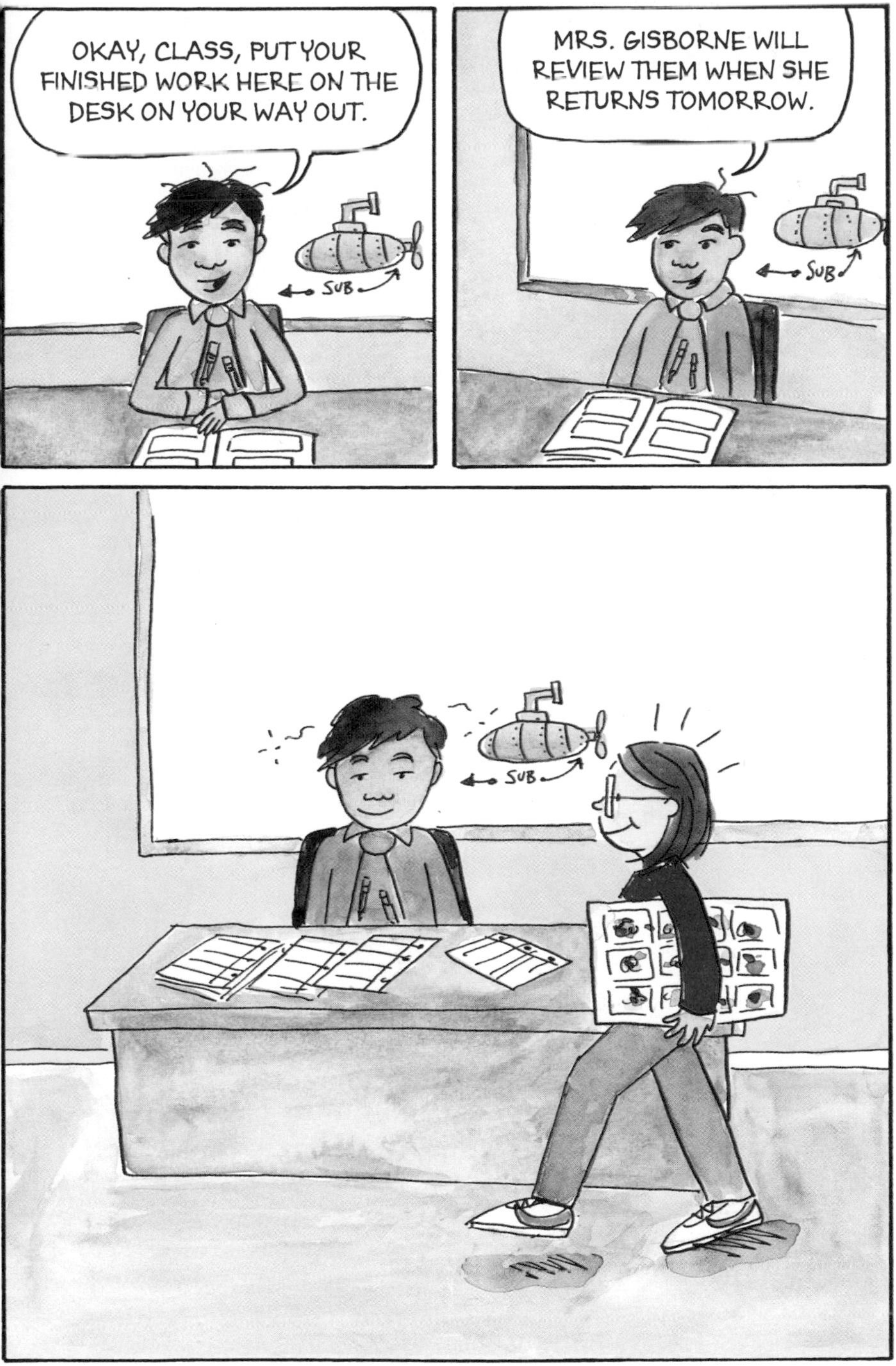
OKAY, CLASS, PUT YOUR FINISHED WORK HERE ON THE DESK ON YOUR WAY OUT.
SUB
MRS. GISBORNE WILL REVIEW THEM WHEN SHE RETURNS TOMORROW.
SUB
SUB

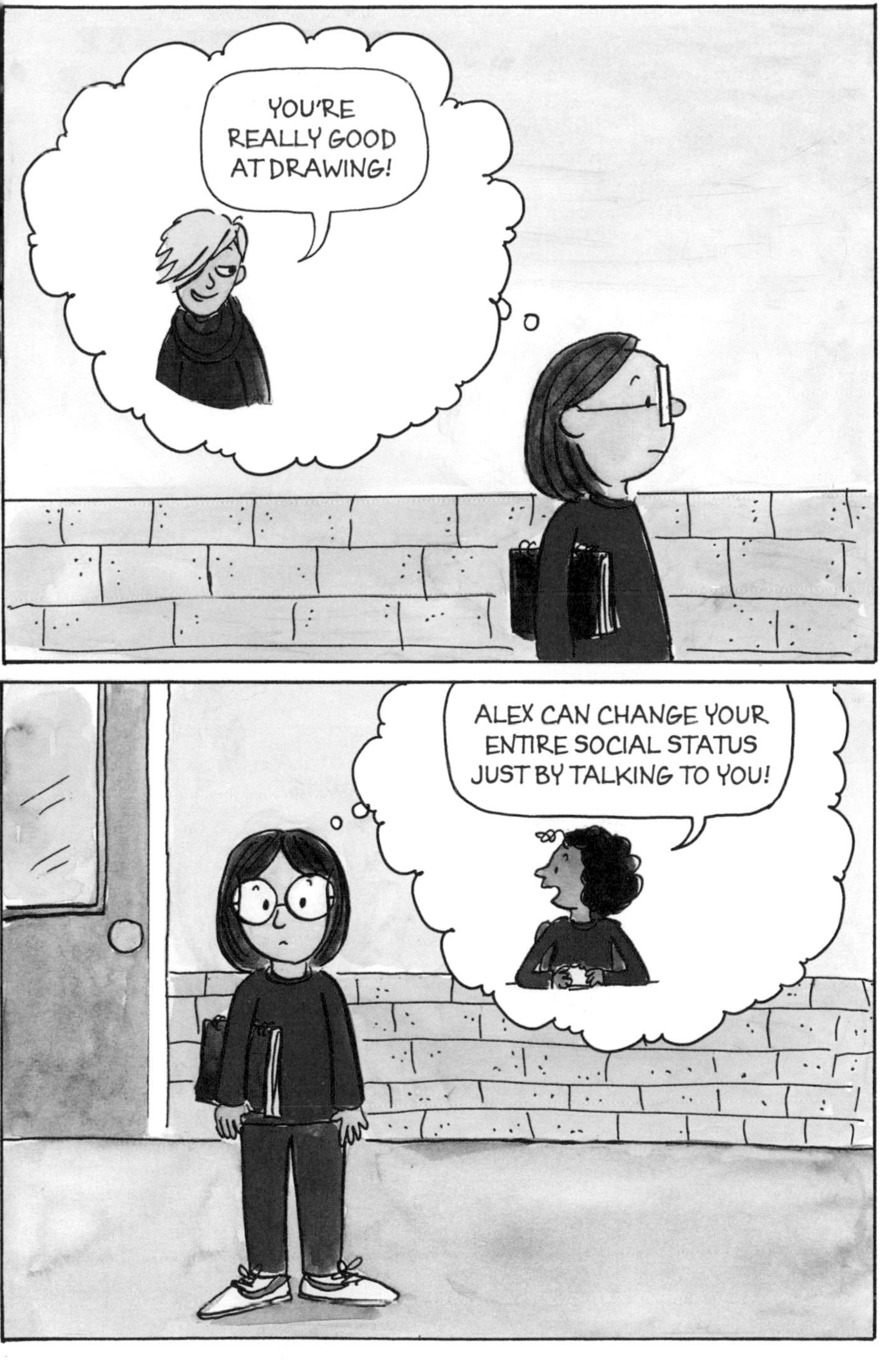
YOU'RE REALLY GOOD AT DRAWING!
ALEX CAN CHANGE YOUR ENTIRE SOCIAL STATUS JUST BY TALKING TO YOU!

I COULDN'T WAIT TO GO TO SCHOOL THE NEXT DAY TO SHARE MY STORY WITH THE CLASS.

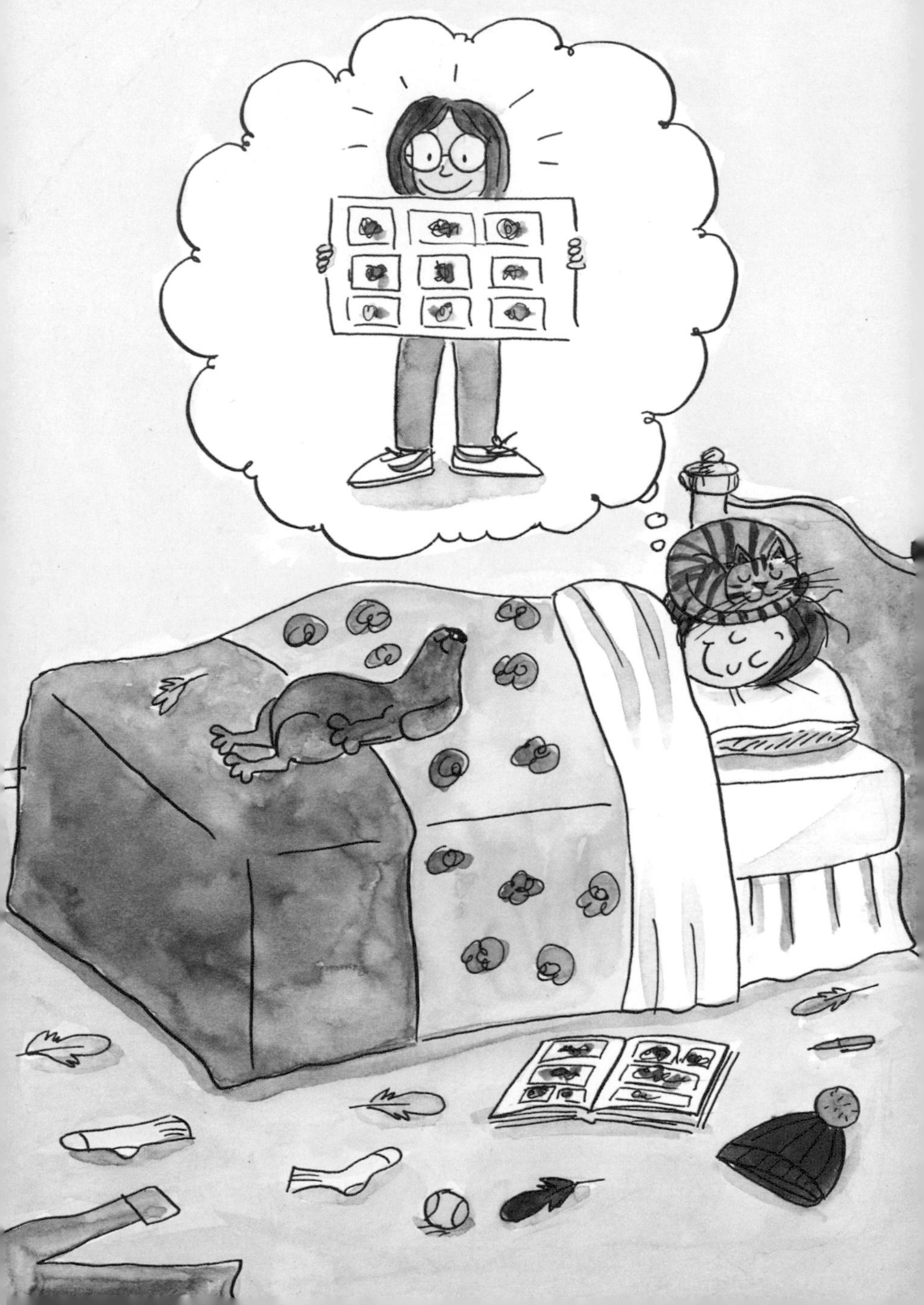

CHAPTER 14
WHAT'S THE STORY?

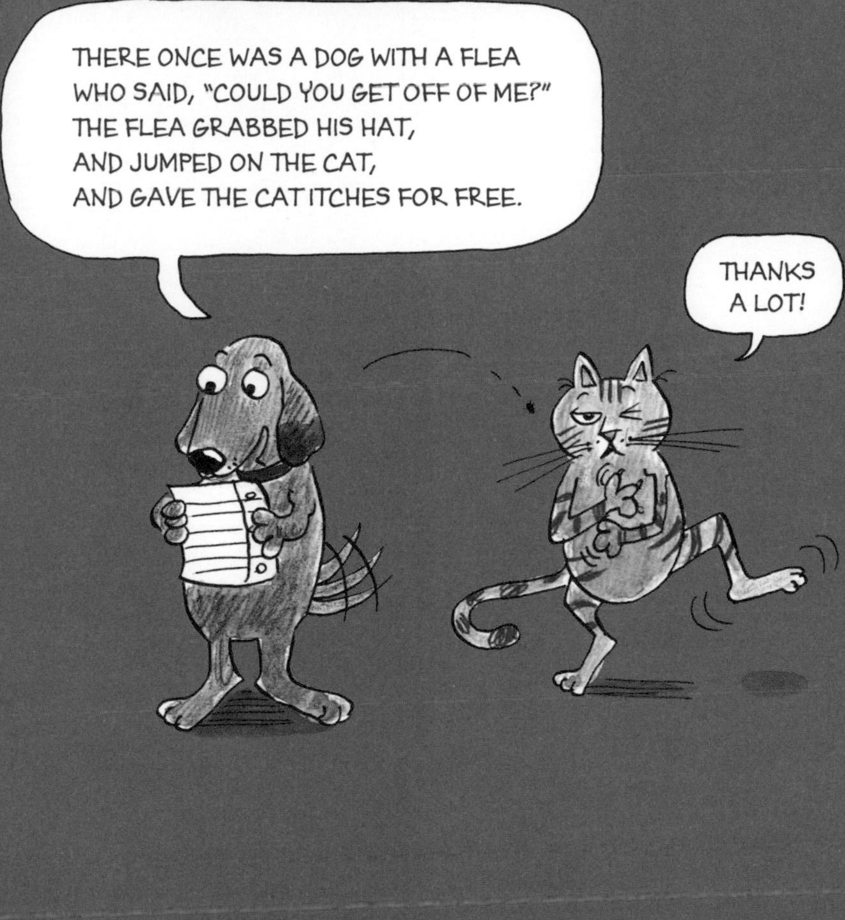
THERE ONCE WAS A DOG WITH A FLEA
WHO SAID, "COULD YOU GET OFF OF ME?"
THE FLEA GRABBED HIS HAT,
AND JUMPED ON THE CAT,
AND GAVE THE CAT ITCHES FOR FREE.
THANKS A LOT!

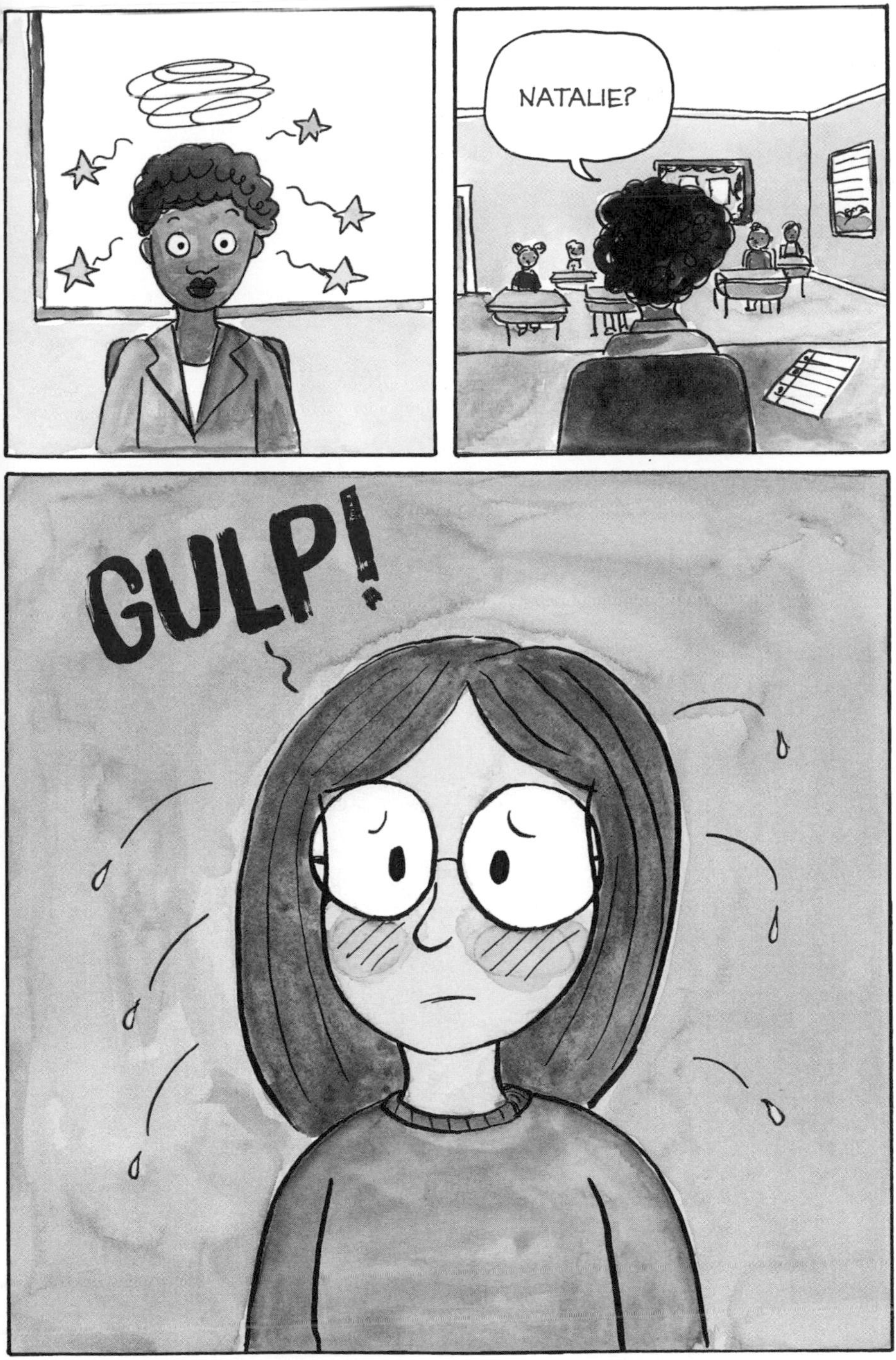
NATALIE?
GULP!

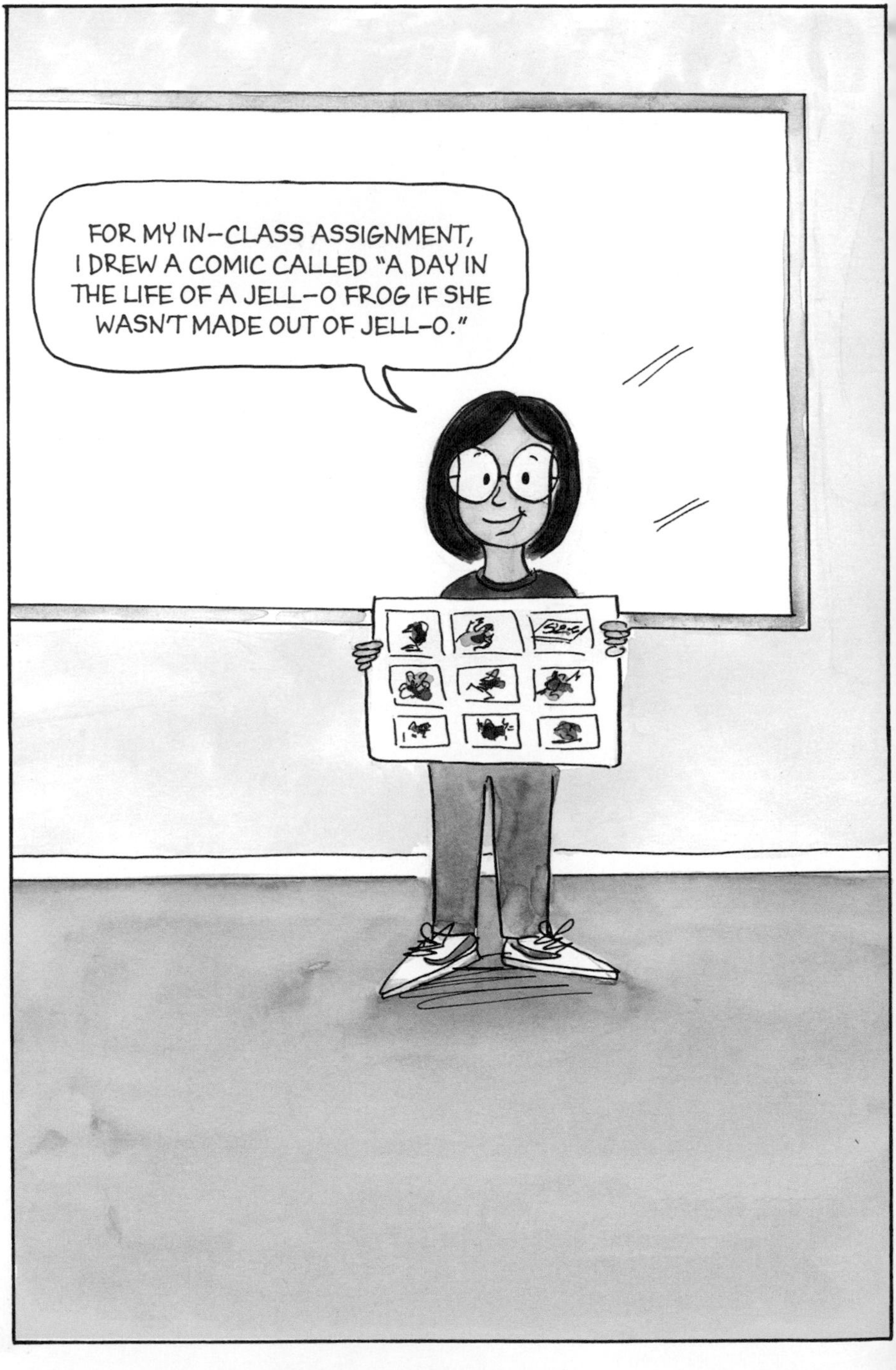
FOR MY IN-CLASS ASSIGNMENT, I DREW A COMIC CALLED "A DAY IN THE LIFE OF A JELL-O FROG IF SHE WASN'T MADE OUT OF JELL-O."

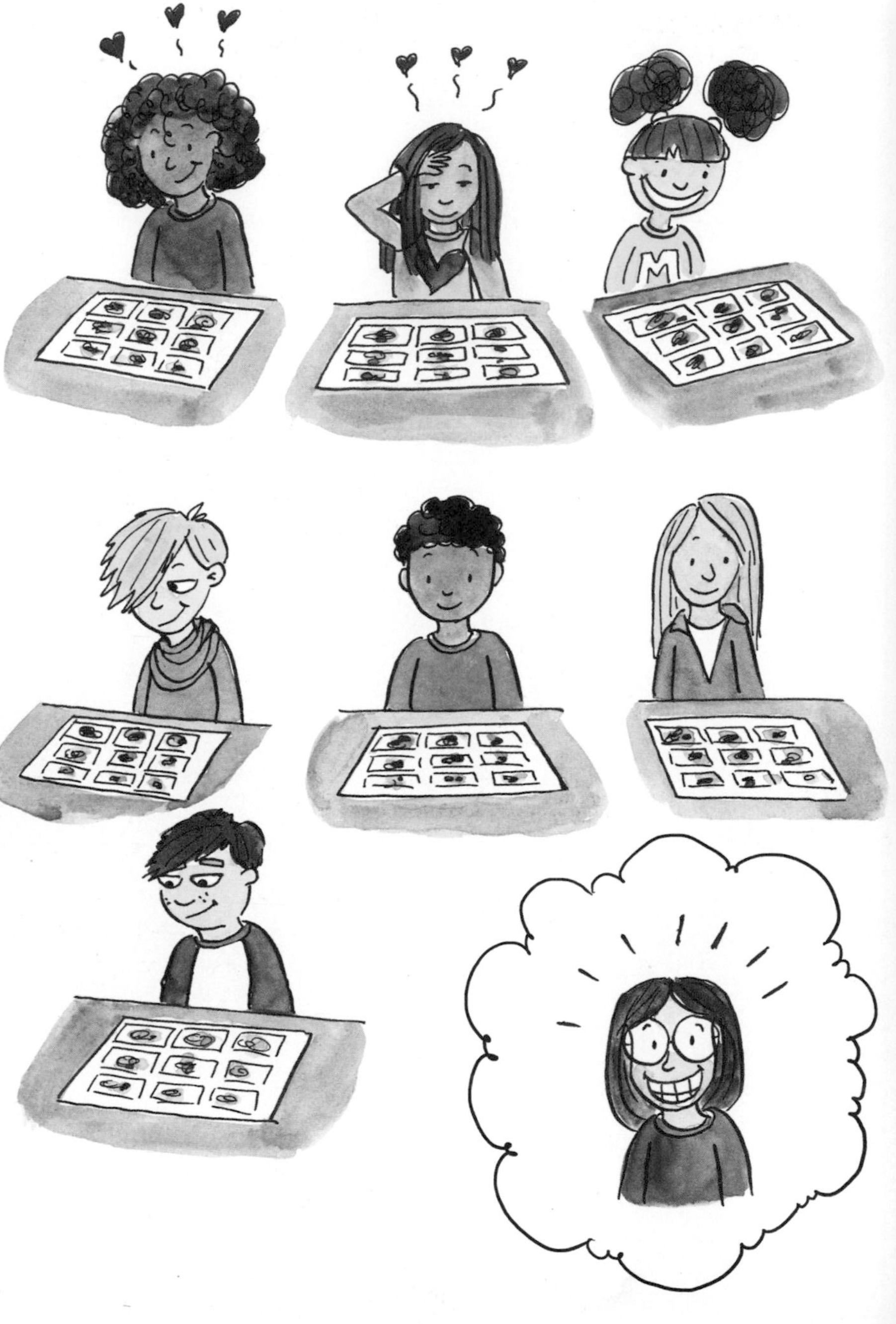

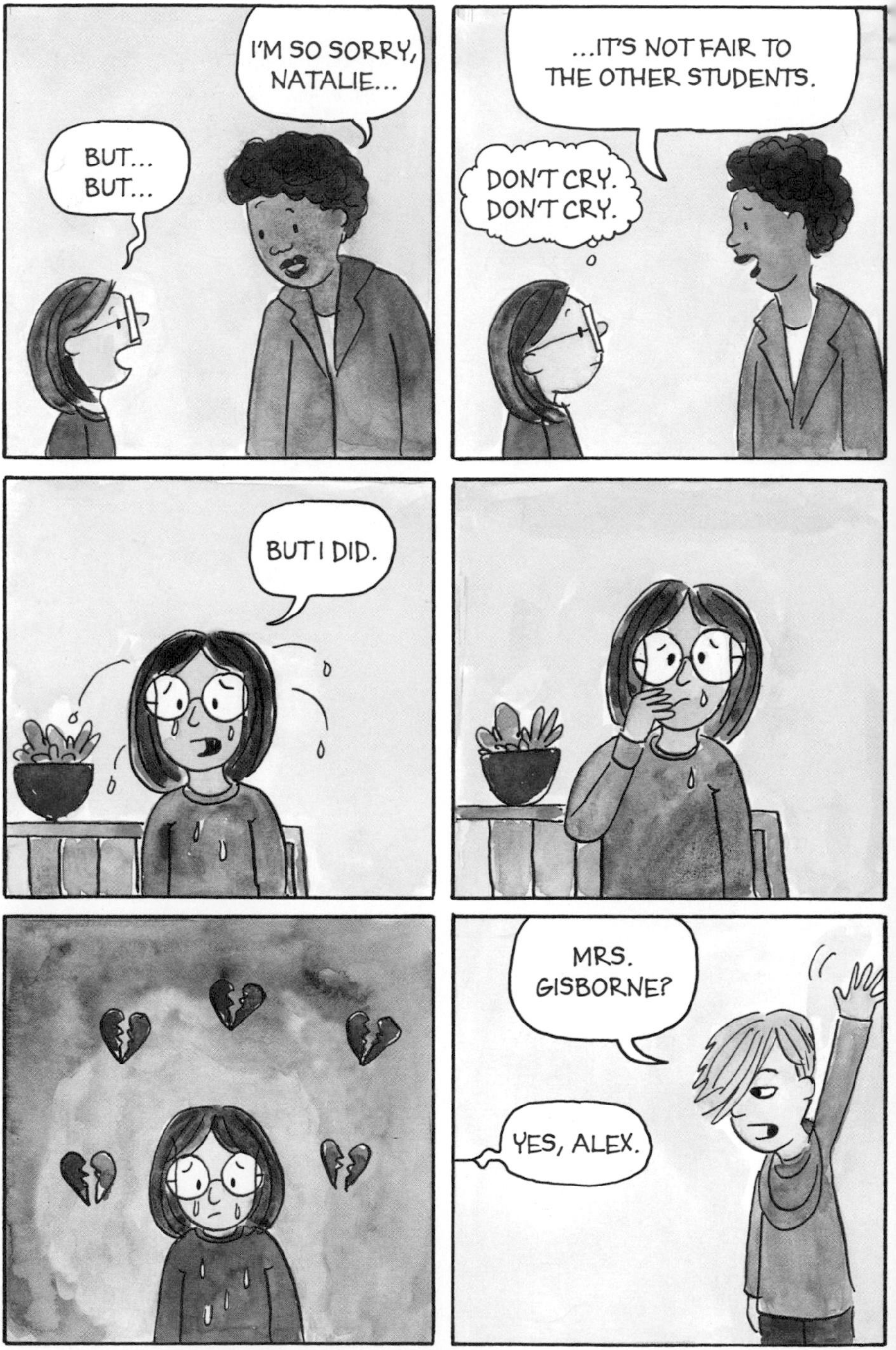
I'M SO SORRY, NATALIE...
BUT... BUT...
...IT'S NOT FAIR TO THE OTHER STUDENTS.
DON'T CRY. DON'T CRY.
BUT I DID.
MRS. GISBORNE?
YES, ALEX.

189

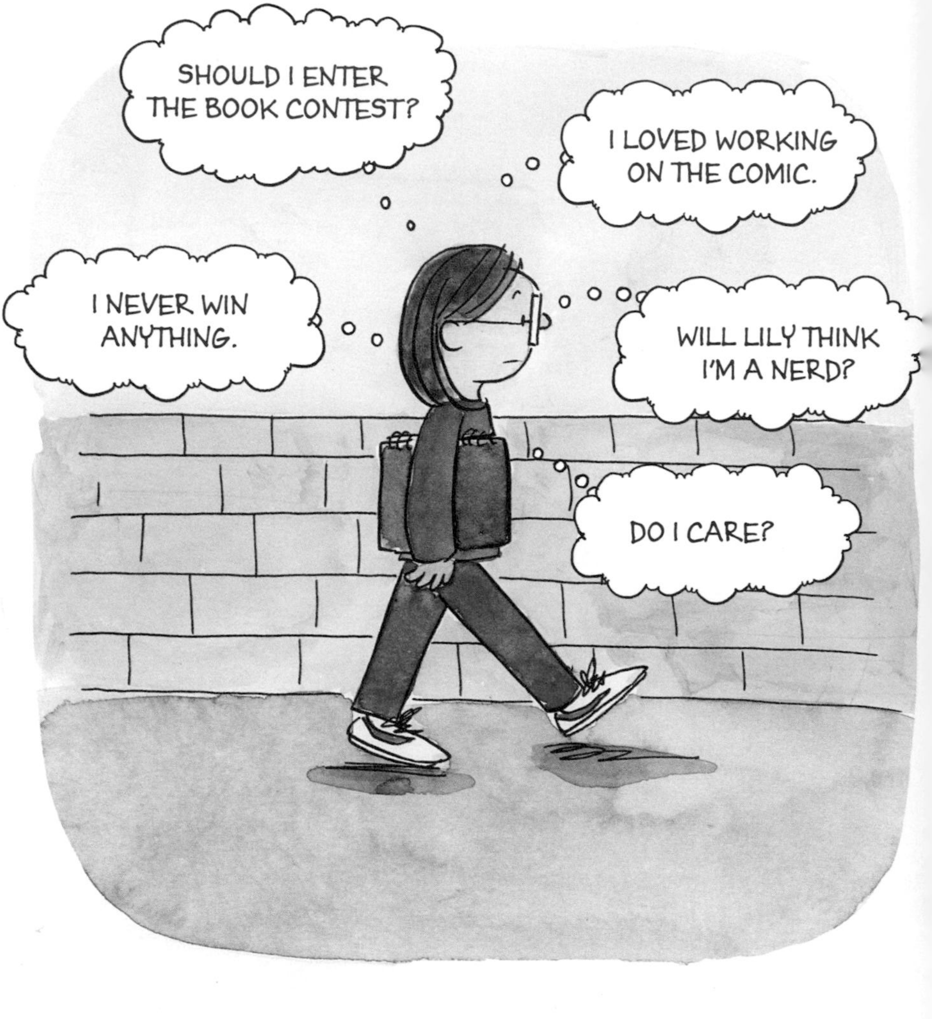
SHOULD I ENTER THE BOOK CONTEST?
I LOVED WORKING ON THE COMIC.
I NEVER WIN ANYTHING.
WILL LILY THINK I'M A NERD?
DO I CARE?

CHAPTER 15
WHAT'S FOR LUNCH?

LUNCHROOM FOOD

MYSTERY MEAT

MYSTERY NUGGET

MYSTERY FRUIT

PIZZA

ANIMAL FOOD

TALK ABOUT A MYSTERY...

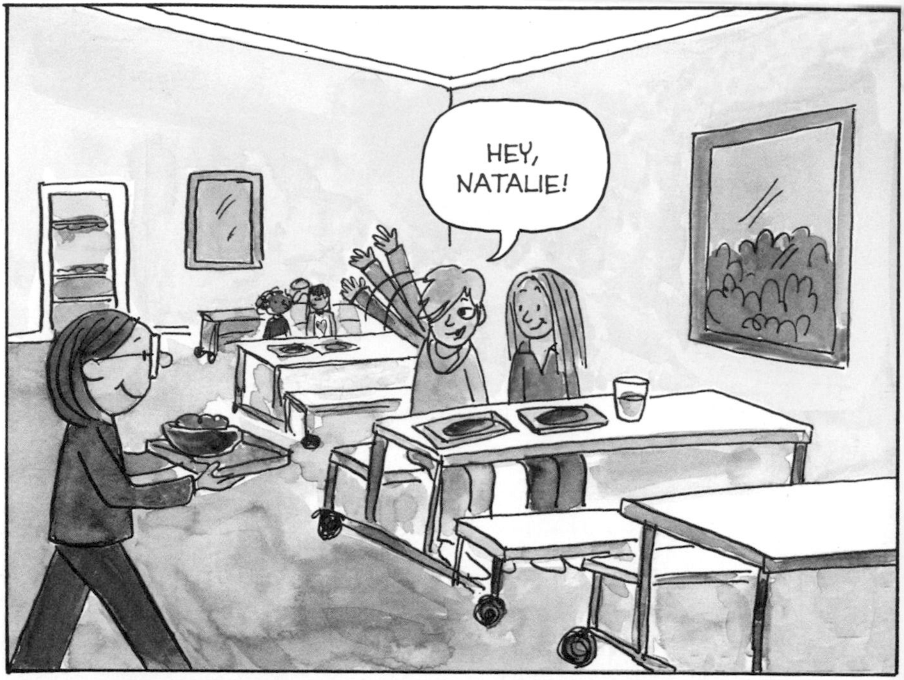
HEY, NATALIE!

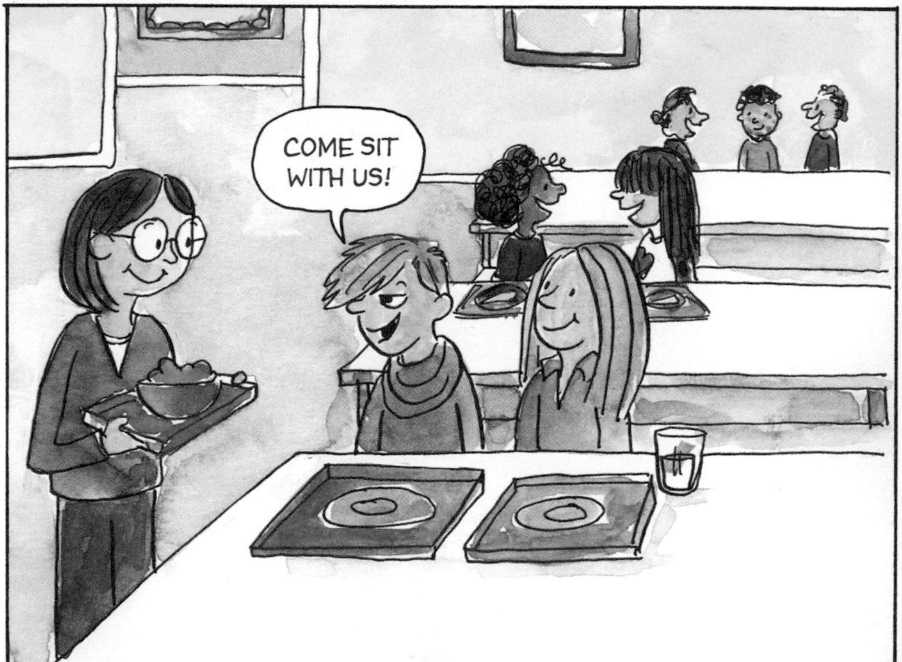
COME SIT WITH US!

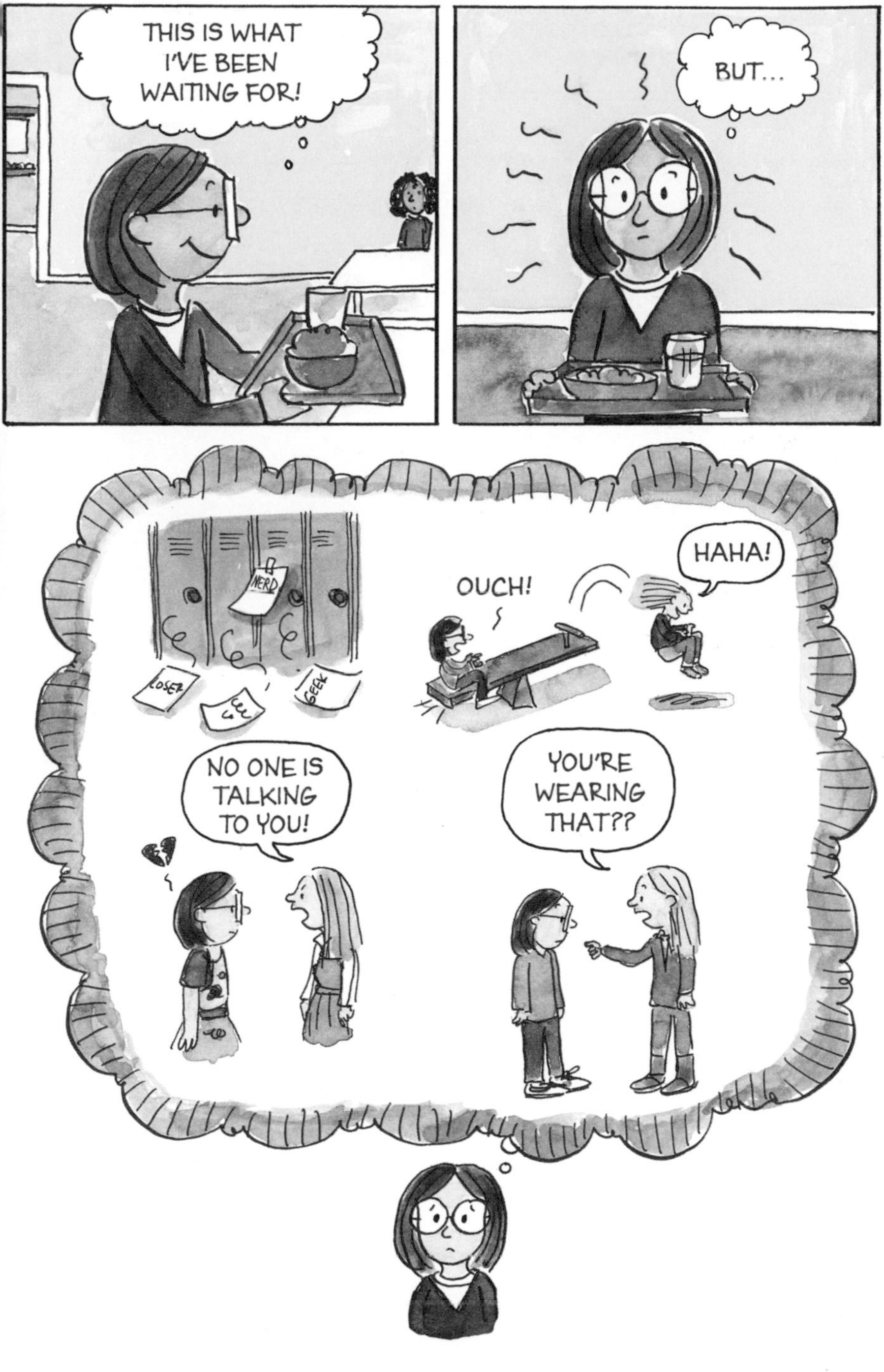
THIS IS WHAT I'VE BEEN WAITING FOR!
BUT...
NERD
LOSER
GEEK
OUCH!
HAHA!
NO ONE IS TALKING TO YOU!
YOU'RE WEARING THAT??

OR...

CHAPTER 16

THE ENVELOPE, PLEASE

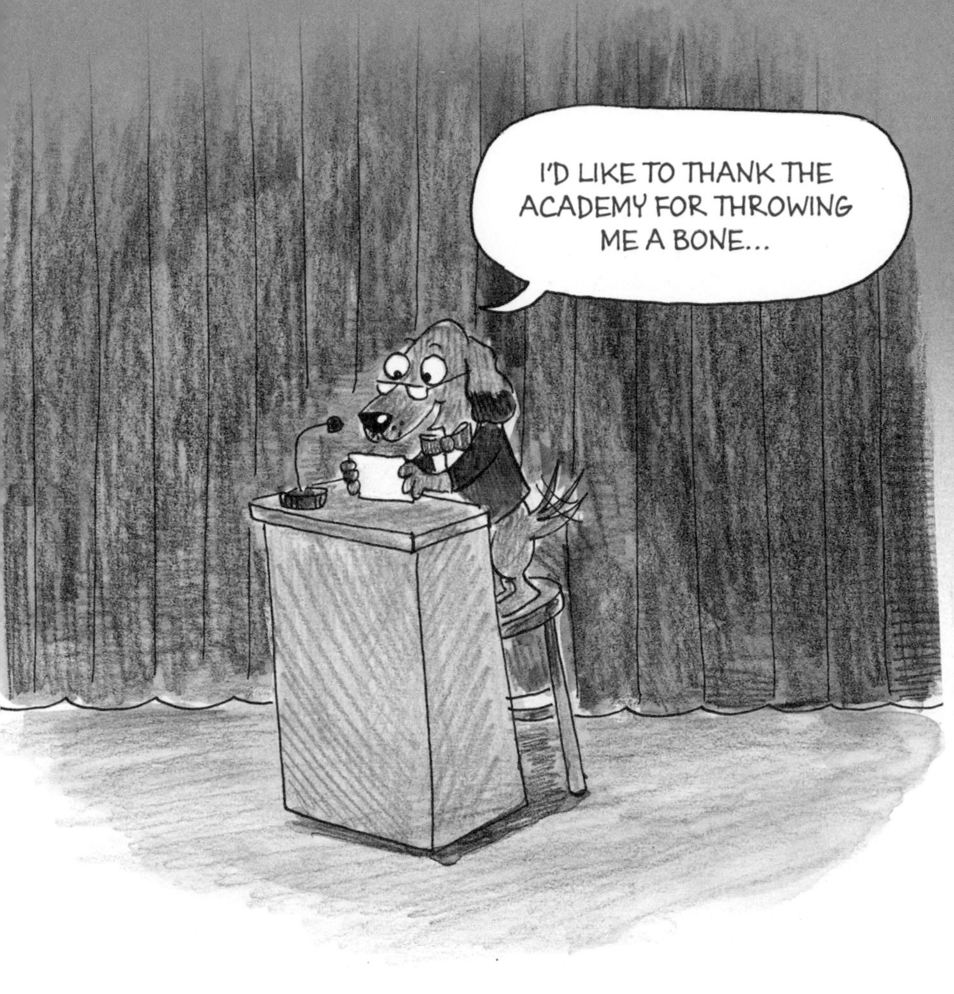

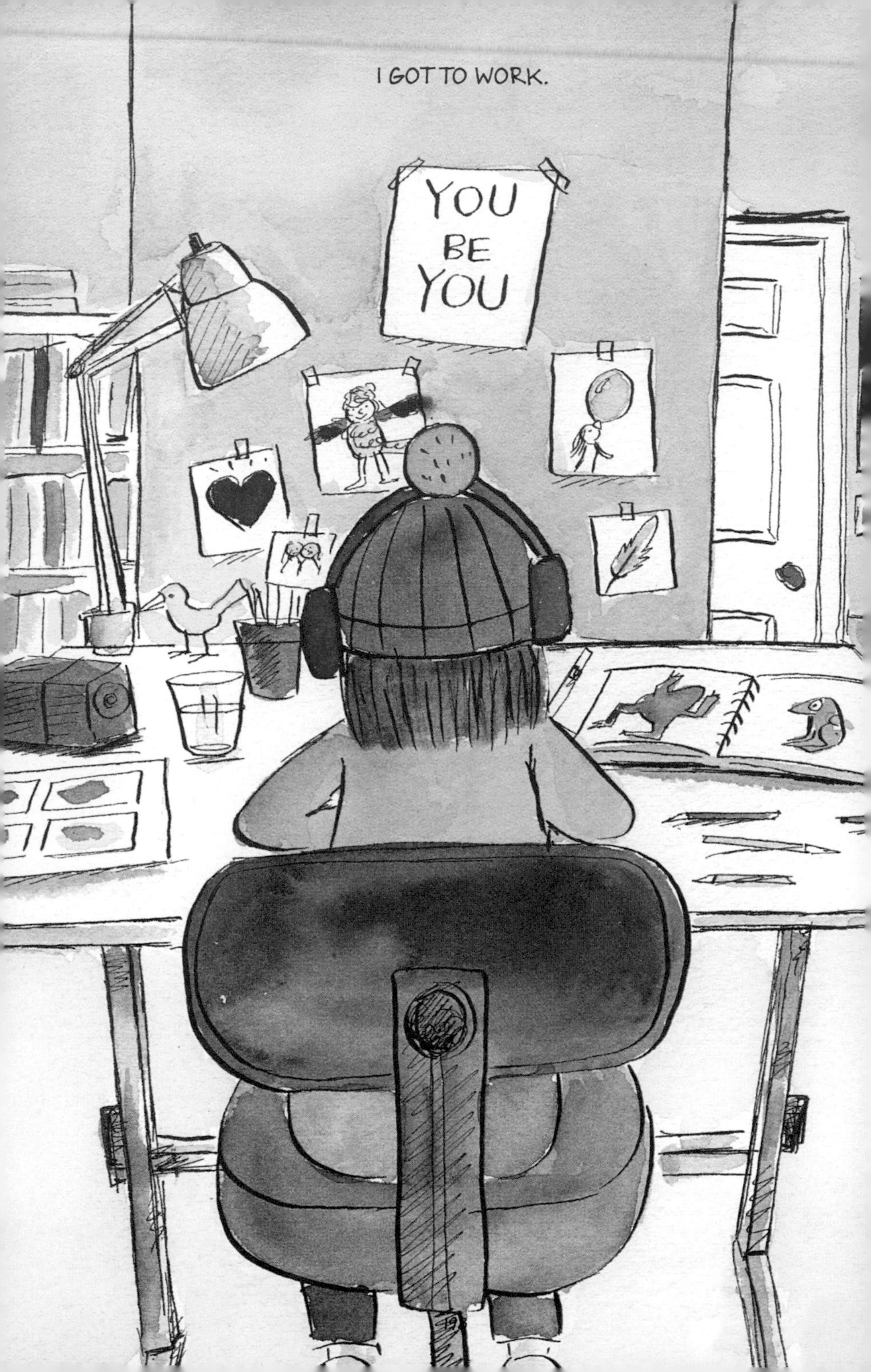
I GOT TO WORK.
YOU BE YOU

HOW TO MAKE A BOOK:

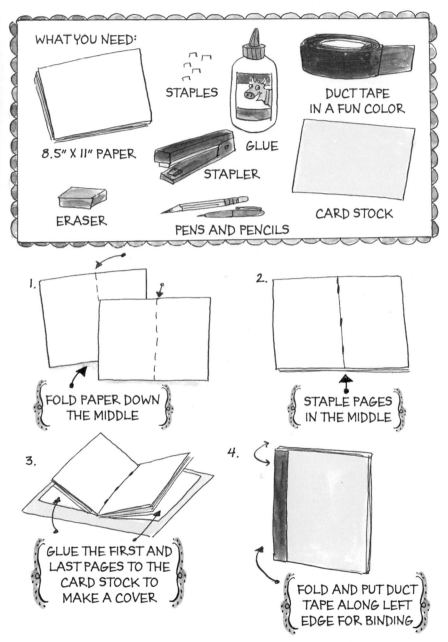

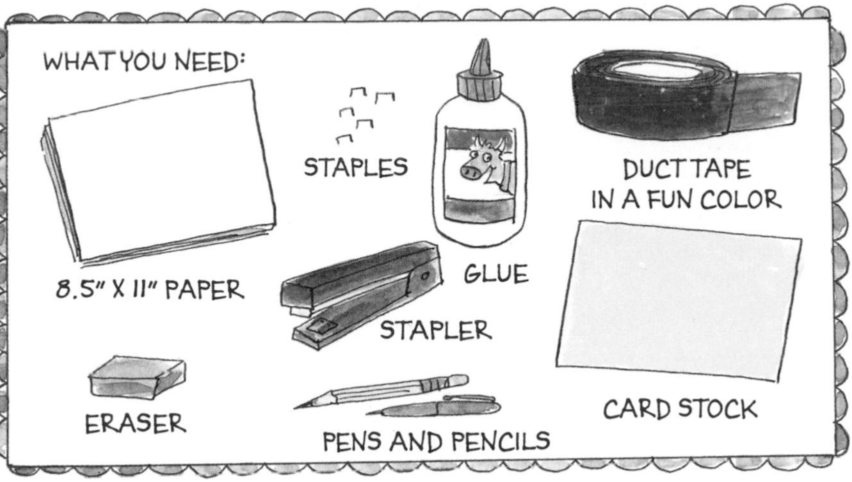
WHAT YOU NEED:
8.5" X 11" PAPER
STAPLES
GLUE
DUCT TAPE
IN A FUN COLOR
STAPLER
CARD STOCK
ERASER
PENS AND PENCILS

1.

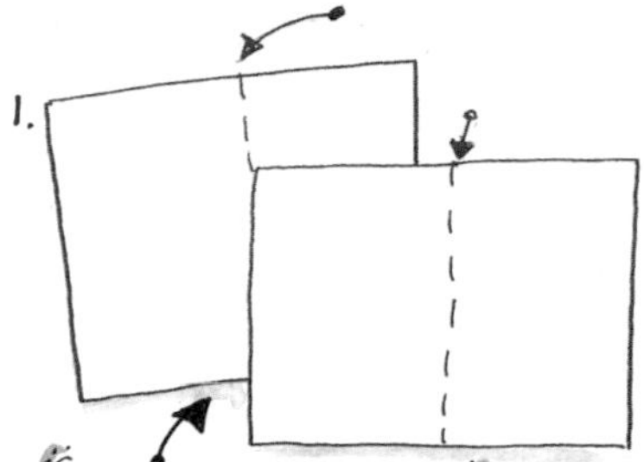

FOLD PAPER DOWN THE MIDDLE

2.

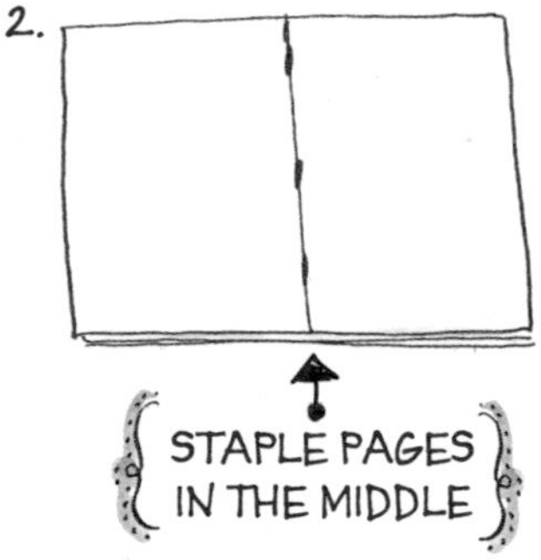

STAPLE PAGES IN THE MIDDLE

3.

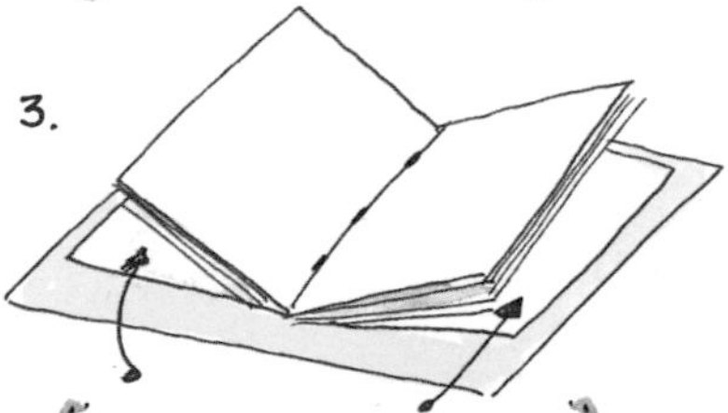

GLUE THE FIRST AND LAST PAGES TO THE CARD STOCK TO MAKE A COVER

4.

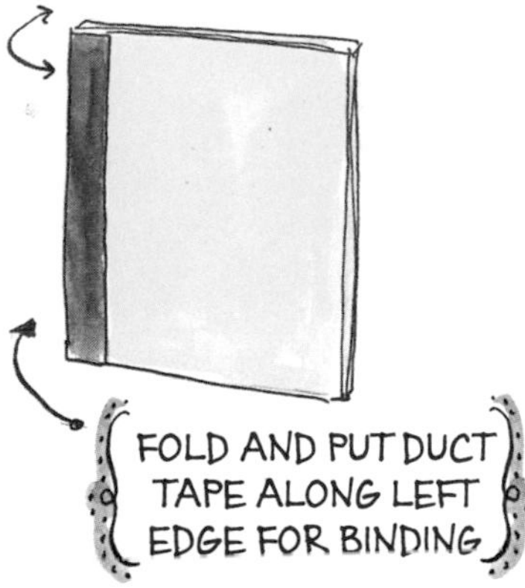

FOLD AND PUT DUCT TAPE ALONG LEFT EDGE FOR BINDING

5. HAVE FUN WRITING AND DRAWING YOUR BOOK!

THEN MRS. GISBORNE HELPED ME MAIL MY BOOK INTO THE CONTEST. WE PUT IT IN A BIG ENVELOPE WITH CARDBOARD AND EXTRA STAMPS.

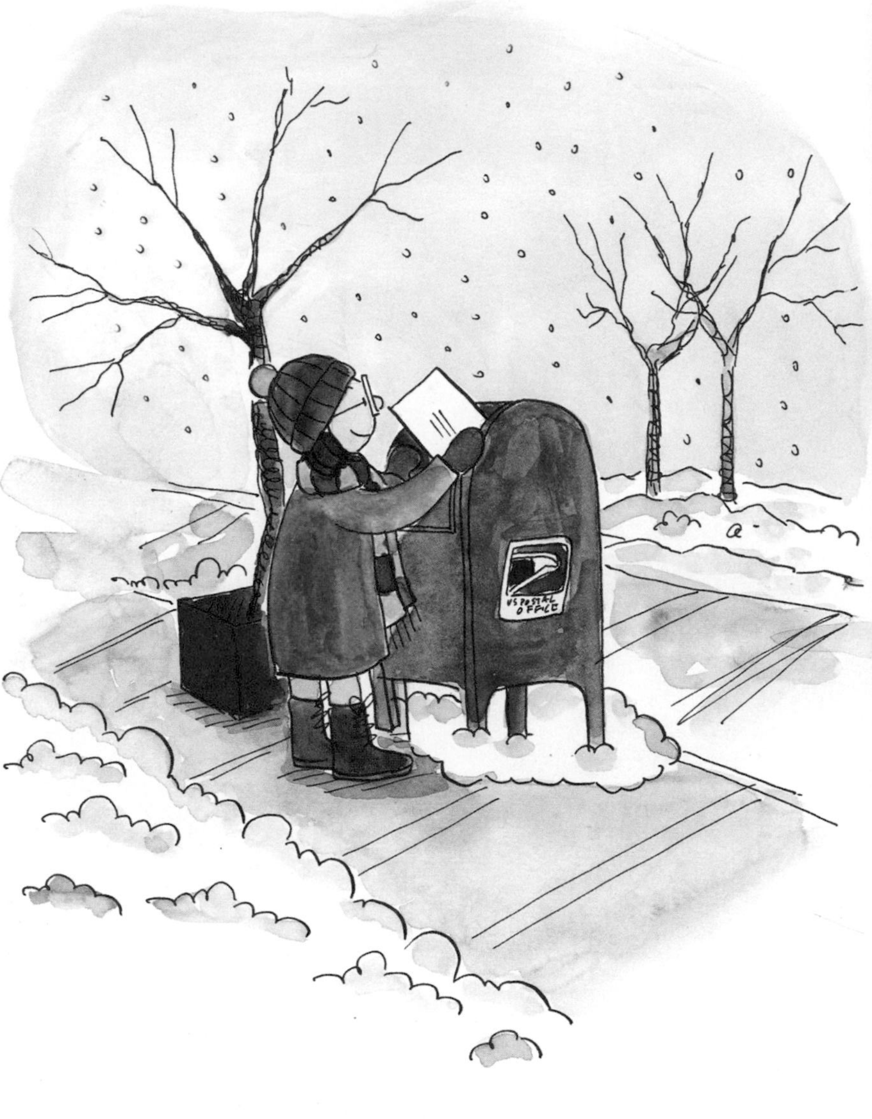

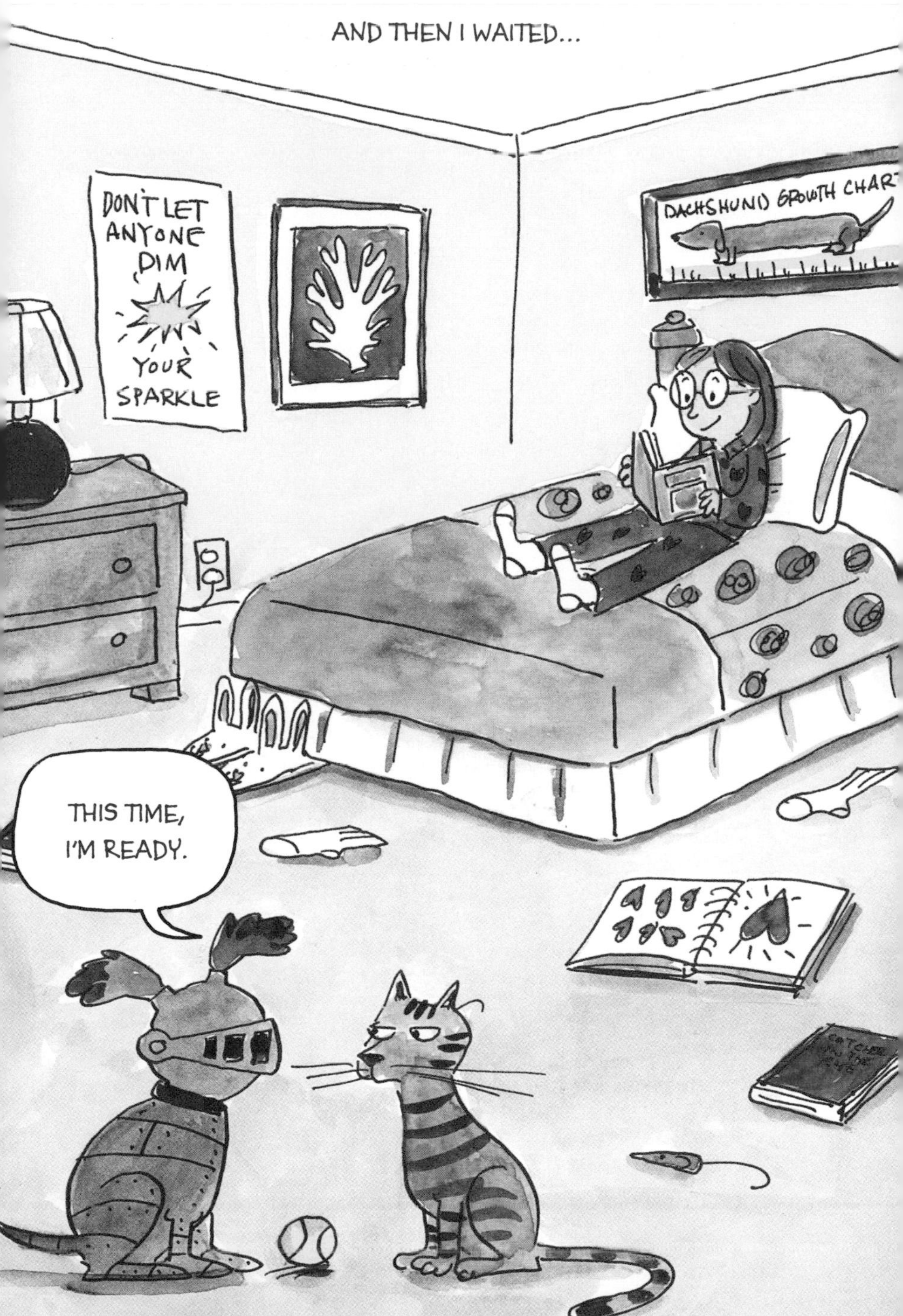
AND THEN I WAITED...
DON'T LET ANYONE DIM YOUR SPARKLE
DACHSHUND GROWTH CHART
THIS TIME, I'M READY.

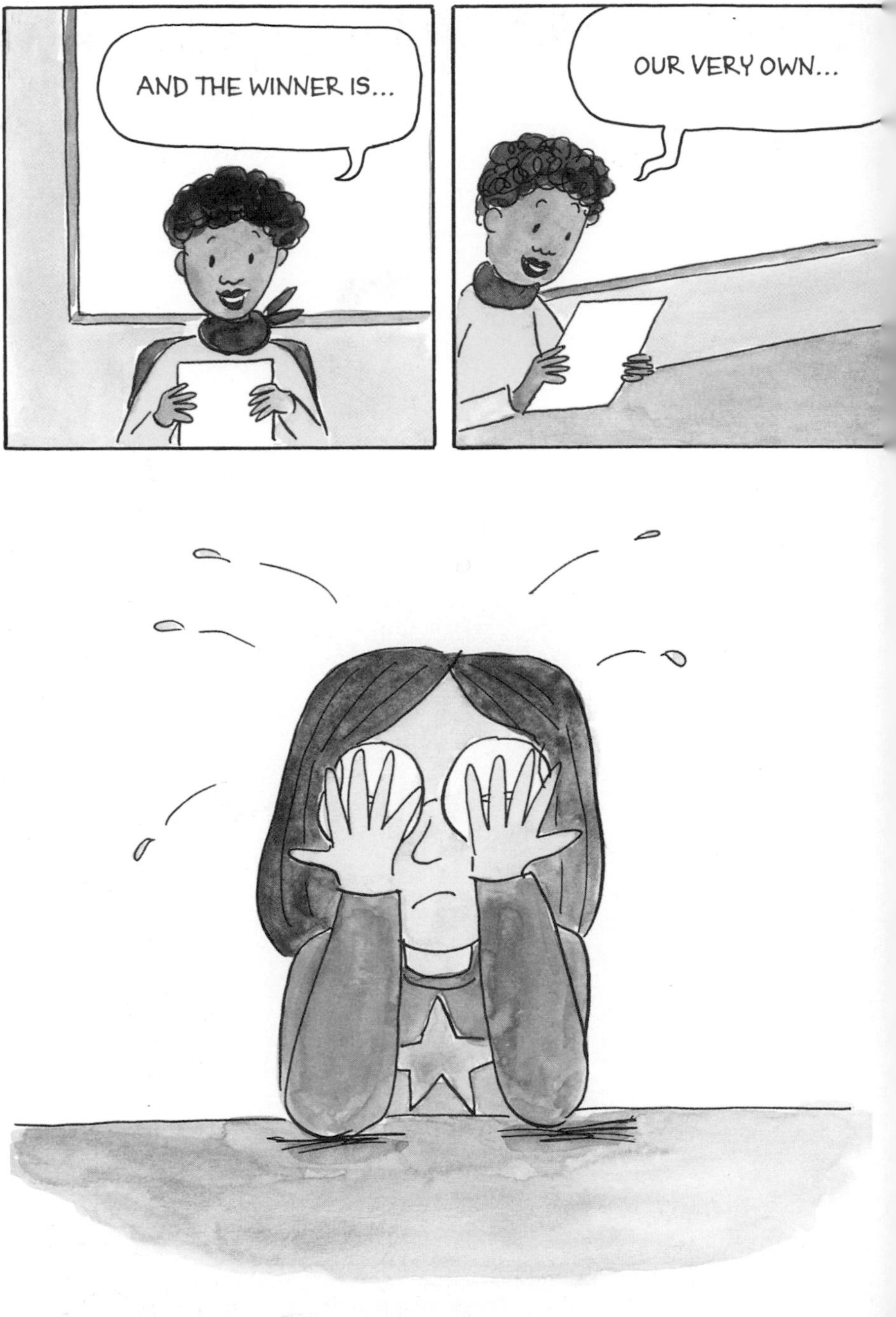
AND THE WINNER IS...
OUR VERY OWN...

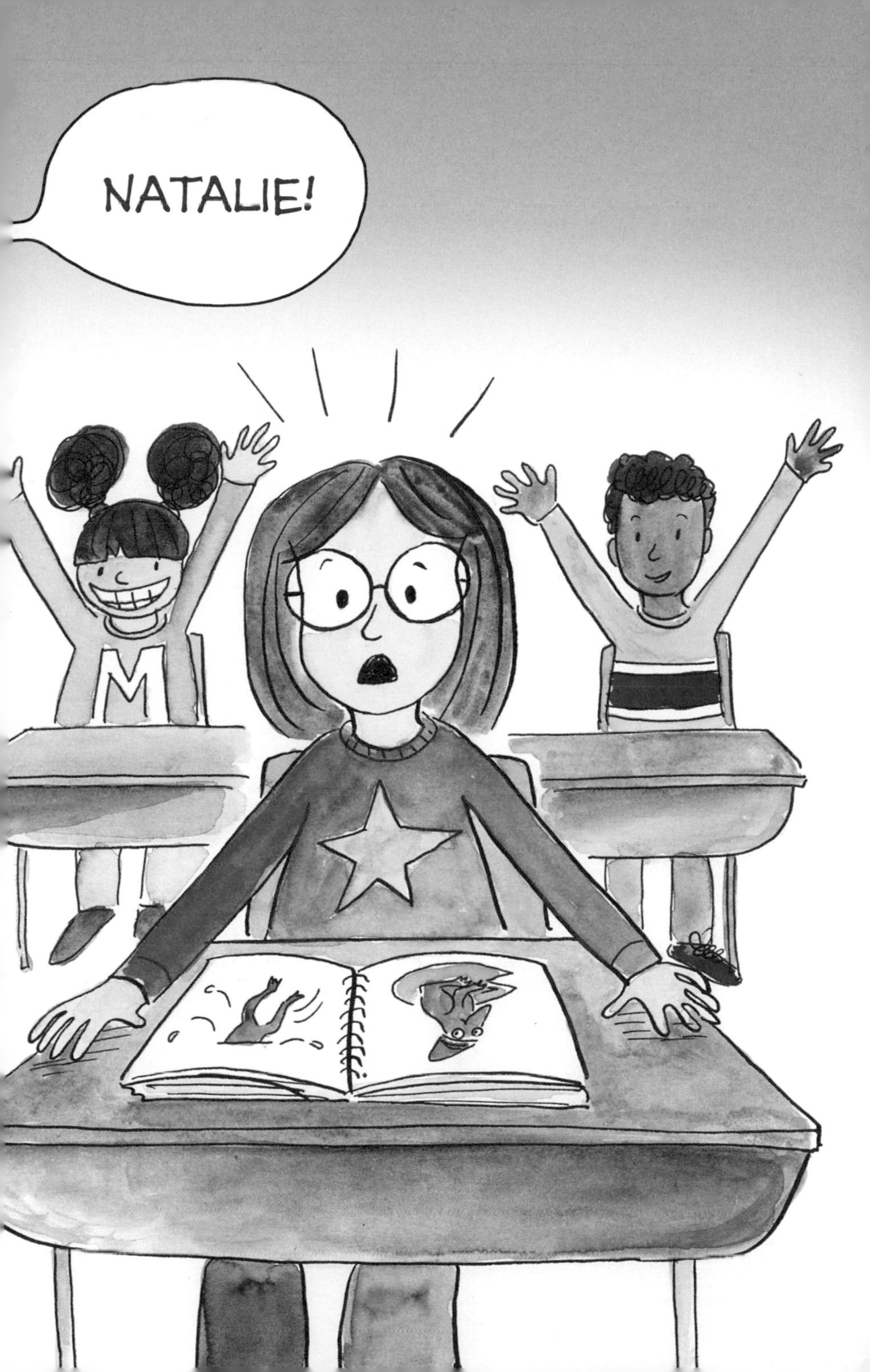
NATALIE!

I WENT TO THE STATE CAPITAL FOR THE AWARDS CEREMONY.

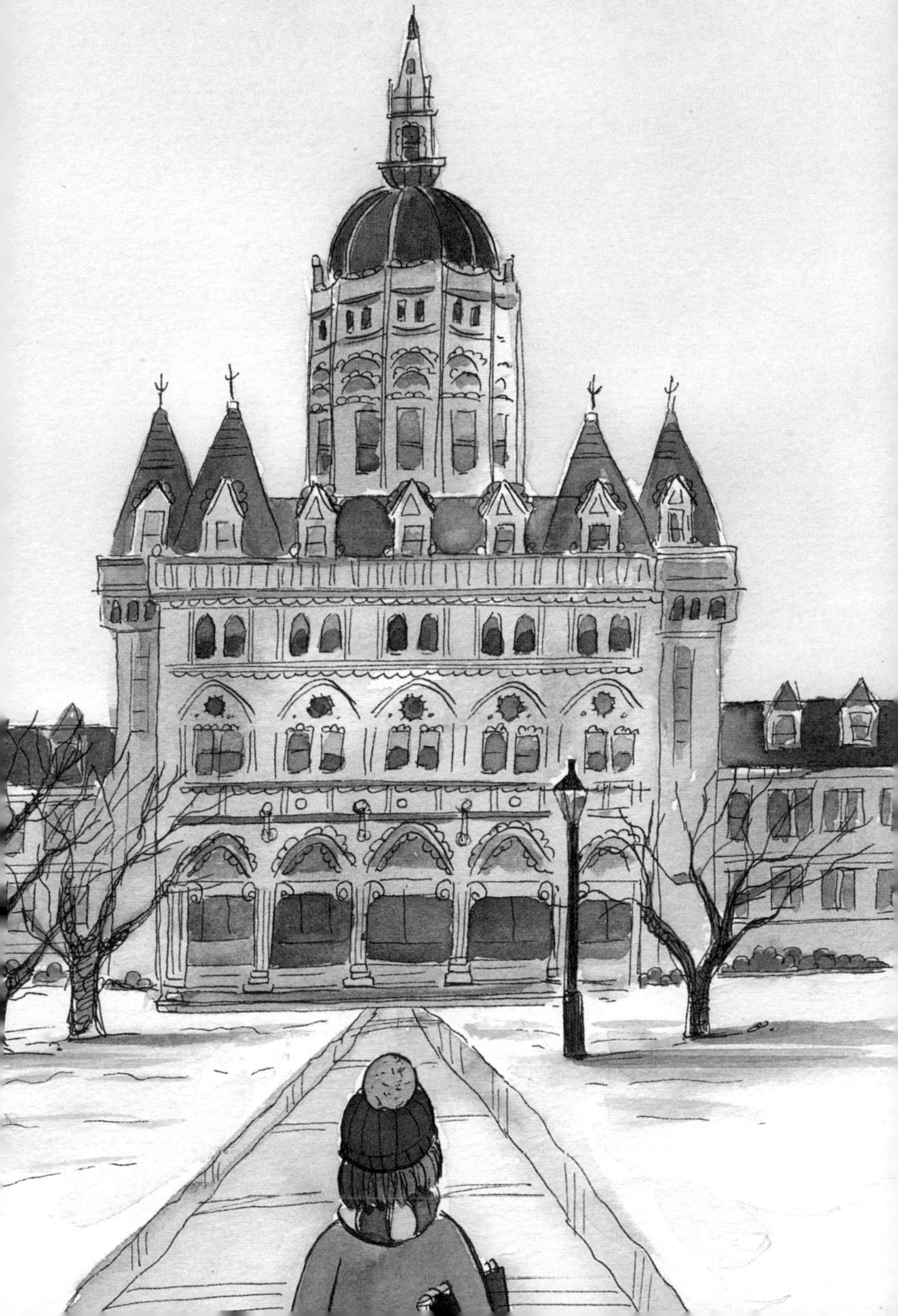

WE GOT OUR AWARDS AND TOOK PICTURES.
EVEN THE GOVERNOR WAS THERE!

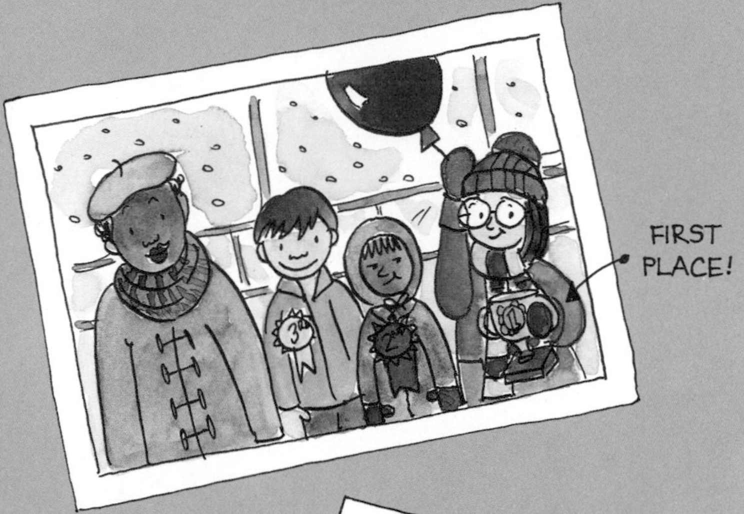
FIRST PLACE!

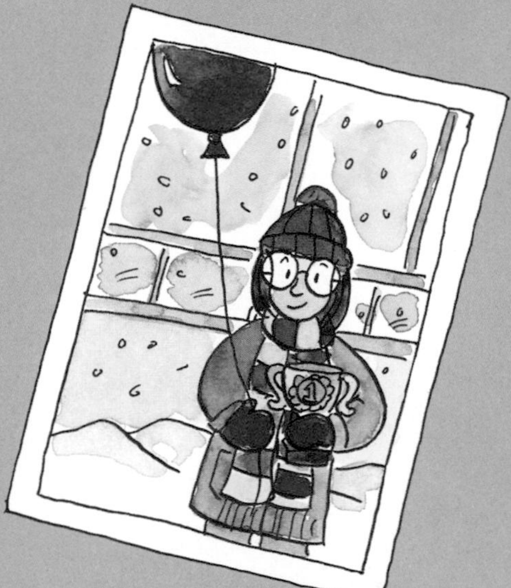

I DIDN'T MIND HAVING MY PICTURE TAKEN.
I DEFINITELY WANT A MEMORY OF TODAY!

MY FIRST PLACE TROPHY REALLY STOOD OUT IN MY SEA OF PARTICIPATION AWARDS.

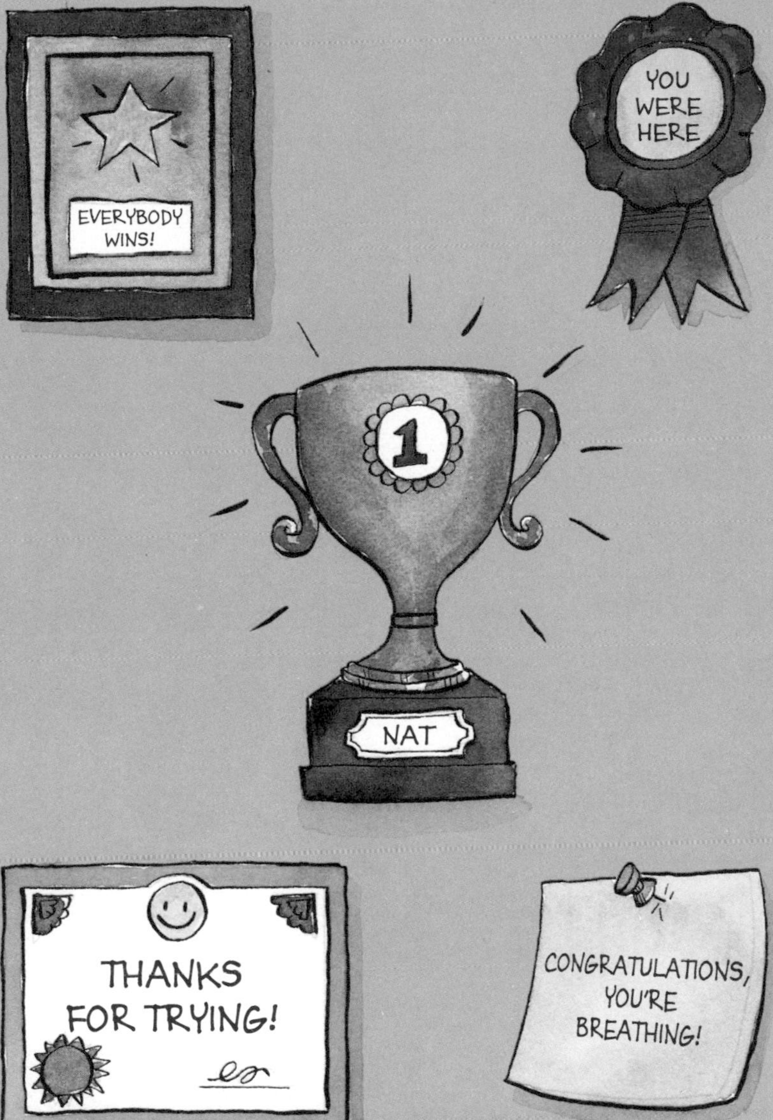
EVERYBODY WINS!
YOU WERE HERE
1
NAT
THANKS FOR TRYING!
CONGRATULATIONS, YOU'RE BREATHING!

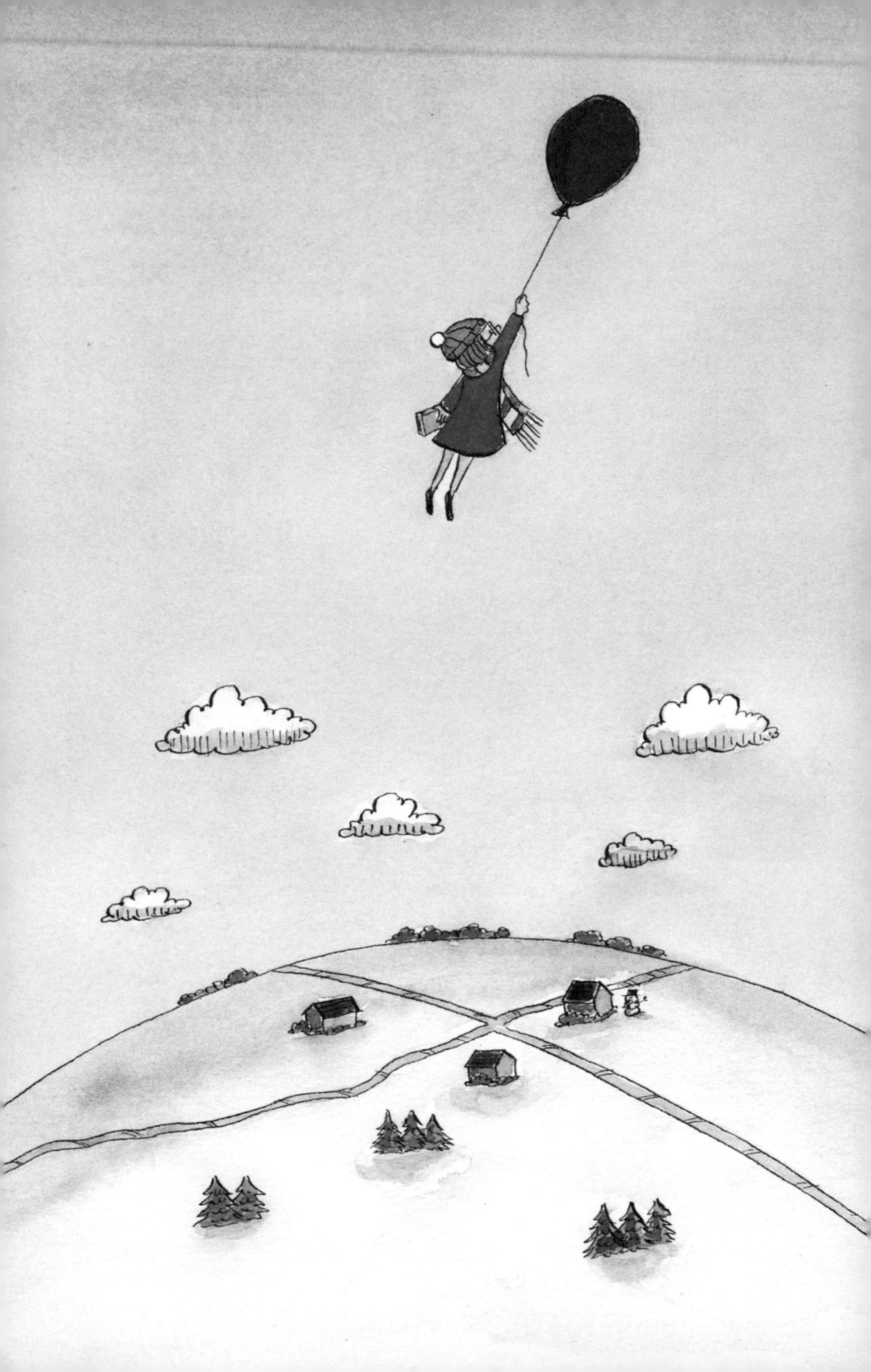

CHAPTER 17
STAND UP

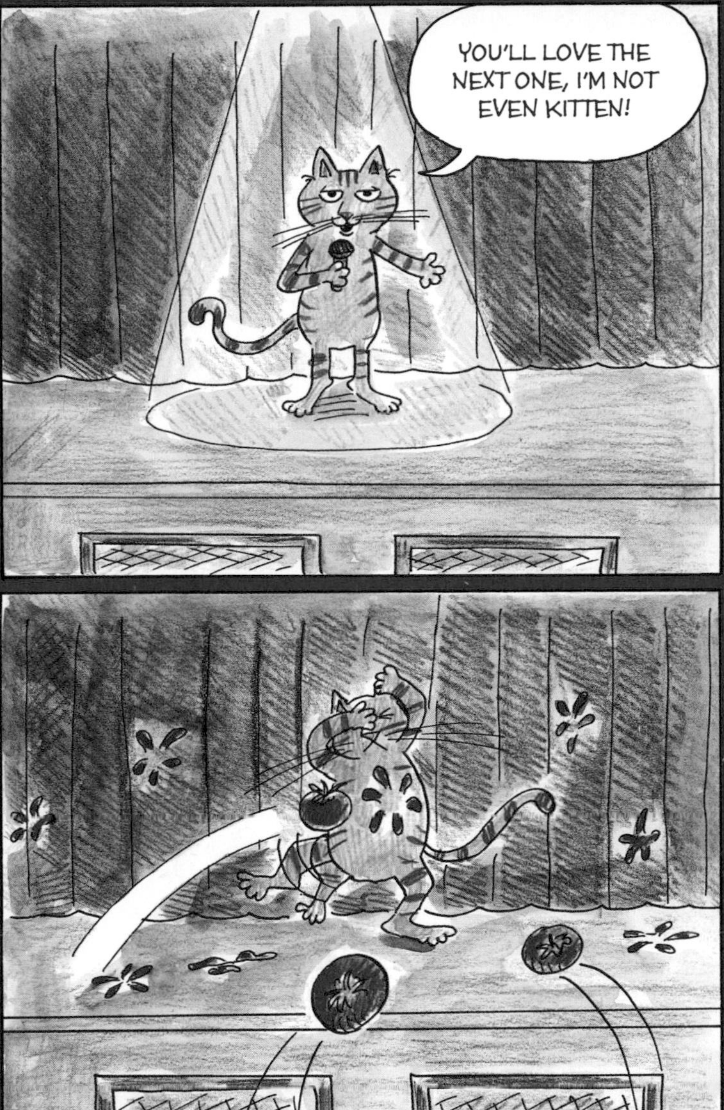
YOU'LL LOVE THE NEXT ONE, I'M NOT EVEN KITTEN!

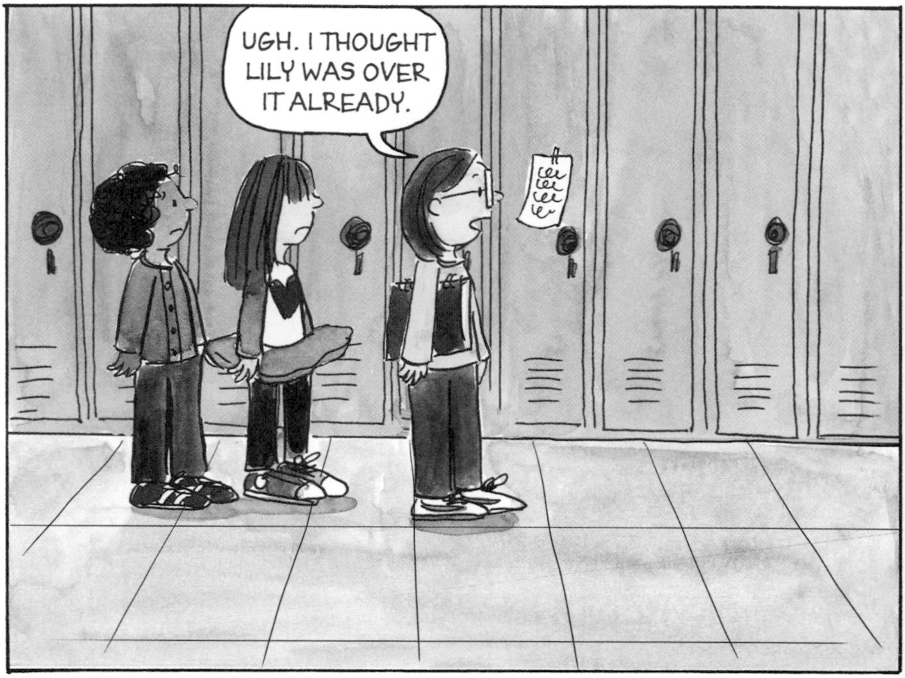
UGH. I THOUGHT LILY WAS OVER IT ALREADY.

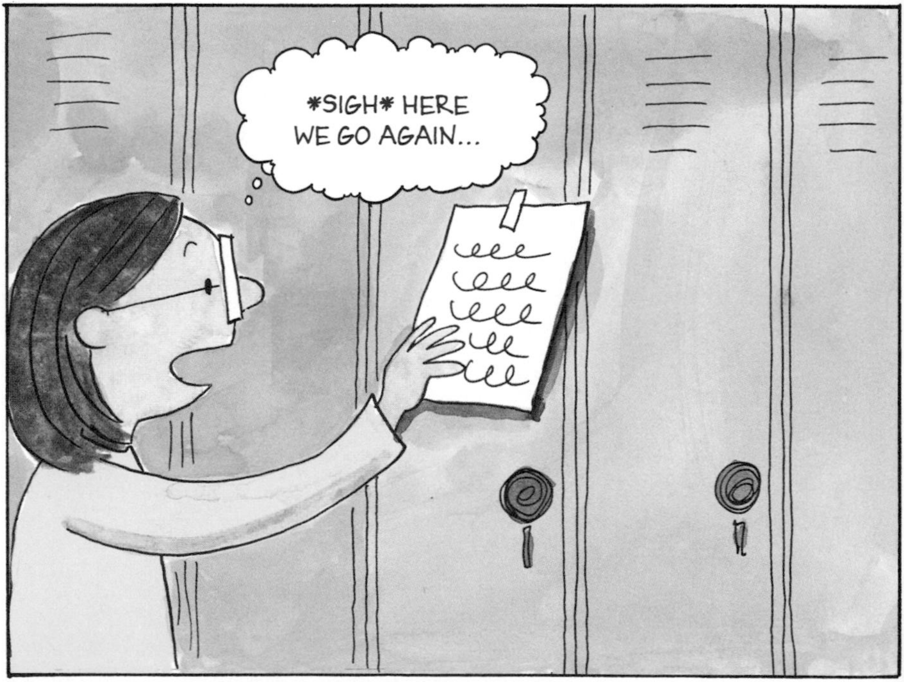
SIGH HERE WE GO AGAIN...

Dear Natalie,
How are you? I am fine.
Congratulations! I loved
your book and I loved
your bird costume. See
ya in class.
— Derek

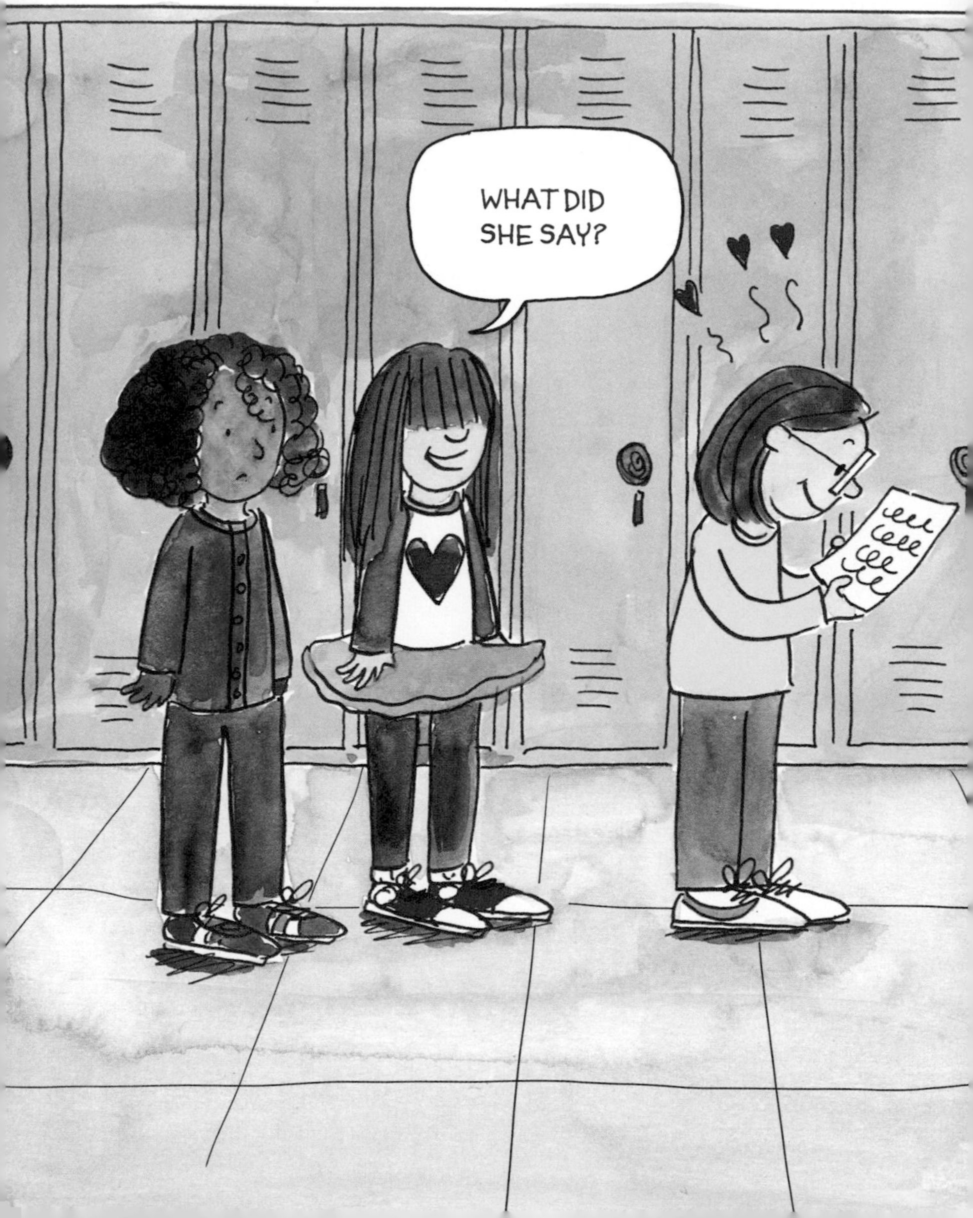
WHAT DID
SHE SAY?

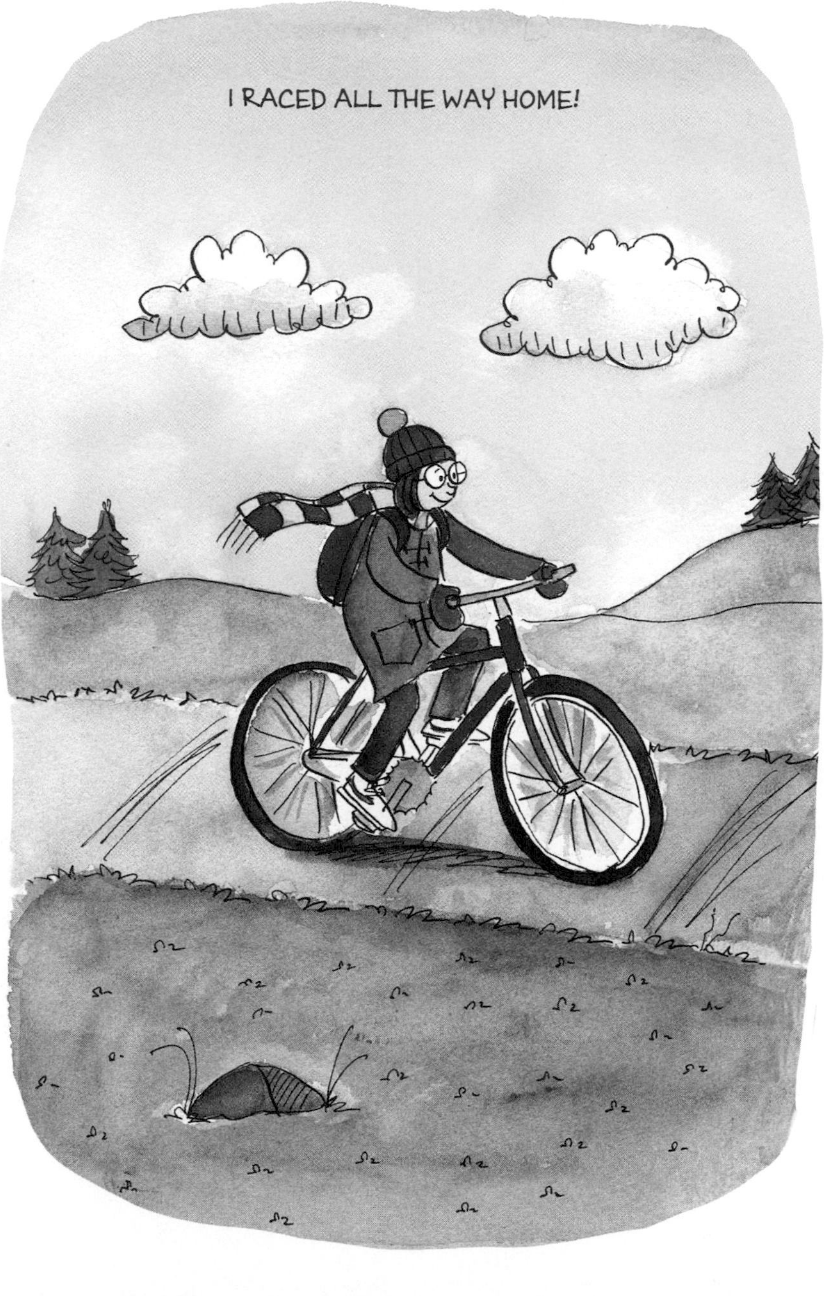
I RACED ALL THE WAY HOME!

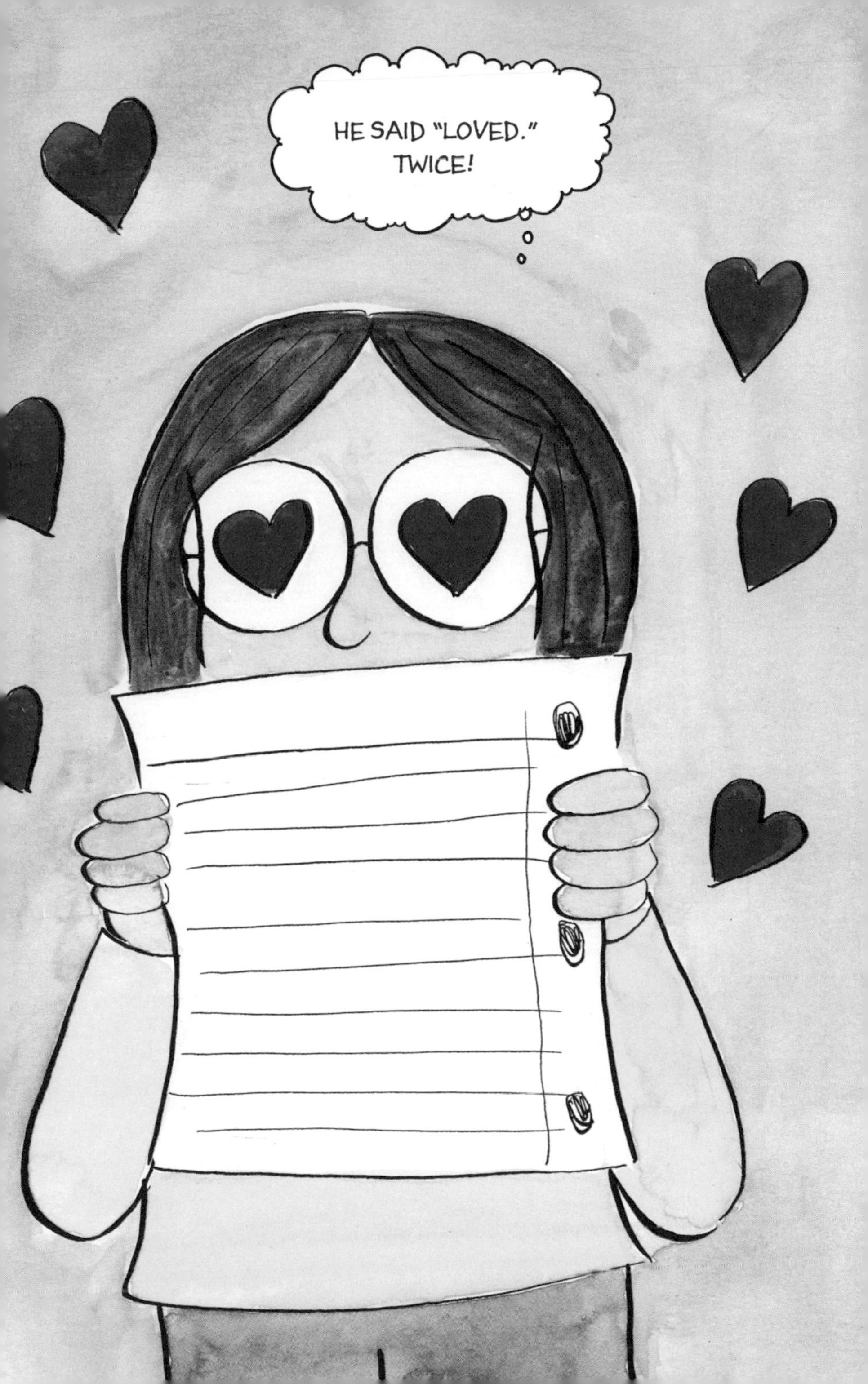
HE SAID "LOVED." TWICE!

STRAWBERRY-BANANA WAS A JELL-O FROG. SHE LIVED IN SCIENCE CLASS WITH THE OTHER JELL-O FROGS: LIME, LEMON, ORANGE, RASPBERRY, AND PEACH.

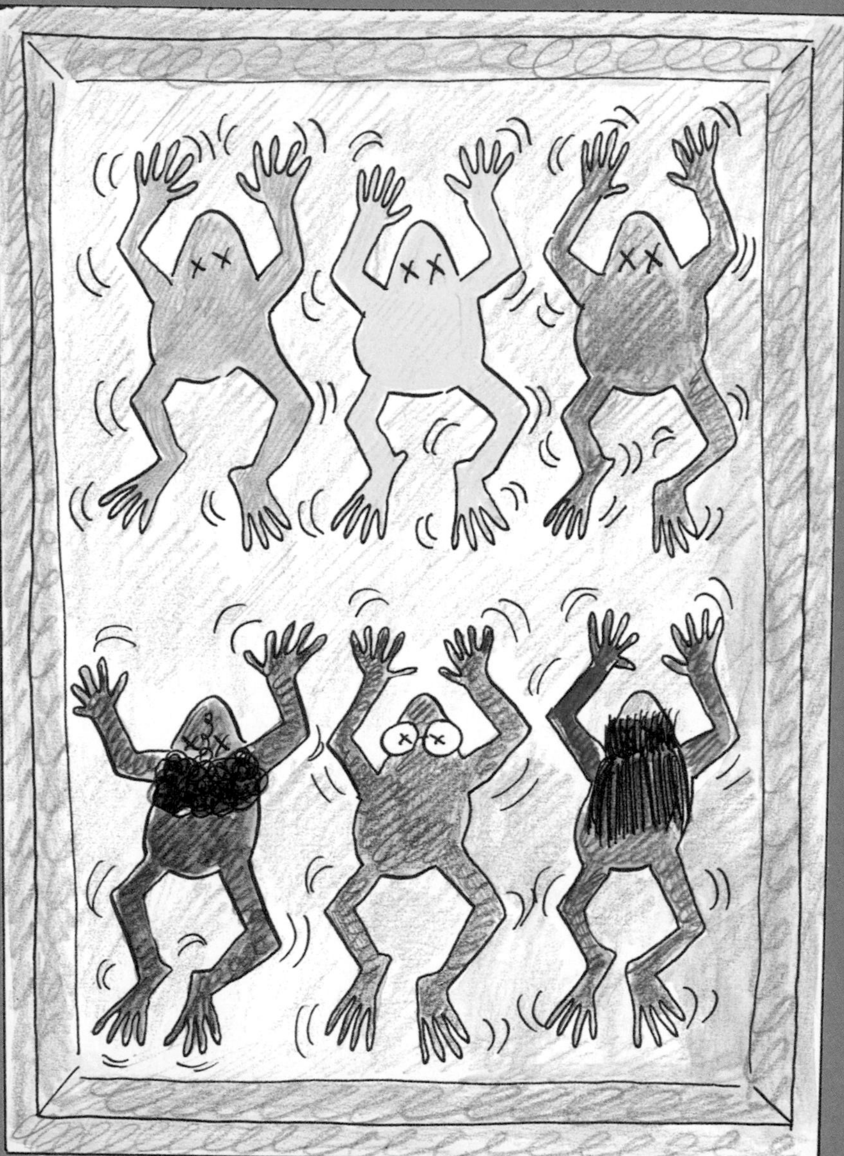

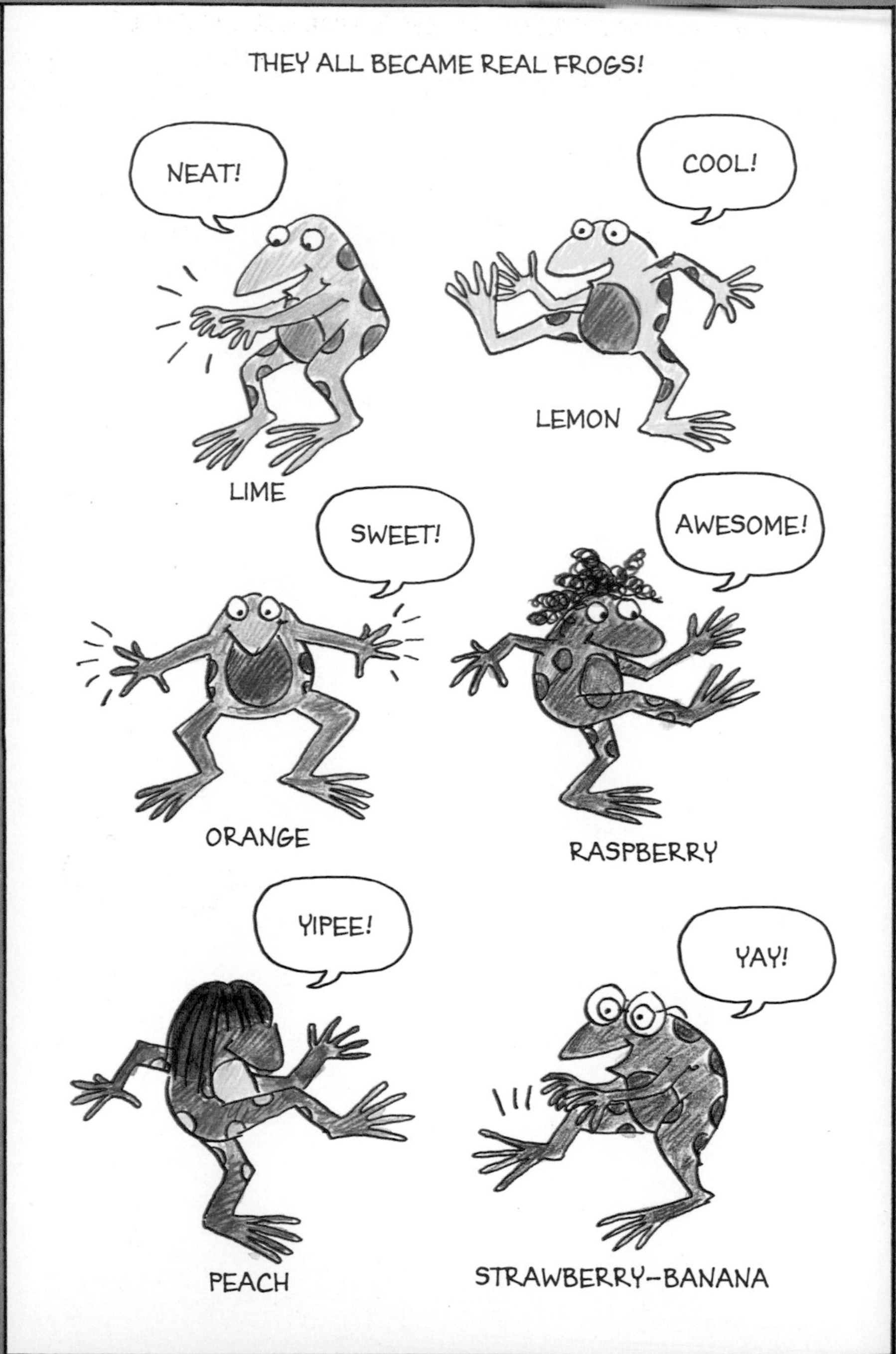
THEY ALL BECAME REAL FROGS!
NEAT!
LIME
COOL!
LEMON
SWEET!
ORANGE
AWESOME!
RASPBERRY
YIPEE!
PEACH
YAY!
STRAWBERRY-BANANA

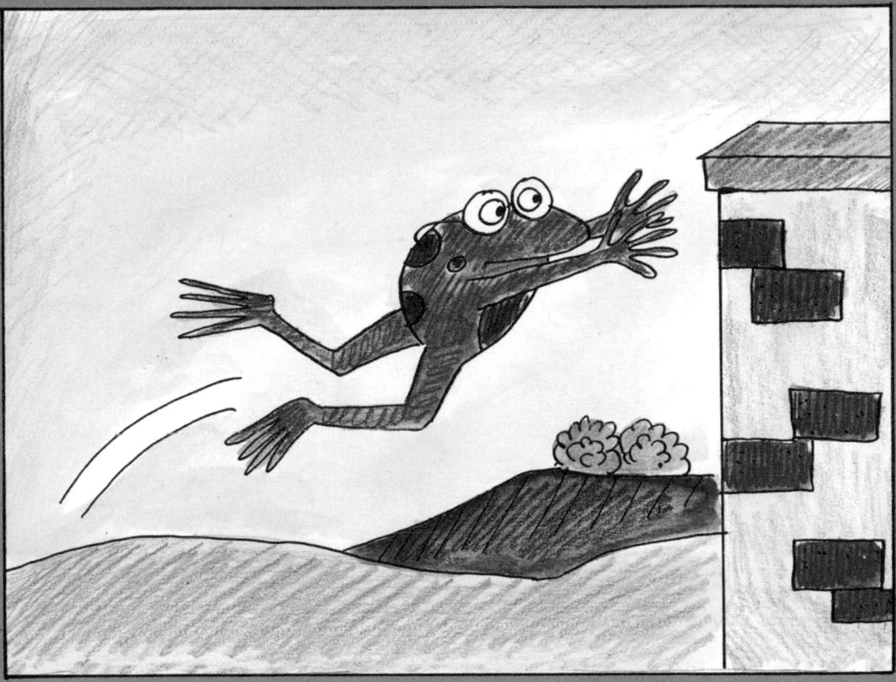

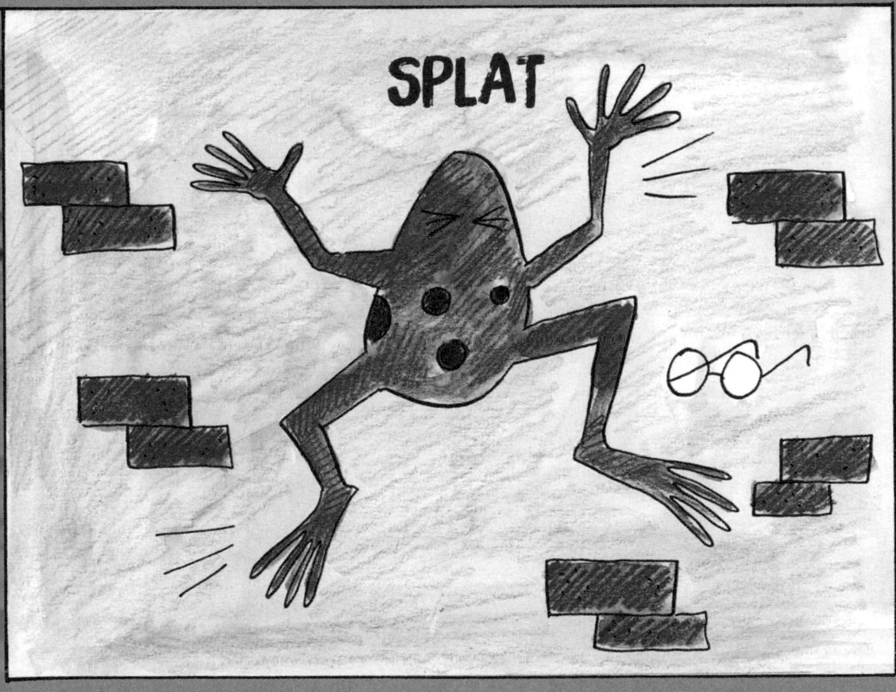
SPLAT

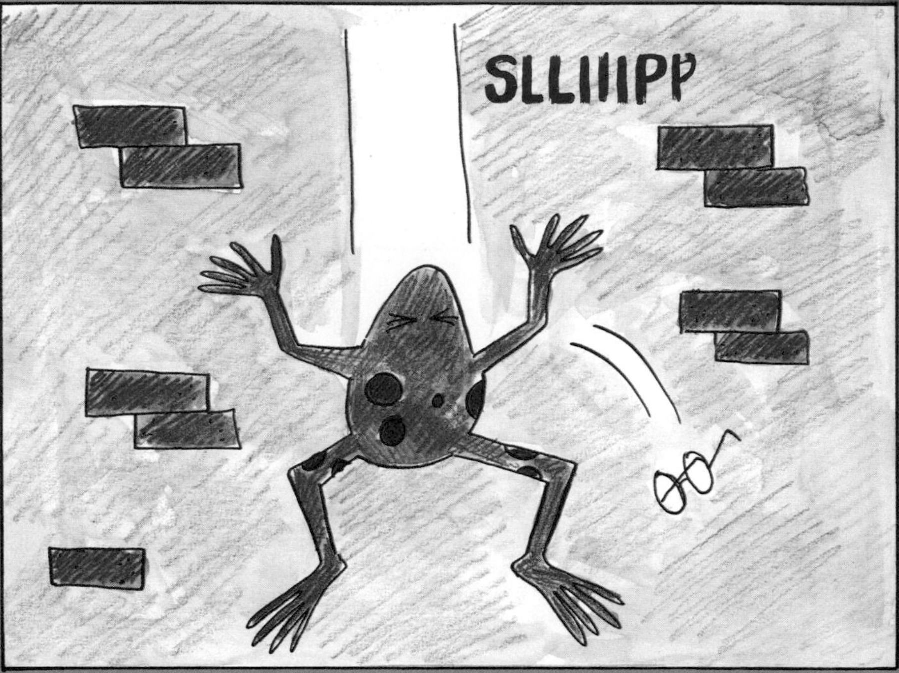
SLLIIIPP

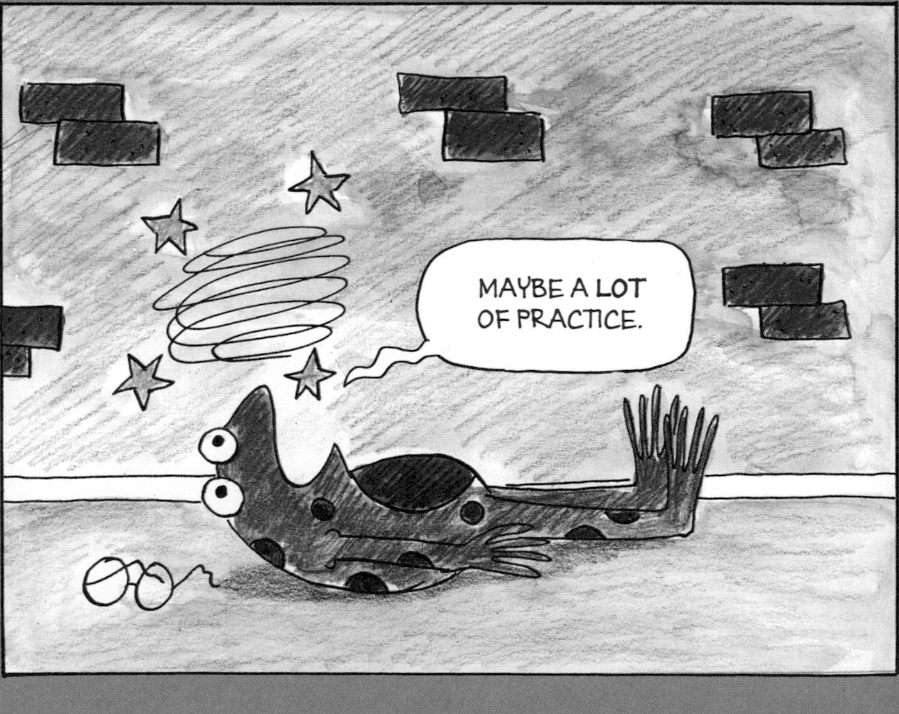
MAYBE A LOT
OF PRACTICE.

UNTIL THEN, SHE WAS HAPPY BEING HERSELF.

MARIA SCRIVAN is an award-winning cartoonist, illustrator, and author based in Stamford, Connecticut. Her laugh-out-loud syndicated comic, *Half Full*, appears daily in newspapers nationwide and on gocomics.com. Maria licenses her work for greeting cards throughout the United States and United Kingdom, and her cartoons have also appeared in *MAD Magazine*, *Parade*, and many other publications. Visit Maria online at mariascrivan.com.